The Templa

Their Secret H

Clive Lindley

VOLUME ONE

THE END OF AN EPOCH 1307-1314

Registered Office
264 Banbury Road
Oxford
OX2 7DY

ISBN: 0957294425
ISBN-13: 978 0957294424

For

Maureen, Daniel, Liberty, Jamie, Archie, Lola, Sophie and Danny

Always my beloveds

February 2015

AUTHORS NOTE

The Templars have excited curiosity throughout the nine centuries since they were founded. In their own time they were a phenomenon and an attraction amongst others, to childless wealthy families- a time when average life expectation was perhaps half of what it is today. Within the hereditary nobility and the gentry, young men for the most part were trained to arms and armour and little else from an early age, which often led on to an early death. Without natural heirs, until the Templars appeared, the church had been the favoured legatee, with their benefactors hoping for an eventual reward in heaven. They all knew of course that the Church was deeply corrupt and here was an alternative, also earning spiritual credits. They now had a choice to leave their wealth to these fine young men, 'Knights of Christ' no less, individually sworn to poverty strictly observed, in an Order of the Church whose sole role was to fight the enemies of religion in the Holy Land and the Iberian countries. This was better, they may have thought, than some fat bishop getting his hands on it.

Hence the Templars soon became wealthy, but keeping and supplying an army in the field and permanently in garrisons, in both the Holy Land and in the separate theatre of war against the Moors occupying Spain and Portugal, was massively expensive. As result the Order having to supply their own troops, mostly overseas, also became merchants on a big scale. As bankers, initially to the pilgrim trade, they invented the same financial 'tool' for the same reasons as the later travellers cheque. Well financed, they could build their castles, supply and remount their troops and remain independent of the acquisitive kings and bishops that brought them down in the end. The end that is, of their formal history from 1129 to 1312.

This book is classified as fiction but incorporates such facts as are known about the aftermath of the Order being suppressed, not for the heresy with which they were accused, but by a 'spur of the moment' executive order of the Pope, on 'administrative grounds'. The assembled Church fathers attending the 1311/12 Ecumenical Council in the cathedral at Vienne had made it clear they simply did not accept the evidence of confessions of heresy which were all solely based on torture. The princes of the church were then about to acquit the Order. This the greedy King of France and his puppet Pope, Clement V, could never allow, given what they had already done in sequestering all of the Templar properties, imprisoning, torturing all the members and leaders they could find and burning many alive as heretics, a charge just refuted by the supreme Church Council.

Most of the cruelty of the suppression took place in France and the small

Papal states, involving perhaps some 2,500 fighting men, yet there were probably at least an equivalent number that survived, untouched or virtually so, stationed and living in countries outside of France.

Their treasure was never discovered. Their impressive international commercial empire largely continued under other names, much of it involved in the dynamic Hanseatic League to which they were close, although within France all Templar activity necessarily ceased.

For example the Templar fleet of sixteen merchant ships and crews, based in the Atlantic port of La Rochelle, had sailed for destinations unknown, by the time the Kings troops arrived to seize them.

It is reasonable to suppose that those fighting men, the elite warriors of their time, having survived in serious numbers outside France, would be outraged and seek revenge on the Dominican Inquisitors that tortured and killed their leaders and brethren, and on the French king who had destroyed their near two centuries - old brotherhood. They would have needed to reorganize themselves and to decide on what their purpose would be in the future - (hardly fighting and dying for the religion). Scotland becomes centre stage. It was the one safe refuge in Europe which attracted those Templars who had escaped the slow-moving papal dragnet in Europe. The Scottish King, Robert the Bruce, was already excommunicated before this time and the nation was under interdict –so uniquely in Christendom, 'the Pope's writ' no longer ran in Scotland.

The role of the Templars in Scotland, traditionally fighting for Robert the Bruce at the Battle of Bannockburn is described here in Volume One. If they were, as it appears in fact present in Scotland, logic supports that.

Since folklore in Switzerland is equally insistent on a Templar presence one year later, at their critical 1315 battle of Morgarten for an independent Switzerland, this is described in Volume Two.

The Templar characters throughout these two volumes, hopefully will share further adventures in subsequent books in the series.

Then there is the masonic connection. Several investigators have scoured Scotland where some came up with good evidence, not only of a Templar presence explained above, but also of masonic activities, then or thereabouts. But how could such a connection have come about in the first place? What, after all, did highly- skilled stonemasons have in common with the European nobility and knighthood?

The answer follows the Prologue to this book. "The Relationship between the Knights Templar and the Freemasons" both as to the ordained connection between the master builders and these warrior knights, and why it was in Scotland where evidence of both Templar and Freemason activities were unearthed.

Just as there was no reason for the Europe-wide Templars to accept dissolution because of a hostile king in 14th C France (who died soon after these events, as did his puppet Pope), it is more, rather than less likely that even now one or more genuine organizations in direct succession exist, as well as within the worldwide Masonic fraternity.

CONTENTS

PROLOGUE:
Troyes 1115: "In the Beginning"

Fifteen years after the First Crusade, Count Hugh of Champagne may well have been the wealthiest magnate in France, and certainly his family was amongst the most powerful in Christendom. The Capetian King Louis VI called the Fat, was by contrast always short of money. His main territory of Ile de France, mainly north of the Seine, was surprisingly small and poor compared with those broad lands of the House of Blois-Champagne, reputed to contain one castle for every day of the year. Ile de France however did include Paris which with around 90,000 people at this time was the greatest city in Europe. Beyond that, the Capetian's kingship essentially was nominal - a struggle to dominate the country's powerful barons and regional magnates, particularly in Normandy to his west, which was in a semi-permanent state of territorial war.

But Hugh of Champagne cared little about the Capetians and were it not that from time to time; Fat Louis' barons attempted a chevauchee into his wide territories, he would have been happy to ignore them. Count Hugh was to tell the truth, somewhat tired of life. He ruled his county fairly and prospered, as did his people, but he was sick at heart, he did not rule his wife. The countess, sister of the Duke of Burgundy, he knew was unfaithful to him, and even more painful, that their son and heir, the only child could not be his.

That was not all. He was unhappy both with his own life and disillusioned with the state of Christendom, within which he was such a great lord. The way his peers regarded the law as a thing that they could impose on their underlings, but need not obey themselves; the fact that most young men of good birth were trained primarily as fighters for war, leaving a large surplus of skilled warriors with often no-one to fight, except their neighbours or passers-by, which they did incessantly.

Religion from which he had hoped salvation would come — and not just in a future life — he had found to be disappointing. The clerical hierarchies, with some notable exceptions, were despicable and worldly careerists, interested in nothing other than the lure of money and power that motivated them. They were often as unlike their founder as was imaginable. But certainly he had known amongst them some admirable and godly men.

The former archbishop in his northern city of Rheims had gone on to become Pope Urban II. He had shared Count Hugh's disgust and concerns and offered his vision of the Crusade as a way to get these quarrelling aristocrats and their knights to fight at least a recognizable foreign enemy. Even now Turkish hordes were threatening the great Christian city of Constantinople and the lands of Byzantium. The various Moslem powers had themselves begun again to fight over the ownership of Jerusalem, devastating the long established Christian pilgrim traffic there. It was an Egyptian garrison that controlled the city and its territories when the Crusade was preached by Pope Urban in 1097 and which had succeeded by the end of the 11th century, in taking the holy city and creating the Christian kingdom of Jerusalem. The conquest was born in blood it was true, but it reversed the trend of several centuries when Christianity had been in retreat.

Count Hugh had sought guidance from his friends and in prayer, and he was convinced that he had been shown a way forward. The key to this, he believed, was to be found in Outremer, the Holy Land now liberated from the Saracens.

Greatly to his disappointment at that time, he had been unable to leave his territory to go on crusade, for fear of the Capetians inevitably taking advantage of his absence, to invade. He had sent in his place a trusted baron and friend, Hugh de Payens, along with a well-equipped warband of young knights and nobles and their followers, some of them from outside his lands but most in fealty to him. They had travelled under the overall command of his older half-brother, Etienne, Count of Blois, another great territorial magnate who was leading a large force.

That had all gone badly wrong before they had even got to Jerusalem. A disillusioned Etienne of Blois had stormed out of the collective leadership of the crusade outside the walls of Antioch, where the long siege had been going badly. He had gone in a fury to the nearby port of Seleucia and embarked for France with his troops, excepting that is, the contingent from Champagne commanded by de Payens. The highly principled Hugh de Payens and his men, having taken the crusaders oath, declined to follow Count Etienne in his personal withdrawal and continued with the crusade, as an independent company within the Crusader army.

When Jerusalem was taken the crusade was over, yet the land still needed to be subdued. Most warriors, their job done, came back to Europe and a hero's welcome. Many of the leaders that remained had captured territory awarded to them, in the new kingdom of Jerusalem. But de Payen's people had stayed. They were mostly bachelors with no strong family pull to return home. Unlike most of the other knights that remained, seeking to serve great lords who were primarily there to acquire lands, they had taken the crusader oath seriously, and could see that there was still much to be done in the years ahead to finally secure the victory. Whilst that was being achieved, their patron Count Hugh, had subsequently visited them twice in the Holy Land, and had continued sending them essential military supplies, remounts and money.

It simply came down to the fact that now the Holy Land was under Christian rule, pilgrims from all across Christendom were flocking to visit the holy places. The King of Jerusalem and his nobles had troops enough to protect their castles, their cities and borders, but so many crusaders had gone home, there were none left to protect the pilgrims. It had been a great crisis, because the lands of Palestine and Syria outside of the garrisoned cities had been swarming with dangerous groups: deserters, bands of undefeated enemy soldiers, cross-border raiders, and simple outlaws, to all of whom these pilgrims were a soft target. Hugh de Payens had informally organised his original group of nine knights, each with their individual followers and friends into mounted patrols of military police, a 'milice' to protect the main pilgrim groups - and it was working.

This morning in 1115 back in France, Count Hugh had an important meeting here in his castle in his capital city of Troyes. The man coming to meet him was a churchman, a monk who remarkably at twenty five years of age was already an abbot of the Cistercian Order. His rapid rise in rank was due to his extraordinary dynamism and charismatic preaching skill. The count believed that if anybody could understand his concerns, it was this young man, Bernard of Les Fontaines de Dijon, whose family also had a blood connection with his own.

The Count was waiting in his solar in the large and rather grim fortress tower where he chose to have his quarters, set into a corner of the Troyes city wall itself. From here he could look out over the well-kept houses of his beautiful city, its streets running in an orderly fashion towards the green where the new Troyes cathedral was under construction. He was reflectively doing just that when his visitors were shown in.

Bernard was an intense, clean-shaven monk, with a light ring of almost colourless hair in the circle of his tonsure, wearing the roughly-woven white fleece robe of the Cistercians. His piercing eyes were a key feature of his powerful personality. His companion was his brother, in clothes that the count recognised, with the close fitting white cloche fabric helmet and plain smock, as that rare creature for the times, an architect.

"My lord Count — cousin," Bernard opened, bowing as he kissed the count's ring. Hugh immediately took the young churchman's hand, and kissed his abbatial ring," Father Abbot — cousin," he replied.

"How is your father, the good Lord of La Fontaine?" the count politely enquired.

"He is fine sir, in fact I think I have persuaded him to take up the vows and join my brothers and myself in the cloister. Here is yet another brother, Achard whom I think you may not have met?" He took his brother's arm and brought him closer to salute the Count.

A steward entered and passed around offering goblets of watered wine, whilst the count indicated his visitors to comfortable chairs, set facing his own.

"So what does your dear mother think about your trying to recruit your father into monastic life?" Count Hugh enquired when they were seated.

"Surprisingly, my Lord, she said that if he does that, she will enter a nunnery."

"Do you know young Bernard, I envy them!" From the vehemence of his voice Bernard knew that he meant it.

"Well you too Sir, if you like," Bernard smiled a broad smile.

"That time may come, but I also have work to do, of which I would speak to you today." He then turned his attention towards the young architect, with an enquiring look.

Achard inclined his head again and said, "I have just returned from Italy, my Lord, after five years, mostly in the city of Ravenna".

"And what were you doing there?" the Count enquired.

Well my lord, it was earlier as you know a Byzantine city and remains the only place in western Christendom with a school of architecture. You may be aware my Lord Count, that there are hardly any architects in all of Northern Europe and very few master builders".

"Do I not know?" broke in the Count. "I had the very devil of a job in finding an architect for our new cathedral here in Troyes. I had to send to England where King William had been building his great fortress of the White Tower and the splendid Abbey church at Westminster and finally found a man who had the skills and had fulfilled his bargain with the Normans." Almost as an afterthought he added ruefully, but shrewdly appraising the young man in front of him, "there are still a few years to go before it's completed, and he is already of a good age."

Achard resumed with his main theme. "Since the time of the Romans the art of building great works in stone was all but lost in the west, except and only very recently, a few rudimentary stone castles and what you just referred to in London. Charlemagne himself built his great church at Aix, based on what he saw in Ravenna, using Byzantine architects and craftsmen, but few followed his example. It is, my lord an intellectual, an engineering undertaking in which training is paramount -- about the capacity for first being able to visualize, such an enormous structure as a cathedral. Then endless work on the geometry, the mathematics of load bearing -- of stress, of foundations, reinforcements to support stone ceilings 100 ft above our heads."

He caught a look from his brother and tailed off. "So, my lord, I have been learning such skills as I was able."

"As you can see cousin, he is an enthusiast. That's why I brought him," explained Bernard.

By the time two hours had passed, Count, Abbot, and Architect had realised that this was a meeting that could change all of their lives.

The purpose of Bernard's request to see the Count was that he had come to petition for a large but desolate tract of forest land owned by the Count, in order to create a monastery there. Forewarned, the Count had already considered the request and the necessary funding with his advisers, and had decided to grant it. It would go formally to the Cistercian Order to build the new monastery, of which Bernard was the first abbot. It was to be named as was the forest, Clairvaux.

Platters of food had arrived and more wine. Bernard explained that like some others of his generation, he had decided to become a monk rather than a priest, because he had been deeply depressed about the state of the Christian church, so notoriously corrupt and self-serving, now it had become rich and long established. Its hierarchy had become virtually a parallel aristocracy. He was convinced that there needed to be a revival and that only a relatively new and idealistic monastic order, like the Cistercians, could see that through. He felt it to be his vocation to create many new monastic settlements around Christendom, and to consolidate that by building beautiful abbeys, and helping to create great churches and cathedrals. To do that, he was first going to have his brother design and build the new monastery at Clairvaux, and then set up amongst their other activities there, a small permanent school of architecture and building, which Achard would lead.

Count Hugh in turn, told the young men about the band of knights he sponsored in Outremer which he had recently visited. How they were religiously motivated, yet trained for war. That they were already protecting pilgrims but that they needed to increase their numbers as they were already stretched, since pilgrimages from all of Christendom were increasing

He said that he would like to establish them in what they wanted for themselves, to become an Order of the Church, observing religious vows and dedicated to protecting pilgrims, for which there was a growing need in Outremer. That way they could recruit new entrants. "God knows", Count Hugh continued, "that there are more than enough penniless young knights all across Christendom, who cannot expect to inherit. Many are little better than bandits, they seem to have no purpose in life".

When Bernard laughed, the Count was perplexed and looked for an explanation.

"I laughed Sir, because one of my uncles on my mother's side, her half-brother Andrew de Montbard, who is out there serving with your Captain, Hugh de Payens, has written to me. He asks if I can help in exactly what you have just explained. Let me say, as I will reply to him, that I will do whatever my poor skills can lead to, within the Church".

"What we have here my lords," broke in Achard pensively, "is a meeting of minds and of wills, very relevant to my potential contribution. Not only does the art and science of architecture serve the glory of God through creating monasteries and cathedrals, but also would serve a future military order with great castles and fortresses".

"We can and should advance together," said Bernard thoughtfully. "We should think of ourselves as one large fraternity, dedicated to God through prayer and good works, and in building miraculous buildings to his glory, whilst defending them against the enemies of God and the Religion"

"Amen!" said both the abbot and the architect in unison.

In 1115 the great Cistercian Abbey of Clairvaux, the donation of Count Hugh was founded. It was only the third establishment of the new Cistercian Order. By the end of Abbot Bernard's life there were sixty five spread around Europe including some of the most sublime examples of the newly introduced Gothic architecture in France and England. The Cistercian Order thrived and continues to this day in many countries, although in England Henry VIII's abolition of the monasteries and in France the 1789 Revolution, caused their great buildings to be vacated and become the noble ruins of today.

In 1118 the Company of Knights of the Temple were recognised by the King of Jerusalem and took their vows as the "Poor Fellow-Soldiers of Christ" in 1119 before the Patriarch there, being formally given their headquarters on Temple Mount next to the royal palace, which had informally housed them for some years. They were now able to increase their numbers from masterless knights already in the Holy Land, and with new recruits from Europe.

Hugh de Payens was duly elected by the knights as their Grand Master, an appointment confirmed and thus made official within the Holy Land, by the Patriarch of Jerusalem

De Payens and other leading knights travelled back to their home countries, first to lobby for the group to be recognised as the religion's first military monastic order; to raise funds and support and to recruit new members. They were greeted with enthusiasm and success.

In 1129 the newly completed cathedral in Count Hugh's Troyes, witnessed the great Ecumenical Council of the Church. There the Church fathers were treated to the inspirational advocacy of Abbot (later to become Saint) Bernard, in favour of establishing this new military Order as a limb of the Church. It was approved and he Bernard, was assigned the task of giving the new Templar Order their 'Rule', part monastic and part military.

But Count Hugh had already left Troyes earlier and forever, having resigned his lands and title of Count of Champagne to his nephew. He travelled for the final time from Europe to Jerusalem, never to return, where he enlisted to finish his days as a simple brother knight, of the newly recognized Templar Order, under its now Grand Master, his former vassal Hugh de Payens. His dream - and that of Bernard of 'a new model knighthood,' had been achieved.

For nearly two centuries 'the Templars' were the military elite of Europe with permanent armies and garrisons in Outremer, the present middle-east, as well as in Portugal and Spain which were permanently at war, seeking to expel the Moors. In order to finance their activities the new order attracted many donations from the devout, often in the form of land. To become fully self-financing and retain their independence from the crowned heads of Christendom, they became international bankers and traders, including owning naval and merchant fleets and ports, in both the Atlantic and the Mediterranean.

This "Secret History" tells the last part of the Templar story, much of it unknown past the point of 1307 and the then treachery of the French King Phillip IV and of his 'puppet' Bertrand de Got, Pope Clement V.

THE RELATIONSHIP BETWEEN THE KNIGHTS TEMPLAR AND THE FREEMASONS

The Prologue to the TEMPLAR KNIGHTS SECRET HISTORY illustrates the close association between leaders and in timing, of the foundation of the Templar Order and the Cistercian Order of the Church. Bernard, as the Cistercian Abbot of Clairvaux, was the dynamic force in the Christian church of that time. The relationships between the Count of Champagne and Bernard de la Fontaine and his branch of the family made access easy. Bernard had joined the Cistercians because at that time most of the other monastic orders seemed to him, to have lost their way, in terms of worldliness and how a monk should live.

An ardent reformer he hoped and succeeded in that the new Cistercian order would set an example of the appropriate monastic life, which involved a regime of daily hard physical labour by the monks, as well as of prayer and study of the scriptures, living in remotely located abbeys.

The Cistercians, still operational today, were critically important in the advent of the new 'Gothic' architecture, which buildings many would claim are the supreme examples since ancient times, of the best in 'western architecture', then at its very beginning. It flourished mostly in western Europe, with some fifty or more great cathedrals and abbeys, like Chartres, Rheims, York, Salisbury, Rievaulx, Fountains and many more. The great spate of building took place between the early 12th and 14th centuries, which more or less co-existed with the lifetime of the Templar Order.

Bernard's own brother Achard, was himself an architect, one of the very first to emerge after 500 years of the Dark Ages, when Europe had been overrun by Barbarian invasions that overwhelmed Rome and their western empire, leaving distant Byzantium, modern-day Turkey as the unconquered eastern empire. This survived around the city of Constantinople for nearly another thousand years after the fall of Rome, but Europe to the west had been over-run by Germanic hordes long before and reverted to savagery and ignorance after the Roman empire collapsed.

The Dark Ages were so-called partly because so little is known about them, in contrast to the well recorded history of Roman civilisation, but 'dark' also because the lights of civilisation were extinguished for half a millennium. The splendid buildings and monuments that were a part of Rome and their empire were left to their eventual collapse, since the barbarian conquerors did not work in stone. The craft of stone-masonry central to this, largely disappeared with them, giving way to the commonplace Germanic buildings of timber, mud and wattle, with thatched roofs. In England and Wales which the Roman legions finally left at about 410AD, no new stone buildings were built for some six centuries, until William the Conqueror commenced the Tower of London, immediately after the Norman conquest of 1066, followed by Windsor Castle. In France, richer and more advanced at this time, once Rome withdrew, very little was created in stone - most of the castles were built of timber, in the 'motte and bailey' format. The Norman Dukes pioneered the use of masonry in their Norman castles, but it was not at first widespread. All of that changed with the new century. Thousands of westerners involved in the First Crusade of 1097 travelled to Outremer overland, by way of Constantinople, where civilization including architecture and stonemasonry, had flourished without a break. The great city itself was defended by vast stone landwalls several miles in circumference, studded with towers and fortifications. To see what that protected — palaces, churches, squares, statues and monuments must have had an overwhelming effect on the visitors. The mighty and ancient Hagia Sofia, the 'Church of the Holy Wisdom,' even now has one of the largest domes anywhere in existence and as then, remains nothing short of magnificent.

As the crusaders moved on into Asia, fighting the Seljuk Turks through Anatolia, into Syria and the Holy Land, they discovered that building in stone or brick was the normal way there in which buildings were made. When the crusaders returned home, some great lords brought stonemasons with them, or hired them to travel from Byzantium. Then the high practical skills of master masonry, would bow to the art and science of architecture, the extraordinary craft of advanced monumental stonemasonry, began to spread throughout the west. The great lords wanted stone castles and palaces, the bishops wanted stone churches and cathedrals. The Cistercians of Bernard and Achard were in the forefront of this, with the new Abbey of Clairvaux having a training school for architects, their Order building for itself a further sixty churches and abbeys in Western Europe during St Bernard's lifetime, with hundreds more built thereafter.

The craft of stonemasonry was truly ancient, as witness the Egyptian Pyramids and as such was an international pursuit, inevitably with knowledge only accessible by being handed on from previous generations. In France, perhaps the most progressive part of Europe in these new times, the stonemasons were organized as a guild: 'Les Compagnons du Tours de France', (and literally, just as with today's road race these craftsmen were itinerant). The most skilled of all the stonemasons were a group within 'Les Compagnons,' named "The Company of the Children of Solomon." These were the Cathedral builders and master masons. To learn the skills of their craft they travelled widely, to work under accomplished experts. Having acquired over years such skills, they travelled again to wherever employment in their skilled vocation had become available. Other trades such as sculptors in wood as well as stone also became Compagnons. Lodges were set up in the towns and cities where such massive building projects as cathedrals, were in progress.

Two important developments arose: the first being their need for recognition, then to lay down the standards of their craft and examine the levels of skill of those who aspired to the greatest projects. This 'skilled worker' status, well rewarded and prized, had the effect of putting them into a rising middle class where hitherto the rigid classes had been Lords, (knights, men-at-arms); Clergy, led by Bishops, (often younger brothers from aristocratic families); priests and monks at the upper level had a monopoly of learning. Then there were the Peasants, by far the majority, often little better than slaves - families tied to the land on which they worked for a Lord who had complete power over them.

Merchants in towns existed in small numbers and after the First Crusade they became more and more prominent. But in these early centuries, the concept of skilled artists and artisans working to a contract, literally free to come and go, was something new. Newly corporate towns often bought out 'local overlord rights' of neighbouring aristocrats, leading to independence from the feudal structure. These basically were the strong points of the emerging 'freeman'/middle class which grew at the same rate and for whom the fraternity of the Masons Lodge was a great attraction.

But the other urgent need of the emerging craft guilds, was recognition and validation in the various territories and kingdoms in which they operated.

Leaders of "The Children of Solomon" operative stonemasons, approached Bernard of Clairvaux asking him to give them their 'Rule' - regulations appropriate for Christian artisans to receive the permanence of the blessing of the church. Abbot Bernard, by now perhaps the greatest man in the church beneath the Pope, agreed but on condition they accepted the supervision of the new Order of Knights Templar.

He very recently, following their official foundation at the 1129 Council of Troyes, had given this new military Order of Knights Templar, their 'Rule.' He gave in turn to the cathedral builders of the Compagnons, ("the Children of Solomon"), an appropriately modified version in 1145. The key item of interest here, is that **he ordained that they would be regulated and supervised, as to the performance of this constitution by the Order of the Temple, who themselves answered only to the Pope.**

Thus from the 1140's onwards, the top-down conjunction of the Templars with the Craft stonemasons took place, with the Order of Cistercians having an enabling role with both! The Templars were assigned by these dispositions of St Bernard, with all of the authority vested in him, to be the protectors, the patrons indeed, of the skilled operative masons and architects, the 'cathedral builders'- and this ensured their close and continuing interrelationship, through the triumphs and disasters that were to follow.

The fact that Cathedral building on this monumental scale across western Europe, largely finished after the Templar Order was extinguished, was probably because the Templars, who were also bankers, would often have been the key financiers in each case, given the vast sums needed over fifty, seventy and even more years, to create and continue such works in some fifty European locations.

'Les Compagnons' over time, attracted other members of the emerging middle classes --other skilled trades and nascent professions. Where lodges had been set up, membership had been available to such, later categorized as 'accepted or speculative masons,' as distinct from the original and continuing 'operative masons,' which process marks the early known history of the Freemasons, as it went on and continued to

develop a history of its own, but not to emerge 'in the world' until 1717 in London.

LIST OF CHARACTERS:

"End of an Epoch"

Volume One: "Templar Knights: Their Secret History"

Sir Paul of Chatillon, Templar Knight, Section commander Templar Fortress of Marash, Cilicia. Asia Minor.

Baudouin, his squire

Sir Mark of Exeter: Templar Knight at Marash

Lionel, his squire.

Brother Aloysius Daly SJ, in Istanbul

Giancarlo: his clerk. Rome

Karl Heinz: Jesuit Father General. Rome

Peter of Bologna, Templar priest/lawyer. Prior: Order of the Temple formerly the Order's representative at the Papal Curia.

Knut Peerson, Templar man at arms, knighted on the field of Bannockburn.

Sir Geraint of Monmouth, Templar knight.

The Marshal, ranking officer (at liberty) of the Order of Templars.

Pope Clement V, in France at Poitiers, later at Avignon.

Joseph of Portugal, Finance manager. Templar formerly attached to Papal Curia.

Sir Olivier de Penne, Administrator, Templar formerly attached to Papal Curia.

Herman, Graf of Mannheim, a provincial master Knights Templar

Sir James Keith of Pitlochry, former Templar, soon to be Constable of Scotland

Peter Proudhomme: Architect. Master of the operative Masonic company of "The Children of Solomon." - The cathedral builder masons of the "Compagnons de la Tour de France"

Cardinal Brancacci, delegated by the Pope to examine the allegations of heresy against senior Templars, held in Chinon Castle.

Cardinal Berenger Fredol, similarly examining the senior Templar prisoners at Chinon Castle,

Jacques de Molay, Grandmaster of the Templars, held prisoner at Chinon Castle.

Geoffrey de Charney, Templar Master of Normandy, held prisoner at Chinon Castle.

Hugh de Pairault, Templar Visitor of France held prisoner at Chinon Castle.

Geoffrey de Goneville, formerly Preceptor of Poitou and Aquitaine, also a prisoner at Chinon.

The Royal Governor of Chinon Castle.

Guillaume de Nogaret, lawyer. King Philip's fixer and minister.

Philip de Marigny. Courtier, Archbishop of Sens, King Philip's puppet.

Sir John de Berricourt. Leader of the Paris lodge of free Templars.

The Bishop of Paris. Subsidiary to Archbishop de Marigny of Sens

King Robert the Bruce, of Scotland.

The Earl of Moray: Scottish general, Brigade Commander at Bannockburn.

'The Black Douglas', Scottish Earl and general. Brigade Commander at Bannockburn.

Sir Peter Breydel. Templar Knight, veteran of the Flemish battle of Courtrai. King Robert's Master of Infantry at Bannockburn, shortly to become the Marshal of the Order.

King Edward II of England, commanding the army invading Scotland.

Sir Henry de Bohun, English knight, the first casualty of the battle of Bannockburn.

The Earl of Gloucester, Edward of England's Cavalry general

The Earl of Hereford, the Constable of England.

Sir Alexander Seaton, Knight from the borderlands with England, supporter of King Robert.

Sir Luke of Pembroke, Welsh knight taken prisoner by the Scots, (Sir Geraint's brother).

Jacques LeGros, Head Huntsman at Fontainebleau.

King Philip IV 'the Fair,' of France.

Prince Louis Capet. Heir to the French throne.

Sir Paul of Chatillon's 1309 journey from Cilicia to Scotland via Paris

THE TEMPLAR FORTRESS OF MARASH

The Armenian Kingdom of Cilicia, November 1307

Sir Paul of Chatillon, Templar knight, looked down at the hilt of his Damascus blade to see why it was slipping in his grasp. The deerskin strips he and his squire had so carefully wound around and glued onto the hilt, then bound with copper wire, should have soaked up his sweat. Only now he realised that it was soaked, not in sweat but in blood - his blood. A string thin rivulet was seeping down from inside his chain mail sleeve.

The night was still dark, but a lightening of the clouds in the east proclaimed that morning was imminent. That meant that the surprise the turban-helmeted attackers had hoped for, was gone with the darkness. This didn't necessarily mean that they would give up. For the moment at least it had gone quiet. Looking down he saw at the base of the wall, amongst the small rocks, weeds and sheep droppings, the wrack of ruined scaling ladders and weapons, with many broken Turkish bodies sprawling around and over them. Most now were still, but some legs and arms were twitching jerkily whilst presenting no threat. The larger boulders further away, he knew, concealed the numerous still dangerous, survivors.

Along the parapet of the castle wall, he saw his fellow Templars, of whom he was the section chief, all apparently upright, although not offering themselves as targets to the Turkish archers. Like him, they had been fully ready, after being alerted to the presence of invaders by the guard dogs, set on long leashes to roam in the darkness beyond the castle walls for that very purpose. The Armenian allies, long used to fighting the Turks in these mountains had taught them that trick, saying that the dogs needed hardly any training and, if slain, were easily replaceable.

Rolling up the steel links of his sleeve he saw the small rent, but the spear that he only now realised had so nearly destroyed his sword arm, had fallen away as its wielder had sunk back below the parapet. Paul, having hacked down into his neck, had then wrestled away the top of the scaling ladder with its cargo of Turks still on the lower rungs. Nevertheless his muscular arm had sustained a slash, which needed a dressing.

With his squire Baudouin nearby, Paul was examining the wound that the spear tip had made and Baudouin was folding a scarf to bind it. Suddenly, out of the darkness the arrow came and took the boy full in the face. Paul caught him as he staggered over and eased him down to the surface of the fighting platform. "Oh no, Jesus God, not Baudouin," the knight mouthed, lifting the head and in dismay examining the wound, the shaft still projecting from it. But the place where it had entered the boy's head spoke of the finality of the event. The arrow must have instantly penetrated the brain.

He regretfully lowered the slight body of his squire down again onto the fighting platform. Then cautiously, this time with his shield before his face, he looked over the parapet at what the assailants below were now doing. His whole long section of the wall was now devoid of attackers, but there was no silence. He heard waves of the surging clamour coming from the barbican to his left. Then he was brought back to his own reality as one arrow and then another, hit the stone parapet to his side and glanced off high above him.

This time, some movement behind a rock told him exactly where the enemy archers lurked; seeking any targets that opportunity might give them. He waved over the sergeant of the Genoese crossbowmen that were the back-up on this section of the wall. He pointedly nodded towards his young squire's corpse. "The bastard that did that," he spat out, "is still shooting at us! There is a silver cup for you if you can get him."

The mercenary sergeant edged over and saw a flash of material as the Turkish archer started to lift his head and fired off a shaft in their general direction, and then ducked down again. "Leave him to me, sir" he said, hefting his crossbow, a steel quarrel inserted, his eye firmly fixed on where the Turk had disappeared.

Paul, ducking below the parapet, signalled with his hand to his nearest Templar neighbor, Sir Mark of Exeter, and they edged towards each other. "Sorry about young Baudouin, brother" his colleague opened, subdued, "I saw it happen and that you now have the Genovesians dealing with it."

Paul nodded in answer, but his eyes conveyed his sorrow, hardened as he was and in the heat of battle. Still only twenty, he had gained most of his experience in a war zone. He was extremely fit and being tall to start with, physically well up to the challenges of campaigning. To be a Templar - the best of the best - had been his ambition since he was a boy in his father's castle in Burgundy. But now this soldier's life had suddenly become very complicated indeed. First principles even, needed re-examination.

Yesterday, the castle commander had convened a meeting of the sixty or so of his fellow Templars serving in this mountainous fortress, possibly the remotest part of the Templar presence anywhere, here where the edge of western Asia met the shores of the Mediterranean. Such meetings were fairly rare. The commander had announced this was to be a chapter meeting, so Paul and his colleagues had wondered what it could be about. Now that he knew, he wished that he didn't. The commander, a thirty-year-old veteran of these Cilician wars, had told the assembled Templars the shocking news. He told them that a carrier pigeon from headquarters in Cyprus had earlier arrived and the news it brought was barely credible, yet if true was devastating.

"The Grand Master and all the Templars in France, some 2000 of our brethren have been arrested by the French king," he told the assembled warriors. "They have been accused of all things, of heresy," he continued incredulously. Paul had met the stern old warrior the Grand Master Jacques de Molay, in Cyprus. He had indeed inducted young Paul, freshly arrived from Paris, into the Order at Kyrenia.

Reflecting on the shocking news, he thought he knew no one less likely than that grizzled veteran to fit the image of a heretic. None of it made any sense. The Templar garrison commander at this Cilician fortress had only been able to tell the congregated brethren those bare facts, from the brief coded message carried on the leg of the carrier pigeon, which he freely admitted, failed to make any sense to him either. There would surely be more information coming, he had said, but all agreed that such news whilst incomprehensible was clearly, disastrously bad

Then the commander had brought them back to their own dire circumstances when he told them that, according to intelligence just received, a large mixed party of Turks and Kurds had been spotted in these Amanus Mountains, and only half a day's journey away. He said that the whole garrison would need to be on the walls that night, with every expectation that they were the objects of this Turkish march into Cilician territory. At least it took them away from baffled speculation about the fate of their Order, and back to the immediate matter of their own survival.

During the long hours since then on this battlements watch, he had wondered in this last remaining Christian fragment of Outremer, if the Templars, the only Christian soldiers anywhere who were still fighting the victorious Saracens, were somehow doomed, for reasons beyond their control. Now he reflected, had the fine young man Baudouin, whose still-warm body lay beside him, died for nothing? Paul and his comrades were certainly in danger of being overrun, if this Turkish attack was large enough. Wasn't it sufficient to be on the front line against these fierce Asiatic enemies, without whatever forces back in France had moved against the Temple?

"Baudouin was a fine fellow," Paul told his colleague Mark, "but what a waste of a young life. He had been with me out here for a year. Candidly now - a good lad, he would have got his mantle after a couple of years and a few more dust-ups like this one. He's a loss to me it's certain, also to the Order. I'll be writing to his family - I think they are in Flanders." His voice trailed sadly, realising that even their Order itself was now in jeopardy. "But this all seems so inadequate somehow." His voiced trailed away and he realised he was speaking to himself. There was no more time. Mourning would have to wait.

His tone became business-like once more. "They won't try scaling here again today, but they obviously want to keep us alert and in place. Why, I ask? I'm going over to look at the gate where clearly the action is," he told Mark. They could both hear the distant roar. "Be ready for a move to reinforce, in case that's called for. Lend me your lad - Lionel, isn't it, and I'll send him back with a message, if necessary." His colleague waved his squire over and instructed him, whilst Paul doubling over to keep his head lowered as he passed, patted the shoulder of the Genoese sergeant, carefully watching the cluster of rocks where the Turks were concealed.

Paul holding his sword and shield ran bowed over, along the fighting platform that curved with the wall away towards the gate, with the squire, Lionel, following in a similar half-crouching posture.

He passed several other Templars in their positions on the walls and slowed each time, long enough to call out his purpose. As he got nearer and rounded a curve in the wall he heard the roar intensify and saw the action outside, in front of the barbican. A large number of Turkish attackers in their mail cuirasses and steel-spiked helmets clustered around an iron-tipped ram which they had got close enough to already be splintering the great reinforced timber gate. The Templar commander stood on the parapet above, urging on defenders who were bringing new loads of missiles to the platform above the gate to others, who were hurling them down on the upturned shields held over the heads below. He saw Paul approaching. "It's gone quiet on our section, sir," Paul reported, "just a few archers keeping us pinned down now, but we saw off their ladders before it got light and their assault troops have gone I expect to come over here, but they are not with us any longer - so I needed to know if you would want us to reinforce you here, or not?"

"Good man, Brother Paul. I was just thinking I would need to send for you," his commander responded. "In case we can't hold them at the gate - and that's now only a matter of time - it will be hand to hand. There are some carts down there," he pointed to where men were unloading and bringing rocks to use as missiles. "Get the brethren off your wall and down there. Leave some of your Genoans to keep watch and stop the Turks over there thinking you've fallen asleep. But get those carts overturned to make a new barrier inside the gate, and then form up your men to hold it."

Paul turned to Lionel. "You heard that. Now repeat those orders... yes, yes, all right, good lad. Now, get back to Sir Mark - and Lionel, for God's sake, just keep your head down!" The Templar followed the youth with his eyes seeing that he was indeed keeping below the parapet. He looked up to the highest point of the castle and was reassured to see that Beauseant, the Templar flag of black and white halves was flying strongly against the lightening sky. The brazier containing the warning beacon was lit and flaming high, a signal to the neighbouring garrison at the castle some twelve miles away across their valley that they were under attack.

Paul scrambled down to the cobbled courtyard where worried looking men-at-arms were watching the great gate bowing and splintering from the impact of the mighty ram. Paul saw a sergeant he knew. "We're going to make another barrier - get those carts closed up and turned over in a line - here." He stood on the spot where he wanted the barrier whilst the sergeant and his squad took the draft horses out of harness, drove them away into the castle lanes, and tipped over the carts end-to-end in a crescent-shaped line, piling up some of their remaining rocks to help fill the gaps.

As they were doing this, the reinforcement of armoured Templar knights and sergeants from his section were arriving, clattering along the wall above, then down the steps to where Paul waited and formed them into line on top of the barrier. He waved at the detachment of Genoese crossbowmen to stay up there, as they followed the knights, and ran up the stone steps to them on the rampart, shouting and gesticulating. He instructed them to stay up on the ramparts to fire down into the enemy, whenever they emerged below. Every bolt they fired should be deadly; but those weapons were slow to rewind and the archers could be overrun unless they could be kept apart from the hand-to-hand struggle that would happen, as soon as the invaders had broken through the gate.

He now had about twenty men at arms transferred from his section of wall - plus some thirty who had already been in the courtyard waiting for any breakthrough, and had them all engaged in erecting the makeshift barrier, and then climbing up to stand on it. He could see some fifteen of his crossbowmen up on the parapet, winding-up their weapons and placing their steel bolts conveniently to hand. He detached four of his men-at-arms with spears, with instructions to stand and defend them at all costs, halfway up the single flight of narrow stone steps leading up to the fighting platform where his Genoese were winding their bows.

Before many more minutes had passed, a great roar announced that the main gate before them was sagging off one of its hinges, as the timbers splintered from the last great impact. Beyond, the defenders could hear trumpets and now see in the gap of broken timber, the maddened bearded faces of battle-crazed warriors, who having had to endure casualties from above, now were able to engage and hit back. Roaring as they ran, the first attackers emerged across the cobblestones from the gatehouse to be surprised and then slowed, with the need to evaluate this new obstacle of Paul's carts, together with a line of well-armoured dismounted knights with shields and swords, standing on top along the length.

As the number of invaders quickly swelled, sheer momentum carried them forward. Above them, the line of armoured Templars standing on top of the overturned carts looked ready for whatever would come their way. Paul now stood, sword in hand and shield on arm in the middle of the line; beside him a young squire holding 'Beauseant', the Templars 'piebald' standard, their black and white battle flag, which on Paul's orders he now dipped and raised. The crossbowmen above and behind the dense crowd of invaders, having had their signal, could not miss.

A volley of fifteen steel bolts tore into the crowd below as the first of the invaders began to scramble up the barrier, as best they could. There the Templar swords took their deadly toll. Within moments, the space in front of the barrier was full of dead and dying men, the air full of screams, shouts and the clash of arms. On the parapet above the remains of the gate, rock missiles were being hurled down by the defenders as well as murderous steel bolts from the skilled Genoese, as fast as they could rewind their bows. The courtyard had become a killing ground, blood flowed and screams and curses mingled, in a frightful cacophony.

Then the first tall horseman was through the gate, an emir to judge by the gold chasing on his steel armour, wearing a spiked steel helmet surrounded by the swathed cloth of a green and yellow turban. Behind him came his mounted standard bearer carrying a metal crescent moon on a spear shaft, with a crosspiece from which dangled two horsetails. More horsemen crowded behind their leader expecting that once the gate was down, their height and weight would carry them through the resisting foot soldiers in the melee, within the broken gate. That done, sheer momentum should have taken them well inside the castle, cutting down any resistance as they came to it. On top of the gatehouse, garrison soldiers who had been shooting arrows and hurling missiles down onto the Turks storming their gates, were now concentrating on the mob already inside below them, crowding the castle courtyard, their momentum checked only by Paul's barricade.

The Templar garrison commander was amongst the crowded defenders above the gate, and seeing the opportunity, grabbed two of his crossbowmen and ordered them to fire only at the enemy emir. His great horse was prancing and his lance had just now found a target embedded in a Templar, bestriding the cart to his front. The roar from the invaders had increased as they saw the gap that this made in the line, and their chance. Two crossbow quarrels almost simultaneously tore through the emir's chain mail, taking him out of the saddle, down amongst the hooves below.

Now the roar came back from the defenders and then grew as the attackers faltered.

At the very height of this drama, a Turkish trumpet outside the walls sounded a signal, which Paul recognised incredibly as their order to retreat. The fierce warrior with whom he had been trading vicious sword blows suddenly disengaged; jumping down from the small progress he had made climbing up the overturned cart, and joined the milling crowd. Paul was not alone in being astonished that they would give up now, having broken into the castle, but those Turks already inside the bailey had already turned and were now struggling with each other to get away. Two horsemen had dismounted and lifted the emir back onto his own horse, their mounted colleagues clustered around him as their horses forced a way through the now panicking foot soldiers, but all the while a rain of crossbow bolts scythed into their ranks, the Genoese now concentrating on the enemy cavalry.

More went down to be lost under the feet of their horses and the frantic footmen, jostling each other trying to escape beyond the shattered gate.

Now the host poured back through the ruined entrance, whilst outside amongst the rocks, Turkish archers gave them covering fire, shooting at any heads that showed themselves above the gatehouse tower. The stricken emir was held in the saddle by two loyal attendants, the three horses moving tightly, their heads grouped together as though conferring, their bodies as though tied together, came out and away and moved out of sight, along with the retreating force, into the rocky hillside outside the castle.

Now above the noise, another, a familiar trumpet, sounded from down the hill below the castle. The very fact that it could be heard above the immediate commotions, suggested it came from somewhere nearby. Paul leaning on his sword, breathing hard from his exertions recognised the signal and the explanation for the enemy withdrawal. He gave thanks for the long column of Templar cavalry riding hard uphill, now coming into sight, with daylight firmly established, having been alerted by the alarm beacon fire on the top of their highest tower. The Templars were saved to fight another day.

THE SECRETS OF ISTANBUL

Istanbul 2010

Brother Aloysius Daly SJ, a small plump cheerful man, who could have been aged anywhere between twenty five and forty five, scurried along the dusty street in his less than spruce soutane - 'lived in' - he would have described it. He relished whatever shade he could find beneath the plane trees that had managed somehow to survive in this unfriendly terrain of run-down buildings, around the sleepy, dusty, down-at-heel square. He had just left the city archive whose worn steps and unimposing entrance lay immediately behind him. It had been two weeks since he had first visited the apparently crumbling building, which he surmised must come close to the tail of any queue for municipal funds. He had been quite surprised when he first met the courteous lady who was chief archivist, with her traditional Moslem ankle length robe and head covering, surprised because he had thought before coming here, that the enthusiastically secular Turkish government, which he knew had campaigned against such un-western apparel, would not allow it to pass in a senior civic appointment.

Not only was he wrong on that point, but also that all the young women assistant librarians were similarly clad, heads covered and bodies apparently as shapeless as Christian nuns. Indeed by the wearing of more or less customary steel-rimmed spectacles, and having well-scrubbed complexions, they resembled nuns quite closely. It was obvious from the textual material that he witnessed them so assuredly handling, that they were graduates and all things considered, probably very poorly paid. But he had been charmed by their willingness to help him in his quest, not of course that they could know what that really was.

He had been in the city of Istanbul and the adjacent township of Galata, on the other side of the Golden Horn for some three weeks, and was nearly ready to move on. The project on which he was engaged was two-fold. The Father General of the Society of Jesus, a German, formerly a Provincial of the Order in the US, had a year before summoned him to his bureau at the magnificent Gesu Church in Rome, and tasked him with a highly unusual project. Beneath Al Daly's undistinguished exterior lay a first class mind. Being an unusually bright scholar in central Ireland, the Christian Brothers who had taught him had advised him long ago, that the Church was the place for him. Yet truth to tell, despite or perhaps because of the physical pressure to recite such schoolroom mantras, as: 'What-is-God?-God-is-Love,' each word punctuated by an ungentle slap to the side of his head, he was not really religious. He had never for a moment wanted to become a parish priest nor a missionary, although having been headhunted by the Society of Jesus it seemed that he was bound to follow the directions of his Order. Fortunately, his intellect and unusual investigative skills had been recognised and his future in the ecclesiastical 'civil service' determined. He was designated a Jesuit 'temporal co-adjutor', that avoided the necessity of being ordained a priest, which suited him fine. For his part, he found the intellectual contrast between the Jesuits and the Christian Brothers of his boyhood, a profoundly different and welcome new experience.

He had been instructed to write an 'eyes only' confidential report on a once mighty Order of the Church that had ceased to exist, seven centuries before in 1312, following the Church Council of Vienne in that year. Although it had been well documented up until then, only two years later in 1314, following three terminal events - the deaths within months of each of the three leading actors in that drama, all further traces of the Order simply ceased to exist. At least, they were not to be found in any ecclesiastical or academic records. From that point it simply disappeared from the history books.

The suppressed Order at that time nearly two centuries old, was a military one - that of the Knights Templar. The deaths, following that last fatal year, included its grandmaster Jacques de Molay, who died in Paris - some said 'martyred', burned at the stake on March 18th 1314. Soon afterwards Pope Clement V, the titular head of the Order under whose ultimate authority this matter came to pass, died following a gastric attack. King Philip 'the Fair', who had ordered the agonising death of de Molay, had survived him only by eight months before meeting his own violent end. He was unloved after a long reign but the circumstances of his death whilst hunting, surrounded by his own people on his own estate, appeared to have been obvious and accidental.

This burning of the last Templar grandmaster introduced Brother Daly's second, parallel project, which was to seek to determine the causes of an extraordinary annual event that had taken place over several centuries past. This was a little known outrage against the worldwide Order of Dominicans, in former years the conductors of the Inquisition. It reliably re-occurred on every 18th March, the anniversary of the execution in Paris that spelled the end for Jacques de Molay.

Usually this took a destructive form, such as the burning down of a Dominican Church or monastery, or other property, anywhere in the world - the last one earlier in that year of 2010 being a seminary in Paraguay. For seven centuries, the Dominicans own research had shown the pattern. No single year on that 18th day of March since 1314, had failed to see such an outrage. Only the Dominicans - and that quite a long time later with the coming of modern communications, had made the connection of the identical dates each year, and eventually deduced from this, a link to the Paris burning.

The friars had confided their suspicions to the present pope, as the General of the Jesuits explained to Brother Daly. But there was something else. Certain records had recently been unearthed in the Vatican Library and published to the world by the licensed researcher, a female lay academic. It was all very embarrassing. The documents described a hitherto unknown episcopal examination seven centuries before, conducted at the then Pope Clement V's behest, by three of his cardinals. It was held at the Fortress of Chinon in the valley of the Loire, where de Molay and his three senior colleagues in the military Order were imprisoned. These, the most senior knights had been extensively re-interviewed there - but this time not under torture. Torture they had already undergone individually, two years previously, when on Black Friday, 13th October, every Templar in France that could be located, was arrested in a country-wide dawn swoop by the king's seneschals. It was well known that the knightly prisoners were all handed over to the black Dominicans of the Holy Inquisition in France, and were grievously tortured. They had either died under the relentless questioning, or had signed prepared confessions under extremes of agony and physical torment.

These recently rediscovered Vatican papers demonstrated, long after the event, that the Templars were not guilty of the sins of heresy or apostasy, which was the widely understood cause of their downfall. For later denying their heresy admitted only under torture- which denial condemned them as apostates, many had died at the stake. Since no mention of this Chinon papal inquiry was spoken of, nor recorded at the 1312 Vienne Church Council only three years later - the Council at which the future of the Order had been determined, it now seemed obvious that the pope of that time must have wanted nothing to emerge that interfered with his chosen outcome for that critical Council at Vienne.

"We may speculate," Karl Heinz the Jesuit Father General, pointed out in his American intonated English, as he long-leggedly strode the room, his hands clasped behind him, "that Pope Clement had ordered his secretaries not to destroy, but merely to definitively 'lose' this game-changing report." He emphasised with a cutting hand gesture, the word 'lose'.

"It was signed and moreover sealed by all three of his nominated cardinals, finding the Templars innocent of the charges against them. My guess is that it was deliberately misfiled amongst the thousands of other records in the Vatican archives. If it were to be discovered, Clement might have thought, it would be too late to make any difference - but he was not to know that as it turned out, it would take a full seven centuries to emerge.

"My dear Al," his general asked, as he was wont to do when they were alone, "the point is that we are not aware that any historical record of all this exists beyond 1314. But, there are some good specialist historians of the military orders, out there. There is also, it is obvious to me, a canvas of sorts, where there are seemingly unrelated factual 'dots' that need 'joining up'. The discovery of this cardinals' commission document may indeed whet a few researching appetites. Your mission is simply to ensure that any 'dots' that need to be connected, are done by us within the Church, and not by the outside laity - not by any investigative journalist or lay historian. That is the whole point of your task. His Holiness, the Curia, and I need to know first!

"To say that there is speculation", he continued, "about the continuation of the Templars and has been for centuries, would be an understatement, as you must know. Many international Freemasons indeed see themselves as their temporal heirs, a continuation down the centuries - and there are other claimants and any amount of other candidates, let alone speculation about the Templar treasure - any good mystery has a treasure." he added dryly. He drew breath and pondered a moment before continuing. "Those who have followed the story so far, will sense that there is more yet to be revealed. The Holy Father has made it clear to me that, next time, he must be the first to know about any developments relating to the Templars, or for that matter any other of the religious orders, past, present, or suppressed. Not, embarrassingly way down the line after the world's media, particularly with any other information, that might emerge about these troublesome knights, if indeed it is they or their ghosts who are pursuing the Dominicans.

"We know for example that the Templar personnel unaccounted for after the 1312 dissolution, amounted to some thousands of individuals. We know this because of the disparity with the numbers who were recorded as being brought to trial. That was compared with the rolls, such as could be painstakingly collected up, from the archives of all the Templar establishments that the Church of those days eventually gathered in. They had help from the Knights of St John, who inherited the Templar properties, including what remained of the Templar records on the island of Cyprus, although the Turks there had obviously had centuries to find anything of interest.

"Your brief is to investigate the events of the last years of the Order and those that followed afterwards, until the story either climaxes, or peters out. You will be familiar with the outline at least, of what I have told you. What I want - more importantly what his Holiness wants, is a credible, demystified narrative on what happened after the dissolution. You will be given modest resources, including access to all Vatican papers and entree to Church officials and affiliates anywhere, but Al, we want no press stories, none, about your investigation. That would be the worst sort of publicity, so be discreet!"

The Jesuit General had suggested some lines of enquiry. He said that the Knights of Malta had recruited many of the stranded Templars from Cyprus after their order was shut down. At that time, long before they went to Malta they had become known as the 'Knights of Rhodes', and prior to that, of 'St John of Jerusalem,' but throughout they were known to the world colloquially as the 'Hospitallers'. They still exist as a sovereign order, now with more than nine hundred years of known history. It was understood that initially there was continuity amongst those Templar knights that they had absorbed. In Portugal indeed, where through all of this, they were still fighting the Moors, the Templars were not 'shut down', but had a modest change of name, and the Portuguese king substituted to be their supreme head, no longer the pope.

Al Daly, considering his brief, was so far, not really startled by the instruction to investigate these events, but later that changed to surprise when his boss then advised him to look further into Masonic histories, which certainly had traditions to offer, and to seek historical facts from before the eighteenth century.

The freemasons, although manifestly older as a society, only 'went public' in London in 1717, four hundred years after the recorded end of the Templars. "There is a Scottish dimension to this story," the general continued, "dating at least from the battle of Bannockburn, and then nearly 150 years later all that business about Rosslyn, the remarkable church of the

St Clair family, built in the Scottish lowlands around 1450. St Clair as a surname seems to have morphed into Sinclair, both versions featured amongst the Templars, as well as Scottish freemasons.

"There is also an historic Armenian angle here too, because of the Western Armenian kingdom of Cilicia, now southeast Turkey. That had held out as a Christian enclave for a further ninety years after the end of the Christian kingdom of Jerusalem, thus sixty years or so after the Templars formally ceased to exist. We know that the Templars had castles and estates there in 1307, but nobody seems to know whether they were still in Cilicia until the end of that Christian kingdom. You may also have heard traditions about the Templar involvement in Switzerland, but none of this has been seriously investigated before.

"And Al," the father general continued, "his Holiness pointed out to me that the reason he was putting this matter in the hands of our Society, was not only because, in the fourth vow of our Society, we are always there to serve the pope of the day, and take on any missions he might designate. But more to the point, because like the Templars, we Jesuits also had powerful enemies and our Order was suppressed. It took forty-one years before the ban was lifted and the Society of Jesus reconstituted, yet, as you will know, during that interregnum our predecessors and our Society didn't disappear at all, but continued 'sub-judice' in outlandish places: Russia in 1773 was certainly outlandish, yet even so, we survived.

"By the same logic," he pointed out, "the zeal and fraternal loyalty of those thousands of surviving Templars, 'esprit de corps' if you will, would surely not have just tamely accepted dissolution and the cruel injustice to their brother knights. I fear that they would have sought revenge, not least for their tormentors - hence perhaps the annual destruction of Dominican properties. Besides, they were very rich, their portable wealth disappeared with them. And if they are responsible for these fires, then they are also signalling, are they not, that in some form, they continue to exist? The implications of that are profound! If it were to be established, think what a media frenzy that would cause!

"There are, it seems, no shortage of matters to be rediscovered, and his Holiness and I expect you to do exactly that."

***

Following that extraordinary briefing of a year ago, Al Daly had a clerk, a computer and a desk assigned to him in the Jesuit HQ in Rome together with written papal authority 'requesting and requiring' help and assistance on his behalf. That hadn't made much difference in Istanbul, where Rome was decidedly junior to the Greek Orthodox patriarchate, but for what he needed to do there, it hadn't mattered. The Istanbul city archives went back from the Fourth Crusade and through straight research had indeed rendered up a missing link, with documents in Latin and in medieval French, from which he had established that - in what was then Constantinople - the Templars had been represented by a trading house, a hospital and a bank, which they had established after that disgraceful crusade, when the city became for a while a Latin domain, a century before the Templar's dissolution.

He had discovered significantly from the city terroir in the archive, that unlike the Hospitallers, the Order of the Temple had de facto survived the restoration of the Greek Byzantine emperors, once the temporary Latin rulers were chased out. Perhaps their being bankers had made the difference, but he also knew that the Templars had refused to take any part in conquering the Christian Byzantine capital. They were sworn to fight the Moslem enemy in the Holy Land and Iberia. To their credit they had refused similarly to take part in the crusades against the Cathars in France and Spain, where their hated rival order, the Dominicans first formed the Inquisition to pursue the religiously deviant Cathars.

The Templars then were possibly still in Constantinople in 1453, when the city fell to the Ottomans - 140 years after the order officially ceased to exist! This in turn tied up with his recent research in Galata, the neighbouring port-town outside the city walls, where the Ottomans allowed westerners and foreigners generally, to live after the conquest, and to do business under a Genoese consul. It was there he had discovered an as yet unproven but probable connection, company names which to him had a pattern associated with the Order, but meaningless to those unschooled in the Templar story. The earlier consular records in Galata were in Latin, and he had recognised 'the Company of Merchants of Palma Balearis' where he knew the Templars in Majorca had their own separate port. Also that being part of the Spanish kingdom of Aragon, they anyway would not have been suppressed in 1312. He also spotted a 'Company of Merchants of Tortosa'. He recalled that this was a fortified Templar town and port that they had owned outright at one time, on the Syrian coast. He had to be sure, but he thought it very likely that this presence in Galata would date back to the Byzantine centuries, before the 1453 capture of the city by the Ottomans. He had already discovered that Galata as a base for foreign merchants had originated under the Byzantine emperors, who wanted the European establishments' resident outside of their city, for the same reason as did the

Turks. There were no clues about foundation dates in this register, but he was hoping that these Tortosa merchants would be shown to have been established in Galata during the period of the Christian kingdom of Jerusalem. Constantinople was then the greatest city in the world and much closer and more relevant to the Templars in the Holy Land than the shattered remains of Rome, near derelict for centuries. The brethren could hardly have been the far-flung traders that he knew them to be, if they had ignored Constantinople.

He had e-mailed Giancarlo, his office assistant in Rome to work up what was known about the Galata trading houses into a report for his return.

So, he mused, now he had evidence of the Templars' probable presence in Constantinople until it fell to the Turks, a century and a half or so after their order was officially dissolved, and it became Istanbul. Moreover, the thought continued, if his deductions were correct, after the Turkish conquest of 1453 they would have continued trading from the neighbouring town of Galata, where these trading institutions, for which he had two prospective names, still to be checked through if that were possible, might have continued until a more recent time.

His work in Istanbul done, the next day Daly flew back to Rome and on the two-hour journey, reclined his seat and turned over in his mind, what he now knew. He had, earlier, through the Cistercians, discovered a 12th century document outlining how the nascent Templar Order had been founded by the powerful Count Hugh of Champagne, together with his vassal Hugh de Payens, with the help of the later St Bernard and his brother Achard the architect, who together had set up the school of architecture at the new Cistercian abbey of Clairvaux.

That did suggest a connection with the later freemasons, then simply called 'The Children of Solomon' a craft guild of cathedral master-builders and architects in France and elsewhere, who like the Templars, had asked for and had their Rule written for them, by St Bernard. Intriguingly, this required them to be supervised, in his instructions, by the leaders of the Order of the Temple.

Daly had made much progress since being assigned his task. Information obtained from the rolls of the early kings in Scotland, together with research in the ruins and records of the castle Aird in Argyllshire, told him that Aird was held by the clan Macdonald, Lords of the Isles, and leased to the Order, became the rallying point for those Templars that had escaped the purge and arrests of 1307 and 1308.

Likewise, he was greatly indebted to the monks of the Cistercian Abbey at Hautrive in Switzerland who allowed him access to their 14th century records, which indicated a Templar connection with Switzerland, dating from as early as 1315. This gave him tantalising leads that now needed further research.

Finally as a kind of continuing thread, he had what purported to be the story of these fugitive years from a lengthy and rambling, but invaluable deposition, made for his heirs, by one Sir Geraint of Monmouth, in the 1340's, held in the library at Wales's Tintern Abbey until Henry VIII's dissolution of the monasteries, and then rescued and placed in a private collection, until much later, gifted to the British Library. Al knew he had enough to put the first part of the story together, up until the Battle of Bannockburn and afterwards.

He had a narrative which took the history of the Order past the nearly two centuries of their known existence, through the first disastrous years of the change in their fortunes following the mass arrests of 1307, their dissolution at the Council of Vienne in 1312, up to and including two years later, the deaths of Grandmaster de Molay; the King of France, Philip IV; and Pope Clement V - all in 1314.

Since his assignment, Al had been living, eating, breathing the Templars, having read all the several histories dedicated to them and of their period; and anxious to miss no clue, a mass of novels starting with Sir Walter Scott's "Ivanhoe," up to Dan Smith's "The da Vinci Code" - and still they kept coming. He found that most of the paperbacks now were modern all-action adventure stories, with the thinnest of connections to such mysteries as the Holy Grail, the Holy Shroud, the Ark of the Covenant, Merovingian dynasties and more, with which the Templar story had somehow become associated.

THE STREETS OF PARIS

Paris, 1309

Peter of Bologna, Templar priest, lawyer and accused heretic, was now for the first time in two years, truly afraid. Physically of average size with a trim beard and, after enduring the plain diet of a monk for the past two years, of spare build, he was being hurriedly marched, late on a cold night through the streets of Paris, down the slope from the Abbey of Saint Germain-des-Pres towards the river. There on the left bank, the bridge at the Little Chatelet crossed to City Island, where lay the palace of King Philip and beneath it, his prison of the Conciergerie. It was there, the escort sergeant had told the protesting Abbot that the lawyer-priest was to be taken.

Early each day for the past several weeks, Peter had been accustomed to the king's guards arriving after matins and escorting him from the Abbey to the papal tribunal at St Genevieve's Monastery on City Island, returning him at the end of each day. At the tribunal he was the main advocate for hundreds of his fellow Templars accused of heresy, most of whom, in the hands of the Dominicans, had been tortured into some form of confession to accusations of deviation, which given this tribunal, their first opportunity, they now wished to repudiate.

The sergeant habitually in the past had made sarcastic remarks about the lawyer's 'silver tongue', but more out of the habit of routinely bullying his prisoners, than from any particular malice. At the time, the Templar priest thought little of it. He had been privileged to be confined as an ecclesiastical prisoner at the Benedictine Abbey of Saint Germain-des-Pres. It was the one favour the Pope, whom he had served as a trained lawyer and diplomat as the Order's representative, was prepared to do for him, saving him from the fate of the other Templars, knights and sergeants alike, seized nearly two years before, on 'Black Friday.' They having been cruelly 'examined' by the Inquisition were still confined in the King's stinking gaols, along with the riff-raff of Paris.

More to the point, Peter of Bologna had expressly been saved from the fearful torture the others had individually experienced, several of them fatally, by his person being given into the responsibility of the Abbot of Saint Germain. The abbot was a perfectly decent churchman, with instructions from his Holiness that Peter was not to be surrendered to the Dominicans for their Inquisition, but was to be held there as a papal prisoner and live the life of an ordinary monk, until the trial.

But it was the same king's men who had come for him, this time at night and now with a warrant to seize him, saying he was to be transferred to the Conciergerie. The Abbot true to his charge protested that Brother Peter was the prisoner of the Pope, but it did no good. These were the king's guards and the sergeant told the abbot that their orders were to take him by force, if necessary.

There was the sergeant briskly striding down the cobbled street out in front with a lanthorn, which showed the rubbish and filth in the thin stream of the surface drain, flowing down the hill towards the river, contributing to the all-pervading city stench. The crowded houses on each side of the narrow way had the uppermost of their four and five stories leaning, overhanging the street below, but at this time of night all the windows were shuttered. His escort, behind their sergeant, was of four soldiers holding spears, two on each side of the prisoner with the sergeant in the lead. But used to him from the daily escort, they did not really expect any more than he did, that their charge would give them any trouble. On this damp misty night they were cloaked against the cold whilst the prisoner in his black cassock with a red Templar cross on the left shoulder had no such overclothes, and shivered - or was that truly, he wondered, trembling?

There were few people about, but then a tavern door at the top of a few stone steps ahead was thrown open and a drinker came out to stagger down the steps, so as to then open his breeches and piss against the wall. Then he was off lurching downhill ahead of them, towards another hostelry. A short column of Franciscan monks, eyes downcast in their brown cowled robes, knotted cords at their waist, their bare feet in sandals on this cold night very evident, were walking uphill towards them in three pairs in file. Suddenly, a horseman, by the evidence of his mount, clothes and sword, a gentleman, trotted up from the rear, his horse's iron-shod hooves noisily resounding on the cobbles. He overtook and passed the briskly marching guards and their prisoner, and moved on downhill towards City Island. Other than that the street was still.

The St Genevieve Monastery tribunal of six senior churchmen in the shadow of the great Notre Dame had been appointed by the Pope to try to reassert his authority over that of the King, in such ecclesiastical matters as heresy, affecting an order of the Church. These churchmen were to take evidence for the future trial of the Order by interviewing any Templar who wished to give testimony. The hundreds of Templar captives had been allowed to elect a lawyer to speak for them and it had been this same Peter de Bologna, a member of their own order and he himself accused of heresy, which they had chosen.

It had all been going so well - too well for the King to tolerate! Philip's ministers had been sitting in court, glowering at each witness giving evidence, whilst taking notes. Peter of Bologna, leading for the defence, had used the same technique with each of the defendants as their turn came up. He had asked them to remove their shirts or prison rags, and show the tribunal the often suppurating marks of their torture. The reverend gentlemen on the tribunal had been genuinely horrified at what they had seen. What value, Peter had argued, was any confession resulting from such vile treatment as that, which flesh and blood could clearly not withstand?

Earlier that very day at the tribunal there had been a shocking development, yet Peter had not been there. For the first time, the escort had not come for him, so he waited in vain to no purpose. Nearly fifty of the defendants had failed to arrive in the prison transports to the normally overcrowded court, and to the shock of the others, the king's representative had then stood up and announced to the court that they would not be coming any more.

The appalling news was that they had overnight been condemned and sentenced to death by fire, as relapsed heretics - the price of withdrawing their torture-extracted confessions before the papal tribunal! This devastating sentence had been passed by one of the king's tame courtier bishops, unconnected to the eminent churchmen on the tribunal, who were powerless to intervene, but which made an utter mockery of their own mission on behalf of the Pope.

The effect was, as intended, to frighten hundreds of other Templars, many of whom had not yet been examined, into withdrawing their 'not-guilty' pleas. Peter now understood that his arrest just now by the king's men, could only mean that they were summarily closing down a process that they had belatedly realised, they could not control. They were, as a part of the reaction eliminating him from the tribunal. Hence he knew fear. He sensed that in such circumstances, once he was delivered to the Conciergerie that he would never emerge alive - and probably, before the king's men killed him, the Dominican inquisitors in the name of Christ, would torment his pinioned body. There was nothing at all that he could do about it!

The tavern door swung open again and another drunk swayed out hanging on it, looking stupefied at the sight of the soldiers who were now abreast of the door and who looked enviously past him into the crowded cheerful, space within. The six cowled Franciscans coming towards them uphill had passed at this moment, showing no interest in the sights and sounds of the nearby tavern. Peter, who alone noticed them as they passed, was the first to see that they had broken formation. The hands that had been buried inside their deep sleeves now emerged holding lethal short-handled hatchets. With these firmly gripped, they sprang straight into action. They leapt on the individual soldiers from behind and mercilessly battered them down, two of them pounced on the sergeant, hacking down on his neck and head and shattering the arm he raised to try to defend himself. The shouts and screams were quickly cut off by the attackers chopping into their throats. The shutters on the nearby houses meanwhile, remained firmly closed.

Within two minutes, the bloody business was finished. All the soldiers, none of whom had either the time nor space to wield their spears in defence, were down. They sprawled on the cobble stones either dead or dying, their blood flowing into the central gutter along with the ordure and household waste.

The 'drunk' hanging on the tavern doorway had closed and secured it behind him, immediately the attack had started, and straightening up, had shown that he was in command.

"Make sure there are none left alive. Clear everything away, leave nothing," he ordered the others as he came down the steps and gripped Peter's arm.

"We are here to save you, Brother Peter. Do everything we tell you, do it quickly and don't argue." he ordered.

The 'Franciscans', Peter could now see, all wore mail shirts with a linen tabard bearing some heraldic device of a stag's head under the blood-stained brown robes, which they were now pulling off and rolling up. They dragged the five bloody bodies down to an alley and into its depths where they dumped them in the dark, away from the corner of the main downhill road. Coming towards the group out of the darkness of this alley, were two more men in mail hauberks leading between them the reins of several horses. "Get you up Brother Peter," said the leader, holding a stirrup for him. "I am Brother Paul of Chatillon. We have a long way to go tonight and first we have to get out of this damned city."

THE HOUNDS OF GOD

Castle Aird, Argyllshire, Scotland 1312

The bare stone-walled room was surprisingly hot with just the body warmth of ninety or so male figures. Mostly they were clad in woollen, cowled robes, some brown, some black, mostly white, but all with the characteristic insignia of the red cross patee of the Templar order, on the left shoulder. They had been gathered there sitting and standing in low-talking groups for more than two hours. The lonely granite stronghold was exposed high above the promontory of Aird on the coast of Argyllshire.

Below the towering cliff on which it stood, Atlantic waves were breaking on the rocks and islets. White foam raced up the shingle towards a pair of large galleys drawn up, well back below the cliff. Castle Aird was not known for its moderate temperatures even in the middle of summer. But such a gathering in the spacious octagonal chapter house, graced with a fan-vaulted high ceiling but without window embrasures, was inevitably generating heat - not least because of the momentous issues to be decided this day.

Decorating the hewn ashlar walls on which beads of condensation were forming and depending from the oak beams above, were long chained, black iron candle holders, emitting a smoky waxen odour, which blended with the body smell of these ninety adult fighting men, to whom such refinements as soap were a rarity indeed. It served to make an atmosphere thick enough seemingly, to cut with a blade, were it not for the Rule, first introduced by St. Bernard, that forbad the carrying of edged or pointed weapons into a Chapter meeting. In sockets set high around the walls there was an array of banners, all with the one device of black above white halves. Beauseant, the battle flag of the Order, floated motionless above these survivors of the treachery of five years earlier - Black Friday, 13th October 1307, forever their day of infamy.

These were by no means the only survivors. The dragnet across Europe was initiated by the French king, who had first launched the surprise mass arrest of all the Templars to be found in his domains across France. This immediately had taken more than two thousand of the brethren including most, though not all, of the Order's high officers and their grandmaster, Jacques de Molay. Like the others, the Master had been swiftly delivered by the king's men to the Dominicans of the Holy Inquisition, to be forced by unendurable torture to sign already prepared - and bizarre confessions of heresy.

It had been a slick operation. No one knew more of the skills of inflicting pain than the Dominicans, who had first honed this black art on the hapless Cathars of the Languedoc, a hundred years before. They had been readily employed ever since, wherever the powerful, be they rulers or prelates of the kingdoms and principalities that made up Christendom, could infer heresy as a part of any resistance to their authority. But it was often enough for these black friars that their own blind fanaticism could find some seeming error, to be sniffed out by those who gloried in being called *Deus Cano*, 'the Hounds of God'.

Breaking the rich and mighty Templars was a detailed scheme devised by those in Paris surrounding King Philip. The Dominican Master, Guillaume de Paris, the Grand Inquisitor in France, was also the King's private confessor and complicit in every detail. He knew that Jacques de Molay, taken by trickery and immediately put to the question was the confession that really mattered. Those experienced torturers overseen by the Grand Inquisitor himself, had not failed to break him. Great warrior and war leader though he was, his body was still only flesh and blood - and nerve endings! Pinioned in chains he too, like his brethren, discovered that unlike blows and wounds taken in the rush of battle, his naked flesh could not indefinitely hold out and withstand intolerable pain, unremittingly and mercilessly applied. The agony was absolute yet he had been told constantly throughout the ordeal, that it would stop instantly if he wished it.

His confession had already been drawn up and all that was required was his pain-wracked assent. This came eventually and inevitably, when finally the man, this leader of thousands, had become reduced to a shrieking 'thing', and all resistance had collapsed.

***

Templar mobility by sea was one factor in the choice of Scotland as the ultimate rallying point, indeed that wild part of western Scotland was barely accessible other than by sea. It was the very frontier of northern Christendom facing the storm-ridden wilderness of the Atlantic, leading only to the presumed edge of the world. It was as remote as could be wished for by the surviving brethren that had made their way there. But there were other good reasons why these ninety fugitive brethren were waiting with growing impatience in this stone Chapter house in the winter of 1312.

They were attending on their leaders conferring in another chamber of the granite fortress. Those men: the Prior, the Marshal from Cyprus were there, and others known only to a few, had arrived during recent days. After some hours in conclave the leaders had announced that they were ready to meet with their brethren in the crowded Chapter house. There, gathered the fugitive knights who had arrived singly or in groups over the five years since the great purge, as well the more recent arrival of those Templar brothers from the revived clandestine groups they called 'shadow houses', summoned as delegates to the meeting from other parts of Christendom to this lonely place. Making their way to Scotland, just surviving over the years, months, and weeks before, had been a dangerous and difficult business, but here they were secure amongst their comrades. Now they were eagerly waiting to make the decisions in Chapter, as was the Templar way, about what was to follow.

***

Many of the brethren had not met before this Chapter meeting, but on the previous night at the refectory whilst some late delegates were still arriving, a group of younger men had found themselves together at one end of the great board table and had struck up conversations. True they were no longer observing the Templar rule about maintaining silence at table, but it was five years since that monastic way of life had been so abruptly terminated. Now their natural curiosity about their neighbours led on to an exchange of their stories and experiences.

None of the older knights were disposed, as in the old days, to call them to order. More, the fraternal warmth and shared dangers of the past years had brought them into a full understanding of the word 'brotherhood'. The curious mingling of purpose that became the life of the warrior-monk was no longer appropriate to the fugitive Templars. On the one hand their days were supposed to be filled with simple tasks and the meek observance of authority while on the other hand they were bound to be battle-ready - undertaking military and equestrian exercises, fitness routines, patrols, weapons maintenance. All these were now becoming faded memories. With the loss of the Holy Land to Christendom, their *raison d'être* - defence of the pilgrims - had become redundant.

Despite their previous privileged status throughout Europe, their power and their money, having been finally expelled from the Holy Land, they had been vulnerable for some time. Recent events in France had merely confirmed what they had feared for many years. Now they knew exactly who and what they were - armed fugitives.

Having avoided arrest, they had failed to submit themselves to the nearest bishop over the five years that had elapsed since Black Friday, and by that omission, anywhere but Scotland, they were outlaws - 'wolf's head' with every man's hand against them!

Paul of Chatillon was in his early twenties. He sat at the end of the table keeping a watchful eye on those around him. As a youth a few years previously, he had journeyed from his father's estates in northern Burgundy to join the Order at their great fortress of the Temple, in Paris. Then after basic training he had travelled with a group of other new recruits on a ship of the Order from Marseilles, to the Headquarters island of Cyprus in the eastern Mediterranean. Soon after his formal admission to the Order, Paul had been posted to a fortress in Cilicia, the mainly mountainous Armenian kingdom not many miles across the eastern Mediterranean, where the Order owned estates and still maintained garrisons, in cooperation with their local Christian allies. There he had earned his spurs and been knighted, rising quickly to the rank of a junior commander. He had, as ordered, made his way back to Western Europe for a special rescue operation, three years before.

Knut Peerson sat beside him, breaking his bread into the wooden bowl of broth. He was also in his twenties, a fair-haired lanky Danish brother with a wispy blond excuse for a beard. He had travelled to Aird from Norway, where after Black Friday five years since, following orders, he had hidden out and been absorbed into the mercantile life of the busy Nordic western port of Bergen.

Prior to that, he had not been long enough in the Order to have had any battle experience, but as a descendant of Viking chieftains he had been trained to arms, and he shared the unquestioned military and naval tradition of his family. He worked with a merchant in Bergen, himself a former Templar, who as a younger man in Syria had lost an arm in battle. No longer able to fight, he had been allowed to relinquish his vows and marry. He had been placed in this port to take care of the substantial Templar mercantile interests there.

Sir Geraint of Monmouth, with a tankard of ale in his hand, looked to be a man who enjoyed life. Solidly built with a fierce gingery military moustache and untamed beard, given somewhat to bulk, and now aged around thirty, he was originally from the coastal town of Pembroke in west Wales, where his father was of the old Welsh nobility. After the conquest, his forebears had suffered a hard time from the Normans and their French allies seeking to dominate this good farming land, but after a century and a half, times had changed. Geraint's elder brother, like their father was now a sworn liegeman of the Earl of Pembroke, and held an estate from him in Monmouthshire where Geraint had lived before joining the Order.

"It is really so strange," Knut told them, "to be back in the habit." He took up a handful of his coarse white woollen robe and squeezed it between finger and thumb. "The quality doesn't improve then - it's still bloody itchy" he grinned. "They loaned me this one when I got here two days ago, it's quite like old times. And hardly anybody, apart from present company …" he nodded in Geraint's direction, "is wearing a beard anymore."

"So where were your 'old times' then young Knut," asked Geraint, himself conscious of being by age at least, the senior of these companions.

"I was in Paris for my induction, and then training for a few months after that. Luckily for me, I was sent to Flanders to make up the numbers there and wait for a posting to Cyprus, because we thought that the new Crusade was what we had signed up for. Everything that happened in France, fortunately for me, was when I was outside of Philip's domains."

"So what then?" asked Geraint.

"The sub-prior where I was in Flanders, got us all to move ourselves. He talked to me about where I could lie low and suggested going north for a while. Then he arranged passage for me to go well to the north, to Bergen in fact."

"Where on this earth can that Bergon be," interrupted Geraint?

"Berg-en" Knut corrected him, "It's as far north as you would ever want to go, but its fine in the summer. It's a busy trading port way up on the wild western coast of Norway. I was sent to the warehouse of a disabled Templar brother whom the Order had placed up there as a merchant. So I was living like a civilian again, no Templar habit and... "

"Does he have any daughters?" broke in Geraint. Knut coloured a little. "He does, as a matter of fact and since we are no longer monks, I can tell you that his daughter and I have an understanding!" He said it defiantly.

"Oh definitely twenty paternosters for you, my boy, just for saying those things, never mind the lewd thoughts," Geraint responded.

"Those were the days - paternosters," Knut ignoring this banter, responded mock-dreamily. "You know they used to do Thor and Odin up where I'm based. Since we are now, it seems, no longer members of any church in good standing, I am thinking of giving them a try."

"You're talking rubbish again," said Geraint. "That young lady you speak of having an understanding with, is hardly going to go along with that. Mind you, it is one hell of an improvement in our lives that we don't have to shy away from women. It's alright for those baldy-headed monks, but not so good for us soldier-boys out in the world, beards or none."

He turned to Paul. "So what is your story then, Brother Paul?"

Paul looked at him broodingly. "Well, I told our Prior when I arrived and I'll tell you now since you ask me straight out, but I would prefer you didn't spread it around." They nodded and waited expectantly.

"Most recently I was serving in Cilicia fighting the Turks, until after the arrest of the French Templars, when I was recalled to Cyprus. They wanted me to get back to the west and join a team doing special operations pulling out key people from Paris - which is where I first met our Prior - and so they sent me back by an interesting mostly land route, to avoid arrest."

"As a novice, I did my time in Paris before being posted out to Cyprus, well before Black Friday, expecting to prepare for the crusade. But it wasn't that. Like the others out there, I heard that the Grandmaster had left Cyprus for France. We were told that he was going to meet the Pope, and plan the crusade with him.

"But it is why they sent me out when they did that puzzles me. I should have gone with my intake a year later, but I was told that I was going on the earlier draft that got me out there, instead of leaving me in the Temple with the others. I know now that that probably saved me from being maimed or burned alive, like the other lads were. Before I left Paris, I asked the sub-prior why I was going early, and he said it was because of a special request from the palace."

"Come on," said Geraint disbelievingly "who did you know, back then a beardless squire, up at the palace - who could be bothered?"

"Ah well, you see," Paul replied, his voice lowering as he spoke. "I told you I was from Chatillon near the borders of Burgundy and Champagne, right? Well so, originally, was the Queen of France, she was Jeanne of Champagne."

His small audience was enthralled.

"You know she was the heiress of Champagne before she married black-hearted Philip. She was some kind of half-sister of my mother when I was just a babe. I knew they were fond of each other, and I think it was down to her. She got me out of it without giving any reason. She sent for me but I didn't know why, and I went, but all she did was ask about my mother and the family; I heard later that she died soon afterwards. I see now that being sort of family, and knowing what was coming - I mean the destruction of the Order, she did what she did for the family, without compromising what Philip was working on."

The silence was palpable.

"Well, blow me down," Geraint finally came back. "So we have royalty amongst us."

***

In the Chapter meeting during the long waiting time, although the volume was low, the conversations were animated as stories of survival were exchanged.

Then the door opened and all talk stopped suddenly. The brethren were seated on the stone benches around the circumference of the chapter house, but some of them, due to the normal capacity being well exceeded, sat on stools, making an inner, less ordered circle. Many of those present had, during the long delay, drifted over to greet old friends, but when the leaders arrived, all respectfully stood. In silence, the wanderers swiftly resumed their places.

The six men that entered made their way to a low podium. The most senior of four white robed leaders was the Marshal, ranking officer of the Order still at liberty, usually war-leader and chief of staff to the grandmaster who presently rotted in the French king's gaol at Chinon castle.

As was the rule, the Marshal would preside over the chapter meeting. His journey over months from Cyprus to this fortress on the west coast of Scotland had been the longest and most elaborately planned of all the leaders and delegates. His presence, however, gave unchallengeable legitimacy to whatever decisions were now to be taken. He had been left in command at the Order's main base in Cyprus, since he was not required to accompany Jacques de Molay to France to visit the Pope.

The Marshal, a solidly built man no longer young, with deep lines etched on his face, his heavy black beard turning to grey, was a bluff veteran of great military experience and considerable wisdom. When the shocking news of Black Friday eventually reached Cyprus via Genoese merchant traders - the arrests, the tortures and the confessions, he had already known of it through the Order's own intelligence system which had much to do with their excellent pigeon-post network. Horrified, he had discreetly informed the more senior of his colleagues and together they had planned and made dispositions. They could do nothing but wait to get official confirmation, then to assess the reaction to the arrests from the new king of Cyprus. That monarch owed his throne to recent help given him by the Order's knights in Cyprus, but his own situation was none too stable.

The sailing season had finished and they knew that the next stage, that of receiving official news from Europe, could take some months.

The Marshal was shrewd enough - given the events in Paris - to know not to trust any crowned head subject to the papal hierarchy, particularly a little king like this Cypriot, when popes and great kings like those of France, or England, could play him like a puppet. He had already used the grace period that the pigeon-post had given him, to secretly move the Order's treasure out of the island. He also transferred away from Cyprus the group of some two hundred of the young knights and sergeants, as yet untried in battle, which had been sent out to Cyprus for training, in anticipation of the new crusade.

He sent messengers to the Armenian King of Cilicia, alongside whom the Templars had continually been fighting in the mountains of southeast Turkey and where hundreds of Templar warriors were still posted.

He also sent galleys with an escort and a senior officer as envoy, on a diplomatic mission to Constantinople itself, together with much of the treasure he was removing from Cyprus. At the Byzantine capital, the Order had long maintained a discreet trading and banking presence in the Genoese controlled enclave of Galata, which also served as a de facto embassy to the court of the Byzantine emperor, also outside of the papal power.

The Marshal now opened the meeting in the Aird Chapter House with a short and peremptory prayer - the prayer was the rule, he pointed out, to open the chapter meeting, but like many others there, his faith in a just deity had been undermined by the events of the last years.

"I want you to know" he told his audience, "that the breach with the Church has clarified my thinking. I have come to realise that they did not deserve our loyalty, the sacrifices we made - and in defence of what? The answer is their comfortable livings, their treasure, and their power competing with the secular rulers, using us as an instrument of that power. For nearly two hundred years, we have served God and the Church. Then the success of generations of our predecessors, who established the means to pay for our armies in Outremer ourselves, aroused the envy of a particularly greedy king and the cowardice of that Pope for whom he had purchased St Peter's Throne. It is clear that this Pope, our supreme commander, betrayed his loyal soldiers to our mortal enemy Philip who sought our destruction.

"What does survive is brotherhood." He looked slowly around the silent warriors, embracing them all with his gaze. "The loyalty we have to our fraternity and to each other. It has been forged over two centuries and it is strong - very strong by the evidence of our presence here today, and those shadow houses that once more are springing to life, all over Europe. I believe that we are over the worst and can now plan for the future. That is the purpose of this chapter meeting. I will shortly pass this meeting over to our Brother Prior, but before I do that there is another thing in which I believe I speak for everyone.

"Hundreds - no thousands - of our brethren have been arrested and passed over to the Inquisition, many of them have been tortured and mutilated. Too many have died. Those arrested in France include our grandmaster and senior colleagues, who even now are still in Philip's dungeons. The word I bring to you to nurture is in our circumstances, the only justice available to us....***revenge!"***

The chapter untypically burst into resounding shouting and applause, unheard of in such a meeting before the assault on the Order.

"The tyrant Philip," the Marshal continued, "the undoubted author of this long and vicious persecution of our brethren must answer for it. The Pope, our commander, who betrayed us - and the Church, which is his vehicle, is now our enemy. So we will regard them as such - how else can it be? But in addition, we will be revenged on the torturers who have ravaged Christendom for a hundred years and more, since the time of the harmless, persecuted Cathars. The Dominicans, educated men hiding behind biblical texts, have cruelly murdered seemingly hundreds - of our dear brethren. If you should ever be so unfortunate as to fall into their hands, they would kill or maim you too, by their black hearts and diabolical instruments.

"As long as there are any Templars left, I charge you to revenge your foully murdered brothers! Do not doubt that we, the Templars, are and will remain at war with the evil Order of St Dominic and their unholy Inquisition."

Again the meeting dropped its traditional restraint as they stood and cheered the grizzled veteran, who now resumed his seat.

By previous arrangement, a man in the black habit of a Templar priest now moved to a lectern at the front. Like all the others he wore a red Templar cross on his left shoulder, albeit atop a black robe. He was of medium build, intense, a rather un-military looking man but nevertheless with an aura of dynamism radiating from him. This was Brother Peter of Bologna, originally trained as a lawyer in the ancient university of that Italian city. When sufficient escapees from Europe, including himself, had been able to gather in Scotland after his flight from Paris three years before, he had been elected by the first chapter meeting that they held to the vacant position of Prior of the Order.

Grandmaster de Molay still lived - during his lifetime he could not be replaced, yet he was lost to them, physically wrecked and confined along with some other senior knights in the close captivity of their persecutor, the King of France in his Loire Valley fortress of Chinon.

Brother Peter was not a fighting man, but may well have been the cleverest and the most worldly-wise within this Order, whose leadership had previously been in the hands of veteran soldiers renowned for bravery, military skills, and devotion to the religion. Against the Moslems in Outremer they had, with some exceptions, been the right men for the job of commanding an efficient military machine.

But they had proven to be like innocent babes when confronted by the machinations of King Philip's lawyers and the Pope's devious advisors, cardinals and others, with cunning men to the fore.

Brother Peter knew something of cunning. He had, before the recent calamitous events, been the Order's representative at the Papal Court, which had not now been in Rome for many years. With the advent of French popes the Curia was at the time of the disaster, established temporarily in the French midland city of Poitiers, before moving south later to Avignon, when that city and surrounding estates were purchased by the Pope. On the east bank of the River Rhone, it technically was outside of the French king's domains, but that illusion would not deter Philip, if he wanted to take it - a permanent reminder to his creature Clement V.

Peter of Bologna's high position in the Pope's entourage had not saved him from eventual arrest, but this had not come until a full three weeks after the fearful events of Black Friday five years before, when the French king's troops had made the infamous dawn raid on the Temple's fortress in Paris and simultaneously on each of their many scattered establishments, spread throughout France.

Brother Peter had been able to see the Pope, after he had been alerted to the events in Paris and elsewhere, on the day following Black Friday, even before the Curia knew of it. As soon as the messenger had given him the first pigeon-delivered news of his Order's disaster, he had requested an immediate audience. It was indeed from him that Pope Clement had first heard of the coup. Brother Peter had remonstrated with Clement, who genuinely seemed not to know of it and had at first appeared shocked and seeming distant, said very little, but the protest was to no avail.

Peter well knew the Dominican's methods. Their Inquisition was forbidden by an earlier pope to 'break bones' or to 'draw blood'; but basting a pinioned prisoner's feet with oil to be roasted over a slow charcoal fire, or stretching their limbs on the rack, both tortures to the point of creating a permanent cripple, no longer able to walk, condemned ever afterwards to agonisingly crawl, were the way they found to get around both those injunctions.

Since all that the victim had to do to stop the torment and the permanent crippling, was to agree to sign the confessions of bizarre heretical behavior, that the inquisitors had already drawn up, it was astonishing that of the several hundred Templars arrested in the Paris Temple on that Friday, the King carried only a small number of such confessions, when three weeks later he came to Poitiers to see Clement. His purpose was to show the Pope this 'evidence' and to enjoin him to issue a Papal Bull addressed to every monarch in Christendom, calling for the immediate arrest of all the Templars in their realm.

The scarcity of confessions spoke of immense courage, but the Templars never lacked that. Yet one of them, Peter was downcast to hear, and it was the one that mattered, was that of Jacques de Molay, the Templar Grandmaster. He had for these early weeks been the principal target of the torments that the Inquisition inflicted, and was now held in close confinement, no one knew where.

Giving Peter of Bologna an audience soon after the king had departed, Clement seemingly sincere, told his Templar advisor that he didn't know where this would all end. King Philip had in numerous ways far exceeded his secular authority. However, the Templars were directly under papal jurisdiction, not that of any king. Only the Church in Council could decide their ultimate destiny, which would he assured Peter, be less than accommodating to the French king, under his own influence.

He also mentioned that King Philip had been shocked to find that the Templar treasure, normally safeguarded in the vaults of their great tower in the Paris Temple had not been discovered there by his troops. Indeed the Brother Treasurer had not been amongst the hierarchy arrested. That news gave Brother Peter some satisfaction, since the seizure of the treasure would have achieved all of Philip's objectives. The King had now officially taken possession of the thousands of farms and estates of the Templars in France, where they had been amongst the greatest landowners.

He had moreover - at a single stroke - wiped out his personal obligation to repay the Order the large debts on loans that he had maintained and increased, since he had come to the throne twenty-two years before. He now took possession of the most powerful stronghold in his capital. The Temple in Paris was more formidable than his own fortress on the City Island, and larger, with 130 walled-in hectares. But his pressing need always was for cash, or valuables that could be converted, and of that - there was none. He had seized the largest bank in Europe - and the vaults were empty!

Almost casually, Pope Clement had told Brother Peter that since every king in Christendom had now been ordered to arrest and confine all Templars, that he, as pope, could hardly have stray members of the Order wandering around as his advisors. So Peter and two Templar colleagues, formerly financial advisors and administrators at the papal court, would be taken under guard to Paris to be confined, mercifully, not in the king's dungeons, but as papal prisoners in the monkish cells of the left-bank Abbey of Saint-Germain-des-Pres. There they would be physically safe, living the monastic life until the time for the trial of the Order was at hand. He assured Peter that the Abbot there had been instructed that he and two other Templars assigned to the pontiff's household, were in no circumstances to be surrendered into the King's custody, or the tender mercies of the inquisition. That much but no more, would he do for his personal staff.

Both of those Templar colleagues from the court were now also in Scotland and on the dais that day. Olivier de Penne, a veteran knight who as a Templar had shown great talent as an administrator, had been a senior official for the Order in Lombardy, but at papal request had been seconded to the Curia to become an advisor to the Pope. He had created a panic in the papal court because he had escaped house arrest alone one night, from Poitiers, before he could be taken to Paris under escort with Peter of Bologna and another Templar colleague from the Curia, Joseph of Portugal, also with them now in Scotland. The fugitive Sir Olivier, despite a reward of 20,000 silver florins offered by the Pope for his recapture had made good his escape and eventually, like the others, got himself to Scotland. He now had made contact, organised and administered the growing network of surviving and re-established 'shadow' houses of the Order, in existence.

Brother Joseph was present in the chapter house and was with him now on the dais. He was clad in the brown habit worn by those members of the order, not members of knightly or aristocratic families, for whom the white cloth had been reserved, the distinction made for nearly two hundred years since their foundation. But knights, obviously the backbone of a military order were not usually schooled; very many - most even, were illiterate. That created a demand for administrative talent; capable of maintaining and expanding what had become effectively the world's first multinational corporation, whose original purpose was to independently fund and maintain the garrisons of their fortresses; their standing army in the Holy Land; and their garrisons in the Iberian peninsula, with the fleets that served them all. Such non-military brethren were often of a high intellectual capacity, attracted by the integrity and scope of the Templars, in a world of corrupt priests and absolute and unprincipled, quarrelling, rulers.

Brother Joseph, like Olivier de Penne, was acknowledged to be brilliant in his own sphere of international financial planning, at which the Templars had no peers. He was perhaps the most skilled financier in Europe, not excluding his Jewish cousins - for he was of a family of Portuguese forced converts to Christianity. At the Pope's request he too had been seconded to the Curia, as they had no one with comparable skills. Now he headed the widespread international mercantile network of the Order, which outside of France had remained largely intact.

***

Within the crowded chapter house smoky with candle-wax, Prior Peter, as he was now known, addressed the meeting, saying that since representatives had come there from all quarters of the Templar world, that he had been delegated to speak for the other leaders on the dais.

The Prior had, undoubtedly, a commanding presence, expressed most obviously by his penetrating gaze. As he spoke, his light tenor voice dominating the assembly, his eyes moved around the room alighting first on someone he recognised, then on another, whose demeanour perhaps deserved his attention.

"I have to tell you of matters which just to speak of, brings sorrow to my heart, as it will to yours." An audible sigh was the response, as if they feared at his words that they already knew what he was to tell them.

"For those who do not yet know me, I am Brother Peter of Bologna, elected as your Prior, a chaplain with the Order and trained as a lawyer. It was my part to represent the Temple at the court of the Pope, normally in the see of Rome, but since the paid-for elevation of this Angevin bishop Bernard Got, who calls himself Clement V, the Curia has been wandering around France. A French pope, it seems, for fear of rioting and violence to his person, would not dare to sit on St Peter's throne in Rome, such is the decay and collapse of the Church of whose body, our Order was a limb.

"I was myself arrested and imprisoned first in Poitiers, and then brought to Paris. To my surprise, I was chosen to represent with three others, six hundred of our imprisoned brethren, some of you are here I see, who wished to renounce the confessions extracted by terrible tortures, of which I know too many of you have had experience at the hands of the vile Dominican dogs."

He looked about at the assembled brethren, some of them actually were survivors of the 'Hounds of God' as the Dominicans styled themselves, more than a few with limbs ruined and their health permanently wrecked from the regime of torture. There was a low murmur of assent and then complete silence as they waited for him to resume.

"So, I and my three colleagues were delegated to speak for them at the Commission of Paris, whose church commissioners were directly appointed by Clement, and surprisingly perhaps, they were not the creatures of the King."

"Brothers of our French houses will know that the King then intervened and stopped that church tribunal, which had obviously been impressed with our arguments. He had his creature, a beardless boy, brother of one of his court favourites himself no more than a courtier that he had created Archbishop of Sens, instantly condemn a great number of our brothers, fifty-seven of them... soldiers of Christ," he articulated the words slowly, "to go alive into the flames!"

He paused to take breath and heard the long low moan amongst his audience. "This mass murder," he continued, "was on the grounds of foul trickery, that by revoking their confessions of heresy, even before the papal tribunal, they had thus become apostates, even though the commission was there to determine that very point - if there was any truth in the ludicrous charges of heresy."

He drew breath, looked around and resumed. "The cardinals, princes of the church, the archbishops and bishops..." Peter paused before continuing, "for generations now have included within their number some of the greatest sinners and hypocrites on earth... "

There was a rising swell of murmured agreement from the assembly. Peter held up a hand for silence as he continued. "But some of them at any rate, even so late as this may have redeemed themselves, enough at any rate to stop Clement from fulfilling his compact with the King, by which he became Pope.

"I have to tell you that we have now had word - our house in Lyons close by is still in shadow existence - from the Council of Vienne... their trusty pigeons, and those of Calais," he added with a smile, "make us amongst the first to know anywhere outside of a two-day march from Vienne. The cathedral church in Vienne, in the territory of the empire, across the river Rhone from Philip's domains, is at this very moment the location of the High Council of all Christendom, there to transact the business of the Church. There is a great drama being played out even as I speak. Foremost amongst their business is the fate of our Order of the Temple."

***

THE COUNCIL OF VIENNE

Vienne 1311-12

The great Rhone River in that late autumn was unusually cold, presaging a bitter winter in the hinterland of the Alpine foothills. In these difficult days for travel of 1311, the river was, however, a highway offering the means by which his Holiness Pope Clement V could reach the city of Vienne, chosen to be the venue of the Great Ecumenical Church Council of that year, from his city of Avignon far downstream. It was not only the pontiff that the river served; in like case it served those that the Council brought together: cardinals, patriarchs, archbishops and bishops, abbots and priors, from all parts of Christendom. The wide river moreover, was at this point the frontier between the Kingdom of France and that of the Dauphine, a principality which at that time was a part of the Holy Roman Empire, within which the ancient city of Vienne was situated.

There were three main points of business before the princes of the Church.

First was an item that generally appeared at all these great councils - the reform of the Church. But since the reforms that were being suggested were the end of simony, the sale of indulgences, and other reliable sources of income for many of those gathered there, it was understood that nothing of significance would change as a result of pious discussion.

The second great topic, which again, nobody took seriously, although that was not apparent from the way they spoke, was the matter of a new crusade. The last bastion of the Christian states in the Holy Land, the great city of Acre, had fallen twenty years previously, to the Moslem powers, ending two centuries of European domination.

Ever since, for forms sake, the matter of a new crusade had been on the agenda. Crusades however devoured money, and lots of it. Further, it had been shown from experience that unless crowned heads were leading the host, then it would probably never set sail. Hence there had been no new crusades within living memory, but the absurdity of even discussing a new crusade was implicit in the third great item to be decided.

That third item concerned the fate of the Order of the Knights Templar, constituted as an Order of the Church in the Cathedral of Troyes in the county of Champagne, one hundred and eighty three years before - it's remit: "for the defence of the faith in the Holy Land and the protection of pilgrims".

Contemplating a new crusade, the only conceivable leader would be King Philip of France who after more than twenty years on the throne, had always managed to avoid going on crusade himself. It was he, as they all knew, who had been the directing intelligence in the destruction of the military order, to which having borrowed for many years, he was overwhelmingly in debt. It was he who had forced the hand of a weak pope who was his creature, by framing charges of heresy, arresting and torturing the Templar prisoners before the Pope even knew of the action he had taken. The Templar's only temporal master was the Pope himself, but as these worldly clerics also understood that this Pope was effectively a prisoner of the king in France, who anyway by bribery had secured his election to the throne of St Peter.

It was these very Templars who were the cutting edge of the Christian armies in Outremer. Other Christian warriors came and served in a crusade, or for a number of years and then returned whence they had come. The Templars, like their fellow knights of the Hospitaller Order of St John, and those of the Teutonic Order, had been a standing army permanently there, building and garrisoning fortresses and patrolling the frontiers.

The Hospitallers were now re-established far from the Holy Land, off the coast of Turkish formerly Byzantine lands, having fortified the island of Rhodes as their new headquarters. They had redirected their efforts towards becoming a naval power. The Teutonics had gone even further away to eastern Poland, where they now employed their crusading zeal against the pagan Prussians and in establishing a new Christian kingdom in the process.

It was a travesty the fathers knew, to consider a crusade without the actual professionals and it was only for this purpose that five years before, the Grand Master of the Order, Jacques de Molay, had left Cyprus for France, at the Pope's summons, in order to offer his strategy and bringing large amounts of money for this very crusade, little knowing he was about to be betrayed by his own supreme commander.

It was apparent then that the fate of the Templars was indeed the only substantive business before them. His Holiness addressed the first session with a sermon on Saturday 16th October 1311, in the great Cathedral Church of Saint Maurice, the martyred Roman soldier who was murdered by the state authorities for his Christian faith.

His Holiness opened the attack on the Templars in an angry voice saying that with over two thousand confessions, their guilt could not reasonably be challenged. The charges against them were classified into 127 headings and he insisted on droning through them all.

His audience was not impressed. They were by no means so sure, and looked for something better to be produced in the way of evidence. They knew well that there were no confessions at all from any of those countries where torture had not been applied, and that although canon law allowed the use of torture, in common sense terms what it produced was worthless, except as a device for awarding punishment. Such points were made over and again by the church fathers, and it became apparent that the Pope and those French bishops, political appointees of King Philip, were the only voices in favour of condemning the Order.

The point was made, and many times repeated, that the Templars should be allowed to represent themselves at such a critical meeting as this, deciding the future of their Order. At last worn down, the reluctant Pope agreed and issued a proclamation to say that any Templar, who wished to do so, could have the opportunity of addressing the Council. He knew that five years after the mass arrests in France and Western Europe, that few Templars if any, could have escaped the manhunt for so long. The chances of any such survivors even hearing of the invitation in this out of the way place, were remote, much less that they would show up.

A few days after the announcement, an Italian cardinal was seated on the dais in the choir presiding over the meeting, his two clerks noting the proceedings at a lower desk before him. Pope Clement in his magnificent pontifical robes was on his throne against the wall, slightly higher up and to one side, with a banner of the Virgin Mary displayed on one side of him and another of St Maurice on the other. Below, in the seats arranged in the body of the great cathedral, the princes of the church in their purples and crimson cassocks and white lace surplices, were intermingled with monastic abbots and priors in a variety of ecclesiastical garments, whilst leaders of the mendicant orders, in cowled robes, the Dominicans in black, the Franciscans in brown, all these were seated in priestly ranks, stretching away into the gloom of the great church.

Then something disturbed the serenity of the place and the occasion. It was right at the back by the western entrance. Papal guards stationed at intervals along the chancel were peering back into the gloom. The presiding cardinal leaned over to tell one of his clerks to go and investigate the noise, when the reasons became apparent to all.

Only twenty minutes before, seven mounted, helmeted and fully armed knights, their brilliant white overmantles bearing the once familiar red Templar Cross, rode through the Lyons Gate into the city. Behind each of them was a squire in a similar white overmantle, these with a black cross, proudly bearing a lance with the black and white pennant of Beauseant. They had ridden through the city gate just ignoring the city's watchmen. They rode purposefully along the cobbled streets past gawping citizens, heading for the dominating bulk of St Maurice. The combined iron-shod footfall of the great destriers and their attendant's palfreys dominated and echoed back from the streets of overhanging houses, through which they passed. As they arrived before the western end of the cathedral, facing the wide River Rhone, a great cloud of pigeons took off in fright and flew high about the pinnacles of the cathedral.

The knights put their chargers to the broad rows of shallow stone steps at the western entrance before arriving at the great wide doors, where they dismounted and threw their reins to those squires that had scurried up behind them. Following their steel-clad leader, this formidable armoured group entered through the double doors, beside each of which stood a papal guard in helmet and half-armour, holding parade-ground halberds. Nervously, they challenged the knights, crossing their halberds, as though to bar entrance. The leading Templar, his helmet visor down, just walked into the crossed staves, pushing them aside like corn stalks. Followed by the other six, he made his way slowly and ponderously down the nave bisecting the hushed assembly, the only sound being the rowels of their spurs noisily trailing along the tiled floor, towards the raised platform in the choir.

It took only minutes, but must have seemed like hours to all those present. These large, completely armour-encased figures, bristling with weapons, swords and daggers in their belts, clanked their way towards the chancel steps. The brightly dressed papal guards nonplussed, stood rooted to the spot whilst the knights approached the dais. It was a moment of high drama. The leader stopped and painstakingly climbed the three shallow chancel steps until he stood in front of the presiding cardinal. His followers had fanned out behind him into a semi-circle, still at the foot of the steps.

The knight raised his visor and displayed a heavily bearded face that showed the scars of battle.

"I am Herman, Graf of Mannheim," he boomed challengingly. As he spoke, with his left hand, he removed the mail gauntlet on his right hand. "I and my brethren are here to defend the good and holy Order of the Temple in trial by combat, or by any other means against those who wickedly traduce us. We are a thousand, perhaps fifteen hundred, camped in the forest behind Lyons."

At this there was an audible gasp from the Pope when he heard "…a thousand Templars"… and only twenty miles away?

With that the Templar knight hurled his heavy steel gauntlet skidding along the chancel floor in front of the presiding cardinal's desk, the traditional challenge of his calling, which clashing sound reverberated up to the lofty ceiling of the choir and throughout the cathedral.

Over to one side the Pope was transfixed with fright. He seemed to be trying to sink down below his desk.

The presiding cardinal kept his head and addressed the knight standing in front of him, but with a voice loud enough to include his colleagues and the churchmen in the pews behind. "Yes, yes Herr Graf, this is correct, we issued the invitation which you and your colleagues have…. accepted." His voice trailed away and then strengthened, "but there is no question of armed combat. We here are all men of the cloth, not of arms. We invite you, all of you to give a defence of your Order. The fathers here have heard bad things but they want only to do what is right, and that which pleases God."

As he was speaking a papal guard officer was stealthily creeping along the sidewall where the papal throne was situated. The Pope still transfixed by shock, hardly noticed as the officer took him firmly by the arm and slowly and steadily walked him sideways away, their backs alongside the wall, and out of the choir, through the vestry then out of the cathedral itself. There his Holiness was helped into his sedan chair and the bearers in papal livery swiftly moved away, with the same officer now mounted, riding escort.

BEAUSEANT VIVAT

Argyllshire, Scotland, Autumn 1312

In the Aird Chapter House, Prior Peter gave out the news to the brethren.

"As usual our pigeons give us a timely advantage on what we propose to do next, but first, a surprise!" He again drew breath and looked around the expectant chapter house. "The bishops had an unexpected intervention in the great cathedral of Vienne. As the business of the Temple and the charges of heresy against us, was announced by the papal clerks, imagine if you will the shock of the assembled church fathers, as seven of our Templar brethren, fully mailed and helmeted for war, their Temple insignia clear to see, pushed and clanked their way past the astonished papal guards and into the cathedral. They strode noisily down the length of the chancel to the dais, and confronted "our master the Pope." he spat those words out. "Their leader the Graf of Mannheim, a provincial master of our Order, removed and flung down his gauntlet stating boldly for all to hear, that they had come to defend the honour of our Order against all traducers of our name - and that there were another thousand of the brethren in the forests behind the city!"

The murmurs in his audience had become a delighted buzz that burst into applause, as his listeners joyously imagined the scene.

"This, my brothers, was more than a small shock to the prelates, five years after the events of 1307, five years over which all of our comrades were supposed to have long been imprisoned and rendered harmless. Needless to say, none of the churchmen availed themselves of the right to answer the challenge."

There was low laughter.

"The council broke up in disorder as the Pope was hurried away to his quarters."

"They did not reconvene the next day, or for some while. His Holiness, it was given out, was ill! Then things took a further unexpected turn. It now emerged that the anticipated sentence of the suppression of our Order - that it be declared heretical, was, after all their planning and vile actions not going to happen. The Congregation of Bishops would not have it - the fathers did not accept at all, that any of these vile charges had been proven!"

The attentive knights were surprised, and some looked suddenly hopeful. "There was nothing like a majority for declaring the Order heretical and no amount of bribery and threats to the Congregation of Bishops could change that."

Many of the brethren looked about and enquiringly caught each other's eyes at the thought of a reverse, any reverse, to the now hated and despised pope, the traditional leader who had betrayed them. They could see he had for political expediency and his own survival, turned on them and allowed Philip to savage them, using another Order of the Church, that of the Dominicans, to inflict the evil of unwarranted persecution, torture and death. This outrage came after suffering countless deaths and injuries, during near to two centuries of frontline confrontation by their Templar Order, with the alien enemies of the religion.

"It left Pope Clement in the deepest trouble," the Prior continued, "with the tyrant Philip, who then came with a sizeable army from the French side of the River Rhone, and took him away from the Council, no doubt to remind him who was his master. In the end it was the papal lawyers," he smiled ruefully, acknowledging his former life as he continued, "who found that if the Templars were not guilty of heresy, then they must be released from gaol, be restored to their former dignities and all of their property - and no doubt compensated into the bargain."

The collective release of breath from the tense brethren was audible. Revenge without doubt was also factored into that list of consequences.

The Prior explained that the Pope must then have realised that they would be all the way back, to where he and King Philip were before that October Friday, five years before, having achieved nothing, except to have made mortal enemies of the most powerful military fraternity the world has seen.

"Briefly after that shock, the lawyers went on to suggest - and the Pope leaped at the idea," he told them, "that he could suppress the Order alone", again a collective sigh swept the chapterhouse, "on his own executive authority, an administrative decision, no more no less, on the grounds of, well… of practicality! That the Order had obviously stopped functioning with all of its members in gaol , as far as anyone was concerned, from that October Friday in 1307 and thus had no longer performed for these several years, any of the founding purposes of their charter of 1129. That we had no more reason to continue, because in practical terms, the Order of the Temple didn't exist, and that it should remain in that condition."

His voice rose impassioned, as he continued. "So the Order has been exculpated of the hateful charges against us. The papal decision was duly announced in the cathedral, but there were key words added at the insistence of the fathers, acknowledging that, 'the Order was without sin'."

"That means and can only mean that by God's law and by man's law, there was no heresy. Our brothers, who died at the eager hands of the Dominican torturers and at the stake of the King's executioners, were simply murdered, and all the time," he repeated his voice lowering, "as we well knew, they were without guilt!"

There was a heavy silence before he continued. "There is however, and this becomes the point of our Chapter meeting here," he added gravely, "legally no more 'Order of the Poor Fellow-Soldiers of Christ and the Temple of Jerusalem." He sorrowfully articulated every syllable of the formal title of the order, as though, as it probably was, for the last time.

"Now it is up to you to decide whether this greedy king and this cowardly pope should have their way, and pay no price to see us disappear from the face of the earth?"

He raised a hand to momentarily stop the eager-to-speak brethren as he finished.

"There is more. The tyrant Philip has not released our Master, nor yet his companions, although legally they are prisoners of the Church. We now have reliable information that they were again examined in the fortress of Chinon, not by torturers this time, but by a delegation of three cardinals. They reported back to the Pope, that the four Templar prisoners had been examined by them and found innocent of all charges of heresy. The Pope never informed our leaders of this verdict, nor indeed any of his colleagues, the other church leaders. This vital piece of evidence was never even mentioned at Vienne. He had clearly suppressed that Chinon report, sealed by each of the three cardinals who wrote it and presumably caused it to be buried and 'lost' somewhere amongst the many thousands of parchment rolls in the papal archives. Even, we believe, most senior churchmen still do not know of its existence.

"Obviously, this Pope's fear of King Philip and of his greedy interests, were of a greater weight than justice, or loyalty to the men of his own Order of the Temple. After the Church Council at Vienne has come to this conclusion of innocence, it is also obvious that now neither king nor pope know what to do with our grandmaster and the others. But we cannot for one moment assume that they will be released, indeed we can be certain sure that now they will not dare to do that. They will I believe, hold them on the personal confessions of heresy extracted by torture, and even though the Order itself has been found innocent, it no longer exists."

He paused, looked around the faces and drew a deep breath.

"So, what is your will?"

Pandemonium broke out, a far departure from the orderly chapter house meetings with which they had grown up. Every man or seemingly so, was on his feet striving to be heard, stools fell over noisily as the Prior momentarily resumed his seat.

But even above that noise, a crash was heard as the great oak door swung open and a fully armoured, helmeted knight, a giant of a man, clattered into the centre of the stone floor. Everyone fell silent. At the sudden intrusion many a white robed brother had groped reactively for his sword hilt, to no avail; swords were not worn in chapter meetings.

As the knight immediately dominated the smoky chamber with his presence the only movement there was from two young squires, the doorkeepers whom he had pushed aside, that came stumbling behind him into the room. On his yellow surcoat they all could see he wore the red lion rampant device of Robert the Bruce, King of Scotland.

The tension eased as the newcomer knight removed his casque, baring a great shaggy head. He shifted his body as he looked menacingly around. Then there were some murmurs of recognition. "Aye", he rumbled in a deep bass voice, "I ken some of you as well."

He turned to address the leaders on the dais and the tension passed. "I was told that my presence here would not be needed, that others were representing the Perth brethren. But also I knew fine that you would be deciding what the future would be for what remains of the Order, and I intend my say on that."

It was the Marshal that had first understood the lack of hostility in the uncalled for intervention. He saw that the timing worked well for the business, but that he must once more take charge. He rose to his feet.

"And you are, Sir Knight…?" The question was not long unanswered. "I am James Keith of Pitlochry, knight, formerly as a youngster, of the Templar garrison of Castle Pelegrin. I came out of there as ordered, to Cyprus, after the Acre fight." He referred to the fall of the Holy Land twenty years before, with the disastrous capture of the last capital Acre, when the few tiny Templar garrisons remaining in coastal castles, were ordered to evacuate them and retreat to their Cyprus base.

One of the other leaders next to the Marshal leaned over to him and spoke quickly.

"Well Brother James", the Marshal straightened up and again spoke authoritatively. "You are not representing your commandery, but you are here and will be heard."

"Aye, that I will," the big man replied. "I come to tell of King Robert, who is no friend of this Pope, and who pretends he doesn't know of your existence here. Now the man needs support against the English King, the second Edward, who is gathering a great campaigning army and boasts that he will soon invade Scotland.

"King Robert sorely needs fighting men. He already has my sword. I promised him that I would seek amongst my fellows, those who might wish to repay in some measure, his tolerance of our presence here for these past years."

The Marshal looked around the assembly and the Prior, his fellow leader, quietly spoke in his ear. He then responded. "We are mindful of our debt. This is the only kingdom in Christendom where the pope's writ does not run. Neither does King Robert have any tie to Philip of France, whilst Edward of England is that devil's son-in-law. We know that King Robert is excommunicated and the nation under interdict, and it is my belief," his fierce gaze raked the assembly, "that if Robert is beaten by the English, that Scotland will be joined to England, papal authority will be imposed, and that we will once more become fugitives. So, Brother James, your point is well struck and we will return to it when we have made some of the decisions that we must now consider."

It was clear that many others now wished to be heard. The Marshal raised his hand for silence - now less willingly given. Speaking above the temporarily lowered voices, he told them that the chapter would take a break and for the assembly to seek amongst themselves, those who could advocate one or another course of action, now that they knew for certain that their Order no longer existed.

The first major decision they had to take, he told them, was whether they should now disperse and for each to go their own way? He was interrupted by a noisy chorus of "no's" and "never!" There were several shouts that swelled into a chant: "Beauseant Vivat!"

He continued, smiling, "We will see what is properly said in Chapter, but if the decision is to continue with our fraternity, then there is much to do. We have, I think, none of us come here unprepared, including those of us up on this dais, but it is clear that after nearly two hundred years, our mission as the Knights of Christ of the Temple of Jerusalem, is at an end. We will need to determine what now our purpose is to be?"

***

BATTLE ORDERS

Castle Aird, Scotland; Autumn 1312

Three days had passed and many voices had been heard. From the dais, the two senior Templars from the Iberian Peninsula had given good news. King Deniz of Portugal had, after receiving the Pope's 1307 Bull, ignored, and later point blank refused the instructions to arrest the Templars in his kingdom. The kings of Castile and Aragon had reluctantly set out to do this, but well forewarned, the knights there had refused to surrender and barred their castles against the royal forces, which then half-heartedly besieged them. That practical point had won time whilst ambassadors of the Iberian rulers worked out a settlement with the Pope, now established at Avignon.

Portugal and Spain had been the second military front of the Order in its centuries-long fight against the Moslem armies, and the Templars had been particularly important in the expulsion of the Moors from Portugal, where, as in Spain, the wars continued. The Moors remained powerful and threatening in the Iberian south - a line of King Deniz's border fortresses and frontier provinces there, were held for him by garrisons of Templars.

A compromise had been found. The Templars in Iberia were brought peacefully before the court of the Archbishop of Taragona in Spain without torture, to answer the accusations of heresy. They all pleaded innocent and he promptly found them not guilty en masse, and discharged them. This farce over, their property in Portugal was assigned to King Deniz who immediately set up a new order, merely dropping the name 'Temple', so now they had been renamed the 'Knights of Christ' with the same rule and officers as before. Their property was restored with their headquarters still in the magnificent convent fortress of Tamar, their master was to be their elected choice, but their supreme leader now was no longer the pope, but the king of Portugal. Similarly in the Spanish kingdoms, parallel Orders had been set up; the existing Templar brethren there inducted into them and continuity assured.

So the Iberian delegates to Castle Aird announced that the fraternity was no longer in danger of further persecution. The invitation was given out to all those assembled: the brethren who wished to continue as fighting men with the Order, would be welcomed in Iberia.

Further news had continued coming in from the Council at Vienne. Individual Templars, it was announced, had not been released from their vows and were to place themselves at the disposal of their relevant bishops. At that news there were jeers and hoots of disdain from the assembly. Also, that their old fraternal rivals, the Order of the Hospital had been awarded the Templar's properties. That information produced a thoughtful reaction as they chewed awhile on the news, but when it was further announced that King Philip was in a black fury at being denied that prize, the tension broke and cheers went up.

Then the Marshal had again taken the floor. The old warrior was in every detail the commander and his statement to this military society, of what was to be, carried the full authority of two centuries of a military hierarchy. These were nothing less than their battle orders!

"We, this Chapter of our Order properly convened, have decided by acclaim that this is not to be an end, but a new beginning. We will, before we leave here, decide on the details for the future of our Order, a brotherhood whose new name, when we have decided on one, will not disguise to us that it is the continuation of what has gone before; but we must learn some subtleties from the disastrous persecutions that have been our lot since 1307.

"We have many jealous enemies out there. Many would deny our right to exist, indeed would hunt us down. I am saying that if we are to survive, then we must do so in full secrecy. We must so structure ourselves that our brethren will need to know when they are dealing with initiates, whom they can trust, and who will trust them.

"None of us are any longer bound by our oaths and the Rule of St Bernard, but your officers do have one powerful condition for those who want our fraternity to continue. We can no longer be an arm of the Church, and after that betrayal by "our master the Pope," he spoke with utter disdain of the treacherous chief who had betrayed them; "few of us would any more wish to be." There was a growl of assent.

"Indeed, be certain sure that the Church now is our enemy. They - in particular the Dominicans - for popes and bishops come and go, have failed to destroy us, despite defiling us without mercy. Now, because we have escaped them, they will fear us, and they will be right to do so. As

Templars, we never turned our backs on the enemy and in this regard we are still Templars. We will pursue them, these cruel Dominicans even after they have forgotten us, and we will exact our revenge."

The crowded room nearly burst apart with the roar of these warriors, who had clearly identified their enemy, and had been promised the vengeance they craved for the many comrades who had died, or been hideously maimed by torture, under these false charges.

"We cannot insist," the Marshal continued, "that any man any longer accepts or does not accept the beliefs of the religion, the defence of which used to be our whole purpose. From now on, this matter of faith must be personal to every man himself. Our fraternity will not tell any of us what to believe, or not to believe.

"But what we do say is this: all here, all of us are outlaws once outside of this realm of Scotland, and your fellows in the shadow houses who are waiting for your return, before you arrive back, they will have already heard that our Order is formally suppressed. We say that our two centuries-old brotherhood has shown itself to be more noble than the formal religion of the priests and popes, and more resilient than any single kingdom from which we came.

"Those secular rulers either fear their neighbours or plan to oppress them. They live in order to raise sufficient money to pay for their armies to conquer, so as to increase the areas they can tax ... to pay for their armies..." he repeated ironically. "For our part, we maintained in Syria and Palestine, the best standing army in Christendom for nearly two hundred years without taxation, entirely by our own resources. We still have many of those resources. In these terms again, it is not an end but a beginning."

The Marshal stopped, clearly going no further down that path. "This, and the nature of our surviving fraternity throughout the known world, perhaps five or six thousand of us remaining, spread across many countries, gives us great potential strength for the future.

"The one condition we make for those who will continue in fraternity or come to join us, is that you do solemnly swear an oath of fraternal loyalty to your brethren. You will promise to do whatever is in your power to aid any of your brethren, even if you have never before met him, yet who identifies himself in ways that will be made clear to you. You will swear the most powerful oaths to keep faith with our brotherhood and our secrets, never to betray us individually or together, against the most fearful penalties."

He paused, then quietly continued to the silent gathering, each man wrapped in his private thoughts. "Knowing as we do, probably better than anyone still left alive, the power of the torturers, we will need to be a society of those who know no more than they need to know. So we will be organised in lodges known to each other, but not to outsiders, except by signs and codes. As there has always been, there will still be a hierarchy and you already have your officers in place. Over time we will develop from there, and we will communicate quietly and without fuss to the leading man in each group, who will be the regional master. They however will only know of their immediate superior within a province.

"So if, in the fearful event that any of our people are taken and put to the question, those who are in danger from this will be alerted. There is *in extremis*, only the name of their immediate superior that apart from their local group they can give, and how contact is made, which," he added with a smile, "will hardly remain the case once it is known that a brother is arrested, and then warnings to others to disperse will be fast, and be made by emergency means.

"Since many of you, apart from the resident brethren, are representatives of the groups of survivors from whence you came, each of you will return to them," he announced, his voice intoning powerfully.

"With our collective authority, each of you will be the first master of your own group, ultimately responsible to Brother Olivier de Penne here by my side.

"Some of us," the Marshal concluded, "may choose to continue with the cloistered life as their way of finding their own peace. Whatever will be their new house, we can say that the Cistercians in particular shared our history and significantly are as white as the Dominicans are black. You will have been told about our history when you were acolytes, that the Templar Order was conceived two centuries ago by Count Hugh of Champagne and Hugh de Payens his liegeman and our first grandmaster. He led a group of mainly Champenois and Burgundian knights on crusade to the Holy Land with a particular mission that became clear thereafter, to protect pilgrims. That this group grew into an Order of the Church through the Abbot of Clairvaux, he that became St Bernard, whose Cistercians received from Count Hugh the land and the funds to create his great abbey. Bernard in turn argued the Templar case to become the first ever military order, and he wrote our Rule.

"The count and the abbot, these two great men," he continued, "tried this way to reform both the Church and the undisciplined bullying knighthood, by the example of our two parallel orders. The Church, however, remains unreformed and as corrupt as it had already become in their day. But although our Order is no more, the Cistercian community remains uncorrupted. They have always been the closest to us of the enclosed orders.

"Others, I believe, who like me, after all of this have lost the faith, will look to other occupations." He paused to see what - if any - reaction there would be and realised that from his senior position, he had given a lead that reflected and emboldened the views of many there.

"The younger men amongst you, no longer sworn to chastity, may wish to marry. Indeed we are told that in the continuing order in Portugal with a king at its head, rather than a pope, it is planned to discontinue that prohibition, so married brethren may join and there we will now be soldiers rather than monks. If we, the continuing brotherhood, are to have any future beyond our own generation, it is essential that we be no longer monks; we re-enter the world and in every way become a part of it, with generations to follow us.

"Yet if it is the full military-monastic life you seek, as of old, we have told you of the other fraternities that would welcome you. In the Mediterranean, there is the Order of Hospitallers if, that is, you wish to continue fighting the Saracens and perhaps one day return to the Holy Land. You can join them through their house at Clerkenwell in London, which will ship you out to their island of Rhodes. Or if it is sunshine you seek, but nearer to here, then there are our own people in Portugal and the new Orders in Spain where you will surely be amongst friends. Our colleagues from the Peninsula," he nodded towards two of his colleagues on the dais, "are waiting to talk to those here who prefer that option.

"In the Baltic and the north, the Teutonic Knights will be glad to receive you and if that is your choice, there will be passage made available on the cogs of the Hanseatic League that trade from Leith, to the port of Lubeck.

"Before this, the last and first Chapter meeting is concluded, council members will meet with each of you to hear your own views and suggest what you might now do. To some indeed, unless they have personal reasons not to go, we may suggest that they travel on behalf of our new order, on sometimes long and difficult missions that are being now worked upon, for the benefit of all.

"Our guiding principle is that neither the Church nor any king holds any authority over us. As guests in any kingdom we will of course respect and observe the king's laws, but our fraternity, as it has always been, remains outside of any feudal system. Each man is now released from his oath to the Order that has been suppressed, and shall be free to decide whether he is with us, or wishes to return to the kind of life he might have had, if he never had become a brother.

"If the decision is to be with us, then no matter what he then does - join the Teutons, or the Hospital, or the new orders in Iberia, or if he retreats to a monastic life, or that of a merchant or a free-lance soldier; he will indeed be with us. In all things he will secretly remain bound as our brother, pledged to help brethren who might seek his aid, whom he will recognise by the signs and signals we will devise, just as he himself may similarly always be free to seek their aid."

This long statement had visibly tired the Marshal, but his colleagues had agreed that his was the continuing authority, that would best leave its mark on the memory of all his listeners.

He had not quite finished. He caught the eye of the burly Sir James Keith, the king's man as he again spoke up.

"I must return to Cyprus - my duty lies there, but it is our intention that before we leave here, your leaders will meet with our friend-in-need, Robert the Bruce, the good King of Scotland, and see how we can best aid him in his wars with Edward of England."

With that he sat down and the resultant hush quickly gave way to an excited outburst of talking. The Prior looking around judged it time for a break, to enable his colleagues to resume meeting with individuals to give them their directions for the future.

Those knights that were there as representatives, had now been here for many days, even weeks, whilst some of the earlier escapees had been here for years. They had each after they had arrived, found a Templar society functioning, for this castle had earlier been leased to the Order by the Lord of Islay, Prince of the Western Isles and a close friend and supporter of King Robert the Bruce, in whose kingdom there had been no persecution of the Templars.

***

In the intervening years the castle had had its interior adapted to receive a large number of knights as with all such large Templar bases, and some of the sleeping quarters were arranged in long dormitories under the eaves of the castle roofs.

On the night of the Marshal's great closing speech that was clearly the only matter for discussion.

"What did you think then, Paul?" asked the young Dane, Knut. They were sitting on their cots which were next to each other, and they were of a similar age. "For me, I think that the Marshal is a great man," Knut offered "I suppose you need that in a leader like him, but he is going back to Cyprus - please God he gets there safely…"

"I would agree with you that he is a leader you would follow anywhere, but this Peter of Bologna", Paul told them that he had helped him escape from Paris in his journey here, "he is certainly a clever man, but, I don't know - a priest after all, even if he's one of ours - and now without the Grandmaster still locked up in his dungeon at Chinon, and the Marshal returning to Cyprus; he as Prior is the highest officer!"

A brown-robed sergeant listening nearby broke in, "I can tell you brothers, both of you, that our Prior is the right man - see he's got brains, and he's the right stuff. Back in Paris I was one of those, they said there were about 600 of us, in the gaols there and about to go before the Church commissioners. We were told that they were independent of that bastard, Philip, and that they would take evidence from any of us who wished to appear before them. It was a trick mind, but we didn't know that - neither I think did the bishops themselves, and those others that were on the bench. Anyway we couldn't find any lawyer to speak for us - none of those in Paris would commit suicide by helping the king's enemies, and besides we couldn't get hold of any money to pay them, but some of the lads knew that Brother Peter was a trained lawyer and he must have been smart, because he was the Order's man at the Pope's court. He was a prisoner, but not in the king's gaols which were truly evil and where the Black Doms would come and go. But he was in custody mind, in the Abbey of St Germain where the Pope had sent him. So he hadn't been tortured and most important, he hadn't confessed to heresy like most of us - which you are inclined to do when you are about to have a red hot poker stuck up your arse." Others of their comrades had gathered around their end of the dormitory and were listening. Nobody was going to quarrel with that last statement.

"Right," he continued, "the Paris Tribunal asked us all legal and proper who would represent us? Apart from a couple of the older knights who were prepared to do their best, Brother Peter of Bologna was the general choice. Well, in all the years and days since Black Friday, this was the first time I had enjoyed myself. Down there was this tribunal with hundreds of us coming and going for questioning by the Bench, and then listening to our Prior in action. He tore the king's lawyers apart. He made them look like the lying slaves that they truly are. He had that bench of bishops really respecting him …you could see that. We were beginning to think that the judges would have to throw out all our confessions made under torture, and that rubbish about worshipping cats and wooden idols, and all that crap. We would be set free perhaps and get back to something like a normal life - to go and fight the Saracens maybe. But it was all dreams.

"French Philip had an archbishop, a courtier, a young aristocrat of only about twenty, would you believe - when he was made Archbishop of Sens, and now bloody Philip wanted his payback. This boy bishop condemns no less than fifty-seven of our lads, taken at random, as far as we could see. Pronounced that they were 'apostates,' they called it, for changing their confessions of heresy. They did this once they were able to explain to the bishops' bench, through Peter, that they had only confessed because of the unbearable pain, and that it was none of it true! Which is what they had thought, the bench was there to judge.

"But the King was told what was happening, and could see what Peter's smart lawyer talk had done and so he had dodged right around what you might call these 'independent bishops' on the tribunal, who Prior Peter by now had clearly won over, and used one of his holy stooges instead. As you all probably know" - he looked around the hushed circle that was now gathered - "within twenty four hours, those fifty-seven men, our brothers were condemned."

He paused, and the effect hit hard. "They were brought outside the walls of Paris tied up in carts, then shackled to stakes and every last one of them was burned alive - all fifty-seven of them. About a hundred of the rest of us roped up together, were brought there and forced to watch. And do you know", his voice cracked, "at the end, not one of them asked to withdraw their denial of heresy, and they died - and that's a bad death - saying, brothers, they were saying, shouting, screaming that they were innocent and that the Order was innocent!"

The sergeant slumped down on to the corner of a bunk bed, where despite himself, the tears came, overcome with emotion and the horror of that memory. The hush that followed, left every one there alone with his thoughts of what he might have done, like them, right at the end. It also made them very angry.

"Well, I had heard some of that before, said one of the listeners", but I only hope that in our new Order, now we are no longer officially Christians," he grinned at the thought, "that we will have the chance of revenge. There is a long list of those who owe us, with King Philip at the top of it and our former master the Pope coming next."

"Aye," said another, "and every Dommy black friar bastard that walks the streets of Paris."

"...Or any street, anywhere..." broke in a big, previously silent, heavily bearded knight.

***

Later that night lying on his palliasse in his box-framed bunk bed, Paul reflected on the sensational events of the day. So now the Templars were no more - officially that is. It was all a long way from when, as a boy, he had dreamed of himself becoming a member of this elite force, which he now realised, had done much to revive the idea of chivalry amongst the knightly class. The thuggish element among that class was certainly always there, as it had clearly been back in the Champenois Count Hugh's time, but he knew now from his own years in the Order, that the Rule and the strict discipline had created a different, somehow cleaner kind of warrior, for a change, not an oppressor of the weak and the poor. He was pleased to count such men as his friends.

What now, he wondered? It was clear there would soon be some serious fighting. They had a debt to pay to this Scottish King, Robert the Bruce, which if he and they were successful, would guarantee their presence in Scotland. If they failed and Paul survived, he would, he realised, again be 'on the run'. But if not, what could he expect his life would now be? He could go to Portugal - some he knew would be doing that, or to the Teutonics in Prussia but what would he be fighting for there? To make heathen Prussians into Christians? Right now he felt more like joining the heathens.

It is true that the Marshal had told him at his interview that he was to be offered an assignment that would involve a future base for the new fraternity. Could it be that the Templars too could find something like the

Teutonic Knight's Ordensland in Prussia, or the Hospitaller's island of Rhodes - both sovereign territories well removed from greedy kings and popes?

Those former crusading colleagues had clearly learned from what happened to the Templars. That all seemed very worthwhile, but he could not begin to guess what place the Council might have in mind to send him. When he asked that question of the Marshal, he had been told he would know all in good time, and that was that, except he was glad to hear that Knut and Geraint, his friends from the beginning here, were also delegated for the same expedition. But first it looked as though they had a war to fight.

There was so much that he didn't understand. Why was it that the Templars had been treated like this, and not the Hospitallers, or the Teutonic knights? It's true he didn't know much about heresy, but he did know that it was absurd that his Order should be so accused - ridiculous in fact. Where would it all end up, he wondered? To have the whole might of the Church arrayed against a few hundred Templars didn't seem like a very good prospect.

He was in his mid-twenties now and no longer a military monk, just the military bit remained - that at least was an improvement. It also raised the prospect of females in his life - now that really was a big improvement. But it seemed the price that had to be paid, to be a member of this elite force, had been raised by these recent events. He wouldn't be able to visit his home. His elder brother was now the baron - Paul had heard that his father had died whilst he was out in Cilicia, but he would have liked to have visited Burgundy again - perhaps for the last time. Now his enemies were the Dominicans, who had dedicated themselves to the pursuit and destruction of the Templar Order. Indeed any official of the Church could be a danger to him, since he had not submitted as a 'stray' Templar to a local bishop, as they would have it. But what he did understand was the comradeship of his order and its two centuries tradition of mutual loyalty. That seemed to shine like a guiding star and that was the direction he would follow. Before he could ponder further, he was asleep, overcome by the events of the day.

A NEW FRATERNITY

Castle Aird, Argyllshire; Autumn 1312

The council chamber was down a short corridor from the larger chapter house, again with granite walls and equally as bare. There were clean rushes spread on the floor, and the only furniture was a refectory table, with fine old oak chairs padded on the seats and arms. Brother Prior as he was to be known, starting for all of their brethren the practice of not using family or given names - that might one day be wrung from them - sat at the end, his senior colleagues spread along the board.

The Prior spoke first. "Well brothers, as you know, our Spanish and Portuguese brethren sailed this morning with some volunteers. They have firm promises from those of our brethren who will put their proposals to their own local groups and intend to go themselves, now they know how to organise their transport.

"Some who are from Northern Europe have told us that the Teutonic Order is more to their taste. They will be easy to transport from the east coast ports from here, into the Baltic Sea.

"The Marshal on his return to Cyprus will make the same proposals to our people there on behalf of the Hospitallers on the island of Rhodes. That will take care of all of those who wish to return to the life of a military monk. But, those who have sat through our interviews with all of the brethren here, know the great majority no longer want that.

"They are the material from which our fraternity will be reborn. To get the fullest understanding of what is possible, I have asked each of our colleagues to take on one area of our future activity and speak to it.

"First, Brother Marshal…"

The grand old man sat up erect. "This will be my last council as I return to Cyprus within days. That is my duty. I want you to then select a new marshal because now Cyprus is irrelevant to the future; you need a marshal nearer to this council.

"There are two areas I have concentrated on: first the question of rescuing those of our brethren still imprisoned, by which I mean the Grandmaster and his companions in the King's fortress of Chinon. We have some ways of getting word to and from the inside, but the prospects of arranging escape are frankly very poor.

"The second area I have discussed with Sir James, who took the Prior and I to meet King Robert, to see how best we could help. Following that, with your agreement, Sir James is due to leave here tonight to join King Robert and give him our final proposals, which are these.

"First we can help him with money - all kings need money! Robert the Bruce has many men at his call. Such is the way of these Scottish tribes, they are formidable fighters but they are poorly armed, and Edward of England can put into the field two to three thousand perhaps more, fully armed, mounted knights and men-at-arms in his train, as well as many thousands of infantry. We Templars probably could not muster more than eighty or a hundred mounted brethren, and we would have to obtain many of the horses from Flanders - those from these parts are ponies, not destriers, but anyway, the absurd odds speak for themselves."

The Marshal continued. "Our offer is that we will provide some thirty of our knights to fight on horseback, but at least another seventy or more as officers and sergeants for his infantry, maybe more than that, if our reinforcements arrive in time from Flanders. The Scots, Sir James agrees, will be trained to fight in schiltron formations with pikes, and as you may recall from Philip of France's defeat at Courtrai, a few years back, it was proven there that well-trained pikemen can stop and then destroy even the best cavalry - but it is the training and discipline that matters. So our Templars will train his infantry and be their officers and sergeants, fighting alongside them on the day. We told King Robert that we have sent to Flanders for an experienced senior brother to train and command our pike battalions. He is Sir Peter Breydel, for some years living as a merchant in Bruges, but he was one of the junior commanders in the battle of Courtrai - he was knighted on the field and joined our Order later, expecting to go on crusade.

"We are also going to present King Robert with three thousand steel pike-heads, which we are bringing in from our Bremen merchant house, so his army will fit them to staves and he will have the weapons to do the job.

Gentlemen, brethren, I ask for your agreement because if we can surprise the English, and if the Bruce can beat them, he will be secure in his kingdom - and so will we!

"We are fighting for our own future as much as his, because if he loses we will surely have to disperse and leave Scotland to try to find another base elsewhere - but where?" He asked rhetorically, his palms open and extended.

"Much better," he forcefully continued, "if we can, by proving our loyalty to him and making the difference in his war, gain the security and the time to get our new order organised."

There was never any question that they might disagree but the Prior called next on his brown-robed former colleague from the Curia, Brother Joseph, who now was known as Brother Treasurer. Before he spoke, his shrewd eyes travelled around the table assessing his colleagues as he was inclined to do, on all such occasions.

"It will never be repeated by me outside of this council," he said his voice quite clear and words articulated, "nor should it be by any of you, but I intend to speak, just this once, of the vaunted Templar treasure that the evil Philip of France so lusted after, but was denied."

He stopped and waited to see the effect his words were having.

Satisfied, he continued, "Yes there was, and indeed still is Templar treasure, quite a lot of it. In fact brothers, it will now be our great strength, because we can no longer be exclusively a military fraternity, and therefore force of arms, as in Syria and Palestine and Spain, is not the way forward for us."

He leaned back enjoying the effect of his revelations. "The world knew of our land holdings - no less than nine thousand estates between the landmass that stretches from the west of the country of Ireland, all the way to Armenia in western Asia - a greater terroir than any in Europe, excepting only that of the Church. Now that has gone to the custody of the Hospitallers - they already had holdings almost as large, so this makes them even bigger than we were, but it was this, that Phillip had expected to receive from the Church Council at Vienne, just as he expected them to find our Order guilty of heresy.

"He was frustrated on both counts - worse for him probably, because when his troops occupied the Temple in Paris on Black Friday, he was appalled to find that he now had captured the biggest bank in Christendom, but with no bars of gold, or sacks of coin, or gems, not even the collateral or documents for the many loans. It was all gone and yes, we know how and where. But even that is not the full story.

"Our banking operations from Paris and all the other cities and towns, together with the income from our many farming estates, generated the money to pay for our fortresses and standing armies in Outremer: Syria, Palestine, Trans-Jordan, Cilicia, and also in Iberia, rotating the troops, supplying them, re-equipping and remounting them, and so on. Maintaining fortresses and financing an army is an expensive business, but apart from our modest activities in Cyprus…" he deferred here to the Marshal who nodded his acknowledgement, "after the fall of Acre, from 1291 to 1307 - a further sixteen years, the same level of income continued to come in from the nine thousand estates, the vast banking business and our widespread merchanting activities, about which more later. But without any troops in the Holy Land or any other major military activity, no substantial expenditure has been going out. We expected a new crusade and were determined to put a major force into the field when that happened, so we had been making sure we had the resources ready.

"Now there was of course portable treasure in the Paris vaults, as always. Indeed more than usual because our Grandmaster had brought a large amount with him - twenty mule-loads of silver coin, in his ships from Cyprus earlier in that year. Although at that time I was in Poitiers on attachment to the Curia, I have the knowledge that certain of our shrewder brethren in Paris quietly removed it all, when certain signs and yes, tip-offs, were received. They had thought that at worst, that the king was going to make a royal raid on the money - that would have been in character, but nothing suggested the dissolution of the order, the torture and the false charges of heresy. We had believed, if we had thought about it at all, that the Pope, our supreme commander could never have allowed such an outrage. We were of course completely wrong about that!"

He stopped to draw breath and looked around the board once more before continuing.

"With our Prior's permission I do not propose to talk about where it was taken and where it is now. Always because there is the danger of the Black Doms, who would burn that information out of any of us that might be captured by them. As we have agreed before, our new principle as with our names and functions, is 'the *need* to know' this is to be the test for information passed between us. But what I can say, to give you, our ruling Council an indication, is this..."

He paused and took a sip of the watered wine from the goblet in front of him.

"What we learned in nearly two centuries of banking was that money must be made to work, not to lie in sacks and strong boxes. The way that is done is by lending to other banks, which work on the same principle. Now apart from us, there have long been some Florentine merchants, the Frescobaldi, organised as bankers. Furthermore, since we were longer able to fund the Plantagenets in London, the Genoese Pesagno clan have been lending to the English king.

"But frankly in today's circumstances, we didn't feel we could trust any of these Italian banks as partners, because their main activity was lending to these kings like Philip himself, and we know that he is utterly untrustworthy. Indeed the Florentines have just now taken a tremendous beating from him.

"Since we disappeared off the Paris scene, he had taken them for as much as they had, until it was time to pay back. He then cheated them and repudiated his debt to them, just as he did with us, and threw them out of France, ruined. Just one year before our disasters of 1307, he had done exactly the same thing with the Jewish bankers and moneylenders in France, and expelled them all, every Jew in his kingdom. He kept all their property for himself, sitting on their collateral and forced their debtors to repay him." He smiled ruefully, as he looked around again. "This is a very wicked - a most greedy man, this King Philip" he murmured.

"No, my brothers", he intoned, enjoying the moment, "there is some specie and gems to be sure, but on the whole the Templar treasure is not only safe but it is working for us, through banks we know we can trust - remember we have been handling large sums for nearly two centuries. Sometimes we even own them or a part of them. More than one is involved in the Hanseatic League in which, through proxies, we play an influential part, and where much of our business now is. Being bankers for near two centuries, it also means that we have long cared for other people's money, but hardly anybody knows who and for how much. That will... and I know the Prior agrees... remain a paramount secret and be released only on a 'need to know' basis.

"We have a substantial, directly controlled - although under another name, commercial and banking office in Constantinople. We're safe there, the Byzantine Empire as you are aware is Orthodox, and therefore, almost by definition, is an enemy of the papacy. Another thing that serves our cause there is the disgraceful Fourth Crusade. When we saw what western Christendom was going to do to their city and their empire, our Order refused to take part in any so-called 'crusade' against fellow Christians and we stood aside. That stands us in good stead now and the eastern empire being more sophisticated than that of the west, when they borrow, it is against good collateral, and even if only because they know they will need to do this again, they don't then seek to destroy their banker.

"You may be surprised to know that several of our international banking partners are Jewish, now of course like us outside of France, from whom we have learned a lot about handling money in different realms. All in all, financially our situation is strong."

Some at the table looked surprised hearing for the first time about the Jewish connection, but it was generally known that the Jews well understood the money business. Since many of the brethren had served in the Holy Land, they did not share the prejudice against them of the ignorant, untraveled, common people of Europe.

Brother Treasurer had finished. He stopped, sat down and looked over to the Prior.

His listeners had individually known some, but not all of what they had just been told, but the scope of the international operations that remained after the disasters of 1307 came as a surprise. Some coughed and cleared their throats; goblets were raised and replaced on the table. Silence resumed.

"From this" the Prior took up the narrative, "you will understand that our strength will no longer be in deploying fighting men, but rather it will be in deploying funds. Just as with Robert the Bruce that is something that he needs and we can do for him - and in return he will guarantee our security here in Scotland, at least during his lifetime. It gives us the breathing space that we so badly need.

"But more than that. What Brother Treasurer has outlined also serves as the background to our future planning and the way in which we will, as the Fraternal Council, seek to guide our brethren for the future. Over two centuries the Templars achieved a reputation of being the greatest fighting force in the Christian world. We need to use that military knowledge and experience as a bridge to our future role.

"What then should that future role be, you will ask? I will ask Brother Olivier de Penne to speak on this."

The tall man in the white habit sat up straighter as he addressed his colleagues around the table.

"As you know I have been given responsibility for administering our shadow houses, where it has been possible to resurrect an organisation, or find a basis for establishing a new one. Although the military side of our work won't disappear overnight, we can see those future generations, the sons and grandsons of our established brethren, will not be joining a military fraternity, although I would speculate that our fraternal bonds would always be attractive to certain kinds of men who choose the path of the warrior in national armies. But that would be their choice.

"Brother Prior and I have a proposal to co-opt onto this Council a new member, himself never a Templar, although his own brother was - a man tortured to death by the Black Doms because he wouldn't sign their hateful confession to absurd crimes. He is named Peter Proudhomme, and is the Master of the 'Company of the Children of Solomon'. He and they are architects - the supreme cathedral master builders.

"This Company, of which you may have heard, is the fraternity of that rare group of men capable of building such great works as a cathedral, of which our Templar order financed so many. The relevance is in our own nativity. As every new recruit learned, our Order was conceived two centuries ago by Count Hugh of Champagne, whose friend and vassal Hugh of Payens was our first grandmaster. But they also know that St Bernard of Clairvaux enabled the adoption of the fraternity into a military order of the Church - there had never been one before. Moreover, it was under the guidance of St Bernard who in 1145 also gave these architects and master builders, 'the Children of Solomon', their Rule of living and of work, although their traditions they tell me, stretch far back to even before the first temple of Solomon in Jerusalem, long before Christianity. But their Rule, given by St Bernard makes it clear that they are ultimately responsible to us.

"So the modern origins of this company also stem from that same alliance of the Count and the Abbot, because it was they who two centuries back jointly founded at Clairvaux a school of architecture for western Christendom, whose first master was a trained architect, St Bernard's own brother, Achard of Les Fontaines. What those three men agreed upon was that there would be an enduring fraternity of their vocations. The Cistercians have always been close to us for this reason. The 'Company of the Children of Solomon', as you will see, can be extremely helpful to us in our new circumstances, and we have everything to gain by extending our own and accepting the fraternal hand, of their master, Peter Proudhomme.

"I talk of their help and will explain. Architects are almost unique in Christendom in being outside the feudal system. They have no master and unlike most people require no passport for travel, because they work under contract for great princes of the realm, and the Church, and take their protection from that. In all cities and many towns there are lodges of stonemasons. Some of these men become masters of works under these architects, some of whose schemes like the great cathedrals, can take a hundred years to complete - that's perhaps three generations of builders. This Company will extend their co-operation to our individual brethren when needed, in terms of a disguise, an identity to travel between cities, since we can no longer travel as individual warriors, and in giving discreet help and accommodation in places where we have no contacts of our own.

"Then, as to the future of our Fraternity, there is a clear prospect of our now taking a lead as merchant venturers in foreign trading, using our already extensive networks and of course, finances.

"We know that apart from Christendom, beyond Byzantium, there are the lands of the Turks and the Mongols and far beyond them, the fabled Cathay. To the south beyond Egypt and its empire, is a Christian country, Ethiopia from where the River Nile flows into Egypt.

"Across another sea, beyond the lands of Syria and Baghdad are the Indies of the Malabar Coast, cut off to Europeans for centuries now, since the rise of Islam. But scholars tell us that the Romans travelled there and wrote about it, more than a thousand years ago. It should be possible for determined merchant venturers to once again find a way of trading with Malabar for their famous black pepper, currently a massively profitable monopoly of Venice, trading with Egypt and selling to all of Christendom and beyond.

"Even outside this very castle's walls, over those fierce waves to the west across the Ocean Sea, there may yet be some surprises - our Danish and Norwegian brethren tell us that there are definitely large areas of forested new land out there, past Iceland and even beyond Thule.

"We have been, and will continue collecting information about this wider world, because if the temporal and spiritual rulers of Christendom have taken our Order and flung it aside, like a child throws away a rag doll, then we will rebuild our fraternity to be as good at merchanting as we were as soldiers.

Those young men out there and our brethren scattered around Christendom are made of the very stuff of exploration and adventure. We have already existed for two centuries. We will be those that are best equipped as merchant venturers to lead in the future world, but never again trusting in a king's crown or a pope's tiara."

THE END OF AN EPOCH

Chinon: March 1308 - Paris 1314

The four chief Templar prisoners held by King Philip were still confined at his great fortress of Chinon in the County of Anjou. They were moved there in 1308 after their initial arrest, imprisonment and torture in 1307 in the Temple fortress itself. Once the Inquisition had obtained its confessions, they were removed to this isolated fortress to be safely away from any interference by the Paris mob. This also had the bonus of protecting their captives from any rescue attempts from rogue Templars still loose, or any other influence not totally controllable by the king and his ministers.

Chinon is in the former Plantagenet county of Anjou - some three days travel by road and river from Paris. Both King Richard the Lionhearted and his mother Queen Eleanor of Aquitaine, are buried nearby in Fontevrault, a foundation supported by that queen who had been Countess of Anjou and Duchess of Aquitaine in her own right. But now the flag that flew from Chinon's highest tower was no longer Richard's leopards, but that of golden lilies on blue, the device of the house of Capet, and of the Kingdom of France.

The long grey fortress sits like an extended grey stone saddle bestriding a ridge, high above the valley of the Vienne, a tributary of the great River Loire. Its towers, bastions and high walls dominate the town reaching up the hillside and down on the flatlands, beside the wide river flowing west into the Loire towards Brittany and the sea. Across that river the lush meadows and extensive woodlands of the Loire Valley stretched out of sight.

There had been an important Templar commandery in Chinon town for more than a century, which, since the purge, had been occupied by royal troops. But over those hundred years various local families had been employed by the Order as serving brothers, sergeants, or grooms. The Temple had some affection from those in the town who had so long been associated with it. Some of those now were employed in the castle up on the hilltop, and whilst the royal commander there was an ambitious and loyal follower of the king, nevertheless he could not know, let alone determine the secret loyalties of his entire garrison.

So it was that the Grandmaster with his three colleagues were able to discreetly keep in touch with the remnants of the Order through survivors of Black Friday, who had across France and Europe slowly and painstakingly set out to re-establish 'shadow houses' - secret cells of surviving Templars.

Of course escape was very much on the prisoners' minds, but so it was always present in that of the governor, who had every expectation that his important prisoners would one day try to get away. Various schemes had been considered both by the prisoners themselves and by the shadow Templar house in Anjou, but none had got beyond that stage, simply because there were simply too many insuperable problems.

The prisoners were intermittently somewhat roughly treated, but all four of them, their guards knew, were supposed to be important and would probably have to be produced in court, so they couldn't be too obviously damaged. There was indeed a torture chamber and it had been shown to the prisoners when they first arrived, in the depths of the tower, on two upper floors of which they were confined, but this was a royal dungeon, not that of the Dominicans of the Inquisition, who elsewhere much earlier, had agonisingly wrung out of them the required confessions of heresy. These four had been put in back in the hands of the king for confinement, within weeks of the interrogations commencing back in Paris. Apart from a lingering fear that more interrogators would arrive from Paris to reopen enquiries into the whereabouts of the Order's treasure, still unaccounted for, or details of the banking business of which they might have some knowledge, the biggest problem for the prisoners was frustration and boredom, as months turned into years.

One day, the governor who made a tour of inspection daily, told them that a delegation of cardinals would be travelling from Poitiers, visiting them to produce a final report for the Pope, prior to a decision on the Order's future that would be considered by a great Council of the Church at Vienne. He was able to answer when asked, that as this was papal business, no king's minister had been notified nor would be permitted to sit in and listen to the proceedings, because that had been held by the Curia to be a great deficiency in getting to the truth, in earlier papal enquiries.

Two of the three cardinals were French and the other was thought to be Italian and that concerned the prisoners greatly because they knew that the recently appointed French cardinals - if that is who these two were - in truth no more than the creatures of King Philip, and their elevation to the College, a part of a bargain between king and pope from an earlier time. As it turned out their elevation predated that event and these fears were not justified. The third cardinal was Italian and they were reassured with his presence, knowing that the Italian churchmen held no brief for the French king, rather to the contrary.

The hearings were held not in the tower that was their gaol, but in a high ceilinged antechamber off the castle's main hall, with the cardinals and their secretaries in attendance, but as they explained, there were also a number of experienced notaries to write down the questions and answers in this enquiry.

None of the castle garrison was present, with guards outside the doors, ensuring privacy. They interviewed just a single prisoner at a time.

For the first time it seemed, the interrogators treated them with some respect, particularly the Grandmaster, who back in the days when he attended the papal court, ranked equal ecclesiastically, alongside the cardinals. For the first time the questions put seemed framed to elicit the truth, rather than give support to preconceived judgements. Short of being able to address the Pope himself, Jacques de Molay felt that perhaps, at last, he and his colleagues might receive some justice.

"So why Grandmaster, did you change your plea - and more than once?" asked the Italian cardinal, Brancacci, who had been taking the lead in the questioning.

De Molay stood up and stripping off his gown, standing only in a loin cloth, showed the evidence on his ageing body of the burns and scars and deep bruises, of the torture he had undergone.

"There your eminences, is the reason," he explained. "Were it not that you have excluded the kings officers from this hearing, for what I am saying to you now, I would after you had retired this evening, have then been taken down to the cellars and racked, or otherwise been subjected to unendurable pain. I am ashamed to say that my body has betrayed me in the past and I fear would do so again in like circumstances. But, without that terror I would as I do now, steadfastly deny any of the charges against me.

"More importantly," he continued pulling on his gown, "leaving my own position aside, I would insist that the Order itself is blameless and without sin. This nearly two centuries old Order, for whom thousands have given up their lives on the battlefields, or in Saracen dungeons, has had the ill fortune to become the object of avarice of a greedy king. Did your eminences know that this king has borrowed heavily from the Order over twenty years past, yet never made repayment of anything at all? The vast amount he owes is now more than twice that of all of the annual revenues of France. We had never pressed him to repay, but you might conclude that there was no way he was ever going to pay it back.

"Indeed" he continued, "it is obvious that if he succeeds in eliminating the Order, he will never even be asked to repay the loans. Moreover, he is - we all know - now treating the proceeds of all our farms and granges across France, the gifts of devout Christians for our work in the Holy Land and in Iberia, as his own for his court, and whatever else. One does not have to look far for his motivation."

The Master's three senior colleagues, Geoffrey de Charney, Master of Normandy; Hugh de Pairualt, Visitor of France; and Geoffrey de Goneville, formerly preceptor of Poitou and Aquitaine; were similarly individually questioned, at the end of which the cardinals were not seen for two days. The governor in his daily rounds told them that they were still at the castle, apparently deliberating.

Then they were informed that the cardinals were to see them once more, before returning to Poitiers. This time all four Templars were ushered in together to hear the senior cardinal, a Frenchman Berenger Fredol, whose appointment as cardinal, reassuringly predated the elevation of Clement V.

"We have asked to see you one more time to tell you not to despair. All of us are convinced that we have heard the truth from you, and so we will inform our master the Pope. He has convened a great ecumenical council of the Church for 1310 - Yes," he exclaimed, as he saw the frustration on the Master's face. "I know it must seem a long time to you, but knowing my colleagues, the Church fathers as I do, I am convinced that they would find you innocent, as you claim to be. Our report…" he waved a parchment which Molay could see had seals already affixed, "is completed. If God saves us, we would all expect to be at the Council at Vienne in two years' time and hope that perhaps even we will meet again, with you there as free men."

"Now I will pronounce absolution of your sins as recorded in this hearing, by which act, individually you are no longer excommunicated, but readmitted to the bosom of the church. Kneel each of you." One by one, he placed his hand on their heads as he pronounced the absolution in the Latin tongue.

De Molay felt the tears course down his cheeks as he and his colleagues remained kneeling for the old man's blessing.

"God bless you my sons" it came, and he and the others remained on their knees, their heads bowed as the cardinals filed out.

***

Two years had gone by and yet a third, when they heard that the council had been postponed by yet another year. They asked the governor, were they to be taken from there to Vienne and he told them he had no instructions except the original one - to hold them safe.

Clearly they were going to learn nothing from the governor, but their principal contact with the shadow Templar house at Poitou, where de Goneville had once been master, was a castle guard who left notes for them in a certain place, a niche in the chapel wall, which was also the conduit for reply. Jacques de Molay was illiterate, but his colleague Geoffrey de Charney was not. It was he who told the others the news as he received it, and who wrote down and sent their questions by the same method. Both receipts and replies were written in the code the Templars used for important messages, so none other but a skilled code breaker could understand this correspondence.

It was in this way that at Chinon, 350 miles to the northwest across France from the Church Council, now occupying the great cathedral at Vienne, they heard from an unusually long message in early 1312 that suppression had been decided upon, as the fate of the Order. They had allowed themselves to hope, but now it was all in ruins.

"Clement knew all the time that the Order was innocent. They tell us that even he had agreed at Vienne, that it was 'without sin.' There was no reason in the religion to destroy our Order." Jacques continually told the others, who knew it as well as he did. "He did it as a pawn of Philip who now has our estates and will hold them as long as he can, even though they were awarded to the Hospitallers - he won't easily let go."

1312 passed and nothing further was told them except that the Governor informed them officially of what they already knew - the decision at Vienne, that their Order was no more.

"And what of us" enquired de Molay?

"His Holiness the Pope has issued a bull," the governor told him. "He says, gentlemen, amongst other dispositions", he read from a paper he was carrying, "that he reserves to himself the judgement of certain senior members of the Order… he names all four of you and one other, a Sir Olivier de Penne but of him I know nothing, he is not in my charge. More than that I do not know, but I have heard that his Holiness is ill and is in his palace at Avignon."

After that information their hopes were once again buoyed. The master would not admit it but he nurtured a hope, even despite all the disappointments. Surely, they agreed, his Holiness must have received the favourable report of the three cardinals that came to Chinon.

Could it be he was making sure that none of Philip's lickspittle archbishops would be making the judgement? Why else would he reserve it to himself? They had suffered too many disappointments in their long imprisonment to be optimistic, but a touch of hope? Yes, there was that.

"Who is this Olivier de Penne?" asked de Molay.

"No idea," said de Goneville, with which de Charney agreed.

"I know who he is," said Hugh de Pairault, himself the Visitor of France, who could be expected to know. "He was for a while our Preceptor of Lombardy. He is an organisational genius of sorts, who worked on attachment for the Pope at the Curia's request. He was at Poitiers when the arrests all came. Before we were separated from the other brethren, I heard that de Penne and the others at the Papal Court had not been arrested because they were still working for the Pope. But they were moved out of the palace so as not to make a scandal. Penne was allotted a house in the suburbs and he obviously picked his moment, because one night he was there, and the next morning he had disappeared.

"Good for him" muttered de Molay enviously.

"His Holiness was incandescent, apparently. He was deeply embarrassed. He was supposed to have said, "They will ask how I can keep 2,000 prisoners when I can't even control one?"

"What happened to this de Penne?" asked one of the old men.

"Nobody knows", replied de Pairault. "The Pope ordered a hue and cry and offered a reward of 20,000 florins for his recapture, no small sum eh? Nobody heard it had been claimed.

"My guess is that he reached the coast and got himself to England, which hadn't closed down the Order at that time. That came maybe two or three months later than in France. From there he would have made his way to Scotland, the one safe place for us, the brethren that I talked to agreed. You may know that the King of Scotland has been excommunicated for years, so the Pope cannot give him orders. That is where our fellows will be, I'm sure.

"The fact that the Pope all these years later, added de Penne's name to ours as 'reserved for his personal judgement', makes it sound as though he doesn't know where he is either, but hasn't given up on catching him, even now."

"Well good luck to him, and how I envy him," said de Molay.

The prisoners agreed that Geoffrey should write urgently to the cell at Poitou, and enquire for anything that they might know. When the answer came back, they heard that Philip would not hand the four prisoners over to the Pope, as he feared they would then be released. He knew that that these Templar leaders were his enemies to the death, and if at liberty, would find a way to bring him down, after what he had done to them.

Christmas 1313 came and went. It was in the New Year of 1314 that the governor told them he had received instructions that the four prisoners would be taken to Paris by an escort being sent for that purpose.

They communicated urgently with the shadow brethren in Poitou and asked what was to be done? The answer came back that the brethren would seek an opportunity to rescue them, once they had left the fortress and were on their journey to Paris along the valley of the Loire.

The message added that if it were possible, they would be rescued, But chillingly it added, if that were not possible, they could be sure that they would be revenged.

That was the last they heard, but buoyed up by hope, they gathered their meagre possessions when they were told soldiers from the King's own guard had arrived at the castle, under the command of Guillaume de Nogaret, one of King Philip's closest lieutenants and no friend of the Templars.

He came into the tower that had been their prison for six years with guardsmen bearing shackles. "Yes," he said to de Molay, "these are for you. We can't have you trying to escape, or your friends seeking to rescue you. I am conducting you to Paris where you will exchange this rather nice accommodation with its good clean country air, for something less salubrious at the Conciergerie."

"We were told," the old man said, "that we were the prisoners of the Holy Father and that we are at his disposition."

"Oh you are, you are," replied de Nogaret airily, "but sadly the holy old gentleman is ill and at Avignon. He has deputed the matter to the Archbishop of Sens and I believe that he has some plans for you!"

The mention of Philip de Marigny, Archbishop of Sens, caused the prisoners to shudder. It was he, a younger brother of King Philip's royal chamberlain and favourite courtier, whom at the time of the Paris commission of enquiry, Philip had made archbishop at the age of 22. In return for this preferment, the infamous new archbishop immediately condemned fifty-seven of the Templar prisoners as relapsed heretics. Their 'crime' was to have given evidence that their earlier confessions to the Dominicans had only been made because of torture, and that they were not true. Ecclesiastical law was so rigged that once heresy had been admitted, no matter if by torture or by any means, that denying it later became 'apostasy' - even worse than heresy, carrying an automatic death penalty for the apostates.

This was that same papal commission held at the monastery of St Genevieve in Paris, in which the Templar priest, Peter of Bologna had so distinguished himself as their advocate, but had then had himself to be rescued, before he too was murdered.

Even as they spoke with de Nogaret, the four senior Templars were loaded with chains and then put on the back of a cart to be taken out of Chinon Castle, downhill to the river. As they left their enforced home of six years past, with the sun bright above the beautiful Loire Valley spread out before them, they feared that their lives were probably over.

When they saw the size of their guard, several knights and perhaps eighty men-at-arms, they could see that any attempt at an armed rescue would be hopeless.

Arriving at the riverbank, they were taken out of the cart and unceremoniously shoved into a long rowing barge with some six oarsmen on either side. The guards re-fastened their shackles looping them under the fixed planks that served as seats, so there could be no jumping off the side, although guards were posted both in front and behind them.

As the oars dipped and the bow turned into the stream they saw alongside them, a similar sized boat with oarsmen and an awning midships, under which de Nogaret and one of the king's household knights were lounging on cushions. On both banks they saw the mounted escort in an extended line, their horses walking, keeping pace, as rowing against the current ensured that the progress of the boats would be slow.

They arrived in Paris after three days on the river and despite the discomfort of the shackles, it was a voyage that they wished would never end, the cleanliness of the water and the verdant banks being so strong a contrast to the stone tower in which they had been confined for so long. But inevitably, the oarsmen picked up their pace as they neared Paris and journey's end. By the afternoon of the third day, the boats landed their passengers on City Island where the Conciergerie prison had its own quay, close to the mighty stone structure of the royal palace whose bulk overshadowed it.

***

De Nogaret had not lied about the comparison between their hill top tower blessed by magnificent views and fresh breezes, with the foul stew that was the Conciergerie. The filthy rushes interspersed with human sewage spread over the stone flags, ensured the permanent smell of a privy, a further degradation for the scores of prisoners confined there. The great undercroft that served as a massive stone dungeon with its thick pillars supporting the floor above, was at river level and consequently always damp.

It was almost with a sense of relief when the day came that they were taken out and loaded into the back of a cart. This then carried them, their escort armed with halberds marching by their side along the quay, until they turned into the open space that was the cathedral close, in front of the colossal Notre Dame Cathedral. There they saw that a large wooden stage had been built on the cobbles right in front of the centre of the three tympana, the western entrances to the church, each surrounded and encrusted with colourful sculpted statues of the apostles and saints. The wooden scaffold was facing west with on one side of the cathedral close, the Hôtel Dieu, the cathedral's massive hospital and almshouse; and on the other, a line of densely built, many-storied merchant's houses.

Jacques de Molay had always loved this great church. The contrast of this carved stone perfection with the sewer adjunct of the Conciergerie, was more than he could bear.

They were hurried out of the cart and taken around outside the great church and then descended a stone staircase to a small candle-lit, sub-crypt. In the dim light they saw already seated at a table, the boyish Archbishop of Sens who looked every inch the foppish young courtier, his great be-jewelled gold chain over his slim figure in a purple cassock, his fingers covered in rings set with fabulous gemstones. On one side of him sat an older priest, the Bishop of Paris who throughout said nothing. On the other was a lay figure they already knew, de Nogaret, in his black lawyers robe, sprawling indolently back in his chair.

The prisoners stood unsteadily, their arms shackled behind them and the Archbishop looked at them in their wretchedness, wrinkled his nose and commented, "By the bones of Christ, you stink." He turned to de Nogaret and said, "Would it not be a good idea to clean them up a little before they go on stage? They look more like a bunch of old tramps than the generals of the Templars."

"Good idea", replied de Nogaret "I have already arranged they should wear clean Templar robes so everybody would know who they are - or used to be!" He laughed at his use of the past tense.

"Alright," said the youthful prelate, addressing the prisoners. "Jacques de Molay, Geoffrey de Charney, Geoffrey de Goneville, Hugh de Pairault, as you already know you're relapsed heretics." He raised his hand forbidding de Molay as he was about to intervene, and continued. "Come now Grand Master, you changed your plea three times as I understand it. Once was enough! You pleaded guilty to the Dominicans and then as an avowed heretic you relapsed and claimed your confession was untrue. *Quo est demonstrandum.* That makes you a relapsed heretic - an apostate for whom the penalty is death. You others, the same.

"However, you will be pleased to hear that in his infinite mercy, the Holy Father has ordained from his sick bed, that you should have your lives spared. Instead you will suffer perpetual imprisonment. We can't have dangerous apostates like you lot, going around like free men."

"But what about the Cardinals Commission that came to Chinon in 1308?" de Molay indignantly demanded. "They found us guilty neither of heresy, apostasy, nor of anything else and we, each of us, were formally absolved of any sin and told we were no longer excommunicated? There were notaries present who wrote it all down, and each of their eminences placed their seals on the document - they showed it to us!"

"Doesn't say anything about that here," the youthful archbishop replied, looking down, casually riffling through his few documents.

"Ah, you must be talking about the guilt of the Order," broke in de Nogaret, waving away their denials. "That was all dealt with at Vienne two years ago. You weren't there, but you must know. The Order was found not guilty, but no more Order, was how that came out - nothing to do with the individual sins of its heretical leaders - you people. Nasty stuff, as I remember. Kissing arse and worse. You should be ashamed."

None of the prisoners had anything left to fight back with. They fell silent and stood miserably in front of the table.

The Archbishop spoke again.

"Alright then, you know your sentences. Nothing more is required of you except that the guards will give you some buckets of water to clean up with, and we have some Templar robes for you to wear, so the people don't think you are just old layabouts we have picked up for the purpose.

"You will be appearing on stage with me, the Bishop of Paris here, and my suffragans and assistants, and you will be called forward by name."

"Then you will apologise to God, to His Holiness, to His Grace the King, to me the Archbishop, to the Bishop and people of Paris.... anybody I've left out?" he asked de Nogaret? "No? ...for your evil doing," he continued. "That's it. Then I take over and will next pronounce sentence. After that you will go your way, back to your abode in the Conciergerie, and I will go mine, and thereafter we will see no more of each other."

***

The prisoners were taken up the steps and outside to the back of the cathedral's stable yard where one at a time; they were unshackled and told to strip off their prison rags. Then a guard tipped a bucket of river water over each naked old man, first to endure the shock, then to wash himself down as best he could, using his discarded clothes to dry himself. Then each of them was handed out a more or less clean, white Templar robe, with the distinctive Red Cross patee on the left shoulder. That prisoner was then re-shackled and the next one treated in the same way.

Strangely, just being newly clean if still damp, and wearing once again the coarse white Templar woollen robe, of which they had been so proud, had a profound effect on the Grandmaster and also de Charney.

All hope gone, the other two seemed paralysed by the sentences they knew they were to receive publicly, that afternoon. The sergeant in charge of the detail told them that they would be placed back in the same small cathedral crypt, to wait there until they were fetched. The stone chamber had only one entry and exit, which was the stairs that they had descended. They saw that a pair of guards was posted at the entrance.

The table previously occupied by the boy archbishop was still there, with the chairs all askew, but the candles were clearly not to be wasted on the likes of them, and had gone. As the day wore on, such light as found its way from the stairwell became dimmer, as did the spirits of the old men.

"So... a lifetime in that stinking privy of the Conciergerie, or somewhere like it? I really can't face that," said de Molay. "Me neither." offered de Charney.

"But what choices do we have?" asked de Pairault. De Goneville spoke not at all. He was already 'out of it'; his mind had given way under the constant assaults that their fate had brought them.

"Come on! We denied it before, and said we only confessed because of torture" said de Molay. "We could do the same again."

"Jacques..." For the first time since he had become the Order's Grandmaster, de Charney called him by his given name. "You must know what will happen. This is the end of the road for us. The Pope has clearly suppressed the report of the three cardinals from their examination of us in 1308. From everything we have heard about the Council at Vienne, this Pope and this King have made a compact. The cardinal's report that we saw already sealed, will have been put aside, burned, or buried somewhere in the Curia archives. Probably only the three cardinals and the notaries even know of its existence, but maybe…" he speculated, "those cardinals had spread the word so that it helped our defenders amongst the Church fathers at Vienne, we don't know. At least we have the satisfaction of knowing that the Order was officially found to be, as we all knew, without sin."

"Yet we the leaders are condemned for all manner of wickedness whilst our Order is unblemished." broke in de Pairault. "We know the infamies of which they have found each of us guilty, and yet the same infamies have quite rightly been dismissed when reviewing the Order itself. Tell me, how could one be true and not the other? The three cardinals" he continued, "were genuine I believe, and they found us not guilty, but here we are, my friends, about to go out on that scaffold and be sentenced to perpetual imprisonment."

De Charney spoke up again. "A part of that unholy compact between king and pope must be to not let us loose with the stories we have to tell, and the influence we still would have, with those thousands of our brethren who were not in France on Black Friday. We know from the shadow cell at Poitou that they are up and organised. I won't count on it, but I would be surprised if there weren't some hardy fellows here in Paris trying to get us away, even now. Personally I have no hope of any success. We saw from the size of the escort they sent to Chinon that they are taking no chances."

"No Jacques," he said it gently now, "they want this over. If we repudiate our confessions on that stage today they will burn us. Make no mistake!"

De Goneville sat still, his gaunt face seemingly transfixed on a mote of dust that swam on a weak beam of light. De Pairault sprawled across the table his head in his shackled hands. "I cannot face the fire, Grandmaster," he said, his voice cracking with fear. "I have seen a witch burned, once when I was a youth. I cannot forget it even now - I could charge twenty Saracens single handed, but not the fire, I just cannot face that."

"So back to the rest of your life in all that shit, with the giant rats," asked de Molay?

"Even that," mumbled the broken old man.

"Nobody can blame you," said the Grandmaster. "Do you know, I feel a most unchristian hunger for revenge? Revenge on the King, the abominable Philip, who has destroyed our Order through his greed. Revenge on Clement, the leader of our Order who did the worst betrayal possible. He sacrificed all of us, like pawns in a chess game."

"And what of God in all this" asked de Charney. "Why did He abandon us?"

There was a long silence. "Maybe the Cathars had it right…" de Molay suggested quietly, "that the devil rules the world and God rules in Heaven. Maybe that is our best hope of justice. That God will have witnessed everything that has taken place and those rulers, too powerful to pay the price here, the King of France and the Pope, will come to know His justice when their time comes. I could believe that!"

They were interrupted by the heavy step of the sergeant and three guards. "Just going to check your bonds, gentlemen. It's time to go up and join his reverence, and the others, at the front of the church. You've drawn a big crowd out there, I can tell you."

***

In the front of the great cathedral a crowd had been gathering for hours, mainly to get a good place to see the show that the church was laying on for them. Families had brought picnics, and before it became too crowded had been able to spread coloured kerchiefs on the ground to place food upon. Hucksters wandered around with trays of hot pies under layers of straw, selling their hearty food.

The forecourt of the cathedral was paved with cobblestones. Despite the size and bulk of the great cathedral, it was right in amongst the city houses with a number of narrow alleyways being the only way to access that open space from the rest of the city. The contrast was highly dramatic, moving between large over-hanging houses along narrow crooked streets, with a slow trickle of sewage and other rubbish flowing along the centre.

Apart from busy people going about their business, herds of livestock - cows, sheep, goats, even pigs, were a commonplace sight. Then these squalid lanes suddenly opened out into the level open space of the cathedral close. From the far end of the square arose a symphony of carved white Caen stone, its frontage brightly decorated with the polychrome stone figures of apostles and saints, and at a higher level still, a line of the kings of

Judah. Even higher on the tower were carven images of grinning devils and mythical beasts, the gargoyles, which often were also waterspouts.

All of this rose sheer to the greatest height of any building then in France. Yet despite its small area proportionate to the building, the cathedral place was one of the largest open areas within Paris, rivalled only by that in front of the City Hall on the right bank of the river opposite, where people came for markets and to watch the civic hangings and beheadings.

The drama of these free holiday events on what would normally be a working day, were welcomed by the citizens as it broke up the monotony of the everyday routines of life. The Church dealt with one class of malefactor, the civil power all others, and both made the most of their authority. These exhibitions were dramatic, dealing as they did with life and sudden death, yet usually there was little sympathy in the crowd for the accused or the condemned, on the simplistic reasoning that they must have done, whatever it was that had brought them to this place, otherwise they wouldn't be there!

The vast façade of the great church, up in its galleries and towers, held another class of spectator: churchmen and senior cathedral officials, noblemen and those, mainly ladies, who would not want to be jostled in the rough crowd. They could see and hear the events below without being discommoded.

Some thousands had now gathered and a buzz went up in anticipation of the principal actors appearing. In front of the stage was a double row of helmeted royal guards standing feet slightly apart, at ease, with grounded halberds held by their right hands.

Within moments the buzz returned, but this time turning to a roar of jeers and shouts, catcalls and whistles as the four old Templar generals, now clad in the white habit of their order, the red Templar cross on their left shoulders. Each with their arms shackled in front of them, were steered by a royal guard holding an arm, briskly up the steps to take their place at the back of the stage.

There were of course no seats for them, and each stood with his individual guard stationed behind him. De Goneville, old man that he was, and aging further by the moment, slumped as he stood, his guard having to steady him. It seemed that he really did not know where he was, or what was happening.

In the great crowd was every kind of citizen - merchants, tradesmen, students, artificers, pedlars, masters and their apprentices. A remarkable number had brought their wives and children. There were also nobles, although they tended to be observing from high up in the galleries on the cathedral's façade. There were knights and country gentlemen in the crowd come to see this, the last act in the story of the military order which they had known all their lives, and indeed had once greatly respected, before all this sinning came about. Scattered in amongst the great crowd, standing in twos and threes, armed and in various disguises, fifteen free Templars now attached to the Paris shadow house, were there, hoping to find an opportunity to snatch back their old generals, if it were at all possible.

Their leader was standing on a low wall as if to miss nothing of the show, but in reality so that his men could see him. He and his companion were dressed as country gentlemen, which gave a reason for them to carry swords. He was Sir John de Berricourt, a senior knight now in command of the Paris shadow house, who had entirely evaded arrest all those years ago, by his good fortune in being away from the city on the day of the raid. He was there together with another knight, Sir Paul de Chatillon, despatched by the council in Castle Aird, as being familiar with Paris. He was to see that everything that could be done in the rescue, was done, and to conjure the prisoners away from Paris, if de Berricourt's team could successfully seize them.

While he had been instructed by Castle Aird to do all in his power to rescue the leaders, he could make no plans except that of getting them away from the cathedral place and City Island, after freeing them. For that, he had no real plan at all; all thoughts were mere contingencies.

He had stationed a boat with several oars in the mud flats, under the Notre Dame Bridge, with an idea of using it after getting hold of the leaders, fighting their way, surrounding the old men, and spiriting them out of the square. Once on the river, with several strong oarsmen and the current aiding their escape, the advantage of surprise should see them get a good lead over any pursuers. The plan was to travel well beyond the city and then land about fifteen miles downstream, where there were colleagues with horses waiting for them.

Paul and de Berricourt at first thought it might be do-able, even though the guards were thick on the ground, an armoured screen between the stage and the crowd. But the crowd itself contained no soldiers, the only possible threat being from their sheer numbers and the danger of some off-duty knights, or armed gentlemen, seeking to intervene. But as they looked at the size and now the placing of the guard around the stage, they realised that the king's men were prepared for trouble. They were so positioned that a frontal assault would be suicidal. They would just have to wait to see if some opportunity arose.

Facing the crowd before him, Jacques de Molay had recovered a measure of his pride. The clean white Templar mantle had made a big difference. He had served in the Order for nearly fifty years. Steadily through his character and qualities, he had made his way up the ranks. Unlike some masters, he had never had kings or powerful patrons lobbying for his promotion. He had reached every stage of office based on merit, and the votes of his peers in the brotherhood.

Until recently he had regarded himself as a religious man, discharging the monastic side of his duties with quiet satisfaction. Now having seen that the good and decent fraternity he led had been so tormented by foul friars, greedy priests and Philip - the Lord's anointed king, he had since the arrests experienced a deep personal crisis of faith. It was all a part of his disillusion with the betrayal of the Order and of himself by his superior, the Pope, whom he had served loyally and well.

He looked out over the crowd who were still jeering and gesticulating but somehow he was beyond any concern at such triviality. For a moment he looked at faces in the crowd to see if any of the likely lads from the shadow house, he and his colleagues fully expected to be there, could be recognised. But no, they would not easily give themselves away. With a practiced glance of his military eye, he assessed the chances of a group cutting a way through to them on the stage, and that was just about none at all. He could see that even if they tried, the guards on the stage behind them would have time to hustle the prisoners away, probably never to be seen in public again.

More than ever before, he felt truly alone. For seven long years he had been in prison. He had always believed that if only he could see the Pope face to face, everything could be resolved. But his frequent requests for an audience went unanswered. Then after the hope he had felt, when the three examining cardinals found him and his colleagues innocent, and told them so, he knew the only possible explanation must be that the Pope had decided that the Templar officers were expendable. So, they had been thrown to Philip's wolves.

Now, he knew, this must be his time. It was his only opportunity. He was not going to waste it!

A sudden buzz of excitement came from the assembled thousands which dropped away, as from the bishops palace by the river side of the cathedral a few yards away, came a procession led by four guards and then a cross bearer preceding the Bishop of Paris, gorgeously attired in his mitre and robes, with his clerks and chaplain nearby. Then came the young de Marigny, Archbishop of Sens, even more sumptuously gowned with an even bigger mitre, and like the bishop, he carried a crozier, his staff of office. He too had his officials in tow.

They made their dignified way to the foot of the stage and ascended the wooden steps for the principals to take allotted seats, with their staffs standing by them, whilst the four shackled prisoners, each with a guard, stood to one side at the rear of the stage. Two rows of guards, each line numbering about twenty, stood in front of the stage, their halberds ready for action, their captain and a lieutenant both sword in hand, pacing in between their ranks, checking their preparedness, glowering into the crowd, scanning faces nearby, clearly expecting and ready for trouble.

The archbishop's clerk came to the front and clearing his throat, was rewarded by a hush from the crowd whilst he shouted out to them the purpose of the proceedings. With the great towering cathedral just a few feet behind the stage the dense crowd was jammed into the available space between, on the one side the large timbered city merchant's houses in this prestigious location, and on the other the long low hall of the hospice and foundlings hospital. Jacques de Molay saw from the stage that the mass of the people even flowed back into the narrow alleyways that opened into the cathedral close.

His would be rescuers had seen the same jamming of the alleyways, through which they had counted to make their getaway. But even without that, Paul could see the impossibility of getting beyond the double line of guards before the stage. He was certainly ready to venture his own life and that of his men, but he knew that there could be no merit in that, unless as a result the elderly leaders could be saved. All the evidence was to the contrary.

The clerk, unable to keep up with the shouting, was talking now, and those near to him could hear clearly, whilst further back the words could hardly be distinguished. Then the Bishop of Paris stood, and taking a text from the Bible, started to deliver a sermon, which he read out. It was mistimed. The crowd most of whom could not hear him, started to become restive and noisy. Observing this, he brought his preaching abruptly to a close, and nodded to the clerk to resume. This worthy now read out the charges against each of the Templars. The crowd strained to hear this and when the Archbishop got up to speak, they were attentive.

He continued to face the crowd whilst addressing the prisoners by name: "You, Jacques de Molay, are by your own admission a relapsed heretic, guilty of the crime of apostasy to which you have confessed, in which you admitted further horrid crimes, too numerous to repeat here, but all of which have been considered."

He paused, the crowd roared and screamed abuse and some rotten fruit was thrown, but discontinued, when the guards angrily gestured that they were in the line of fire.

Sens then spoke against each of the other Templar leaders in turn, repeating the charges and each earned a similar storm of abuse from the crowd. De Molay felt a curious numbness, as though he was merely a spectator and not a leading actor in this drama.

He saw his friend, de Charney standing tall in his clean Templar robe and disciplining himself to take the abuse, without breaking. Hugh de Pairault stood erect and iron faced, but the master knew he was in an inner turmoil. Poor de Goneville was unaware when he was addressed, that it was anything to do with him. As he staggered, his guard needed to take a grip on the back of his mantle to stop him from slumping over. The pitiless crowd seemed to take that as a sign of his deep guilt, and howled the louder.

From his vantage point within the crowd, de Berricourt had signalled his men to force their way in ones and twos, through the dense crowd, to get near enough to the front to be useful, if he, the leader, signalled an attack. Paul was struggling to move through the crowd, constantly looking fruitlessly about him to see if any space was opening up.

The archbishop proceeded to the sentencing. Each in turn he addressed by name and gave an identical sentence.

"Jacques de Molay, for your crimes you are sentenced to perpetual imprisonment."

The crowd sounded angry, they wanted more. Imprisonment was too lenient. As each sentence was pronounced, the crowd seemed to become angrier.

Then, the sentences recited, the archbishop took his chair. He leaned over to speak into the ear of the Bishop of Paris, sat beside him. "I thought that went rather well," he murmured, and turning, looked expectantly at the Grand Master as his guard shoved him forward.

Jacques de Molay had commanded armies. As a young knight he had shed his blood in Outremer and survived several seemingly impossible confrontations. Twenty-three years before, he had taken part and been wounded in the last great battle fought by the Templars, at the city of Acre where his predecessor had been killed. Soon after that, he had been elected Grandmaster by the survivors.

Then he had been tricked into returning from his headquarters and power base in distant Cyprus, to enter the King of France's realm, and thus his trap. For seven years now he had been his prisoner, first in the dungeons of the Paris Temple itself and then in the fortress of Chinon. For the first four weeks he had been interrogated and tortured by the accursed brothers of the Order of St Dominic under their master in France, Guillaume of Paris. He it was, who had personally conducted the torture of de Molay, seeking and eventually finding the point at which he would break.

The old soldier, who had sustained many wounds and injuries to his flesh and limbs in a lifetime of soldiering, had learned that pinioned naked to a torture table whilst the Dominicans probed his nerve endings, he could not sustain the seemingly endless white pain, which he himself had the power to end, as they kept telling him. "Sign the confession," they kept saying, with each increment of pain! They had already written what they wanted him to sign. He had dared to hope - then his only hope, that the Pope, his sole chief in the world, would rescue him.

After the three cardinals had examined him at Chinon and found him innocent, he had wrongly thought that perhaps Clement was playing a waiting game, until Philip had dropped his guard. Then the long nightmare would be over. This event today however, of being produced before the Paris mob, would he now knew, be the last time he would ever appear in public.

He stepped forward near to the edge of the stage, his guard also taking two paces forward, whilst the crowd screamed their hatred and insults: "Idol worshipper!" "Devil's spawn!" An over-ripe pear sailed through the air and broke up on his white mantle over a thigh.

He wiped off the remains thoughtfully, then threw back his head and roared contemptuously at the crowd, "I once took a Saracen arrow there in the Holy Land." Suddenly, he found his cry had earned him a moment or two of silence.

He continued loudly, summoning all his reserves of willpower.

"You have all heard my crimes and of my confession. You know the penalty that has been awarded. But I am telling you now that this so-called confession was a lie, as all of the charges against me were a lie. I confessed, because I was tortured, until I said whatever it was, that would make them stop the unbearable pain."

Sens shocked, was looking around the stage for the captain to have him interrupt the Templar, but that officer was down amongst his halberdiers, facing the crowd, which now seemed in an uncertain mood.

"There is no truth in the awful charges against our ancient and honourable order - the very idea that the same Templars who would accept being beheaded by the Saracens - and hundreds were - rather than deny Christ, that they would worship a cat! How could anyone believe that we, who built great cathedrals full of beauteous things, would bow down before a crude wooden idol, like a child's toy?" His contempt came through powerfully.

Clearly the mood in the crowd was changing. It seemed to be moving towards a tide of respect for this elderly warrior.

"I repudiate this farce of a so-called 'holy tribunal' that sentenced my brethren and me. I totally deny the charges that were laid against us, and I insist that the Order of the Knights of the Temple is an honourable and godly brotherhood, without sin!"

He stepped back, his guard with him whilst his friend, De Charney took his place. The crowd suddenly respectful, now was quiet.

"You have heard our Grandmaster. I too deny all the charges against me - and my so-called confession, which was given under torture, and which I hereby revoke.

"I too say the Order was without sin, and that this horrible crime against our Christian Order was the work of King Philip of France - your king, abetted by these priests and bishops you see here on this stage." His guard was now pulling him back before he had finished, whilst the Archbishop and his suffragans were stealthily stepping down from the stage, and retreating to the bishop's palace behind them.

Now the crowd were throwing their rubbish missiles at the departing priests together with their full-throated abuse. The four Templars were hurried off the stage and away, back to the crypt they had previously occupied, whilst the lines of halberdiers in the front had lowered their halberds making a wall of steel points against the crowd surging towards the stage. The guards in good order retreated slowly backwards, their points still extended, until they were all behind the railings of the bishop's house.

The crowd took out their anger on the timber stage, tearing it down and throwing chunks of it over the bishop's railings.

Paul had rejoined de Berricourt, now surrounded by his men, with weapons still concealed, as the great crowd began to break up and drift away. They had never had the slightest chance to intervene and now could only wait on events, to see if an opportunity might still occur.

On the very fringe of the crowd, Philip's minister Guillaume de Nogaret had waited until the end of this disaster. It had been intended as political theatre to show the crowd the wickedness of the Templar Order, whose appropriate suppression their king's diligence had made possible. With the crime being heresy, it was to have been entirely a church tribunal so it was agreed he should keep off the stage. He had waited with his horse, so that he could promptly report to the king. Now he angrily thought, due to de Marigny's incompetence in letting the Templars ramble on - once it became clear what they were going to do, it was a total balls-up!

He took hold of his horse's bridle and walked him to face around, before mounting and riding down the length of the small island to the king's palace.

***

The royal palace of the Capetians occupied nearly all the land at the western end of City Island, and outside its walls there were farm animals grazing on the sloping field, down to where it gave way to the fast flowing waters of the Seine. But on the other side of what could be called a channel, of some twenty feet in width, was a small tump, which like similar small islets in this part of the river, adjoining the City Island itself, had no buildings on it but was used for grazing and vegetable gardening. This particular island was owned by the monks of St Germain, who did not discover until the following day that the King in his wrath had ordained that the two old men, who had so publicly repudiated the Church's judgement and named him, should be burned there. This would be in sight and perhaps sound, of his palace balcony, from where he proposed to see the thing done.

When de Nogaret had reported the disastrous bungling of the condemnation of the Templars, Philip had nearly suffered apoplexy in his rage. He had summoned the archbishop, Philip de Marigny to attend upon him immediately and when that terrified prelate presented himself, the King gave full vent to his rage as he paced around the trembling archbishop. "I made you, de Marigny, and I can break you. Right now, I am greatly tempted to do just that."

The young archbishop, who had known nothing other than privilege, did not realise that he should just bear this humiliation and not answer back. To say anything would just bring about the same storm, but with renewed vigour.

"But I have had them cast into the deepest dungeon in the Conciergerie, Sire. They will never see the light of day again." His voice faltered as he saw the King was about to explode.

"You are just a damned fool, and you are supposed to be a leading churchman. Don't you know what even the Paris mob knows, that the penalty for a relapsed heretic is death by burning, not vegetating inside a strong building to be forgotten. I don't WANT them forgotten, damn you. I want them remembered, so that the manner of their death will be known as the price to be paid for crossing me, or indeed...," he added as an afterthought, "defying the Church.

"Those two that spoke out, must die today - tonight, and I shall deal with it myself. Now, get out!"

He turned to his dependable man of affairs. "De Nogaret, see to it. Put up some stakes on that little islet of the St Germain monks, just off the tip of City Island. I want to see this done and I expect it to go smoothly. I want them to suffer, do you understand? So no executioner's tricks to help them die before the flames reach them. In fact build up their fires on a good thick base of charcoal around the stakes, and pile up some green branches. No one at all is to be on the island, other than guards and executioners, and a priest, I suppose. And we don't want any of those rogue Templar bandits out there on the streets, to think they can rescue their leaders. I want a ban on all river-craft up and down the river until tomorrow morning, excepting only those involved with the execution. Now get on with it!"

***

Jacques de Molay, in the aftermath of his final defiance, had become almost cataleptic. Nothing any more seemed real. He knew he would die a terrible death and that it could be at any time from now. The four old men had eventually been put in a cart and hurried with a large guard through the now empty streets, taking them back to the Conciergerie. There, their new accommodation was lower down and even damper than the previous great prison chamber, and completely without light. Both he and de Charney were physically and spiritually spent. After their few cathartic minutes of speaking out, each had turned in upon himself, knowing what this would cost them. When Hugh de Pairault congratulated them both, with genuine admiration in his voice, neither of them could find the words to readily respond.

Later when the iron door swung open, the gaoler called out just the two names, "de Molay … de Charney," they knew that their time had come. Quickly they each embraced their companions as far as the iron shackles would allow. Their mind-injured friend de Goneville made as if to leave with them, but de Pairault held him back. "May God be with you" he said to his two doomed old colleagues, but they didn't hear him.

It was six in the evening before the executions took place. De Nogaret with his normal competence made sure of all the details, choosing experienced men to handle the executions and ensuring that the King's specified choice of slow burning green branches was used on the pyres and stacked amidst the two pyramids of spars, which had hurriedly been erected around two solid stakes. It had not taken long for these to be driven into the place of execution, the soft earth of the tiny island.

Word had of course got out that the burnings were imminent, and on both banks of the river, narrow at this point the left bank particularly close, large crowds had gathered. The palace grounds and its pasture land on City Island ensured none of the citizenry could be closer to the islet than the riverbanks. It seemed eerie that the river, normally swarming with vessels at this time of the day, was completely empty of craft, large or small, excepting only the small barge transporting the prisoners and their escort.

The Grandmaster was walked off the barge by two burly guards half holding, half lifting him and then up onto his pyre. There the waiting executioner opened the wrist manacles, and took the linking chain around the stake before refastening them.

Looking over at de Charney, de Molay saw he was likewise being secured to a stake. He found himself facing down river, but asked the executioner if he would move him around, so he could look on the distant towers of Notre Dame as he died. But before those giant equal towers came into view, he could clearly see in the foreground, rising above the palace rooftop, the slender and elegant spire of the tall Royal Chapel, built to house the relic of 'the crown of thorns' by a sainted ancestor of this king, pointing like a finger to heaven.

He could see that the executioners were close to completing their preparations, including placing two burning brands in a small brazier between the pyres. He tried to prepare himself, knowing that he could not, for what was to come.

On the left bank, Paul and de Berricourt were at their wits end. Once they knew of the place of execution, they had agreed that two boatloads of armed Templars descending on the island, might be able to swiftly save the leaders, fighting off the guards and then back into the boats and continue with the current, towards their pre-planned landing point downstream. But he knew that it would have to be spilt-second timing to rescue the leaders before they were fatally burned, and that he would inevitably lose some men in such a wild venture. Then their boatmen reported back that there were two guard boats already moored, one each side of the little island, crammed with heavily armed soldiery, including crossbowmen, clearly to prevent any such rescue as he had envisaged.

The waiting Templars knew now that they were beaten. Their only remaining duty would be to witness the deaths of their leaders and to somehow try to signal them, that their comrades were with them at the end. Berricourt spoke to a colleague who hurried off into a nearby warehouse building, amongst the crowded frontage of the straggling left bank.

De Molay watched as the executioner took a flaming brand and touched it to various points, low down in the piled wood. Then he thrust the brand into the pile and moved over to de Charney's stake and did the same there. Wisps of smoke were rising.

"Goodbye Geoffrey" the master called out through cracked lips. "Goodbye and God bless you, Grandmaster," came the reply and then he shouted, "look over there, over at the bank. God bless those boys." As the old generals strained their eyes, they could see not one, but three Beauseants, the black and white battle flag of the Templars being furiously waved from the dense crowd on the riverbank, and the people there were cheering at the gesture of defiance.

De Molay could feel the heat now on his legs and lower body, but as yet there was little flame. He knew that he would lose control once the pain started, and increased. Looking over towards the palace, to fasten his gaze on the slender spire marking the Crown of Thorns, he could see light and people emerging onto the terrace of the palace.

He didn't know whether they could hear him, but he would try: "You, Philip Capet, evil king without honour…" he roared! "You have destroyed what was good and holy, for the sake of your insatiable greed.

"You, Clement false pope wherever you may be. You traitor! You betrayed your own faithful followers!

"We could not get justice in this world, but you both will surely face God's justice in the next."

The heat was building up and hurting now around his lower half, and smoke was entering his lungs.

With one last effort he shouted, which tailed off involuntarily into a hoarse scream, as a tongue of flame licked up and seared his groin.

"I charge you evil king… and false pope… to face me… in the court of heaven… before… this year end!"

From the palace balcony, the King had seen the Templar battle flags waving defiantly, over on the left bank, and furiously ordered his captain of guards to send men over to arrest whoever it was, but knowing that they would be long gone, before that could happen. Now he could hear that the condemned man de Molay, was shouting something. He could hear some, but not all. A trick of the wind caught the final words "…face me… court … heaven…this year..." He could hear no more, he expected it would be curses, no doubt he would be told, but what he heard, such a prophecy from a dying man, was enough to slightly dent his ease of mind.

In the dawn's first light, Paul released the two carrier pigeons that he had brought with him with identical messages, en route to the Flemish coast for a relay to Castle Aird. He had sent volunteers early whilst it was still dark, to swim across to the island and bring back the charred remains - scorched skulls and bones of the two leaders, which he would immediately take back in his saddle bags to Scotland, to become the first relics of the new fraternity.

***

BANNOCKBURN

Scotland, 23-24 June 1314

Although it was not that cold, Paul shivered in the wet June afternoon as he stood on the fields before the city of Stirling. The long grass was soaking, as were his boots. After today it would never make the hay that its farmer had intended. A pair of ravens wheeled overhead, their aggressive caws echoing from the line of trees that bordered the broad meadow, as if they had some knowledge that here was to be a bloody battlefield and a scavengers feast.

The young knight wore his knee length chain-mail hauberk above his chain-mail breeches and over this the long linen surcoat displaying the white diagonal cross of Saint Andrew on a blue background. His sword belt slung from right shoulder to left hip across his body, and sheathed dagger found him equipped for war. Over all in the drizzle, he wore a plain, now sodden woollen cloak, trailing on the wet grass. On top of the chain-mail hood of his hauberk he merely had the spacious cope of his cloak. His steel helmet was until needed, hooked onto his horse's saddle-bow, and the palfrey un-required, was contentedly grazing back not far away at the rear tree line.

The Fraternal Council had ordained, not without protest it should be said, that their warriors in this battle would display nothing that could identify them as Templars, and the Scottish Kingdom's emblem seemed the appropriate insignia. Brother Prior had forcefully maintained that it would not help their cause, now that the Order was passing into history to demonstrate otherwise, whether or not they were to win or lose on this battlefield.

Paul looked at the mighty Stirling Castle on its rock only three miles away, with rain clouds scudding past its battlements. It looked impregnable, but it was not. It was one of only three great castles in Scotland that the Bruce had not yet captured. Already it had been under siege for more than a year by his Scots, who controlled the town surrounding it. No frontal assault was now likely, because its English commander had many months ago agreed on terms of surrender. He had offered to capitulate if the castle was not to be relieved by an English force before midsummer's day, 24th June, which now was the very next day.

This is why the two armies were destined to converge at that place and at that time. If the garrison was now to be relieved that meant that the Scots had lost; yet if that were to happen, raising the siege would be the least of their worries. Less than five hundred yards away, across rolling grassland from where Paul now stood facing south, was a long line of dense forest, pierced by the narrow divide of the Roman road from Falkirk. It was along this road that the enemy must advance.

The Scottish scouts had informed their commanders that the forward contingents of the mighty English army had arrived, and their advanced elements all mounted, of some 500 knights and men at arms would be within striking distance later that very afternoon. They were now some five miles distant but with their main army strung out over twenty and more miles behind them.

Having returned to Scotland from Paris in early May, where he had witnessed the execution by fire of Grand Master de Molay and another top leader, quite unable with his Templar colleagues to rescue them from this terrible death, used as he was to success, Paul had tasted there the bitter gall of failure.

He had brought back their scorched bones and skulls, relics from the death fire; had made his report on his return to Castle Aird, and was glad to have been sent off almost straight away, to go to Stirling. There, as had been arranged, he took command of one of the pike battalions forming up near the city, with King Robert's army, to meet the anticipated English invasion

He had now been in these parts for several weeks together with other Templar knights and sergeants, training the battalion of 750 foot soldiers assigned to him, especially in the tactics and drill of fighting with the long pike, the cruel steel blades of which the Temple had imported from across the North Sea. In Scotland sixteen foot long, stout ashwood staves had been carefully fitted onto the ferocious cutting, stabbing, hooking pike heads.

They made a formidable array indeed in the schiltron formation, as old a fighting posture as Alexander's Macedonian phalanxes. Eight ranks each of 90 men, next to another like-sized battalion commanded by his friend and fellow Templar knight, Sir Geraint of Monmouth, would stand together presenting a bristling forest of one and a half thousand steel spiked staffs, in the face of everything that the English would throw at them.

Together these two battalions, each with a band of highland skirmishers and a small number of archers in support, made up the brigade of the Earl of Moray, a well-experienced leader and nephew of the Scottish King. There were two other brigades to be arrayed behind them, one under the Black Douglas, and behind this force, the King under his direct command, had pikemen in an enlarged brigade, including most of his archers. There were also some 500 light cavalry, a fraction of the number in the English army, the Scots commanded by Sir James Keith, the same knight who had attended the chapter meeting and rallied the Templars at Aird, in the cause of his sovereign.

Apart from all of these were the mass of pictish blue-painted, half-naked highland clansmen under their chieftains - ferocious, if undisciplined light infantry. King Robert the Bruce commanded a total of about 8,000 fighting men who were defending their own soil, heavily outnumbered by the invaders from the south by perhaps as many as three to one.

Paul's battalion under Templar officers and sergeants, were now moving up into position. They had assembled a month past and up until the last moment, were still exercising under cover of the woodland behind him. It was a measure insisted upon by King Robert who knew that training on open ground would be observed by English spies. They would then be able to alert the invading army to the Scots main tactic of a well-drilled force using pikes and the pike wall, as their primary weapons system, of which it was known that the English, like most militaries at this time, had little experience.

He was now pacing out the ground assigned to his command in the carefully prepared defensive position, which a heavily outnumbered King Robert had personally chosen and now supervised. Across the whole front in this seemingly innocent rolling meadowland, there were a series of pits dug, each concealing sharpened stakes to entrap charging cavalry, hidden under coverings of sailcloth covered with light grass sods. The Falkirk Road itself and its verges as it debouched from the trees, was heavily mined with such lethal pits.

Then, in between the lines of opposing forces, on the land to be contested by the two armies, came thousands of the anti-cavalry weapons, randomly scattered steel 'hedgehog' spikes, called caltrops, that would pierce a charger's hoof or a man's foot, again imported by the Templars from their Hanseatic factors across the North Sea.

Paul with his Templar colleagues from Castle Aird, had himself been intensively trained in the tactics to be used, by the senior Templar commander, Sir Peter Breydel and his veteran master-sergeant, brought in by the Council from Flanders. Sir Peter had fought and had been knighted on the field of the Battle of the Golden Spurs, just twelve years before at Courtrai, where Flemish pikemen, 'citizen soldiers,' just like these Scottish volunteer townsmen, had destroyed the flower of French chivalry. Later, two years before Black Friday, he had joined the Templar Order, expecting to go on crusade. He had been attached to a north Flemish Templar Commandery and thus had missed being caught in the French king's dragnet in France on Black Friday.

Brother Prior had sent to Flanders for him months before, where he had been living in the city of Bruges since Black Friday. Within the few years since that purge, helped by Templar resources, he had settled down to become a substantial merchant in that city. Once summoned, he had crossed the sea and taken up his new command in Scotland. There he had first discussed tactics and instructed his officers and sergeants. Then he had taken overall command of the Templar battalions with their assigned pikemen, under the generalship of King Robert who had appointed him to be his Master of Infantry.

He was probably the leading exponent in Christendom in the use of the infantry pike, as he had demonstrated at Courtrai's famous victory against heavy cavalry, still the backbone of all of Europe's medieval armies. So King Robert had given him strategic command of the schiltrons under himself, to which his brigade commanders with tactical responsibility would defer, when the time came to turn defence into attack.

Courtrai in 1302 had been the first great victory in western history by infantry levies - in this case from the Flemish towns' middle classes - over well-mounted armoured knights. The 'golden spurs' for which the battle was named, were those of the hundreds of French knights who had died that day, which thereafter were displayed in the local church.

The memory of this was all the sweeter to the Templars, who had long talked of it, because it was the army and heavy cavalry of their persecutor, the hated King Philip of France that was defeated at Courtrai. It was the despised townsmen of Bruges and Ghent and other Flemish cities that performed the miracle. There it had been a feudal quarrel that did not at all involve the Order, but as Europe's outstanding military professionals, the Templars had not missed the lessons that it taught. They knew that it was about discipline and drill and the belief for these pike men, that now they could defeat these vain aristocratic warriors of English King Edward, who held them in such disdain.

The young Templar, Sir Paul, had at the very first, been surprised that the troops over whom he was given command, were not to be the wild, highland Scots tribesmen that he had expected. They had been mostly allotted to the king's direct command, except for a few score skirmishers assigned to his and the other pike battalions.

Paul's pikemen volunteers were mostly lowland townsmen, a very different breed. Many were from in and around Edinburgh, Dundee, Perth and from Stirling itself. Whilst they lacked the fire and ferocity of the clansmen, what they did have was an acceptance of discipline and a commitment to drive the continually invading English, from their land. They also knew that if the English won this fight, that home and hearth would be laid waste, their women and children raped, enslaved or killed. In a word, he thought, and agreed with the other young Templar professionals as they had assessed their chances, that these lowland Scotsmen were 'steady' - steadiness being the key virtue in infantry, in the face of the shock of attack by superior forces.

Now, after weeks of hard and repetitive training, the men themselves had come to believe that the deep forest of bristling steel points with which they would greet the charging cavalry, would defy their adversaries, and even defeat them.

The Templar officers leading them just hoped that it would be so, but they knew that battles turned on many factors. The Scots had few archers, numbered in the low hundreds - the English were reputed to have many, perhaps 3,000, of the famed Anglo-Welsh longbowmen, from the marshland valleys of the Wye, the Monnow, and the Usk, known as Archenfield, in the borderlands of South Wales. The Bruce had no more than 500 cavalry at his command, mostly light cavalry, their mounts no match for the heavy war horses of their adversaries and outnumbered at least six to one by the English foe. Apart from his scouts, King Robert held this small force in reserve, commanded by his sturdy friend from Pitlochry, Sir James Keith, strengthened with a small leavening of thirty mounted Templars on their destriers.

The English also had brought in absolute numbers, many more men, some 22,000 to attack the Scots. Quite aware that the fields would be wet and heavy going for cavalry, they had with them an unusually large force of infantry, mainly billhook men, who carried a close-quarters weapon with a wicked axe-like blade not unlike a pike, but shorter.

Although well outnumbered, the Bruce had showed his mettle as a general in many battles and was the unchallenged leader of his unified host.

The English Edward II had no such military history, quite the contrary, and had a surfeit of mutually jealous commanders, from amongst his great - and often vain and quarrelsome barons, each with their own liegemen who would accept no orders other than those from their lord. It was a general failure that the grandees were plagued by their own concept of honour, notoriously quick to take offence, yet not slow in turn to taunt their fellow knights.

It was inevitable that Paul, like every man there, wondered if today would be his last on earth, but none of that could be shared with his men, now only hundreds of yards away, marching towards the front from the main camp, on higher ground within the woodland behind him, about a mile away. Instead, he contented himself by concentrating on the coming battle. He could feel the suction of the wet ground beneath his feet as he paced the field. The ground really was soaked and the soil beneath too soft to suit charging armoured cavalry.

What the English really ought to do, Paul mused, would be to dismount and fight on foot, but he knew enough about the knightly class, within which after all, he and the other Templar knights had been raised, that such a decision would not sit well with them. Their tactics against lightly armed infantry, had always depended on the shock of heavy armour and big battle-trained horses, plus individual feats of bravery. It had nearly always worked for them before.

Paul was not alone on the field. He could see others doing what he was doing, with Geraint off to his right, pushing sticks into the soft earth as markers for his men when they formed up. Then he noticed a lone rider emerge from the training area in the woods behind him and over to one side, walking his palfrey across the wet meadow.

With growing excitement he recognized him by the simple gold circlet on his head over his chain-mail hauberk, reflecting the sun. It was the King. Some distance behind, near the rear treeline, clearly under orders to stay back, was his herald holding aloft the golden silk flag bearing the rampant red lion of the Scottish kings. The King, apart from a gleaming chain mail hauberk was unarmoured, except for his shield painted with the same red lion device. He held a short battle-axe. The small grey palfrey from which his long legs dangled was clearly not his warhorse.

Then Paul caught his breath as he saw another figure emerging directly opposite, just a few hundred yards away, where the Roman road emerged from the dense woods - the direction of the oncoming English army. Here was a single, fully armoured English knight with his brilliantly coloured quartered surcoat and horse trappings. He had come out of the treeline to see better, but now decided, was already charging, alone and gathering pace, his great horse's hooves pounding on the wet earth. His visor was down and long lance couched. Far behind, the smaller mounted figure of his squire followed his master. The English knight was Sir Henry de Bohun, nephew of the English cavalry general, the Earl of Gloucester. He had been the first of the advance guard to reach the edge of the woods, intending to scout the battlefield from cover. From that position in the bright sunlight, Bohun had seen the gold circlet over the commonplace hauberk on his head, the unescorted Scottish King, out on his own. No doubt dreaming of his own king's gratitude and the glory that must be his, he had made an instant decision and thought that he might single-handedly end the battle - indeed the war - there and then.

Paul watched horrified, immobilised from a hundred paces away, but then started running towards his leader, unsheathing his sword as he ran. He was conscious of others further away, doing the same; a mounted Geraint behind him was closing fast. He was amazed that the Bruce, who must have seen everything, did not seek to turn and escape, as Paul was willing him to do. He sat there on his small horse, his axe in hand just waiting. The distance closed and whilst Paul and Geraint were still yards away, the English knight was upon him. With a mighty crash and a tangle of limbs and weapons, it was all over.

King Robert's horse had smartly sidestepped one pace, obviously a trained manoeuvre, and with his shield the King deftly parried the lance point away. The momentum of the charge had brought the two horses almost into collision, as the King rose up in his stirrups, his timing immaculate, raised his war axe and brought it down with a mighty blow onto the knight's helm, crushing it and tumbling him quite dead from the saddle. His frightened destrier driven by the force of the blow to its knees in the mud, recovered, staggered up and then galloped aimlessly away, stirrups flapping against the horse's flanks.

Paul had now reached the King who seemingly unconcerned, was calmly looking down at the dead man. His herald was now there with him. Other mounted Scottish knights were arriving. In the woods opposite, from where the English knight had come, a small group of other brightly caparisoned armoured horsemen emerged.

Taking in the scene, they had just witnessed Sir Henry de Bohun, leader of their scouting party go down defeated - the Scottish infantry battalions now entering the field and the King's numerous escorts riding hard towards the scene. They hesitated and then wheeled around walking slowly, to return with their sad, even ominous story to the English camp.

King Robert looked askance at his tardy escort as they rushed to surround him and reproached them, "You had better do it differently - and better than that when their main army arrives," he said harshly. "There was just me and these likely lads here, against half the English army. Still, I can see that they are Templars", he smiled at Paul and Geraint.

King Robert watched de Bohun's squire ride after and catch his frightened warhorse and return a certain distance, then wait, dumbly seeking permission to recover his lord's body. The King waved him in and told his men to load the dead knight's bloody corpse onto his horse. "When they see that passing through their camp," he said, "it will somewhat lower their high spirits!"

"Congratulations Sire" a voice came from among his mounted noblemen. "The bards will sing of this."

"That's as maybe. I just ruined my best battle-axe." the King grumbled in response to the sizeable group that now surrounded him. It was split down the length of its wooden haft and he hurled it away towards where the English cavalry had been, and would surely soon be again. He then turned, followed by his chastened escort and rode off.

Within the half hour, Paul's schiltron was drawn up in a classical formation of eight ranks, each about ninety strong. Geraint commanded the battalion on his right, together making up the brigade. Their commander the Earl of Moray was however at the rear, conferring with his king.

Somewhere behind them two other battalions were drawn up in reserve, the Earl of Moray's Brigade, had earlier been ordered to move across to face the Roman road. They knew that the small English force they had seen was merely scouting, not yet their main army. That was still strung out in a long column many miles back on that road from Falkirk. The scouts had reported that those nearby were all heavy cavalry, at most, a few hundred in number. No archers were seen to be in their party.

It was unusually cold for midsummer, although no longer raining; the grass underfoot was well soaked. The orders had come down earlier from Sir Peter Breydel that every pikeman should remove the shoe of one foot. They had done this in training and despite the grumbles and some ribald jokes in the ranks, they discovered that it was to individually get a better purchase on the wet grass, when the shock of heavy cavalry came, with each mounted knight about a ton in weight, smashing into their levelled pikes.

The Scots took comfort that these conditions favoured them over the opposing cavalry, but they knew with a leaden certainty that sooner or later they would be confronted by a much mightier army, whose leading drums they could hear rolling like distant thunder, still far off.

Paul's battalion smartly formed into their assigned ranks with officers and sergeants shoving and haranguing the tardier individuals, but then it was done. The ranks were formed, the pikes bristled, and each man was alone with his thoughts as they watched the tree line and waited.

Then in an anti-climax came a frenzied mass of activity. Bursting from the treeline was the exodus of numerous fleeing forest creatures, rabbits by the hundred, hares skipping madly away and an unsuspecting startled herd of red deer, their splendidly antlered leader being the first to burst out of the wood. He was followed by as many as twenty delicate hinds, some with tiny, recently born followers, with just occasionally another antlered juvenile, a tolerated male, not yet a challenge to the forerunner. They ran at considerable speed in a straight line towards the unmoving Scottish ranks before the stag realised his error and wheeled, at speed, sharply off to the right, without changing step, his herd flooding along behind him strung out along the battalion's front.

The tension broken, the Scots cheered and waved their bonnets. Before long he was out of sight, the whole herd close behind. That brief diversion over, the sobered Scots troops viewed the cause of the animal evacuation, as the long sinister line of the emerging steel-clad enemy, magnificent on their great horses, came out of the forest right along the tree-line, as it bordered the meadow.

Expecting it though he was Paul was still shocked to see the number and pageantry of the knights emerging from the woodland opposite. Led by the

Earl of Gloucester, they had clearly entered the trees in strength, probably suspecting an ambush some way back along the Roman road. They looked magnificent, Paul could not help but reflect; but he knew from his own knightly experience that with the visors down, inside those steel pots on their heads, they would be uncomfortably hot. With the restricted vision through narrow eye slits, each man, no matter what his rank or experience, right now would feel very much alone.

They would also all of them know that, although on their great horses they were like individual mobile fortresses, if their horse failed or was struck down, then they were in the deepest trouble. Many of the horses, he noted wore face armour, since infantry nowadays were trained to stab at a horse's vulnerable face.

The Scottish front rank of the two battalions now braced to receive the charge, was of 200 men wide taking up about a yard each, defending the width of the open meadowland. Immediately behind them, there were still more lines of similar strength to complete the pike wall in depth, with reserves, a few archers and the highland skirmishers waiting the chance to engage.

The lines curved back at the wings, which could close to complete a circle, if the cavalry should manage to lap around them. Now, although impeded by the slippery wet surface, with little delay, a disorderly mob of some 300 heavy horses and their riders clustered together in depth, were coming at them and building up momentum in the charge, their hooves sounding like heavy thunder, churning up the wet earth. More followed, but the pit traps were already claiming their first victims and by the screams of horses, the caltrop spikes were taking their toll, disabling some of the great animals. The air was rent with shouts, war cries and challenges, the screams of the wounded horses and the Scots bellowing their defiance, as the front line came ever closer.

The rhythm of the charge had been broken up by the obstacles, into uneven clusters of armoured horsemen, now trying to maintain cohesion. The leading knights in a slowed and ragged line, rode right up to the forest of pikes where the caltrops had been most heavily sown, taking more victims. At the last instant without momentum to deceive them, most of their horses refused to impale themselves on the hundreds of steady pike points and blades facing them, and shied off. Their riders had no answer. They had lost their essential momentum, they milled around frustrated, having to avoid trampling their own fallen colleagues and the dead or injured horses. They tried to wield their heavy lances to beat aside the rigid pike shafts, but these were each anchored with the angled shafts buried a few inches into the ground behind each braced pikeman, and were unyielding.

The scene before the line of pikes was a melee of horses and men, which after the initial shock, is how most such cavalry confrontations resolved themselves. But here there were hundreds of frustrated horsemen, confused, because there was no opponent for them to trade blows with, the implacable defenders were tantalisingly out of reach. The pike wall was unbroken and many of the horsemen already were down with both horses and men pierced by the spears, or horses disabled by the caltrops. The few archers in the Scottish ranks were shooting at point blank range finding a victim with every arrow. When the riders repeatedly came in too close, trying to engage, the cruel hooks on neighbouring pikes were used to try to tug them off their horses, for others to finish them off. Once they were unhorsed, they seldom would rise again.

Interspersed with the ranks of pikemen were a number of the nimble blue-painted clansmen, skirmishers with the battalion. They waited for a lull, or any opportunity along the line to dart out and finish off the fallen knights, sometimes trapped under their stricken horses or otherwise immobilized. The knights knew that even their massive armour was cruelly vulnerable in the groin, or their helmet's eye slits, and the slim dirks brought final agonizing destruction to their victims, if not always the comparative blessing of instant death. Always the danger to the clansmen once out there, was that some amongst the frustrated mass of mounted knights would spot them unprotected, out on the wrong side of the pike wall and ride them down, before they could dodge back behind the pikes.

By now the sheer number of fallen horses and riders had created another obstacle, a line of destruction - bodies of men, and of horses kicking out their lives, broken armour, shields, shattered lances and other weapons, all along the front of the bristling wall of men and pikes. The stink of blood and entrails and ordure, was added to the horror of the dying shrieks of disembowelled horses, and of mortally injured, dying men.

Gradually the depleted mounted force, now completely stalled, withdrew frustrated, unhurriedly it seemed, even though their leaders were urging them back to their start line. Single dismounted knights limped or dragged themselves back as quickly as they could, fearing to be cut off by pursuit, but there was none.

For a while the Scots braced themselves as they prepared to receive the next assault, but the milling crowd of horsemen turned and waited a while at their starting point by the edge of the woods, then eventually disappeared, first in groups, and finally one by one, until they were gone into the trees. They did not re-emerge.

***

The Earl of Gloucester led the remains of his bloodied advance guard, of which two-fifths had fallen, back to join the main army. This had progressed, moving away from the Roman road to make an overnight camp, planning on this being in a direct line for the few miles remaining in tomorrow's short journey to Stirling Castle. They fully expected that the main battle would be joined once they were strung out in column, in order of march.

King Edward II had called his senior generals and courtiers that evening to entertain them in his marquee, including Gloucester and his uncle, the Earl of Hereford, but also with a crowd of others. Amongst the senior officers were interspersed some younger gentlemen of no known military merit, distinguished by nothing more than their good looks and gorgeous courtiers clothing, easily distinguishable from the many wearing chain-mail, dressed for war.

Edward was homosexual and had he not been king, his exotic behaviour would have been regarded as intolerable - but he was also the son of a famous and warlike father Edward I, known in his time as 'the hammer of the Scots'. If the son could produce the victories of the father, the grim barons on whom he ultimately depended could ignore his personal peccadillos. Which was not to say they would tolerate his favourites, when Edward over-promoted them - as he was inclined to do - to positions of real power.

None of those present in that assembly in the King's splendid marquee had seen action that day except the Earl of Gloucester. He was aching, tired and worried, as well as saddened by the loss of his impulsive young nephew, Henry de Bohun. His worry now was because he had seen at first hand that the Scots were going to rely on pikemen. It was a form of warfare of which few even of the battle-hardened English, including himself, had previously experienced.

His concern was also that the rigidity of the Scottish line and their discipline in standing firm was quite unusual, compared with many previous battles over past years when they had not done so. He had fully expected that when he ordered his horsemen back after they had been frustrated in the attack, that the Scots line would dissolve as they pursued the fleeing English in search of the booty, which for many was their reason for being there. Then he had been ready within moments to turn his horsemen around. Without a pike wall to stop the horsemen, the Scots out in the open would have been annihilated, easy targets for his cavalry. But this time they hadn't moved. This was worrying - a new kind of disciplined, Scottish fighting man.

His concern was that he knew that now the English order of battle should, with this knowledge, rapidly be re-organized to neutralize these pike formations. It was obvious to him and to those of his officers he had discussed it with, that the lightly armoured pikemen were vulnerable to missile troops.

There should, he now knew with the certainty of experience, be no more frontal attacks by the cavalry, until there had first been a massive assault by the archers, to drastically thin the enemy ranks. They were somewhere back along the long line of march, some 3,000 Welsh bowmen; but before entering the king's tent, Gloucester had searched the encampment and had seen no sign of any of them as yet, having arrived.

Inside the luxurious pavilion its interior draped with cloth of gold, Edward was in a frivolous mood and was surrounded by the laughter of his pretty favourites, as he moved around his followers. When he saw Gloucester standing with some of the more senior barons, his brow darkened and he spoke loudly and slightingly.

"So Gloucester, I hear that you got thrashed by the jocks today. Sorry about young Henry, but he at least showed his courage. That seemed to have been in short supply, amongst your followers."

"Not so, Sire," the earl indignantly replied. "I lost 200 of my own following today - two in five of those that came with me."

"Well then what do you suggest our army should do now?" Edward sneered, "Go back to England, let the traitor Bruce have the victory?" He looked around at his sycophants for their inevitable chorus of jeers.

"Of course not Sire, but I do suggest that we wait until the whole army is here and then re-organise the line of march. Let the troops that have arrived rest and tomorrow, as the others catch up, we organize for an advance on Stirling the next day. We need archers to the front and nobody has seen them yet arrive - they could be miles back. Sire, the Bruce will have chosen his preferred location - he knows the ground where he will try to block our advance. Meanwhile we can scout the country around here and decide where we can outflank the Scots when battle is joined."

"I fear you are getting old," the King responded as some of his gaudy favourites snickered at the thrust. "I have near 3,000 mounted knights and men-at-arms here already, Gloucester, and more on the way. There's no force on earth that can stand up to that massed charge. Tomorrow we move on to Stirling. If they still resist, which I doubt, we will brush them aside. If you have no stomach for it, then leave it to the younger men."

Leaving a stupefied earl behind him trying to stifle his outrage, he and the cloud of perfumed intimates moved on, amongst light laughter, to another group of warriors.

***

About four miles away in a large but rather plainer tent, King Robert had called in his brigade commanders together with his other generals and senior noblemen. Amongst them he addressed the Fleming Templar, Sir Peter Breydel.

"That was a convincing demonstration your fellows gave us today, General. I thought - indeed, I feared - that when Gloucester pulled his men back, that your line would break, that they would chase after him, and then of course he would have turned and rolled them up. I know my countrymen and having won the fight, as they would see it, they would think it was fair play that they got themselves some booty. But it never happened. It seems that they have at last understood the point of discipline. Well done, Sir."

"The officers and sergeants were well aware of that tendency, your Highness," the Fleming replied, "and clearly they had drummed it into the men how the English would have just turned around, and out there in the open, with no pike wall to protect them, then they would be dead."

"What about tomorrow gentlemen, friends, what should we do?" the King then asked.

The giant leader, an earl called the Black Douglas, on account of his dark complexion and great black bushy beard, one of King Robert's closest and most loyal supporters, intervened. "We should attack, Highness. We have bloodied them and we will never be in a better position. We should use our knowledge of the terrain around here and attack them, rather than defend against them."

"Yes, Sire," said Breydel. "They now know that we can defend solidly but they didn't use archers today. Will they make that mistake again? They know nothing however of the schiltron in attack. It is time to show them, Sire."

"I have to say that on the other hand," replied the King," today we have raised our men's morale. If we depart now, we can continue to fight the kind of swift raid on the English in their lands, in northern England, and withdraw. These tactics have served us well for five years past. If we attack now and don't succeed - and he has four or five times as many troops as we have - we throw away everything."

"This," he insisted, "is not a simple decision." He knew however that a large part of the enemy had not yet arrived, and he too feared the impact of the archers on his schiltrons. Either way there was a risk, but with the high morale after today's fight, he had really made his mind up. It was time to hit them hard.

He signalled a servant to pass around, charging the wine goblets. There was an interruption at the entrance to his tent, as his guard barred someone who clearly wanted to get in. The officer there told the King, "It's a Sir Alexander Seaton, Sire." he said. Someone there surprised, expostulated, "Seaton is with the English, Your Highness!"

"No, he's not," responded a tall, distinguished knight, who unbuckling his sword belt and throwing this and a scabbarded dagger onto the floor, before entering the tent, went down on one knee, before the King. "This was my first chance to join with you Sire, so I took it. I have left the foolish Edward and his disreputable young friends."

King Robert went to his attendant, took a goblet of wine and turned to the new arrival, and raising him up, thrust it into Seaton's hand. "Welcome Alexander," he said. "Tell us of the English camp, or does your very presence here denote the state of their morale?"

Despite being midsummer, it seemed a long night. Those Scots that managed to get any sleep were aroused at 2.30 am, an hour before dawn which came early in these northern climes. They had eaten some oats porridge and those who had it, swallowed a dram or two. Now a column, two battalions wide, was formed up and advancing in close order towards the meadow where the English had camped, still a mile away, as dawn was breaking.

The English had made their overnight stop on a large water meadow bisected by two streams, a tributary of the River Forth, known as Bannock Burn, and a smaller watercourse, the Pelstream. The ground declining down to these watercourses soon became marshy and unsuitable for camping. On the firmer higher ground could be seen the English king's pavilion pitched, surrounded by those of his magnates. To the northwest, lay tomorrow's route, through the Bannock Valley with the ground rising towards the city. A mile further on were the roofs of the outskirts of Stirling, the great castle beyond, dominant on top on its great rock.

Stretching away from the two watercourses, back towards the Forest of Torwood, from which units continued to emerge throughout the night, was encamped the main body of the English army. In the western part of this meadow, facing where they believed the Scots army lay, rested many of the thousands of English heavy cavalry with their servants and squires. There an outer ring of knights had slept in their mail, with their horses nearby, already saddled, anticipating a night raid on their camp, for which Robert the Bruce was infamous.

The great mass of the remainder of the English army, the infantry, were nowhere close, many being still a day's march away and those already arrived being crowded out of the narrow field by the sheer bulk of the cavalry, the horses, knights, squires and grooms and their tents, kitchens, carts and pack horses. Mixed up, far back amongst these distant infantry as though irrelevant, were such small groups of archers that had arrived overnight, crucial to the English cause but with most of their number still far to the rear, destined to miss the battle.

The English picquets in the path of the Scottish advance over to the west raised the alarm once the rolling drums were heard and the attacking Scots were spotted on the move. Urgent trumpet signals turned the sleeping English camp into a hive of activity. Tired fighting men cursed, knuckled the sleep out of their eyes. Those that had them pulled on pieces of plate armour in the near dark as they made their way to their horses, some of which were reacting skittishly against the sudden mayhem and bustle. Squires were fussing around their irritable masters, trying to fasten buckles and hand them their shields, whilst grooms frantically tightened the saddle girths on the horses and helped the riders to mount, with the distant sounds of the rolling Scottish drums stretching all of their nerves.

The two English cavalry generals, the earls of Gloucester and Hereford who had been awake for some time, sat their horses at the front, but as their household ranks filled up behind them, they were, as usual, arguing about precedence. Gloucester still outraged by the king's humiliating treatment of him the previous night, was insisting that he should lead the charge. Hereford equally claimed that it was his right as Constable of England. Neither would give way.

Then through the early morning mist, they had their first sight of a relentlessly advancing line of pikemen, two hundred yards wide, with a depth clearly of many ranks behind them, not yet possible to count. Already they were less than a half mile away, the English could see the Saltire - the white diagonal cross on blue of St Andrew - and the rampant red lion of the Bruce, on the gold of their banners, also other banners with the three red lozenge cushions on white, of the leading brigade general, the Earl of Moray. Now on the word of command, the Scottish drummer-boys started to increase the pace.

Inexorably steady and strangely quiet, the dense body of Scottish infantry carried their deadly pikes angled upwards, their pace constant, and were attentive to maintaining their line. Sergeants and officers bustled among them constantly dressing the line, as they encountered minor obstructions to their advance. They made a brave sight and it was unnerving to these watching English veterans that they were uncharacteristically so implacably well drilled, and keeping to their ranks. They were not behaving like the battle-eager, surging clansmen the English were used to seeing. Paul's battalion with the Pelstream on his left marched in front, with Geraint's keeping pace to his right. Then came that of the Black Douglas, his white banners with three red spur-rowels, were the phalanx behind them.

These three pike battalions together with reserves were more than 2,000 men strong, with the king's own mixed force somewhat further back. The sergeants and officers along the whole column were continually dressing the ranks, as they skirted the obstacles of trees and ditches.

The Earl of Gloucester took in the sight as he finally reached the end of his patience with his co-general, the Earl of Hereford. Their household knights were milling around behind both of them, getting in each other's way, trying to form up into the correct formations behind each of the two earls, their generals, as they continued to argue. Some five hundred yards of fairly regular grassland with a gentle slope favouring the oncoming Scots, was all that now separated the two armies. After a final barrage of insults fired off at his uncle of Hereford, as though in emphasis, Gloucester lowered his visor, eased his horse forward and in his silent rage jabbed his spurs, without first ordering his followers into the advance.

Every eye amongst the oncoming Scots watched the magnificently accoutred knight, a belted earl no less, leaving the English lines alone with only his squire to hand. He spurred his charger out in front, not to just to lead it seemed, but as though to charge singlehandedly, with his large scattered personal following clearly unprepared for the assault, as they emerged late from the meadow behind him, spread out and following him raggedly.

Try as they might, there was already a dangerous distance separating the household knights from their earl which they could not close, as bracing himself he lowered his lance and accelerated into a classic full charge, which they could only match, but already from well behind him.

The first rank of Paul's Scots pikemen, were ready, if apprehensive. On the order they halted, the front line each went down on one knee on the wet ground, their spear butts bedded deep enough in the soft earth besides them, braced to withstand the shock of the oncoming cavalry.

The supporting ranks behind them, their 16-foot hafts topped with steel blades, made a dense, seemingly impenetrable thicket of sharpened steel points. Once again, most of the men had bared the back foot, to get a better purchase on the muddy ground in the life and death struggle to hold back the weight of the advancing cavalry. "Steady lads…" The rallying call came from Paul and could be heard up and down the ranks, every one of his officers and sergeants took it up, as the English drew closer.

The second and third rows remained standing, their pikes angled above the heads of the front men. Many of their pike heads had hooks, to pull the riders down from out of their saddles once their horses had refused to be impaled, as most would if the Scottish ranks held.

The third line of Scots and those behind them would fill any gaps in the ranks ahead. Their formations were interspersed with a number of the wild, half-naked clansmen from the far north, whose work this day as ever, would be to dodge out from under and between the pikes and kill dismounted knights, before they were able to get up and start to fight on foot.

It was the standing order drilled into the pike battalions by the Courtrai veteran, their Templar commander, that they must first seek to kill or wound the warhorses, which would not be as well armoured as their riders. To help with this, they had some fifty archers with them with orders to fire at the horses and only at point blank range, so every arrow would tell. Once the horses were down, the clansmen were to dodge out and seek to despatch the dismounted riders thrown clear or more likely struggling under their dying horses.

Paul was suddenly conscious that his infantry commander, the Fleming, Sir Peter Breydel was there. He had ridden up into his rear ranks, accompanied amongst others by Knut, who was serving as his aide.

"They never learn," the general said wonderingly, calling out to Paul as he approached, then sitting his horse and watching the magnificent solitary horseman, lance couched, riding full tilt towards the waiting pikes. His following, hundreds of them, were coming on strongly but scattered all over the open meadow, well behind him.

"These bloody snobs think that infantry will just run away, because they are not wellborn, destined to be warriors - like them… and that one, who's got himself too far ahead of his men," he raised himself in the saddle the better to see his heraldry, "is none other than the Earl of Gloucester, whom we saw off yesterday."

He raised his voice, "Steady lads - go for his horse, remember."

Sir Peter stood his horse by Paul. He had quickly noted that the defence was fully ready and made sure that all the men saw that he, their commander, was with them.

In his frustration, now at full gallop, the earl now knew that he had clearly misjudged. He had realised too late, that he was far ahead of his own people and these miserable Scots peasants weren't running away. After Edward's insults the previous evening, his blood was up. Instead of prudently reining back, allowing his men to make up the distance, he would just have to show them how it was done.

He charged on for both his horse and him to have the maximum momentum, inevitably to be brought down in a mighty crash, he and his mount pierced by unwavering multiple points. With that impact, as they tumbled to the ground, his great horse brought down a pair of Scottish pikemen in the melee which left him inside the Scottish ranks. Almost before they hit the ground, two nimble kilted men were there beside him, slashing and stabbing, as his leaderless group came up behind, now numbered in scores and then hundreds. These were the earl's own liegemen.

Disgraced, they had seen with horror their lord go down to ruin, without them at his side, his wreckage beset with blue painted savages stabbing at him, over and again. They now looked only for revenge. They came in fast, in ones and twos, fruitlessly hurling themselves and their horses, if they didn't refuse, onto the unyielding spears. They died as he had done.

Now the mass of the main body of horsemen were there, but already the momentum was lost, the bodies of the fallen horses and their comrades, cut their volition before they could hit the pikes. They could not penetrate the steel bladed wall, although some of Paul's men inevitably were down in the fury of the charge.

Rear rankers were pulled forward by sergeants to fill the gaps in the Scottish frontline. The English cavalry milled around frustrated, just beyond stabbing point, some in their fury hurling lances like spears, battle-axes, even shields, anything to move the impenetrable wall of spikes. Arrows flew from the Scottish ranks, each archer getting off around four shots a minute, at a range almost impossible to miss. The screams of stricken horses and men rent the air, together with oaths and war cries with all the while, the relentless clash of steel on steel.

Slowly the English backed away leaving their dead behind - the wounded did not long survive as the Highlander's knives found their way around the armour into their groins, or their faces through the slits in their visors. Paul had paced his lines, pike in hand, looking for any vulnerability, calling and encouraging reassuringly, but his men stood firm and now were gaining in confidence. He could see that Geraint's neighbouring schiltron were still there in good order and had also repelled their attackers, who were streaming away demoralized, back to the line of their camp where they purposelessly milled about in front of the wagons and tents. Some, whose mounts had perished, were limping back to join them, or running, holding on to a comrade's stirrup. In the clear ground that was all that now separated the two armies, a number of riderless horses aimlessly milling around, as though to mark the futility of the last charge.

Paul ordered his reserves to take skins of water along the Scottish ranks and rejoined Sir Peter, still mounted with his small group. "First blood to us" the Fleming dryly commented, from his height able to see more of the battlefield.

Paul leaned on Sir Peter's horse to take a quick breather, whilst the general dismounted, slipping down beside him and passed him a small silver flask. "Take a mouthful of that my boy," he said. "We call it schnapps; it's the Flemish equivalent of whisky."

"They should never have attacked," he continued, "without giving us an hour or so of archery, which is what I was afraid of. Look at the damage we did to them all massed together, with just our few archers." He lowered his voice as he confided to Paul. "We don't have much of an answer to that - we've so few archers of our own, and not much in the way of cavalry. We have some waggon loads of wooden shields at the rear, but pikemen cannot fight one-handed. Luckily for us, the English are so over-confident. They looked around their host and saw thousands of other courageous, armoured horsemen just like themselves, and they really believe that they are simply unstoppable against any force on earth."

"That brave idiot who came first was indeed the Earl of Gloucester, a leading general," Sir Peter told the young Templar. "Even now some new leader, an earl, or the king, will be telling them they must try again and try harder - and they will. So I am afraid young Paul…" the commander remounted and turning his horse was in the process of moving off to inspect the rest of his force, "…your day's work is not finished yet, but well done!"

"Obey the trumpet signals" he called as he departed. "Keep the line moving until it is time to receive an organised charge, but don't stop for a little harassment. Don't let your men break ranks under any circumstances - go for the horses first, and we've got 'em!"

"Well done all of you and stand to your ranks - always." he repeated, his voice now raised, as he trotted away with his aides, towards the neighbouring formations, the rows of pikemen watching him.

"Let's have a cheer for the general!" Paul called out, and the men newly confident, those with bonnets waving them, lustily obliged. It was a cheer taken up by the neighbouring battalion as he rode in to their ranks.

"They'll be back, lads" Paul called out clearly. "But this time we don't wait - we're going after them! We've got the beating of them this day." Another cheer went up as the well-drilled battalion formed up, the drums returned to beat the steady marching pace, as the pikemen picked up their steady step and moved on towards the English line, itself scrambling to reform.

Within another hour, another full assault by the horsemen had followed, this time preceded by no single champions, but an implacable wall of armoured men and horses, riding stirrup to stirrup, steadily in line formation, gathering speed for the maximum shock, as they closed on the lines of pikemen. But still the line of spear points held. The horses just could not be forced over the barrier of the rapidly growing heaps of their own dead and dying men and beasts, to then be impaled on the endless wall of spikes that confronted them. The Scots archers kept up a withering fire as the English lost their initiative, unable to go forward and getting in each other's way, as they attempted to ride up and down the line, looking for a way through, probing for a weak point. There was none.

Once their momentum had gone, if they got too close, second rank pikemen would try to hook into their armour or harness, and drag them off the horses for the clansmen to go after on the ground. The northern men took casualties that way, but they seldom left a dismounted knight alive, although they dragged several back alive behind their own lines - if the quality of the armour, or the heraldry- suggested a fat ransom.

The English cavalry once again drew off, whilst their commanders went back to confer with their army's leaders. But they no longer had the initiative, they were not now to be allowed the luxury of a respite. The trumpets blared and once again the Scottish schiltrons resumed their steady advance, the drumbeat implacable and their levelled pikes steadily pushing the milling horsemen back.

Although still well back behind their cavalry, newly arrived English infantrymen were trying to get into the battle, but were impeded in the rapidly diminishing space, by the continuing press and weight of constantly arriving new cavalry, eager for battle, forcing their way forward in front of them. A company of Welsh archers, the first to arrive, had earlier come up to some fifty yards back from where they believed the English frontline to be. Unsighted on low ground, they attempted to fire arrows over the heads of their own cavalry, but they hit as many of their own as the advancing Scots, whilst most shots were wasted.

A cool-headed English commander stopped that, shrewdly withdrew the archers and took them further back, until they could loop around the back of the cavalry camp and cross the Pelstream. There they were divided from the advancing schiltron by the narrow watercourse and its steep banks, as well as from their own army. Immediately they started to pour arrows into the exposed flank of the leading battalion. For the first time in the two days, as the Templar general had predicted, the archers were hurting the Scots.

Paul was losing men and his momentum was slowing, when he spotted Knut on horseback a few ranks back, and called him to the front. "Knut, for God's sake find the king, or the earl, and tell them what these archers are doing. See if they can deal with them. My orders are to keep ranks with the other schiltrons, and keep pushing the English back. We can't both do that and also cross the stream to deal with those bastards, but we are losing too many men."

Knut took the point. He had saluted and gone before Paul had finished talking. Paul's men were faltering looking up to try to dodge the descending arrows and he called out to his officers, "Push up the pace, we must get mixed in amongst their cavalry. That will stop the archers." The drums took up the faster beat and his front lines doggedly pushed their pikes forward, continually moving forward but apprehensively looking upwards.

The hard fight continued and still arrows were coming down. Then he heard a cheer from along the flank of his battalion. Looking across the stream he saw the Welsh archers were running before the lances of the Scottish light cavalry of Sir James. They were scrambling to save themselves, back to where they had come from across the stream, to rejoin the English infantry behind the crowded armoured cavalry.

Now the battle was taking shape bordered by the two streams, where the leading English cavalry were being gradually pushed back by the pikes into an ever-diminishing space, within which they could not deploy. Their infantry were still shut off from the action by the sheer mass of horsemen in front of them, wheeling about, their front rank mixed in with the detritus of their own camp, the tents, carts and kitchens, which now impeded their horses movements. They still were unable to make any impression on the lines of advancing pikemen. Steadily they were giving ground, preventing the many eager horsemen behind, and the infantry further back behind them, from getting close enough to engage.

Then coming from behind him, Paul was startled to hear a new and menacing sound. It was the noise of a large number of men and the metallic jangle of weapons, coming up fast. Alarmed, he pulled back from exhorting his troops from just behind his front rank and looked back to see what was happening.

To his enormous relief he saw that a fresh schiltron, the red-spur banners of the Black Douglas prominent, had moved up from the reserve to reinforce his own. They were making their way at the double, pikes at the slope, through his tired ranks to get up to the front, to be greeted by the cheers of Paul's weary troops, which further depressed their English opponents. Their officers, his brother Templars, that passed near Paul, were calling to him, "well done," as they moved ahead to form a new front line.

King Robert had seen the damage caused by the English archers and had thrown in the new schiltron reinforcement, to increase the pressure on the English. The newly doubled strength created a surge in the Scottish progress and Paul's troops were able to draw breath, whilst their comrades brought fresh energy to the front of the fight.

From somewhere behind the English force, even above the clash of battle, Paul could hear the thunder of many hooves. Then looking across to the rising ground beyond the Pelstream, Paul had the worrying sight of Sir James' Scottish light cavalry patrolling there, being scattered by an approaching body of heavy English horse. As a solid wedge of some fifty tightly grouped English horsemen, splashed across the stream heading for Stirling Castle, he could see that they were not after all in attack, but escorting who had to be the English King, tall in the saddle of his magnificently accoutred warhorse. Yet it looked to Paul that the reins of that horse were in the hands of two escorting knights - they were forcing him to leave against his will, it appeared.

The memory suddenly came back to him, of years before, the wounded Turkish emir being rescued in the bailey of Castle Marash in Cilicia, with three horses heads so close together as if to be conferring. The departure had to be to avoid the total disaster of his capture, but at the inevitable price of shattering the morale of his own troops, to see their fleeing king desert his army! It could only mean, whatever else, that they had abandoned the prospect of victory for that day.

It was still only midmorning and already the sun was high and hot. Paul remembered that it was midsummer's day, but both he and his men were feeling the elation of success steadily giving way to exhaustion. A small knot of riders came up from behind them and Paul could see that this time it was his own brigade commander the Earl of Moray, with Sir Peter Breydel. The earl nodded. "Well done de Chatillon," he said to Paul, who reflected that the rather stand-offish Scottish aristocrat did actually know who he was. But it was Sir Peter who said more.

"We have new orders for you." Sir Peter told him. "The English commander has left the field and many would have seen that, but there remain many brave men out there. We are still well outnumbered. They will come again, but this time, after you have beaten them back, we will immediately and without delay - before they regain their ranks - widen our front and we will advance all along our line and keep on moving. We must herd them down to the stream." - he indicated the neighbouring schiltron moving forward from the Kings battalion, closing gaps and falling into line beside his and Geraint's battalions. "It will, we hope, be our final push."

"Here is the situation and why we need to finish this thing. They did start to use their archers from across the stream and they were hurting us, your people particularly, as they were bound to do. But our good brother, Sir James, brought up his cavalry boys and sent them running. Amazingly the English had given their archers no infantry protection. You saw it, yesterday and again today, so you will believe it when I tell you that the bloody fools started this whole attack, whilst their infantry are *still* spread out over ten or twenty miles back from here. They have a huge force of footmen including many archers, but most of them have not yet even arrived at the battlefield. That's why we need to settle this now, with a new attack. We have to defeat them before fresh troops and the bulk of their army get here!"

The earl asked Paul if he had taken many casualties. Was he in a state to be able to continue to attack? The young Templar realised that not only numbers, but also time was on the side of the English, with their reinforcements on the way.

"Yes, my Lord," he responded. "These are good men. They came here to win and they will do what it takes, as will we all."

"Good man yourself," said Sir Peter, his own commander. "The schiltrons are to advance on my trumpet signal. Timing now is everything! Make sure your people keep their ranks, keep your points up and steady, and keep on pushing forward.

"I will send young Knut to tell you when to go, or if our objectives change. I want your unit to lead the push, the others will close up on you from each side… and by the way, you had better get that fixed." Paul saw where he had looked and noticed a thin trickle of blood down the chain-mail sleeve of his left forearm. He hadn't felt anything, but something metallic had clearly pierced his forearm somewhere in the chaos of the fray, again he had a fleeting memory of Cilicia, and of his poor dead squire, Baudouin, when his other arm was wounded.

This last, more controlled, cavalry attack had taken a toll of his front rank, but was in no way comparable to the hurt inflicted on their attackers. Behind his part of the Scottish front line, there were now some twenty bodies of pikemen stretched out, for whom nothing could be done. A similar number of his men, each to some extent damaged, were taken to the back so that their wounds could be attended to. But immediately to their front now, the highlander's knife work had stilled the ghastly cacophony of the scores if not hundreds, of dying cavalry, men and horses. Amongst the last jerkings and twitchings of the settling corpses, the kilted men still were picking over the bodies to collect the loot, such an important part for them of going to war.

Paul had a nearby pikeman tightly wrap a scarf around the slash on his arm and tuck it under the chain-mail sleeve of his hauberk. He ordered the rear ranks to take food and drink to the front, but he dared not stand the men down. They could see what still seemed to be more than a thousand of the English horsemen, milling around, presumably waiting for their leaders to give the orders.

"Here they come, sir." A pikeman pointed to him, whilst he had been straining to see the newly forming schiltron, off to his far right flank. This time, the English charge started out as a disciplined trot before the trumpets blared out in support. The line, as it advanced, could be seen to have been reinforced and was a controlled mass of gleaming armour, splendid great horses, bright pennants and in such numbers, it seemed even more magnificent than before.

Formidable though it was, Paul knew from his own experience the loneliness of each of those riders, encumbered sweating inside their heavy steel armour, each helmet stifling the need to breathe clean air, and the rest of the world and indeed the battlefield, only visible through the narrow slits of the helmet's visor. He had chosen to wear an infantryman's steel cap rather than a knight's casque, mainly so his men could see who he was and that he was at one with them, in terms of the risks of injury.

He knew that above all, the approaching horsemen feared that they would be unhorsed, and thus move to the vulnerability of an upended crab out of its element, lying helplessly on its back even worse perhaps, pinned down by their dying or injured horse.

But now all Paul could think about was to thank his luck and their bad judgement, that they still hadn't brought back the archers against his people. Most of his men had steel hats of various shapes and ages, but only boiled leather jerkins with odd bits of chain mail. They were extremely vulnerable to the arrow clouds, of which the enemy was known to be capable, but presumably their archers remained elsewhere.

After the battle, as he talked with the others, it turned out that apart from the men who had shot at them from across the Pelstream, other archers had been there but in the crowded space, had been stationed well behind the cavalry. They had been stopped from shooting because they had no high ground to occupy, could not see their target and were striking the backs of the advancing English rather than the Scots defenders. The army leaders by now were anyway too blinded with the particular rage of the frustrated military elite. Their notions of dignity and shame insisted for 'honours sake' that they themselves, the knightly class, clear away this obstruction to their feudal splendour, rather than call on the lower orders in the infantry to do the job for them.

The advancing cavalry had however learned this time, at least to have a plan. That was clear when their two wings crossed the greatly diminished space between the armies and sought to stream down his flanks to take the Scots from the sides and the rear; but he had been trained to expect that and seeing his neighbouring schiltrons doing likewise, he had closed the formation into a hollow square using his third and fourth ranks to extend the line. His seamless lines held unbroken until one impaled knight's dying momentum took the pike, himself and his charger crashing a way through the front line, destroying two pikemen and all landing in a heap behind it. But his comrades could not exploit the gap because they were obstructed, casting about for a way through the massed, heaped-up barrier of their own dead and dying, between them and all along the Scots front rank. The line of pikes swiftly closed up as the solitary intruder was swiftly dispatched by swarming clansmen.

It seemed like forever, with screams of pain and rage from men and horses, the battlefield stink of blood, entrails and ordure, with the ghastly sight of gaping wounds, but eventually the now exhausted survivors of the cavalrymen broke off, and followed their leaders yet again, backwards. Now the battle had driven them in amongst the tents and carts and flimsy shelters of their own camp, pursued by arrows from Paul's bowmen and the jeers and catcalls of the Scots infantry, who had yet again repulsed them.

Paul stood legs akimbo, breathing hard, when he saw his rear formation open up to let in a mounted messenger, his friend Knut. "It's time, Paul; it's time." he called as he approached. He had obviously had to fight his way back into the battalion, as his hauberk was covered in gore. "Not mine," he reassured Paul, who had looked worriedly at him.

Then they heard the clean clear notes of a trumpet signal rising above all else.

Paul pulled the now dismounted Knut along behind him, his horse sent to the rear. Seeing he was holding a skin of wine he grabbed it and took a pull before handing it back. He had briefed his section leaders on what they had many times rehearsed and what was now to follow. His dry throat eased by the sour wine, he called out in a stronger voice than he knew he had.

"Battalion will advance points up! Up, you hear me. You know what to do. Keep your formation men. It's time to finish this thing. Now Move.... MOVE!"

The entire front line moved slowly yet deliberately forward into and through the English camp, as they passed around the canvas tents and other impediments, dressing their ranks as they had been trained. The third and fourth ranks had reformed and closed up on them, so the formation of many hundreds of men had now become like a giant moving hedgehog, its spear points, and the wicked blades of the pikes reflecting the bright sun that had risen above them.

The last of the retreating horsemen driven from their camp were limping ahead of them, some dismounted, looked around and quickened their pace. They were afraid, and more than a little puzzled; this wasn't supposed to happen, none of it. The Scots were known for making wild reckless infantry charges, their version of shock, as distinct from that of the English heavy cavalry.

Now after standing firm in the face of continued attacks from Christendom's finest cavalry, this relentless many legged beast, bristling with spikes and blades, was moving onto them, drilled like a Roman legion. Over to Paul's right he could see Geraint's battalion was now a little ahead of him and within it the mounted figure of their Flemish commander directing the movement. Whilst it's left was still closing on his right, Geraint's men were wheeling, turning the enemy's scattered flank across the face of the hill, into open though marshy ground, towards the Bannock stream, across which the retreating English in increasing numbers now sought hopefully to escape the slow-paced, relentless Scottish advance.

All the schiltrons had together formed a steadily moving front, a column now some three hundred men wide, their points held outstretched before them and no English formation stood to oppose them, to inevitably be spitted, or rolled over. Instead, they were herded downhill towards the stream. Streaming out from behind the pikemen, the retreating English now well demoralized, could see and know fear, as the Bruce's highlanders at this point, were unleashed by him. Great numbers of howling, bare-chested wild clansmen, brandishing dirks and claymores, poured along screaming, shouting, running, towards the swollen stream. As the retreating English, turned to defend themselves, with a mighty clash the forces once more engaged, the English trying to stand with the highlanders nearly upon them, the pikemen not far behind. The closer the ground got to the muddy banks of the stream, already chewed up by the body of cavalry that had crossed it, the softer the ground, getting worse by the minute. Even there, hopeless for horsemen, the English had been able to deploy few infantrymen, most of whom in their useless thousands, were still hours away, far behind the line of battle, leaving only the foot soldier retainers of some of the great magnates in the vanguard.

Inevitably, with the overcrowded muddy banks of the stream, the heavily armoured horsemen with their big steeds and excessive weight, struggled for their footing, which as a result, quickly churned wider and deeper, swiftly becoming even worse. Then with their horses in the stream itself or on the banks, they attempted to stand on this unsure ground and fight off the swarming lighter footmen of the Scottish army. Breydel's trained pikemen could now use their lethal weapons for attack. Hooks snagged on armour, and then a heave pulled mailed men off their mounts into the mud and water, meaning almost certain death. As those that fell struggled to keep their helmeted heads above water and mud, and just breathe, yet the slim steel points of the clansmen and broad pike blades sought and found the gaps in their armour. It was moot whether more died of the swift blades, or from drowning in even that shallow depth of water and mud.

Blue painted clansmen, their fighting rage stimulated by their potent whisky, now soaked and covered in mud, ducked and weaved, mobbing each horse and rider, trying to avoid the horsemen's flailing weapons, whilst they stabbed their dirks upwards into the chargers' bellies, bringing their riders crashing to their ruin. But it was still not over. So narrow was the fighting front, there were a large number of the English even now, not yet engaged, many of whom were battle-hardened, armoured veterans, who knew now that they would be fighting for their very survival.

Then the screams and oaths and wild cries, and the monstrous clash of weapons, all at once suddenly and inexplicably stopped. Whilst the bogs sucked and squelched and muddy water swirled about those in the streams, men even in mid-thrust halted. It was as though the sky was about to fall in. All of them: mounted knights, highlanders, archers and pikemen; both armies were as if frozen, looking up at the ridge behind the Scottish camp, far away it seemed.

A muddy Paul, his helmet lost, was now up near to his waist in the burn, fighting short-armed with an axe which he had just chopped into the sword arm of a rider and toppled him screaming into the water, when he too saw what they saw.

Amazingly, what had appeared from the Scottish camp on the far slope, was another army, a great mass of new troops, lines of them, thousands seemingly, spread across a wide front, hundreds of horsemen led this host with their mounted officers in front, their bright banners flying, still at a distance, but now steadily moving together down the slopes towards the river. Distant trumpets were heard and a steady low rumble that could only be drums. Who they were, and from where they came didn't matter, they were not the English.

A wild cheer, growing in intensity, went up from the Scottish fighters. It was enough, too much indeed for the English attackers who now in desperation redoubled their efforts to reach the further bank, and the escape that this promised. They scrambled not as earlier to engage, but just to get away from the steel blades of the swarming wild clansmen, or if that was just not possible, in their despair to just give up and surrender, rather than drown. It was for all practical purposes over.

The fight was done; the battle was lost - and won!

***

BLOOD ENEMIES

Bannockburn, 24 June, 1314

Not far away, Geraint felt that he had had a good day. His battalion had stood. The Lowland Scots had shown what they were made of, to the cost of the English invading their land. But primarily he was elated just to be alive. Although he had taken some knocks, which would mean bruises and a slice across his shoulder, the wound was not deep. Yet he was sorely troubled.

In the melee at a distance, he had seen something he had never wanted to see. It was unmistakable to him. An oak tree on green and white quarters, the escutcheon of his own family, emblazoned on an English knight's surcoat. The knight's helm was closed but he knew that his father was too old to be campaigning, so it had to be his older brother, Luke. Fully engaged in his own fight in the muddy river, he had barely seen that the small group of knights, which had included Luke, had managed to scramble away up the further bank, once the distant relieving force had appeared, and so settled the day.

Profoundly glad though he was, that they had not confronted each other with bare steel, it had been a close thing. But now that particular worry was overtaken by another. The English had lost - and badly. Their king would certainly get away - his type always did. The great nobles would be held for the ransoms that would balance King Robert's treasury for a year or two. But the ordinary knights, like Luke... Now if he wasn't killed then he would certainly be captured, and once the Scots had sorted out who was worth ransoming - and who was not, the lowly Sir Luke would likely not be on their 'list of the saved'.

The pikemen were halted here by their commanders, they did not pursue the retreating English - that was left to the teeming clansmen who took off in hot pursuit, luckily for those exhausted English in the stream now without hope of escape. They had no option but to seek to surrender, in which they would not have succeeded with the kilted men. The pikemen were more minded to take individual surrenders of these armoured knights, and the immediate plunder that came with it, whilst at last being released to search the bodies of those they had slain for their valuables - the booty of war.

***

Sir Peter Breydel had called the senior Templar officers to attend his tent late in the afternoon to debrief them, and give them their orders. Meanwhile having consulted with the battalion commanders, he started out by calling forward three of the younger brethren, including Knut Peerson, who now had his sword arm in a sling. In front of their cheering friends and colleagues he dubbed each of them 'knight', for their gallantry over these past two days fighting. The general also had not failed to despatch a pair of Aird's carrier pigeons giving the good news, after the battle was decided.

The evening was dry and the sky clear and the Templar warriors, now tired but happy, were told that King Robert had allowed a few score of the English cavalry to escape along the Roman road to Falkirk, so as to spread the news of the extent of their defeat to the many oncoming English soldiers, who had never reached the battlefield. That news of course turned them around, particularly when they heard that their king with a sizeable escort had already run, long before the battle was over.

Breydel's servant passed around mugs of wine, whilst a boar was roasting on a spit before them. King Robert, they were told, had accepted the surrender of Stirling Castle and would temporarily take up residence there.

Geraint had mounted beforehand and ridden through the lines to where the English prisoners were held. Nearly all them were from the heavy cavalry and were either knights who might be worth a ransom, or other men-at-arms who had little chance of rescue.

The Scots guarding them were retainers of the Earl of Moray. He would himself be arriving to decide who among them were worth money and would live, as distinct from those who could not raise a ransom and would not be worth feeding. The exhausted prisoners were confined in the reinforced cattle pens of a nearby farmhouse, their plate armour and their chain-mail stripped from them; many were wounded and all deeply dejected, understanding that their tenure on life right now was slender indeed.

They also knew full well, that had the day been theirs,that few of their prisoners would have been allowed to live. That even any great noblemen amongst the captured might have been put to death, as an example to all. The Scots were no more known for acts of clemency than were the English, so they rightly expected the worst.

Geraint, having been one of Moray's battalion commanders, was known to the Scottish knight of Moray's household who was in charge of the prisoner compound. He had commandeered a shed for his office, where Geraint explained his problem to his colleague.

"His lordship looks to ransoms to provide some of the necessaries for the cost to himself of being at the disposal of His Grace the King," he told Geraint noncommittally. But he was at the same time looking down the lists of names he had in front of him.

"Aye, this would be him," he said, his finger stopped where it had travelled down the list. "Sir Luke of Pembroke is the name you gave me."

"Might I speak with him?" the Templar requested.

"Aye, I can do that for you Commander, I'll send for him. I can'na allow you into the pens where they are confined. These are desperate men. They know most of them now what their fate will be, and most are bitterly regretting they didn't fight on, until they were killed in battle."

Luke, a big man like his younger brother, arrived within a half hour with two grim Scottish soldiers each holding one arm, his wrists being pinioned behind him. He was dressed only in his soiled undershift and drawers. He was dirty enough, but appeared unwounded.

Geraint asked the soldiers to sit him down; his arms still shackled behind him facing the table, where he sat along with the Scottish knight, after which he asked them to withdraw. The knight looked at the brothers, and said, "Alright Commander, I'll give you twenty minutes alone. Then he must return to the others."

Luke didn't recognise Geraint immediately, but sat puzzled, glowering across at him and then his eyes lit up as he slowly realized that this Scottish commander was his younger brother.

"Are you a traitor then?" he challenged incredulously. "Fighting against your king? We thought you must be dead since the idolatrous Templars were all destroyed."

Geraint swallowed that jibe, but then spoke. "We don't have long," he said. "He told us we have twenty minutes and there is a lot to say - so just don't jump to conclusions; just listen to me while I tell you what is important. But I am not a traitor. I never was a subject of your King Edward, so I cannot be false to him! Likewise the Templars were not idolatrous, nor are they destroyed."

He explained that he had escaped the rather leisurely round-up of Templars in England, and had made his way to Scotland where they had regrouped; that the King of Scotland had tolerated them where seemingly no other crowned head in Christendom had done so, and that their remaining in Scotland depended on King Robert surviving this invasion by Edward of England. It was, he said, as simple as that and an easy choice.

"Now Luke, unless the family has come into a lot of money since I last heard, they won't be able to ransom you. The Earl of Moray will not feed you a day longer than necessary- so you know what will happen."

Luke who had heard all this in silence and said, "I feared as much. I never thought to surrender, but my group was trapped - my horse was killed under me and I was pinned underneath him. But instead of cutting my throat they made me a prisoner. Look, I'm sorry Geraint I shouldn't have called you a traitor."

Geraint quickly dismissed that episode and talked practicalities.

"Now I know you are alive and seemingly fit, I am going back to my chief and see if they will let me ransom you. If I can secure your release it will be on your oath that you will never reveal that it was Templars who fought against you today, or that I was here except perhaps to Father, on the same condition - how is the old man anyway?"

"He is good, but too rheumatic to go on the king's campaigns anymore and yes, I accept your condition willingly."

As he spoke the Scottish knight returned and looked at Geraint enquiringly. Geraint told him that he was returning to the camp and would ask his commander if he could be allowed to ransom his brother out.

"Well he will nae be going anywhere before the morrow, so I will look out for you then." He called for the escorts and Geraint got up and, before the soldiers came back, embraced his brother who, with his arms still bound behind him, could not return the hug.

"I will walk you back to your horse" said the earl's officer and, once out of earshot of the guards, confided in Geraint saying, "I have to tell you privately that the earl takes ransoms very seriously. Don't rely on him being generous, despite the fact that you have given him excellent service."

***

After the de-briefing at Sir Peter Breydel's gathering, Geraint sought out Paul and told him what had happened; also how the Scottish knight had warned him about the earl's grasping nature. Paul thought about it and said, "Let's you and I together see Sir Peter, and ask for his good offices in this matter. Come on." He had just seen the Fleming come free from a group to whom he had been talking.

The two young knights who had so distinguished themselves in commanding their pikemen, quickly had Sir Peter's attention and they told him the problem. He considered for a minute and then looked up at the approaching sound of many horses.

"We can ask him here and now," he smiled.

"Who, the Earl" asked Geraint looking over towards the approaching riders?

"Yes, but I see that he is with the King," their general replied.

The group dismounted and a beaming King Robert walked over to embrace his Master of Infantry. Behind him, his courtiers followed respectfully, including the tall figure of the rather dour Earl of Moray.

Wine was produced and there was much good cheer and laughter. Geraint and Paul on the fringe of the group wondered how they could get to speak to the earl privately, but apart from perfunctorily nodding at the two commanders, he made no effort to include them in.

Then they heard Sir Peter tell the King that two of his battalion commanders had a problem and could he tell the King about it. The Bruce happily replied, "Of course. Are they here? Bring them over!" As they made their way to the King's side, they heard Sir Peter explaining the situation, but the King's eyes were fixed on them.

"I know you two," he said. "When that fool de Bohun saw me without my bodyguard yesterday, and the idiot charged before the battle had even commenced, you were the two Templars who came to join me in the fight," he looked reproachfully at his military attendants. You had a battalion each of Moray's men did you not, Monmouth - and de Chatillon, isn't it, if my memory serves me? You both did brilliantly well today, I have to say."

Sir Peter took the opportunity. "You see Sire, we Templars still have families, often a half a world away from where we serve, but Sir Geraint here was shocked to see his brother's arms in the battle, and subsequently has discovered he is a prisoner of the noble Earl of Moray. Now Sir Geraint tells me that his brother will not be able to raise a ransom and we all know what that means. Sir Geraint would ransom him himself, except that Templars individually do not have any money and …"

"Moray, you heard all that?" cut in the King. "You have a prisoner with no means of being ransomed, except that his brother, one of your excellent commanders would like to ransom him, but has no means either. What do you say?"

"Well Sire," the haughty Earl replied. "I depend on those ransoms. I cannot go around plundering the dead on the field, but the income from ransoms does help me to keep my estates working. I could in this case give Sir Geraint time to pay."

The King, his brow furrowed responded, "That is not at all what I had in mind, Moray."

Sir Peter intervened, "Perhaps I could lend the ransom to Sir Geraint, your Highness?"

"Enough," rapped out the King testily, now with an edge to his voice! "My Lord Earl, I want that man your prisoner, his arms and armour restored, supplied with some decent clothes, some food for his journey, a good destrier and a palfrey, leaving your prison tomorrow morning.

"You, Monmouth and you, de Chatillon, with your general here's permission, will escort him with safe passage through our lines…and give him some coin for his journey, which I shall give you. You my Lord Earl and I, will agree a sum in compensation, in lieu of the ransom that you were never going to receive. This is my last word on it! And Sir Geraint", he turned to the Welshman, "wish your brother God speed from me.... Oh, and tell him never to invade my kingdom again."

THE FRATERNITY IN COUNCIL

Castle Aird, Autumn 1314

In the castle forecourt all was bustle as grooms took charge of the horses of the last of those to arrive. It made a lively and colourful scene with groups and individual brethren arriving and departing. Now that Templar livery was no longer worn, many of the knights customarily wore what they had deemed appropriate at Bannockburn, the arms of King Robert's mesnie, or the saltire of the Kingdom of Scotland itself. But some had managed to replicate the armorial devices of their family escutcheons, which drawn as they were from across Christendom, would have taken a team of genealogical experts to identify.

The noise of iron-shod hooves of the several horses on the cobbles, the numerous grooms and other servants, the persistent hammering metal on metal from the castle smithy, hounds loping about, even chickens scratching amongst the odiferous horse droppings, combined to give an impression of activity and bustle, even normality, in what was now a cheerful place.

Prominent amongst the latest arrivals was Sir James Keith, the bulky former Templar and much admired leader of the King's small body of cavalry at the great battle at Bannockburn. Stationed on high ground before the Scottish main camp commanding the reserve, he had witnessed late in the day that the mass of fighting men below were wheeling away from the great meadow where the main shock of conflict had taken place, down into, and across Bannock's stream. As he watched, an equerry rode up with his horse well lathered. King Robert had sent a despatch for Sir James to use his own judgement, for the moment when to intervene.

Released by this, almost immediately seizing the moment, at a point when the battle was still not won, he made his decisive move. Organizing not just his cavalry, the squires, grooms and servants but also the camp followers, telling the women to leave their small children with the old ones, take off their coifs and tie up their skirts - there were perhaps together two thousand or more, to whom a chance of the early pickings of a defeated enemy was lure enough.

He had personally uprooted the banners that stood in the camp before each nobleman's tent and handed them out to this motley crew of grooms, cooks, women and half-grown youths, with orders to wave and display them. He pressed some drummer boys into action, and then ahead of them across a wide front, he spread out his entire remaining reserve of near two hundred armoured horsemen, pennants flying from lances, moving them forward at a slow trot, leading this newly created infantry running down the slope behind them, towards the wide Bannock stream.

There, less than a mile away, desperate close quarters fighting had put the whole battle into the balance. This was the new army whose appearance at a distance had so dismayed the undefeated English, hard pressed but still numbered in their thousands, had led to panic and wild retreat for those who could get away. Surrender, the last option for those that were left behind, depended on whether their - by now blood-crazed - foes would accept it.

Sir James had, after the battle, been created Constable of Scotland by the triumphant King, an appointment in which his fellow Templars rejoiced.

The leaders of the Council of the Fraternity were now expected to be in session for several days. After this meeting, it would be a long time before the full council would meet again. Some members were in residence there, but other brethren of the new order had been summoned to be in attendance on them, to appear as required.

Prior Peter of Bologna opened the proceedings but no longer was a prayer intoned. The simple words, "Let us remember," signaled one minute's silence for reflection, and silent prayer for those who wished it.

The outcome of the great battle had drawn a line under the past. His notes in front of him, the Prior called the meeting to order to hear the many planning matters to be discussed, and if possible decided. The mullioned windows gave enough light for now, although candles guttered in wall brackets. A fire blazed in the great stone fireplaces at either end of the long oak-beamed room. With him around the heavy waxed oak table was the brown-robed Brother Joseph the Treasurer, Peter Proudhomme the master of masons with his white close fitting plaincloth 'cloche' helmet, the mark of an architect or master builder; Sir Peter Breydel their veteran from Flanders' 'Field of the Golden Spurs', who had trained and commanded the schiltrons at Bannockburn, Sir Olivier de Penne controller of the network of shadow commanderies, and the new Constable of Scotland, Sir James Keith.

First the Prior spoke of the awful death in Paris of the Grand Master, Jacques de Molay, together with Geoffrey de Charney, the Preceptor of Normandy. First hand detailed news of this had reached Castle Aird, with the return of their envoy, Paul de Chatillon from Paris, prior to the Bannockburn fight. But this was the first full Council meeting since before that time. It was indeed a grim story the Prior had to tell. The most senior Templar leaders in the French King's custody had been brought blinking in the unaccustomed daylight onto a stage built for the purpose, he told the hushed council members, in front of the great Notre Dame Cathedral in Paris.

Above their heads, high up on the cathedral façade, the famous gargoyles grimaced down on them, their stone ears deaf to the drama taking place below.

The much abused old warriors, he told them, already locked up for seven years, were there to play their part in this predetermined tragic farce, to publicly repeat the pain-wracked confessions of their grievous sins - above all, heresy and apostasy. They were supposed to beg for clemency and to hear the judgement of the archbishop, widely expected to be perpetual imprisonment.

But events took a very different turn. At this, the first opportunity to speak out in public after seven years, the Grand Master had shouted out to the multitude of Parisian folk who had come to see the end of the Templar Order, that his alleged confessions were entirely untrue; that they were extracted by unbearable torture, that he and his fellow Templars were innocent of all the charges against them. More important, he said, was that the Order was entirely innocent of these false charges - it was without sin!

As his guards dragged him off the stage still shouting, his colleague de Charney took up the refrain and also shouted out he too was innocent and, as the guards sought to restrain him, fiercely repudiated the confessions given through torture. The crowd first reacted in surprise and then their sentiment turned in favour of the two elderly and distinguished knights, even in their damaged state.

It came near to pulling them away from their guards and rioting against the king. The Church dignitaries standing on the stage were horrified at the turn of events, and that it was they and not the prisoners that were attracting the abuse and the missiles of the crowd.

The king had not been there, but when they brought the news to him at the city palace nearby, it was said that Philip's fury was unimaginable. He ordered that the two Templars should be burned that very night as apostates, and this indeed took place. As a sign of his vicious nature he specified that the fires, on which the two old men should be burned to death, should be on a charcoal base and the pyre stacked with green branches, to prolong the agony.

Prior Peter told the Council all this and that the Order's shadow Paris commandery had planned a last minute swoop, risking everything to try to rescue the victims, but events had moved too fast to prepare a move with any chance of success. The King's careful instructions to burn the old Templar generals on a small islet in the Seine, opposite his palace on City Island from a terrace of which he had watched - and listened - had made rescue impossible, with all river traffic of any kind being banned before and for the duration of the execution.

"There was something else," the Prior told them, "our people together with many others on the river bank, were helpless to do anything, yet duty bound not to go and leave them at such a time. Whilst the fires were lit and the executioners stepped away, this grand old man our Master, called out to heaven for justice in the life to come.

"Then with his last words, in his final agonies, he called out that Philip of France and Pope Clement should meet him within the year, before the 'Court of Heaven', there to answer for their crimes." That was the last, he told them, that was heard from Jacques de Molay. "Many hours later before the dawn, when the fires had cooled, two of our young men swam across to the isle and bundled together the charred bones and they were brought back here to keep safe, as relics of our two martyrs."

The meeting listened, mostly with downcast eyes and then it was Sir James who quietly said "That whoreson Philip must pay for this!"

Prior Peter resumed quietly, "Of course I knew how you would react, and I think you will approve that I had set up a small group entirely for the purpose of achieving the justice we assuredly must have. It is now our mission to simply ensure that our Master's last order, that these two 'should within this year meet him at the Court of Heaven', shall be fulfilled - and brothers, we can hardly leave that to providence!" He grimaced at the idea and looked around the table to be sure they had understood his meaning.

"We will take this just revenge on both the tyrant Philip Capet, and on our traitorous commander, who betrayed us, the arch-priest Bernard Got Pope Clement, and send them on their way to this final rendezvous" he declared. A solemn silence fell, which he himself interrupted.

"Some of you already knew of the events I have described, but now there is news that you cannot have heard", he smiled, "unless you have a private pigeon post, competing with our own."

***

THE TASTE OF REVENGE

Avignon, 1314

The summer of 1314 had been exhausting for Pope Clement but that had been the situation every year since his election. He lay feeling ill, flat on his back in a night robe, spread-eagled on his great bed, whilst his eyes idly wandered across the high stucco ceilings and over to the long narrow windows overlooking the river.

There always seemed to be a shortage of money, he reflected, and always a struggle with the princes, secular and ecclesiastical, just to obtain the bare necessaries to support the Curia. It is true that the Church had unique access to certain fund raising schemes - the sale of indulgences, for example, but Clement's judgement was that to be most effective, this should be used sparingly. Pilgrimages were another great source of funds, but so many of the houses of the monastic orders had dominated the well-trodden routes to Santiago, that there was nothing much available for any new initiatives.

Of course Rome had been the greatest pilgrimage route of them all, measured by the people travelling it, and that had done wonders for the papal coffers, but here he was, in Avignon, unable to even go himself to Rome the centre of the faith, his capital, simply because of the Roman mob. They were, he was told by the Italian cardinals, living in a state of outrage because the papacy had gone outside Italy to him, a Frenchman. "They would destroy him," Colonna said, "if he were to even set foot in the eternal city." Yet he was their one and only bishop! "Well," he mused, "we know who Colonna wanted to be pope, but even so, in this matter others had confirmed that he was right."

At least he was theoretically not any longer in France, although that was just over on the western bank, across the wide River Rhone. "God how I hate Philip," he thought, an often repeated private lamentation. He had never had one single meeting with the King, which when remembering it later, he could say that he had enjoyed. Except once, when he was an archbishop and he had met surreptitiously by night with Philip, both disguised, at Santonge in an inn at St Jean d'Angely, just over the border of his archdiocese of Bordeaux, then in the King of England's domain. That was when Philip had told him that he was going to 'arrange' the papal election in order that Bertrand de Got, as he then was, should fill the two year-long outstanding vacancy.

At the time his reaction was to think what an outstanding monarch Philip was, compared with his own suzerain in Bordeaux, the Plantagenet Edward II of England. That one was married to Philip's daughter, Isabella, and from what de Got had heard, she was a real bitch, in every way Philip's own daughter. But she clearly despised her royal husband's well-known pederasty; which might, he mused, explain something.

Philip had told him then at this, their first meeting, that there would be a price to be paid for his elevation to St Peter's Throne, a part of which was that he wanted to restructure the military orders within his own political sphere. These were the military Orders of the Templars and Hospitallers, both of whose top commander at present was the pope.

The Teutonic Order was more problematic being primarily faithful to the German emperor, rather than to the pope their nominal chief, and certainly not to Philip of France - no love lost there. At the time, it all seemed sufficiently distant that he had no great problem in agreeing - it was not a big price to pay for the papal tiara. But this was before he discovered from his spies that Philip's plan was to make one giant military order with himself or one of his sons as grandmaster, and the whole thing, including their immense wealth and property and all manner of ecclesiastical and civil tax privileges across Christendom, becoming an appendage of the House of Capet.

Philip already fancied himself as the Master of Christendom and with such additional power and wealth, and with the papacy already in his pocket, he would be near invincible.

So many things had happened since Clements election, that he had half-forgotten about Philip's price until late 1306, when Philip had asked for a meeting and said it was time that Clement should invite the masters and top officials of the Hospitallers and Templars to prepare plans for a crusade. They were to urgently come to France to present themselves to the Pope and his senior cardinals. At the forefront of his mind, the King was seeking to merge the two military orders.

De Molay had come from Cyprus, full of ideas and plans, and with ships loaded down with silver coins. But the Hospitaller's Grandmaster, John de Villiers, had sent only excuses from his new island fortress at Rhodes, just off the coast of that part of Byzantium conquered by the Turks. So one out of two, walked into the bag. But Philip then pre-empted everything that might have been negotiated, by making his own arrangements to destroy the Templars, and grab their treasure at the same time. That was a shock!

He moved restlessly on the bed. As usual he was feeling unwell in his bowels - it had been three long days since he had been able to pass anything and this condition always made him depressed. He helped himself to a Smyrna fig from the dish beside his bed, indeed he took another, they sometimes helped and he was partial to them. But apart from that, he was always living in dread of one of his attacks of stomach cramps, which caused him to double up, seeking to relieve the pain.

He had felt the symptoms earlier that evening and had made his excuses to the apostolic delegates of Armenia, who had already been to Rome, and now were waiting on him here, at his new capital of Avignon. They were back after a tour through France's southwest, seeing how things were done down there. It wouldn't have done to have sent them there a century ago, he mused, with the Cathar business coming to its inevitable resolution in the flames of Montsegur. Two hundred burned on one day. It must have made those bloodthirsty Dominicans very happy! Extraordinary, he thought that all those Cathars chose to burn, rather than abjure their nonsensical beliefs. Nobody would have known if they were sincere of course, but so long as they didn't start up again, practicing their evil ways, they could have gone back to the world - after enduring a prison sentence of course.

Thinking about burning heretics put him in mind of the despatches delivered by the courier from Paris. So, old de Molay is dead, he reflected. It's been a terrible business all round. He could have settled for imprisonment - two of them did - but the obstinate old man and his friend the Templar Master of Normandy, turned down the arrangement he had made for the four of them. He wasn't called Clement for nothing, and clemency is what he would like to be remembered for.

True, Philip's gaols would be no bed of roses, but if they were alive, then maybe, one year or another, something might have been done. Alive, there were possibilities; with death there were none. He chose not to continue along this train of thought because he had just remembered the report he had received from the cardinals he sent to Chinon. The old Templars must have known that their verdict was one of innocence. He had decided before the great council of the Church at Vienne two years ago, that those arrangements he had with King Philip had now gone too far, that this dangerous report must never see the light of day.

After an important meeting with Philip, who was unmistakably clear in his demands, the Pope had instructed his secretary 'to lose it.' It was to be misfiled in the archives, amongst the least visited of the vast number of unrelated Curia papers, going back for centuries. Clement had then insisted on meeting the three cardinals individually, requiring that each of them swear an oath to him, never to speak of the report they had made, to each other or to anyone.

"It was all a matter of politics, not finer feelings, but necessary for the survival of the Church," he had told them. None of them remonstrated with him, but he still remembered the dumb insolence in the attitude and looks of disgust that the individual cardinals had given him, which he ignored as he took their oaths.

Now Philip was off his back for a while, no doubt driving the Flemings or the Luxemburgers, or some others of his neighbours' crazy, with his schemes to get money out of them.

He remembered there was a personal message from Philip in the despatch from Paris. It seems de Molay at the stake had cursed the king and himself. Well, no surprises there, but also he had prophesied something, which Philip had thought the pontiff would like to know, he remembered. It was short enough.

"Meet me false pope…" the old man had shouted as the flames grew higher, "….at the Court of Heaven…. before this year-end!" That story would be all over France by now, Clement guessed. 'The condemned man's prophecy', they would call it.

He felt a griping pain, one of the worst kind that seemed to have a sharp edge to it.

It would surely help if he could move his bowels, his stomach was quite distended. He reached for more figs - the seeds had been removed - and he crammed his mouth with them.

If he called for the doctor, Brother Timothy he knew would want to bleed him. Doctors always did. He had once had an Arab doctor sent to him from Spain, 'Abu something', highly recommended by the Queen Dowager of Aragon. That fellow had prodded him about as all these physicians did, examined his urine and stools, but hadn't bled him at all. His judgement had been that there was a solid of some sort, obstructing his intestines, but that it could be broken up by frequent massage of the belly, plus a diet of citric fruit, figs for the digestion, and little else.

That was in the days before acquiring the city and palace of Avignon five years ago - he and his large curia had been constantly on the move, but mostly based at Poitiers, so as not to be too close to Philip's capital of Paris. He had thought to permanently retain this Arab fellow, but his close colleagues had said that it would never do if a pope had an infidel medical practitioner, who couldn't possibly know the right passages of Holy Scripture to use in the cure. He had seen the folly of ignoring that advice and so sent the man back to Spain, duly rewarded. The diet had in fact made an improvement, but the fruits were not always available, in northern France in particular. It was not a cure, but it helped. He himself had planted fig trees in the kitchen gardens, once he was established in Avignon, and tried to stick to the diet.

Another sharp pain wracked him. This was the worst yet. He sat up and stretched out for the silver hand bell on the table beside him and within moments the old nun who looked after him was by his bedside.

"It's bad." he said, breathlessly.

She gave him a silver goblet of fresh well water, the chill causing beads of moisture to form on the outer surface and then plumped up his pillows to try to make him comfortable. He had moved onto his side, and then into a foetal position, clutching his belly with both hands. She fussed around him mopping his neck and face with a wet linen cloth and making soothing noises.

His belly felt as though it was full of lead but with a hot knife slicing at it. A moment of terror came. He knew that this was serious. "Better get my confessor," he said, through gritted teeth.

Two hours later, his bed was surrounded by functionaries. He had mumbled something as a confession, and had duly been shriven. He was rambling on about 'the Court of Heaven,' he wouldn't let it go, but nobody knew what he meant. The nun was applying her wet towels trying to cool him, as his temperature was soaring.

Suddenly he stopped writhing, stopped mumbling, and stopped breathing, but even then the dignity of death eluded him. Nobody wanted be the first to move. There was a prolonged reverent silence from the spectators around the bed, but then came a startling if muffled, explosive sound and a noxious odour as his distended bowels finally voided, as nature offered its own crude testimonial to his passing.

Two days later a pigeon arrived at Castle Aird in Scotland with a short message, which decoded said only, "Departed Avignon for eternity, via Smyrna."

***

NEW PLANS AND AN EXPEDITION

Aird Castle, 1314

"You cannot know it yet," the Prior told the Council. "Our carrier birds arrived here only today, but two days ago the Pope died; you may not be too distressed to hear that he passed in quite considerable pain. It is believed that he died of a stomach complaint that has been plaguing him for some months past." His grim-faced listeners caught each other's glances at this, as the Prior continued. So he is already dead. One of our two main enemies - the treacherous leader who betrayed his own followers, the thirty-second pope to preside over our order and he who destroyed it, has gone to answer for his crimes.... at the Court of Heaven" he added drily.

"Now we need to deal with the arch-criminal, the greatest enemy our Order ever knew who for his greed and ambition alone, destroyed the Order of the Temple. An evil man who set himself above popes and all other kings, whose wickedness brought down this mighty, and in its way, magnificent order of chivalry and religion. Let us also honour the memory of the earliest of our predecessors, those humble knights in Jerusalem, two hundred years ago."

The Prior paused to hear and understand the will of those listening.

"Two questions" interjected the Flemish brother Sir Peter Breydel, now hero of two battles where trained foot-soldiers had defeated armoured knights. "How is that to be done? "How? Is there a plan," he repeated, "and my second question... May I have the honour of leading the team that will execute the tyrant?"

The Prior reflectively examined the liver spots on the backs of his hands, before he replied. "I cannot deny, Brother Peter that you have earned high honour in this new order. Of course I can understand why you, like any of us, would want to be the one who risked all to rid the world of that monster, but I think not, is my answer to your second question - for two reasons that will become clear." He squarely met the Fleming's gaze.

"I am going to put it to this Council to agree that we ask you to become the Marshal of our new Fraternity. There are still battles to be fought where your great skills and experience will be vital to our success. I will explain that, but your first question can only be answered in a general sense. Unsurprisingly, King Phillip is the best-guarded man in France."

The men assented as the Prior added, "The honour of the task will fall to our French brethren. They do have a plan and it is underway. If this idea of theirs works, there will be few regrets and much rejoicing!"

"Brother Prior," spoke up the burly Sir James. "You mentioned creating the office of Marshal to our Fellowship, but two matters arise from this. What of our revered Templar Marshal, who was here at the time of our last and first Chapter meetings? How has he fared - did he get back to Cyprus? I will speak of the other matter later, but what of Brother Marshal?"

"The news is not good", the Prior replied. "Our 'pigeon road' has closed. There are no Templars at liberty any more in Cyprus, information comes very slowly but what does get through does not look good. I will ask Sir Olivier to speak on this."

The tall knight took over the narrative without hesitation: "He did return to Cyprus some months after leaving us, the same way that he came to us, through the Empire to Venice disguised, together with some of our German knights as his escort, as if of the Teutonic Order, with I can say, their full co-operation. Then he sailed to visit our two commanderies in Greece, a country that is still lawless. We still have places in Chorinte, and in La Cremonie that the ancients called Sparta. There are others, all happily outside the papal dispensation and without overlord, as the Greek Emperor at Constantinople is in yet another civil war.

"And this war, you should know, involves some of our former brethren who having survived Black Friday, or even before that, went their own way as mercenaries. One of them, you will have heard of, or may even know, Roger de Flor, formerly a sergeant of the Order and ship's captain of 'the Falcon' was at Acre, and made a fortune for himself, it was alleged, ferrying rich refugees out of the city across the sea to Cyprus, before the Mamelukes broke in. He was in deep trouble with the Order for using 'the Falcon' for his own squalid purposes, gouging money out of terrified refugees and he was ordered to surrender himself to the castle at Limassol. He knew that he would have almost certainly have been hanged for these extortions and unsurprisingly was never seen again, nor yet was our ship until years later. It was found to have been sold in Genoa, with Roger long gone.

"Then he turned up in Spain, years after that. He was recruiting for a mercenary force to go to fight for the emperor at Constantinople. He has gone from strength to strength, I can tell you. They call themselves 'The Catalans' with a lot of their men raised from that province of Aragon, and this is a story for another day gentlemen, but Brother Roger, our wayward Templar sergeant became a prince of the empire, married a princess; fell out with his master the emperor and started a rebellion, in which he has been doing rather well, as I hear.

"Enough, except that there are several former Templars in senior positions amongst his free-lances - bound to be some old comrades amongst them, which may or may not have a relevance to us at some future time.

Sir Olivier glanced around the board as if to wait for questions. There were none.

"The Marshal", he continued, instructed the Templar sub-prior in Greece to open contacts with these Catalans, on the principle that we are former comrades and that our enemies' enemy might well be our friend. In particular I had heard that the Catalans had taken over great areas of these parts where our own remaining commanderies are located, so we may anyway need to treat with them. Better I think than the alternative of the King of Sicily and Naples, a Capetian, who is one of those would burn us, rather than live alongside us.

"Returning to the Marshal," he continued, "I now have the pieces of the puzzle together. He was back in Cyprus for about a year; long enough to put in train certain matters relating to the few hundred brethren in the east whose dispositions he organized. His last messages to us said strongly that since the Knights Hospitallers were now well established behind their own battlements on the island of Rhodes, and the Teutons similarly at Marienburg in Prussia, which they had made into their own territory, the Ordensland, as they call it, that our Order ought similarly find our own safe place beyond this realm of Scotland. The problem here, being of course that our safety depends on the long life of our good friend King Robert." He caught and questioningly held the gaze of Sir James, the king's great loyalist who shrugged his assent, but did not speak.

"But the story in Cyprus has changed. Our last news in fact was that the king there, who was favourable to us, was overthrown by his brother, who now reigns. Our beloved Marshal was arrested by the royal forces and imprisoned. The military remnants of our order there mostly got away, scattered between Cilicia and Greece and our merchant house in

Constantinople, to the extent that now we no longer have contact with Cyprus at all. Brother Marshal was already sick and the likelihood is that he will not emerge from that gaol alive. You will remember that he foresaw some of this, and enjoined us to appoint his successor. These are the reasons my brothers, that I believe we must - and we know that he would wish it, move on and appoint a successor."

The Prior turned now to squarely face Sir James, "Brother James, you spoke of another matter. What troubles you?"

"Simply this," the bluff Scotsman replied. "I have as you know been appointed Constable of this realm of Scotland, pledged to uphold the military affairs of King Robert's government. That will involve expeditions beyond our present frontiers to places such as Ireland, the Isle of Man and disputed lands in Northern England, indeed who knows where. My concern is that a Templar Marshal..."

"No longer Templar," broke in one of the others.

"All right" he answered brusquely, "but you know fine what I mean. I don't want to see any clash between my duties to the King and... the Order." He glanced across the table at Sir Peter as he tailed off.

Outside, the light finding its way through the mullioned windows was failing, but the blazing fires gave a cheerful glow and crackled from time to time.

"I can reassure you on that." the Prior spoke again. "We will always be grateful to King Robert. He may always look for and be sure of our support, both in the field and in his purse. We wish him a long life. But one day his crown will pass to a son or grandson who will by that time regard us as no more than a curiosity, perhaps an embarrassment. King Robert is excommunicated and has no contact with Avignon, where currently, as you have just heard, there is no pope, nor yet in Rome, although unless the next pope is an Italian, I would expect his seat to remain in Avignon. But King Robert's descendants will not be excommunicated, and although most churchmen will have forgotten about us - and if they remember will not care - never forget *Dominum Cani*, the blood-hounds of the Dominicans.

They will not forget us because they do not forget, any more than we will forget them. I have heard by the way that although the Hospitallers were awarded most of our estates, there were exceptions. As a reward for their pitiless use of the rack and red-hot iron on the living bodies of our comrades, the Black Dominicans asked for and have been given our houses and estates in Vienna, Strasbourg, Worms and others." Around the table, eyes met in disgust.

The Prior continued in full flow as with any discussion of their loathed inquisitors. "As we know them to be our mortal enemies, so we will be their worst nightmare. We have a great price to extract from the Dominicans and that account will be paid in full!

"The anniversary of the burning of our two leaders this year is likely to be marked in Paris, perhaps elsewhere, by the burning of Dominican properties. That I regard as a local matter best left to those who feel the need to take such action, but buildings are no recompense for the flesh and blood of our brethren. The message however is clear to them. We are still here and now it is us that are hunting them!

"We know the fate," he continued in sombre tone, "of any of us of the Temple, who might ever have the evil fortune to fall into their hands. But quite unlike the helpless, crazy old women they call witches, those that they routinely sniff out, torture and burn alive, we are now in no way helpless. Never again will we be off our guard, so they cannot know when we might strike back. But we must heed the characteristic wisdom in the last message of our imprisoned Marshal, about an 'Ordensland'." He looked fiercely around at his colleagues and saw on their faces nothing other than approval.

"So," he continued quietly, "in a sense this must be our main business at this Council. We must have an alternative plan for a safe refuge. Of course we have looked at some alternatives. This is what I want to discuss with you. Our banking brethren with their wide contacts and information networks have identified a possible new base for us, which seems to have many things to commend it. It coincides with an approach that has been made to us for practical assistance by a group from those parts, that has fallen foul of the church and been excommunicated, who occupy the area that I am now proposing as a possible Ordensland. That could be a long term solution for us, as well as for them."

His audience, frowning with concentration mostly had no idea of what he had in mind. Observing that, he turned to Brother Joseph.

"I will ask Brother Treasurer to explain."

All eyes turned to Brother Joseph, who unrolled a parchment onto the table. Not a big man, he stood up the better to illustrate his message: "As you know we have long had private banking houses and discreet partnerships in many parts of Christendom, including Constantinople, even in Outremer cities, and through agents in Alexandria and Cairo. In my time in the Curia I have myself travelled in several parts of the eastern and western empires and even further afield, ostensibly on papal business, but also that of the Templars.

"Now gentlemen, you will see here," he tapped the parchment, "where we are proposing to perhaps create a near impregnable base, militarily highly defensible, yet well placed to continue to carry on and expand our commercial interests, central as it is to both the French kingdom and the German and Italian states of the empire."

It was a river he was showing them on the unfurled parchment. He pointed to the several ill-defined mouths of the Rhine and using a dagger point to illustrate, he showed the North Sea and how the great river, draining northern Europe before debouching into the sea through several separate routes, further back into Flanders flowed as a broad flood.

He slowly drew the steel point upstream along the winding river and named cities near to which it passed: "Utrecht, where we have an important presence; Arnhem here, where there is a bridge across the great river; Wesel, again a bridge; Duisburg; Dusseldorf; Cologne the seat of an archbishop; Bonn; further upriver, Koblenz - these are all established cities and in many of which we still have friends or better, our own people. Wiesbaden, Mainz - another great cathedral there; Worms - we have just heard, that our commandery there is now occupied by the cursed Dommies; Mannheim where the river Necker joins the flood, that way is to Heidelberg; but we continue on, upstream past many towns and villages, eventually to the great city of Strasburg."

He paused. "Looking at the map, apart from the Rhine's exits to the sea and that hinterland which belongs to the Count of Flanders, virtually everything to the south west of the river loosely falls into the lands of the Franks, for which the French crown claims suzerainty. To the east - and the river itself is the boundary, this is the Holy Roman Empire, made up as you know of numerous small and large states ruled by princes, some of whom are electors, whose function it is to choose from amongst themselves, the 'Holy Roman Emperor,' as they would have it.

"You will appreciate that this broad river, the greatest in Christendom, is also a highway into the centre and on to the east. Our predecessors, the first crusaders two hundred years ago, on the way to the Holy Land started in

Flanders and then travelled along the Rhine River playing havoc with the well-ordered cities of the Empire. It was everything the magistrates there could do, just to keep them moving on.

"Beyond Strasburg, on the western bank are the lands of the Dukes of Alsace" he commented, "who do not recognise the house of the Capetians in Paris as suzerain - although that can always change - and opposite, all the land on the eastern bank there is the Empire.

"Now here on a hill right by the river," he tapped the place with the knife point, "is Breisach, an ancient free city and river port, which means they have no overlord except the emperor, for whose protection of course they pay taxes. It is a busy trading port. There we have a commercial agent, a merchant, by the name of Simon the Jew, who is key to helping us in organizing what we propose. The eastern area behind it, passed by the River Rhine is mountainous and densely wooded. It's called the Black Forest, a truly enormous area, thinly populated. It is one of the great forests to which our comrades escaped years back and we still have military groups there, with whom I believe Sir Olivier is in touch.

"From Breisach just a few miles inland from the Rhine River, see here on the edge of the forest, is the great city of Freiburg, again a free city, well known to Peter Proudhomme here" he nodded to the master mason, who acknowledged with a nod back, "who even now has work in progress there.

"I would add..." he continued, "that Master Peter is of all of us, the one who best knows the area. We will be proposing that he takes joint command of the advance group we wish to send, along with our Brother Marshal who will remain in full military control.

"Following the course up river" the treasurer continued, tapping his knife on the indicated place, "we would then arrive at the city and great lands of the Bishop of Basel, a Prince Bishop in fact. The River Rhine bends there, and recently there has been built a great stone bridge - the river is still about a quarter mile wide and continues higher up past Basel. It flows from a lake and a city named Constance, fed by the snow-melt and streams of the great range of mountains.

"Across the river to the south and east behind Basle, it is still the empire, but it is restive, it can be said. The territory is very mountainous with the greatest peaks in Christendom and with large lakes and hidden valleys. In Roman times it was called Helvetia and whereas in the west we have counties, there they have cantons - but there is a big difference! Now to the south, gentlemen…" he illustrated with the dagger point again, "once we leave the river behind and move to these heavily forested mountainous regions, known as the Forest Cantons, here the feudal practices that we all know cease, as there are no great lords and no feudal duty - or to be more accurate, there is a continuing conflict about that.

"The foresters are free men. They elect their leaders from their own and it has ever been thus as they will say, because they were never conquered. These people are simple but robust foresters, hunters, herdsmen and the like and the lands are their own. They pay some nominal dues to the Duke of Austria who leaves them, or hitherto has left them alone."

He nodded bowing to the Prior, to take up the story and sat down. The listeners transferred their attention to the opposite end of the great table.

"In short brothers," the Prior explained, "the detail is for another time. These foresters from three of the cantons have openly declared themselves independent. The Duke Leopold of Austria is planning an expedition, to conquer them, hang their leaders, and enforce their duty. The free foresters of Schwyz, as it is called, have every intention to resist. Like us, gentlemen, and rather fortunately as it turns out, they are also excommunicated, so the Church cannot intervene. They fight as foot-soldiers, and the Duke is raising a great host of mailed chivalry to break them and tame them."

He smiled. "Perhaps this situation is beginning to sound familiar to you?"

Brother Joseph at the further end of the table again continued the story whilst the prior took a draft from his pewter goblet. Not a tall man, he preferred to stand up whilst addressing his colleagues: "Through our commercial people we have established the following: The Schwyzers need help. Being under interdict they cannot go far outside their own region to get it, anyway they don't have enough money to pay mercenaries. Moreover, no feudal lord locally will openly help them by defying his suzerains, who thereabouts are the Hapsburg family and this Duke.

"They are foresters, not rich but freemen. They are a self-sufficient race and many of them are exceptionally good with the long bow. Even more are they experts with the crossbow. In close fought action, they favour the woodman's axe. They realise however that pitting footmen against mailed knights is usually a mismatch. Even so, they are prepared to fight for their liberty. They also know from recent history in Flanders," he nodded towards Sir Peter, a victor of that earlier 'Field of the Golden Spurs', "that trained pikemen, well led, can stand up to and defeat a King's armoured cavalry. I think", he smiled, "that they may or may not yet have heard about the Bannockburn fight, but they surely soon will, as will all of Christendom!

"But now they need weapons, skilled trainers and experienced officers. Also silver. We can supply all of those things," he pointed out, as he resumed his seat.

"In return," it was the Prior who resumed, "providing they - and we - succeed, they will agree to our becoming established there and living amongst them. We will become the core of the new military they will need, training all of their men, making sure they will be properly equipped and able to safeguard themselves, and their independence. So we will stay on.

"At the same time we can - without fear of persecution - build up our banking and commercial services both on our behalf and on theirs. In truth, if we are to have our 'Ordensland' there, we will become very close to them, we can bring there our many isolated bands of soldiers, continually waiting for our directions. No doubt many of our men will marry amongst them, and in the new scheme of things, that would be in everybody's best interests.

"Our military knowledge and connections will mean that our new Schwyzer friends will be a well-organized force, stiffened with former Templars. If we do it right they could be the best infantry in Europe, and in this mountainous terrain, powerful enough to keep jealous neighbours away. That is the reason we now need a war leader and this is why I formally propose as Marshal of the Fraternity, our brother here Sir Peter Breydel, to whom I have obviously spoken of this." He nodded expectantly to the new marshal. "He will, he tells me, accept the charge."

Sir Peter smiled around the table, as all there smiled and spoke their assent. "It will save me going back to a boring life as a merchant in Bruges, at any rate."

Sir James spoke next and with undoubted enthusiasm. "I will entirely support the project and the appointment. It was my privilege to serve in the same army as our new Marshal, Brother Peter. Since I was commanding the reserve up on the hillside, I was able to watch with great admiration the way that he deployed the schiltrons in that hard fight at Bannock."

"Gentleman, brethren, we have many things to discuss", the Prior spoke again. If you agree to this expedition, there is much to do for Sir Peter, now Brother Marshal, and Brother Treasurer to start to make ready."

PHILIP AT FONTAINEBLEAU

Fontainebleau, October, 1314

Philip, King of France surveyed the gloomy weather outside his country palace of Fontainebleau. Not that it was much of a palace by his standards, compared with his great hall on City Island in Paris's River Seine. It was however, a splendid royal hunting lodge, big enough that it could take many of the court. It was mainly a place that he could relax - he was born there after all, and the hunting was just superb, as he hoped for the morrow. But the heavy clouds on this dank Michaelmas day did not augur well for his favoured sport, for which the party had been gathering since the previous day.

That was another thing, he reflected. No sooner did he say he was going to spend a few days hunting than his brothers, their hangers-on and all the other so-called courtiers, all hoping for some kind of favour would be angling for an invitation. One might think that being a mighty Christian monarch as he was, already more than twenty years as the Lord's anointed, that he could get away alone, and go into Fontainebleau's mighty forests and lose the world and its cares, with only his professional huntsmen along with him.

At least, he thought, once they were mounted and out there, the *cannaille* of courtiers had the good sense to keep their distance and not to try to keep up with him. That way he was alone in the clean uncomplicated world of nature, whilst they concentrated on what was seemingly most important to them, or to most of them, the pursuit of the opposite sex.

He was sitting in his solar at a covered table looking out at the damp forest and was in a sombre mood. He chose to use this chamber when he became bored with the company of others - which was often. All knew that he must not be disturbed when there alone, which knowledge was reinforced by the presence of guards outside the door.

A large fire burned steadily in the stone and oak-beamed chamber. Before it basking in the radiated heat, sprawled a massive grey wolfhound, a studded broad iron collar around his neck. A silver goblet of best Pauillac wine and a jug with more, lay untouched before the king, his still handsome visage clouded by concern.

When he had left Paris two days ago, his last visitor had been an English bishop, the emissary of his son-in-law, Edward II of England. The quarrel between them had not been improved by the fact that Edward's queen, Philip's daughter Isabella, had now openly left him, to live at her own properties, or other royal residences where he was not in occupation, yet no doubt where her lovers were to be found.

He had heard that she had a relationship with Earl Mortimer, which seemed to be lasting. He had, through his own ambassador remonstrated with her, but she had replied that Edward would not - or could not - serve her as a husband should, in bed. They had managed between them to beget his grandson, young Edward, who would be the third of that name. Then, their duty done, as both Edward and Isabella seemed to view it, they could now pursue their own desires, his now being exclusively pageboys and young male courtiers, whilst she sought brawny warriors.

Isabella had no time for the Provençal poet type, who would worship the pedestal on which they would place her, who would treat her as though she were a delicate vase. His confidential spies assured him, choosing their words appropriately, since this was about his daughter - that Princess of France and Queen of England though she be, she liked rough sex, the very opposite to courtly love - "all words, lutes and no action" as she had dismissively described it to her women. Not that he could care less about her sexual tastes, but if, as it appeared, that she and Edward were now permanently disunited, then this Roger Mortimer might be worth some help, given the news from England.

Edward and he had just about become irreconcilable, he now believed, since the Bishop of London had delivered the latest messages from his son-in-law. He recalled Mortimer as having visited his own court. He must be an ambitious man, he mused - he would arrange a discreet meeting.

It all inevitably meant war and Philip had already engaged in enough of those to know how expensive they were. Money! As ever, he needed money and for the first time in his twenty-year reign he really had little idea for sure where it was going to come from. Taxation could not be increased - his ministers had sounded the alarm at the present rate. The Florentine bankers: he had dispossessed them, given them a taste of his prisons and expelled them, minus all their substance. All very satisfying, he recalled, but of course there would now be no more Italian bankers coming to France.

He had cleaned out the Jews, thrown them out of France forfeiting all their possessions eight years back in 1306 and collecting the debts owed to them for years to come - that worked well. And the debtors were people who didn't dare refuse to repay debts to the king, whilst they might have defied the Jews to do their worst. The Templars came next in '07 - what a disappointment that had been - a massive effort and then the coffers in the biggest treasury in Christendom, as he had always believed, were empty when his boys had gone in there on that October morning.

And then after five years of 'feet to the fire' and pulling out Templar finger-nails - getting all the confessions they could ever have needed, the bloody bishops at the Vienne Council had given their estates away to the bloody Hospitallers; not as he had carefully instructed the miserable ex-pope - may he linger for ever in purgatory - that the estates in France, at any rate, must be returned to the realm of France. But then, as he reflected, it had been recently pointed out to him that there was still a source of money in that.

It was now seven years since his Templar *coup de main*, the last chapter of which had been written back in March of this year when that crusty old idiot de Molay, had missed his chance of saving his life by bawling out, denying his heresy - playing to the Paris mob - of all audiences. He had chosen the fire, as did his comrade, de Charney, so that was what they got!

Now his useful fool of a prelate, Bertrand de Got, Pope Clement V, had died in Avignon, leaving him with another expensive problem. It was unthinkable that the papacy should return to Rome. Now that there had been a French pope, then he must ensure the succession to another such candidate. He had just the man in mind. But as he had discovered with getting Clement elected, the majority in the College of Cardinals would simply vote for the highest bidder - that after all, was how they recovered some at least, of what it had cost them to be sitting there, receiving in their turn their cardinal's hats. But they knew, even the Italians, that this king would not be gainsaid as to his own status. He had established early in his reign that it would be him and only him, as an anointed monarch by succession, and not by bribes like the money-grubbing prelates, that would make the big decisions, so far as they affected France. And by ensuring a Frenchman had the post, paid for by Philip, a pope unable to travel to the eternal city, where the Roman mob would lynch him, he would at Avignon be physically within the power of France, as Clement had known all too well.

But what of the Knights of Rhodes, as the Hospitallers were starting to call themselves? They might have set-up their banners in an impossibly remote place, so absolutely no chance of a re-run of the successful Templar coup with them. He greatly doubted if France would be seeing much of any Hospitaller Grand Master paying visits to the 'old country'. But if they wanted to take up their amazing good fortune in becoming the biggest landowners in France, apart from the Church, then they would have to physically be in France, in much larger numbers than they were already, to station perhaps another thousand or two of their Hospitaller brethren to take over the 2,000 Templar estates to add to their own. That, after what had happened to the other military order, at least would make them cautious of offending him.

Now there were no crusades any more, he thought with relish, no one who mattered could object to him taxing them. But meanwhile, one of his bright young men had pointed out, that over these seven years since the Templars had been broken, the King had needed to take on the irksome responsibility of managing these two thousand estates spread across the realm, as well as the cost of imprisoning the thousands of Templars in royal prisons.

It could be argued, young de Bayonne had rightly pointed out, that the profits of the farming estates might have defrayed some part of the costs of imprisoning the heretics, but someone, be it Church or whoever, owed the French King a fortune for managing and maintaining the 2,000 estates for all the seven years past. A bright lad, that Bayonne, thought Philip. But he knew now what he was going to do. The Knights of Rhodes, or Hospitallers, or whatever they liked to now call themselves, were going to pay him Philip, a very fat fee indeed, before they would be allowed to enter any of the splendid estates his agents had so carefully managed for so many years.

He looked again out of the window and observed that the clouds had lifted and there was every chance the next day would after all offer some good hunting. With that cheerful thought, he lifted the goblet and swallowed a good draught of the best wine in France.

***

The early November morning was misty but the signs were of it clearing. Philip had breakfasted lightly - his appetites for everything seemed jaded, a penalty he reflected, of holding supreme power over such a lengthy reign. As he left his chamber, valets were fussing around him even though it was not long after dawn, and there was a welcome bustle throughout the manor.

Most of the women still lay abed but a few of the more audacious, or ambitious to be noticed, were being assisted to mount by the grooms. Everyone knew that Philip would wait for no-one and when he was ready he would be gone, if only with the huntsmen and the fifteen couple of hounds whose excited baying filled the misty air, competing with the steel-shod hooves of half a hundred horses on the cobbles of the great courtyard.

Jacques LeGros, for twenty years the head huntsman at Fontainebleau, was on a tall mount alongside his assistant, the staghound's kennel master, walking his horse amongst the excited hounds, reminding them with his curled whip of their discipline. Together with another assistant with a curved horn on his shoulder, they were nearest to the courtyard gates now open, with the great forest looming a mere meadow's length away.

A groom knelt to enable the King to step up on his back to mount his great black stallion, which, clearly ready to be off, was held in check by another liveried groom. Philip, a tall man on top of his horse of eighteen hands, quickly looked around at the milling throng of his court and nodded to his grown son Louis, not yet mounted; then he caught the steady gaze of his huntsman and almost imperceptibly gave a nod.

As though drilled, the well prepared horses of the professional huntsmen with the King, took off at a brisk walk out of the great courtyard, which became a gentle trot as they emerged onto the lane, leading to the forest. Ahead of them the hounds loped along, their kennel master riding amongst them, his shouting occasionally audible above their deep-throated baying.

The chief huntsman rode marginally less than side-by-side with his monarch, available to hear and respond but not so forward as to be on a par with the king's horse.

"So what have you got for us today, LeGros?" came the expected question.

"Sire, we are heading east into the Barbison quarter", promptly came the reply. "We have a fine 16-pointer located over by the Gorge of Apremont, and my men are now beating in this direction. We should expect to put him up within about twenty minutes of now. We'll head him towards the plain of Macherin where he should give us a good run."

Philip turned in the saddle and observed disapprovingly the long strung-out line of riders that followed, dressed in a miscellany of clothing of fashionable colours in contrast to the King's sober woollens and leather, suitable more for the weather than a fashion parade. But he knew well that any event involving the court also involved fashion - as a young man glorying in his nickname 'the Fair' he had once undoubtedly set the tone. But no more. He cared nothing for such trivialities any more, in fact as he sometimes reflected; he cared about very little in life. His pleasures were few, sometimes they involved sex, but on those none too frequent occasions not with the ladies of the court, who always expected rewards, favours and preferment. He had agents who procured for him - uncomplicated quality liaisons with a beginning and an end, so that part of his life was organised.

He had, as a young man, thought to take religion seriously, but the trouble with that was that the bishops and priests, with whom he talked, were all revealed more as aspiring politicians, than holy men. The Church was rotten to its core, just a career path for second sons it seemed, and had been for centuries, as far as he could see. Some of them, he would concede, did have spiritual values, and no question…some even were very clever, who could be useful to him with his problems of state.

As a contrast he did enjoy a day's hunting, however. That could sometimes be an untrammelled delight, particularly after the pack with him and LeGros and the huntsmen, had distanced themselves from the others, as would shortly be happening.

His horse's pace picked up as though reading his thoughts, but Philip knew that the great beast was as aware as he was that there was a fine gallop for a stretch coming up, of about two miles. He could feel the powerful shoulders beneath him, tensing up, waiting only for his hand to relax the rein. "Sire," he heard from just behind him. "Remember Sire, the grass here is very wet and your mount could lose his footing."

He didn't deign to answer, but as the trees formed a glade in front of him, he let the horse have his head. The excited baying hounds were by now far ahead, streaming along with their mounted attendants amongst them, as the King and LeGros charged some distance behind.

Within some thirty minutes as the forest grew denser, the hounds were well ahead and out of sight, then the sound of the horn and quite close - 'a view,' came back through the damp trees. Both Philip and LeGros went for the trail that led in that direction.

Within minutes the trumpet sounded again and minutes later, where the trail divided, the King looked swiftly over his shoulder at LeGros, who pointed to the right hand path. It was narrower, forcing them into single file. As though in encouragement, the horn sounded once more - they were close.

The King's great black horse powered on at full gallop, oblivious of the vine-like rope that suddenly jerked out of the mass of fallen leaves. It took the beast down at knee height into a massive crash against a tree trunk, as he tried to regain his balance, smashing the undergrowth all around. Philip had been precipitated straight on over his mount's head, as it dived beneath him. He had hit the ground face down and lay there sprawled flat.

The huntsman was out of his saddle and running to the King. He knelt by his side and tried to find if there was still life there. He was not alone. Two woodsmen, as it seemed, appeared, one still holding and coiling the vine rope in his hand as the great horse thrashed nearby in agony, a leg broken.

"Is he dead, father?" one asked.

LeGros moved from his knees and straddled the King's back, placing one knee on each shoulder. He moved his hands and gripping Philip's chin with one hand and the back of his head with the other, sharply pulled his head around until they all heard the snap above the forest noises.

"He is now," the big man said. "Your brother is avenged. Now get you gone!"

When the first of the courtiers arrived some ten minutes later, it was the King's son Prince Louis who led. He saw LeGros on his knees, his bonnet lying beside him, apparently praying besides his recumbent royal father still sprawled across the track, whilst the great black horse half in, half out, of the shrubbery, whickered in pain and fright as his legs reflexively spasmed.

"My God", his shocked tones reverberated around what had now become a clearing. "In God's name, what happened to his Highness?" He demanded from the huntsman.

"I fear he's been killed, Your Highness." LeGros replied. "I was just behind him, and it was a fox ran out of the bushes, right in front of his mount. The black checked, but on the wet grass he lost his footing, and his Highness took a dreadful tumble. When I got to him, he was just like this, I tried to bring him around, but I reckon sir, that his Highness's neck is broke."

More riders had joined them and quickly took in the scene. The silence was shattered by the black horse, once more screaming. Ironically at that very moment, they again heard the distant horn.

"Put the beast down, damn you LeGros", demanded the King's son in a strained voice.

The huntsman unsheathed his great knife and stepped over to the stallion and swiftly sliced open an artery on his neck. Killing the magnificent beast was all that he regretted about murdering the King. His elder son, who had been a sergeant in the Templars, had been arrested in distant Marseilles and tortured, then burned by the Inquisition, all of five years before. He had not known anything of his boy's gruesome fate, not even that he had been arrested until about two years ago. Then two of the sergeant's former Templar comrades had visited him by night, at his estate cottage, and told him the evil news.

All of France knew that Philip was the architect of these terrible events. LeGros remembered with regret that he had even advised his boy to go ahead and join the Templars, when the opportunity had first arisen. The former comrades that had visited, very discreetly, kept in touch. They had discussed with him what might be done.

Wiping off the blood onto the mosses underfoot, he re-sheathed the blade and stepping back out of the broken shrubbery he saw that the several courtiers had sunk to their knees whilst the prince remained standing. LeGros paused and then joined them.

It wasn't only out of reverence for the dead that they knelt. They had realised that they were witnesses not only to the death of a king after a long reign, but that they were in at the very beginning of the reign of King Louis, the tenth of that name.

THE CLOSING OF THE CIRCLE

Jesuit headquarters, Rome, 2010

Relaxed after his flight and with the story clear in his head, Brother Aloysius was preparing his interim report to the Father General. He was now confident he could sketch out the events that followed the purge of 1307 with the rallying of survivors in Scotland. Pieces of evidence, which standing alone were mere curiosities, like random jigsaw pieces, began eventually to gather coherence. He began to write:

"The death of Pope Clement was well attested from several witnesses. The end of King Philip whilst hunting in his forest of Fontainebleau, however it seemed at the time, did not appear at this distance to have been an accident, since a modern researcher (at my instigation), had found the records of membership of the Templars of that region, and discovered that a man by the name of LeGros from the Fontainebleau district had been a Templar sergeant at the right time, who was also listed as a relapsed heretic in Church records. Together with others, he had met his fiery end in Marseilles, far away from Fontainebleau. He almost certainly was the Le Gros son.

That provided motive enough, which when compared with the document that had survived of Sir Geraint's recollections, seemed to confirm much later that what the knight had heard within the fugitive order, was indeed how it had happened.

The battle of Bannockburn had been covered in 'broad brushstrokes' by several historians, although very little detail of the fighting of seven centuries before had been available. Here again, Sir Geraint's unique memories were invaluable, particularly as to how Robert the Bruce had pardoned Geraint's brother Sir Luke of Pembroke, and set him at liberty, which did have the 'ring of truth'.

The Welsh knight's account of what came next with the voyage up the Rhine and thereafter, was all new material except that an antiquary in the city of Edinburgh had a fascinating early parchment map of Netherlands provenance, on which was marked the great river all the way through central Europe to its several mouths debouching into the North Sea. It passed certain German and Alsatian cities along its length, including the Swiss city of Basel, far from the sea. This map Al had acquired after touring Edinburgh and Stirling antique shops, in search of anything from that period, when visiting Scotland to see Castle Aird for himself, and the battlefield of Bannockburn, now largely developed as a housing estate.

The story of the 'camp followers brigade' that appeared at a critical time in the Bannockburn battle, is an explanation of where the 'new troops' referred to in existing histories came from. No other adequate explanation has been advanced. But made up for the most part as they were, of women and boys, it is understandable that English historians of the period, seeking to explain the ruin of Edward's powerful magnates and great army, would not wish to dwell on that perhaps embarrassing point.

The Council's decision to send troops to Switzerland, in answer to the appeal from the rebellious foresters of the three cantons, was described in Sir Geraint's document. As he says, he had been told only after arriving in Europe, of the purpose of the mission (his 'pay grade' had not previously entitled him to that information), and with the ever present fear of individual capture and harsh interrogation, by the Dominicans, 'need to know' was clearly an intelligent policy. It is not clear if Sir Paul, who was of a higher rank, did or did not know the details of the mission before leaving Scotland.

Next, Brother Daly wrote what was primarily an aide memoir: "At this stage I can verify that the expedition to Schwyz, was led by the Fraternity's Marshal, Sir Peter Breydel (who first attracted historians interest with his role at the battle of Courtrai in Flanders, in 1302). His co-leader was an intriguing civilian, Master Peter Proudhomme, a leading architect of the period whose great work was the Freiberg Cathedral in the Black Forest, who was also the Master of the Architect's fraternity: "the Company of the Children of Solomon."

He is notable as the first non-Templar to serve on the Fraternity Council. He appears, whatever else, to have represented what might be called a Masonic interest and to be a link to the longstanding connection between the two fraternities, going back to the 1130's.

I am now concentrating on what I will call 'the Swiss Expedition,' which I believe will explain where the Fraternity's leaders went to, in the period before Scotland was relieved of the papal interdict in the early 1320's. That was of course after the 'Declarations of Arbroath' and Scotland was restored to enjoy normal relations between Edinburgh and the Papacy.

The death of King Robert came in 1329. It seems that the Constable of Scotland had earlier reported to his sovereign that Castle Aird was now uninhabited and had been returned to the MacDonald, Lord of the Isles; so the remaining Templars had dispersed some while before the date of his report in 1320, before Scotland came back into communion with the Holy See."

Al closed his notebook and drew back from his desk. Stretching his arms above his head he decided to call it a day - for a short while at least.

***

The Templar Knights

Their Secret History

Clive Lindley

VOLUME TWO

BIRTH OF A NATION 1314-1316

CONTENTS

Birth of a Nation 1314-1316

LIST OF CHARACTERS:

"Birth of a Nation"

Volume Two: "Templar Knights: Their Secret History"

Peter of Bologna. Prior, Order of the Temple

Sir Paul of Chatillon. Templar Knight

Sir Knut Peerson. Templar Knight

Sir Geraint of Monmouth. Templar Knight

Brother Aloysius Daly SJ

Giancarlo: his clerk. Rome

The Very Rev. Karl Heinz: The Jesuit Father General. Rome

Sir Peter Breydel. The Templar Marshal

Jan Ansbach: Templar top sergeant to Sir Peter Breydel

Peter Proudhomme: Architect. Master of the operative masonic company of "The Children of Solomon." - the cathedral builders division of the Compagnons du Tour de France. Co-opted Member of the Templars new 'Fraternal Council'.

Simon the Jew, Merchant in Breisach. Templar business agent

Baron von Stauffen in the Black Forest, ally of the Templars

Master Herman: Master of Works at Freiburg Munster

Brother Joacquim: Dominican Inquisitor

Master Franz: Waggonmaster from Schwyz

Sir Heinrich. Leader of the Templars contingent from Germany

Sir Martin his deputy

Ludo Von Stauffen, the Baron's son,squire to Sir Paul de Chatillon

Birth of a Nation 1314-1316

Archbishop of Constance.

Lady Melissa, daughter of the Baron von Stauffen betrothed to Sir Paul

Lady Helene, younger sister of Melissa

Underofficer Gurt, Deputy commander Town Guard of Rheinfelden

Pippin, servant to Sir Paul in The Black Forest and Schwyz

Duke Leopold von Habsburg, Austrian Army commander

Baron Otto von Cham. Officer of Duke Leopold, Castellan of Zug

Arnold Neirmayer: Leader of Schwyz resistance fighters

Werner Stauffecher: Leader of Schwyz resistance fighters

Walter Fuerst: Leader of Schwyz resistance fighters

Sir John of Potsdam. Paul's prisoner and then liegeman

PREFACE

It was a clear June day and Al Daly was on the autostrada heading north towards Switzerland. He had set out from his office in the Jesuit headquarters at via del Santo Spiritu in Rome's Vatican City, after an early morning meeting with the Jesuit Father General, The Very Reverend Karl Heinz.

Al's boss a year earlier, on instructions from the Pope had assigned him to the task of tracing the subsequent history of the Templar knights following their formal dissolution at the Council of Vienne, seven centuries earlier in 1312. Although it was true that the Templar order was officially dissolved, it was believed that many members had continued their elite heritage secretly under another name. 'The Fraternity,' as it appears to have been known.

This task, research on which had already occupied more than a year of his time, was not just a matter of resolving an academic point; there was clear evidence that the descendants of that ancient brotherhood were still settling scores with their mortal enemies, the Dominican friars who had conducted the Inquisition, that had so cruelly tortured and persecuted many members of the Order of the Temple. Then of course there was the famed Templar treasure - but that was another matter.

He was heading for the lakeside town of Lucerne in Switzerland but had decided to take his time in getting there. The previous evening he had gone down to the Via Prenestina and hired a brand new blue Fiat Panda for the journey; now he had left Rome and was on the open road, loving every minute of it.

To look at him, you would not have picked Brother Aloysius Daly SJ - to give him his full identity - as a somewhat clandestine member of the Jesuit order, a clerical secret agent in fact. Rather he had something of a tradesman's look. In his middle thirties, and standing just over five feet seven inches tall with badly cut salt and pepper hair, he was slightly stocky in appearance with a face perhaps made rugged by the fact that he had quit smoking two years previously. That had aged him ten years, he joked. But his outward appearance belied a first-class mind and an uncanny knack of finding things that others might easily miss. He had not become a Jesuit to enter the priesthood. He felt no vocation to that end, but rather born and raised in central Ireland, of course a Catholic, he had been invited to join 'the Society of Jesus', and had accepted because he admired their intellectual ability (as they had noted his), and indeed their individual courage, as demonstrated historically. Besides, he had no other plans. But for that he might well have become a researcher, a detective, or a professor, such was the enquiring nature of the man.

He was dressed for his trip in a pale blue open neck shirt and wore a pair of new dark blue jeans, purchased just for his 'holiday'. It was not really a holiday of course, he was on papal business; but after the extended tourism involved in his investigations over the past year - first in France, then Turkey, Cyprus, Crete and latterly in the British Isles - he had become tired of sitting for hours in long powered aluminum tubes and felt good at being behind the wheel, pretending at being the master of his own destiny, even if this was to be only for a few days. Besides, he was traveling incognito so as not to draw undue attention to the purpose of this visit, which was to investigate the extent of a continuing Templar connection with Switzerland, in the aftermath of the Knights' official dissolution seven centuries before.

During his visit to the UK he had uncovered tantalizing evidence of the connection between the Templars and the ancient order of freemasonry or 'the Company of the Children of Solomon,' as the Architects and Master Builders fraternity were first known in France, within the wider organization of master craftsmen known as 'Le Compannonage du Tours de France'. While researching Templar history at the British Library, Daly had unearthed the facsimile of a parchment written in the 1340s by a retired Templar warrior, one Sir Geraint of Monmouth, a form of a journal, in which he had told of a Templar expedition up the Rhine Valley to the Swiss City of Basel and beyond. That expedition, according to the Welsh knight, had been led by the Templar Marshal, Sir Peter Breydel who it appeared may have adopted that rank soon after the Battle of Bannockburn, *two years after the Templars had been formally disbanded.* Breydel was an historic figure, being one of the leaders of the resistance to King Phillip of France whose army the Flemish rebels defeated at the Battle of Courtrai, aka "The Battle of the Golden Spurs."

But what intrigued Daly even more, was the fact that accompanying Sir Peter had been a leading architect of the time, Master Peter Proudhomme, one of the builders of the Cathedral at Freiberg, in Germany's Black Forest. Proudhomme, he discovered, had close connections through the 'Children of Solomon' with the knights, and had been the first non-Templar to serve on the Fraternity Council.

The great Freiburg cathedral known as the Freiburg Munster dedicated to St Mary, is a magnificent edifice entirely dominating the ancient Black Forest city. After checking out Schwyz and other points in Switzerland, Al thought he might pay a visit to Freiberg and dig around a bit for any Templar evidence that might have lain there unnoticed. Yet if truth be known, he had wanted to make that Black Forest visit as much as a tourist, as he did for his mission.

But there was another factor playing on his mind as he drove past Genoa that day, towards his planned overnight stop at the Swiss city of Lucerne. The Templar's 'Swiss Expedition' as Daly called it, of seven centuries before, was in response to an appeal for help from the foresters of three cantons who were resisting annexation by the Austrian Habsburgs and an imminent invasion.

The Foresters had recently been excommunicated en masse by the Abbot of the neighbouring Abbey of Eisienfeld, over nothing more sinister than a longstanding quarrel over grazing rights. The spectacular abbey was to be another stop on Al's route

That Templar expedition to Switzerland had come about, shortly after the Scottish King, Robert the Bruce, had quite unexpectedly defeated the English armies of Edward II at the Battle of Bannockburn. That battle had taken place in June of 1314 and a bland childhood history rhyme went around in his head as he drove along: '*The English thought the Scots unsporting, at Bannockburn in 1314'.*

The 'unsporting' aspect as Daly now knew, was the unexpected help the Bruce had received, from the former refugee Templar knights, fetched up at Castle Aird on Scotland's western coast. But then, the Swiss connection Al Daly had discovered, came just a year after Bannockburn, coinciding with the Rhine expedition outlined in the British Library's parchment.

It culminated in the November 15th 1315 Battle of Morgarten, the event that enabled the independent republic of Switzerland, to become established.

Morgarten could well be the defining connection Al was seeking. This battle took place when foresters from the Swiss cantons of Uri, Schwyz and Unterwalden fought and defeated the mighty Austrian army of Duke Leopold. There was a scant 17 months between the two seminal battles and there were some remarkable similarities, apart from Templar involvement, not the least of which was that as a result, both small countries had been able to convincingly assert their independence from an over-powerful neighbor.

Traditionally, the victory of the cantons over the apparently all-powerful Habsburgs was attributed entirely to the spirited free foresters who had famously resisted the Austrian occupiers of their country. Al had a hunch that the intervention of the Templars, Europe's finest soldiers of the time on the side of the 'civilian' foresters, might be a more plausible explanation for the sheer extent of that extraordinary victory.

It was now late afternoon. Al had much earlier passed up the opportunity to divert from his trip and enjoy a leisurely lunch in Florence, one of his favourite cities. He was now approaching Lucerne on its eponymous lake, where he would spend the night.

Al had pre-booked a room at the Hotel des Balances on the waterfront and as he pulled off the busy lakeside road to the entrance of his hotel, he was feeling very satisfied with himself. He had skipped lunch but decided that he deserved a good dinner that evening. How better, he had mused, to enjoy that dinner than watching the sun go down over the snowcapped Swiss mountains! That prospect had actually eluded him, since sundown had already taken place, but he resolved to enjoy it the next evening when he expected to be in Schwyz on the eastern shore of the lake, a key part of his research. But anyway, the drive itself once he had left the plains of Italy behind, had been quite spectacular.

He had driven up the Alpine foothills from the south through the late afternoon, climbing above the North Italian plain through the St Gotthard pass, the road stretching ever higher until he finally saw the mountain girded, immense body of water, that was Lake Lucerne. Already in the dusk a myriad of lights shone from points around its shores and from locations dotted along the sides, even at the top of the surrounding mountains, but these were dominated by the lights of the city itself and of the traffic, much of it at this hour, leaving the city.

Tomorrow, he reflected, would be his first day proper in Switzerland. Schwyz was not much more than an hour's drive around the southern shore of Lake Lucerne. The HQ of the Swiss resistance to the Austrians, this town had been the Habsburg's target when their mighty army advanced from the castle of Zug in November 1315.

***

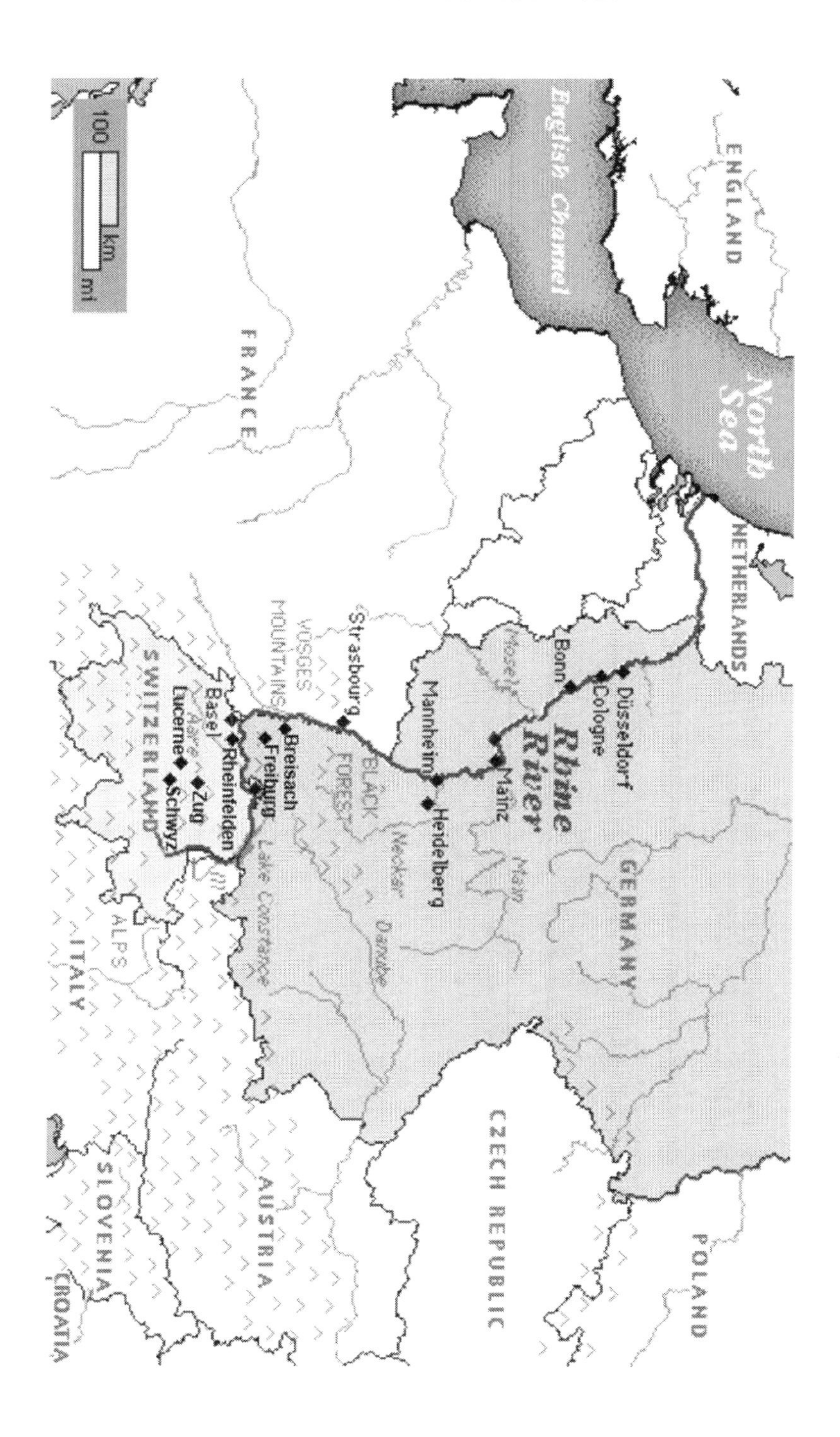
ENGLAND
English Channel
North Sea
NETHERLANDS
FRANCE
Düsseldorf
Cologne
Bonn
Rhine River
Mainz
Main
Mannheim
Heidelberg
Neckar
Strasbourg
VOSGES MOUNTAINS
BLACK FOREST
Breisach
Freiburg
Basel
Rheinfelden
Zug
Lucerne
Schwyz
SWITZERLAND
Lake Constance
Danube
GERMANY
ALPS
ITALY
CZECH REPUBLIC
POLAND
AUSTRIA
SLOVENIA
CROATIA
100
km
mi

THE RHINELAND. 1315

The master mason stretched out, his back against the weathered plank bulwark of the great Rhine barge, his legs propped up on a coil of rope. On the riverbank, the two Flemish bargemen with the tow rope over their shoulders and trailed through the harness of four horses in line behind them, hauled their weight as the vessel made steady progress against the light current. Peter Proudhomme was taking a break from hauling, as was young Paul of Chatillon, sprawled opposite him, leaning back on a bale of the horse's fodder, enjoying some late afternoon sun. Paul's shoulders felt raw, as did his hands from the hours, when taking his turn he had carried the taut rope, helping to haul the barge. Both the master mason and the young knight had decided to take their turn spelling the bargees, mainly to keep exercised on the long slow journey east into central Europe, but haul vigorously though they did, they knew that it was the horses that did most of the work.

There were long reaches of the great river now in high summer, at its most shallow, where its course took it away from the bank between long shoals that would be submerged later in the year when the river was in full flood. At such reaches the barge could no longer be hauled. Then the draught animal teams would be unhitched and led along the bank. That was when the bargees used their skills and whatever wind was available to fill the small sail on the stubby mast, to keep moving east against the weak current, poling off the mud banks and shoals. If the wind was too feeble or contrary to them, they made little progress.

In other circumstances, it would sometimes have been better just to moor and wait. But the expedition's leaders were highly conscious of the fact that there was a war to be fought that wouldn't wait for them, nor would the wind oblige. On such occasions they asked Sir Geraint, or the Marshal commanding the military column half a mile to their rear, to send some well-muscled volunteers up forward to them, who with sturdy poles could join in and follow the example of the bargees. With help on this scale, even when becalmed, they were able to maintain a steady momentum up the great river. Nothing in the young knight's clothing - a long plain smock over breeches and boots - marked him out, except the close fitting white cloth helmet worn by such as architects and master builders. His role and costume on this mission was to travel as pupil to the master mason, who on behalf of his fellow master masons and architects of the fraternity of 'the Children of Solomon', for reasons of a shared Cistercian parentage, earlier patronage and family connections, amongst others, had not hesitated to reach out to the persecuted Templars in their time of trouble, then joined with them in their new fraternity. A second barge followed. In addition to the vessel's crew of two regular Flemish bargees, this vessel carried two more of the brethren, one of whom was the Danish knight Knut Peerson; the other a young Flemish Templar, not yet knighted.

The river was broad, though in these summer months, not powerful, as it flowed against them towards the now distant sea. High above, a pair of buzzards hardly more than specks in the sky, slowly wheeled, patrolling the verdant riverbanks below them. At various reaches the stream divided, exposing mud flats with long-legged water birds striding, their slender beaks picking for food. Between the flats, both shallow and deep currents moved steadily, yet slowly, always westwards. Along the whole length of the tow-path - all the way back down river to Flanders - the maintenance of which was the pretext for the local lords levying tolls at the way-stations, there were spaced out many other bulky river barges with teams of horses, or of oxen, hauling patiently against the light current. From time to time for the upstream travelers the monotony of the slow journey was relieved, by watching west-bound craft coming towards them fast down river, liberated on the favourable current, making a fair speed, some with a sail, others heavily laden where haulage beasts were used as much to brake and steady, as to propel.

No more than half a mile behind the two eastbound barges along the same towpath, followed the Marshal's column of half-armoured Templar horsemen in chainmail, two by two, walking their mounts, helmets on the saddlebow and wearing a motley but effective collection of steel accoutrements, without surcoats or heraldic devices, consistent with their cover story that they were a 'free company' of men at arms, otherwise known and widely feared as 'soldiers of fortune' - mercenaries. Few would presume to question these serious looking men of violence. Their purpose, they would have said (if they had deigned to even answer), was to take up paid employment with the Habsburg Duke in his forthcoming war against the rebel foresters of Schwyz. There were in this group some twenty-five knights and sergeants, together with squires, grooms, farriers and servants, all men and boys, perhaps sixty souls in all, together with carts carrying their tents and supplies bringing up the rear of the column. There were in total some eighty horses, with the individual heavy chargers being led by squires, whilst the fighting men up front bestrode their riding hacks.

The new Marshal of the Order, here using his real name Sir Peter Breydel, was in command. Sir Geraint of Monmouth was his second and the Marshal also had with him Jan Ansbach, his leading sergeant, another veteran of the 'Battle of the Golden Spurs' at Courtrai, in Flanders. Jan had originally come with him when summoned by the Templar chiefs, to Scotland from Bruges, to fight at Bannockburn. The 'Golden Spurs' fight 12 years prior to Bannockburn in 1302 was a European 'first,' where disciplined foot-soldiers, armed with 16 foot pikes, together with their archers, had triumphed over a large, aristocratic and disdainful, cavalry army that failed to break their line, the victory an unprecedented event in medieval Europe. Bannockburn just one year ago, had seen a repeat of the same phenomenon.

The top sergeant forcefully dealt with the daily detail of the march, which included posting sentries when stationary and always, when on the march, having scouts out both ahead and behind.

The master mason's barge was low in the water carrying as it was, twelve heavy crates of statuary destined for the great cathedral being built at Freiburg. But beneath that cargo, separated by a framed layer of wooden planks, were steel pike heads, greased against rust and packed in straw, each with elongated sharp points, a wicked blade and a hook. They were of the same kind that had done such damage at Bannockburn. In addition the barge carried a supply of the many pointed caltrops, the anti-cavalry weapon of steel spiked balls that strewn before them, had wreaked such damage on the English cavalry there.

Knut's barge, traveling close behind that of the master mason, ostensibly for security, was laden with bales of a heavy wool covered with a roped down canopy of sailcloth, stacked high above the level of the hatch in the deck, for all to see. Knut had earlier trained at a merchant house in Bergen and could hold his own in either idle conversation or trading talk as to this cargo, the heavy oily water-resistant Norwegian wool, with its ultimate destination in Northern Italy. But below that deck, buried beneath the baled wool, were more pike heads with chests of steel caps, steel link chain corselets and other armour, intended for their new allies.

The journey had started out some five weeks before, crossing the North Sea on a trading vessel from the Scottish port of Leith and entering one of the waterways that made up the mouth of the Rhine where they took on a pilot; then journeying via rivers and canals - it was not always clear which was which - as far as Utrecht. There they disembarked.

Those of the military party were taken off to a stud farm, which had long been discreetly owned by the Templars, where they were equipped with trained warhorses. There were very few such great animals in Scotland and the carts and servants recruited by the local agent, joined the travellers there. Those traveling on by barge were taken to a nearby town called Deventer, where the two river barges and their cargoes had been prepared, ready for them. The bargees waiting there were employed by the merchant who owned the river barges, a mercantile brother of the Templars. He now fulfilled the same role for the Fraternity, and personally brought them there along the waterways from Utrecht. The master mason's cargo had been arranged for him by people of his own masonic fraternity, who had an important lodge in Deventer. From there they imported selected stone and building materials for the town's craftsmen. In this charming town of Deventer, completely encircled by water, the travellers were clearly amongst friends.

The local agent of the Fraternity, who was responsible for getting them on their way - himself a prosperous river merchant, efficiently saw to the reunion of the two parts of the expedition, and the journey east commenced.

The long slow journey up the great river Rhine would have been tedious in the extreme, had it not been for Paul's discovery that Peter Proudhomme, the master-mason, was a remarkable man with an endless wealth of tales to tell of his journeys and adventures in foreign parts.

On those long lazy afternoons whilst the barges were being hauled and the two of them had been relieved by the bargees leading the big draught horses, they resumed their relaxed sprawling on the sunlit deck. Then the master mason and the young knight would fall to conversation.

"Brother Paul", the older man started, "until we arrive in Schwyz, it is agreed that you are officially pupil to a master mason, so I need to tell you some of the things that you should know about the craft, of which you are now a temporary member." "Better that than I fall asleep, Master Peter", the knight replied, "but if you see me nodding off do please give me a dig - I will take no offence."

"Well, since your life might depend upon it - we shall be travelling amongst people shortly, some of whom might have suspicions of our party, so staying awake would be more than a good idea," the master responded briskly! Paul quickly sat up, apologetic, now fully awake and all attention.

"First about my calling - also yours at least for these few months. That world of which you are now a part, is one that is almost unique, since there are still so few of us architects here in all of western Christendom. The craft of building in stone was completely lost here in the west for some five hundred years until two centuries back, when in Northern France the barons started to replace their wooden castles with stone. Now, I expect you have never seen even one wooden castle." Master Peter caught the nod of agreement and continued.

"After the conquest of England, William of Normandy built the White Tower on the River Thames to keep a grip on London. I think it was the first wholly stone new building in England, for five or six hundred years - since the Romans had left.

"But mostly, building in stone restarted later from about the time of the crusades, with warriors returning home and the beginning of your Order of the Temple. For hundreds of years, since the Romans were over-run here in the west, the Germanic tribes that invaded our ancestors did not have the knowledge to work in stone other than simple structures - walls with wooden or thatched roofs ; nor yet the good sense to keep alive those who did have these skills. They had all been killed off or made into slaves.

It was after the Crusader conquest of Jerusalem, when stone building, both of fortresses and churches once again appeared, that architecture as a profession and stonemasonry as a trade, which had long thrived in Byzantium and eastern Christendom, started up once more, here in the west.

"Back in Outremer, where there was not much wood, stonework had always been important. From then on, stonemasons were highly valued by both sides. When a city or a castle fell and there were prisoners, the stonemason's lives would usually be safe, because they were going to be working for their new masters. One day perhaps I will tell you of the Mongols, who take such skilled prisoners thousands of miles back to their remote country to build for them - when otherwise they will kill everything that breathes, in any city that has resisted them."

It was summer, hot and blissful. After a strenuous morning helping to pull the barge, stretching out now on the warm wooden planks, listening to the intriguing story, Paul reflected drowsily, watching the birds wheeling overhead against the azure sky, thinking how far away this all seemed from cities under attack by Asian warriors. He had himself some experience of being under siege by Kurds and Turks in Cilicia - happily his castle with its Templar garrison did not fall, but now as he listened to the older man, it all seemed rather distant and unreal.

They both heard the horse being ridden hard along the riverbank, towards them. That sounded like trouble. They sat up and peered over the bulwark to see one of the scouts, normally a mile or more ahead, nearly abreast of them, heading back to the mounted party. As he passed they stood. He saw them looking, slowed and shouted, "A large group of horsemen coming along the riverbank, this way." He then spurred his mount and continued on towards their armed group riding slowly not far behind, in column of twos, with the kitchen and baggage carts at their rear.

As the scout approached, the Marshal riding alongside his master sergeant raised his arm to halt the column. Having received the report he gave some orders in quick succession to Jan Ansbach who fell back, giving out these orders rank by rank, as he moved down the column. Two riders broke away from the column and rode fast inland, away from the river, so as to scout the flank of the oncoming party for any surprises. The reporting scout had told the Marshal, that the group they had spotted, would at their present pace, take a further twenty minutes or a half hour to reach that point. They were he said, looking at all the barges preceding the two Templar vessels - not methodically, like inspectors - but probably, he thought, to see whether there was anything to which they might want to help themselves.

The Templar ranks were now abuzz with activity as the horsemen dismounted from their palfreys, the grooms quickly saddled the great destriers, their squires helped them don their plate armour breastplates, greaves and gauntlets over their customary chainmail. Then they mounted and were handed up their helmets and lances. The main body reformed as two parallel steel-clad ranks of twelve, no identifying surcoats, lances upright and helmet visors open. With the top sergeant barking at them, the two lines moved forward only as far as to stand about thirty yards ahead of their first barge, which had now halted. The bargees had held back the four-horse team whilst the second barge caught them up. They then secured the two vessels to the riverbank, unhitched all the draught animals and led them back, behind the lines of horsemen. Out in front, the Marshal sat his charger staring up river, with the top sergeant once more beside him. Sir Geraint similarly led his squadron, positioned behind the Marshal's line. They remained silent, their upright lances anchored on their stirrups, and rather eerily still, except for minor movements of some warhorses, their heads tossing, reacting to the irritation of summers' flies.

Altogether their steel-clad readiness and grim professionalism, unquestionably menacing, made them an impressive sight.

As this potential threat to their onward progress came into sight, for all of their bright heraldry of surcoats and pennants, they were not really impressive. At least, this was the common assessment the watching Templars made of them. The apparent leader, to whom older men deferred, was a well-built youth wearing expensive gilded armour, in so far as a breastplate and greaves over plain chainmail could be so described. He wore no helmet, none of them did; but at his saddlebow hung a large gilded helmet with a prominent and ugly beak, surmounted by orange and white ostrich plumes. His appearance spoke of wealth and ostentation.

His people were of two categories: several lively youthful companions were surrounding him with a degree of careless flamboyance. Apart from them and to their rear, a more restrained older group of men-at-arms in plain armour, in the livery of the young leader, made up, together with squires, about thirty mounted men.

During their slow journey through this part of the Rhine valley, the Marshal's men had sometimes seen as many as two or even three castles each day, some in apparently impregnable situations on heights above the riverbanks, or on islands in the great river. The Marshal assumed that this group were from one such castle, probably seeking to relieve their boredom by harassing the passing barges, and to see if there was anything worth purloining from their cargo. It was clear to the Marshal from their relaxed appearance that this was not the kind of interception against which he always had to be on guard, in accompanying the war supplies. Indeed he immediately understood that he held the initiative and had little to fear from these riders, quite the contrary provided that they showed a modicum of good sense.

Still fifty yards or so away, the Marshal called out for Geraint to join him and when he had arrived, commented, "They look like a bunch of lordlings out for a jaunt, presumably the local baron's brood."

"A familiar enough sight, anywhere there are travellers," Geraint agreed.

The oncoming group did not change their leisurely pace, but neither did they show any belligerence. On the leading barge Paul and Peter Proudhomme were standing up watching from the river, merely spectators. Paul had his sword out of sight, but close to hand. As the two groups closed, the tension that had mounted at this face-off was broken by the Marshal's courteous greeting, "Good afternoon, young gentlemen."

That was enough for their leader to halt his party whilst he swiftly reviewed the twin immobile ranks of plain armoured warriors facing him, their lances resting on their stirrups. He swallowed hard and tried to appear serious.

"Good afternoon to you", he managed. "I am Sir Ruprecht von Danizen and these are my father, the Baron's lands. That is our castle," he indicated a strongly situated fortress on a cliff face on the opposite side of the river. Now less certainly, he added, "And who might I ask, are you?"

"I am Sir Peter Breydel of Bruges", came the answer. "Yes, I will tell you my business, but it is my understanding that the riverbank is a highway with travel rights guaranteed by the emperor, just as my people paid some fee at the last way-station."

The younger man nodded agreement, but waited expectantly to hear the rest.

"My people whom you see here, and I are on our way to join the service of the Duke of Austria who has a small war coming up in his domains."

"Mercenaries - that explains it," mouthed the young leader to his nearest companion, who appeared to be a younger brother.

"But tell me Sir Ruprecht, since your family castle is on the other side of the river, is this side also the Baron's property?" It didn't matter one way or the other to the Marshal, but he wanted to signal that he recognized that if the young man's party were to become aggressive, that they were cut off from help by the wide river. The young man muttered something about it being his uncle's land, but the point had been made - and taken. He asked another question.

"Are you then, Sir Peter, a company of freelances? - I see no blazons", he added by way of explanation.

"That we are," came Sir Peter's terse response, with the unspoken challenge - "what of it?"

"And the barges", broke in the younger brother, "what are they to you, are they yours?"

"Well not exactly", the Marshal replied civilly, "but as I have explained we are professional fighters, which includes escort work, and since we are traveling in the same direction, and the cargo of one is for the Archbishop of Constance, we are providing protection for them… and now young gentlemen, we would like to be on our way."

He spoke to the sergeant who rapped out orders. The bargees who had heard everything took hold of the draft horses and ran to hitch them up, so the barges started to move again.

The two lines of mounted Templars moved forwards in their existing wide formation so the miscellaneous mounted men facing them had to back off to give ground and move wide, to let them pass. The Templar squires and grooms all mounted up behind them, together with the luggage and kitchen carts, were immediately mobile. As the knights passed the local Baron's men, the young Sir Ruprecht spoke up again, in some attempt to regain the initiative, in the hearing of his following.

"Very impressive, Sir Peter. My father would be interested to meet you - and perhaps discuss some future employment by him.

"We go now to the lands of the Duke Leopold," came the reply over his shoulder, "but perhaps next year we may be returning to Flanders and if we are free, I know your family name and that is your castle across the river."

"How to make a promise sound like a threat," was the way Geraint summarized it to Paul later.

***

Riverine life returned to its familiar slow pace. The master mason continued with teaching Paul the outlines of the mason's craft, so he could pass muster in the role the hierarchy had decided for him, to explain his wide ranging travelling, both now and in the future. He also showed some hand signals of recognition and spoke phrases used by travelling brethren of the Masonic fraternity, to identify themselves, which the High Council had decided to adopt for the whole fraternity

It became like a series of tutorials as after their morning exertions with the hauling team, they relaxed in the summer sun of each afternoon. "St Bernard was the great man of the Cistercians," the master mason repeated, "just as it was he who arranged for your Templars there in Jerusalem to become an Order of the Church. He probably, more than any other man revived the stonemason's craft in western Christendom, which moved quickly forward to the great Gothic cathedrals. But you cannot just take a bright lad, a monk, let's say, who could maybe read and write but could hardly understand the principles of selecting the rock, quarrying and transporting it, shaping it to an exact set of mathematical measurements, and then fitting it together - as a piece in a complex puzzle. It probably started that way since back then, hardly anyone else had an education, but it couldn't go on. Bernard, the abbot of Clairvaux's own brother, Achard de les Fontaines, who had been in Italy was a trained architect, and at about the same time as your Templar Order was becoming organised, Bernard's new abbey at Clairvaux included the first school of architecture in the west, since Roman times.

That forest of Clairvaux in which the abbey stands was donated by his cousin and friend, the Count of Champagne, the first patron of the Templars, who sent a company of knights to the Holy Land with the First Crusade, as you will have learned as a squire at the Temple. When it was over many crusaders returned home, but that group of knights from Champagne and Flanders stayed on and became the first Knights Templar, with their first Grandmaster being another cousin and former vassal of the Count.

"Another factor, very often, great cathedrals might take fifty or a hundred years or more to complete. That meant that a family, or a lodge of particular masons would contract to design it, start it and to finish it, and that usually meant generations of the same families, which after all, monks do not have. Besides, doing heavy labour training as stone workers, was not what bright literate young men, of any intelligence or education, would think of doing. The Italians describe our work as '*sciente*' - it is for intellectuals. But, tell me, did you when you were serving in Paris, visit the great Abbey Church of St Denis?"

"I did," Paul assented. "I was just a squire, part of a Templar escort for some member of the King's family who had died. As you know, they mostly go there to be buried."

"Well then, you may already know that this was one of the first great churches in stone in the west, but of course many more have been built since then, all over Christendom. You may not know however, that it was your Order that made that possible. They arranged the finance for many a bishop who wanted to outshine his neighbours - bigger and better cathedrals, no? That could be done because amongst the rather sparse collateral these bishops could offer for loans, the holy relics they offered were acceptable to the Templars, and often..."

The conversation lapsed by mutual consent, as they paused to watch a large and majestic flotilla of stately white swans glide past them in V-formation, riding the downstream current and ignoring them completely.

Paul returned his attention to the master mason looking puzzled. "But going back to the question of where did the craftsmen come from? As you said, nothing had been built for several hundred years and a monk with reading skills isn't going to build St Denis out of looking at a book."

"Exactly! Now we are getting there," came the reply. "The skills existed alright, but not anywhere in western Christendom. From what I will be telling you now about our shared origins, you can work out some other things like why I am on your Council, although I was not of your military Order."

"Yes, quite a few of us have wondered that", Paul interjected with a smile.

"I am sure they impressed upon you the history of your order before you were accepted, and I think you will know the beginnings, but forgive me for perhaps reminding you." Paul smiled his acknowledgement. "You know that your Templars came into official existence when the Church fathers at Troyes Council, agreed it should be so, and you probably know that this was due to the special pleading of the brilliant churchman of his day, of whom I just spoke, the Abbot of Clairvaux, the later Saint Bernard. Now apart from being the unquestioned patron of your order - he willed it into being; he was better known as the great leader of the Cistercian Order, which over the centuries since his time has built hundreds of Cistercian monasteries - still they are building - all across Europe - and in stone! Are you hearing what I am saying?"

"I know a little of this already. I know", Paul told him, "that Count Hugh of Champagne gave critical help to Bernard's Cistercians at the beginning. He gave him the very land and the finance to build his first foundation, and that same Count of Champagne was the original founder of the Order of the Temple, long before it was so proclaimed. The first of our Grand Masters, Hugh de Payens was his cousin and vassal. The Count in his old age eventually passed on his title and his estates and worldly possessions back in France, and retired into the Order in Jerusalem where he lived and died as an ordinary brother knight."

"So," the master mason intervened, "when I tell you that it was this combination of the Templars and the Cistercians that brought training and teaching modern stonemasonry, and all its related skills, back to western Europe, then you won't be surprised." Master Peter suggested.

"I never thought of it," Paul told him, "but now you explain… please tell me more."

Before he could do so, a shout from one of the bargees on the towpath interrupted. "Masters", he called pointing to the far side of the river, about eighty yards wide at this point. They saw a long line of armoured men helmeted and carrying upright lances moving slowly along matching the barges' slow progress. "Well, well," muttered Paul, "it looks as though the young Sir Ruprecht is wanting to make a point." The gilded, beaked helmet reflecting the afternoon sun, with its orange plume, confirmed the identity of the leading knight, "I think he needs us to see that his following is more than we earlier encountered - there must be a hundred of them across there, but at least he has the good sense to keep the river between us."

Minutes later, they heard and saw two Templars riding fast overtaking the barge, followed by another knight riding up behind them, who slowed to a walk as he came abreast.

It was Geraint. "The Marshal asked me to come and tell you to pay no attention to the lordlings over there. However he is sending out scouts, to see where the next bridging point is and to pick out a defensible campsite for us, for tonight, just in case it gets serious, which he doesn't think it will. But then he's not known for taking chances. You chaps look comfortable, lazing in the sunshine", he added enviously.

"Alright Geraint," Paul responded, "but just come and see us in the mornings when we haul this damn tub - and then offer to change places."

The escorting lordlings had disappeared from sight, as the far bank they could see was now heavily wooded to the river's edge. They had not emerged before late afternoon, when the Marshal himself rode up and said that their party would be camping about a mile further along, which duly happened.

***

"More will follow another time, in what I will say," the master said, " but I now move on to the important part of my story, which is of the craft, which you, as my presumed pupil, are supposed to know about. You have seen St Denis and maybe other cathedrals, probably also Notre Dame in Paris." the younger man nodded. "You will then realize that there is a rare science involved in engineering these great structures of stone blocks, building roofs of stone, and doing it in such a way that it doesn't just fall down when a strong wind blows. What knight have you ever known, or priest, or nobleman, or merchant that would know how to even start to do that, I ask you?" He stopped only to draw breath whilst Paul was already hungry for more - he found it hard to believe that he had never before reflected on these things.

The architect resumed, "The ancient science that makes this possible is called mathematics but because we have talked about the ancients understanding these skills and their having been lost in the Barbarian ages after the Romans, that was in the west. Yet it is obvious that they survived somewhere. That 'somewhere' is in the great city on the edge of Christendom that straddles east and west, across the waterway called the Bosporus. It is the city of the Emperor of the East, Constantinople, the capital of what they still call Eastern Rome. It has stood for a thousand years already and contains some of the most magnificent buildings in the world - not in ruins as you may see in Rome, or Greece, or Syria, but as a living city surrounded by mighty walls twelve metres high, five metres thick and several miles around. The present walls are eight or nine hundred years old and even now, still in daily use.

"I was lucky," Master Peter continued, "to be born to a family of a long line of master-builders - architects, as they are called by the Greeks of Byzantium, and grew up in Italy in the city of Ravenna, where they were well established. I also spent some years in the city of Constantinople like my brothers, my uncles, and my own father, with never a thought to be anything other than such a person myself. But enough, Brother Paul. It is close to dusk and we will continue this talk and let us hope we will have dry warm afternoons on this deck to do so."

***

The next day however it rained and the rain again persisted through the following day, so it was half a week before they once again were private and unhurried, sufficient for the talk to continue. It was in the morning, after they had washed themselves in pans of river water, that first the master told Paul of his discussion with the Marshal at the campfire, on the previous evening.

"Before we talk later today of the ancients and the craft of us masons, there is word arrived via a messenger who came from Worms, the last city we passed, to catch up with the Marshal yesterday. He told me of it last evening and asked that I should tell you discreetly and our colleagues behind on the wool barge. Our friends in the city of Worms back there had received a carrier bird alerting us to some bad news. The Dominicans have caught one of our brethren who had travelled from Scotland to France, presumably returning to his own people. How he was found out, we don't know, but he was seen being taken as he came off the vessel he was travelling on, by soldiers supervised by a pair of Black Dominicans, in the harbour at Boulogne.

"We must assume that they now - or soon - will know whatever that poor man knew, which may not be a lot, but we must understand that they must certainly know the following items," he reeled them off, "that the Order is continuing, despite the Church's ban; that we played a role at the battle of Bannockburn; that Castle Aird is our headquarters - although they probably knew that already. He also would have known that we ourselves, a sizeable body of fully equipped knights and sergeants left Scotland by sea before he did, to travel across to the European continent, but since our party themselves did not know where or why until they arrived, then he couldn't have told them much more, than that we were headed off somewhere."

"From what I understand about the way they work," Paul volunteered, "the Doms will now despatch a letter to all of their main houses, right across Christendom, telling them of these things and instructing them to keep watch for us - the Marshal's party at any rate -it will take them months to get the word out. But tell me, Master Peter, do we know if the Black Doms have houses in the towns where we are going?"

"I fear that they do," he replied. "They have a small house in the river port of Breisach where we dock, but it's the sort of place where they would put some of their elderly brethren out to grass. In fact, I was told that they intended to next use it as a nunnery. However, in Freiburg, they have a big thriving monastery, right in the city centre, close in fact to where you and I are delivering this load," he banged on the deck with one heel of his outstretched leg, "at the Freiburg Munster, which you would call the cathedral. So young Paul, although they can know of no connection between us and the missing Templar knights, you had better listen and well remember what I am telling you, the knowledge of which might serve to establish your credentials as pupil to a master mason."

Master Peter patiently explained that it was the crusades that had opened up the appetites amongst magnates of the west, for great buildings in stone. Leaders of the crusades had included kings, dukes, even the western emperor and many great regional leaders of wealth and power. The meeting point for early crusaders from the west had been the great city on the Bosporus, Constantinople, capital of eastern Rome. It had been normal for the eastern emperor to re-provision the western armies and expeditions on the way to Outremer, and whilst the masses of largely undisciplined troops and camp followers were kept outside the walls of the great city, the noblemen were admitted and shown around.

There amongst other marvels, they saw the amazing Haghia Sophia, the Basilica of the Holy Wisdom, by far the greatest church in the entire world. Its wide dome, defying gravity, measures more than thirty metres across, and this mighty church was, even back then, 500 years old. The main water cistern, another marvel nearby, itself the size of a small buried city, is a miracle of engineering with its forests of classical columns supporting the stone roof, many of them taken from the ruins of ancient Greek Mediterranean cities. Here was the clean drinking water fed by a piped underground stream, for the city's one million inhabitants - the means of surviving protracted sieges. There were palaces, monasteries, churches, merchants houses, docks, warehouses all built of stone or brick. Water was channelled in clay pipes, including fountains in many public places. Sewers likewise buried below ground, to outfalls beyond the city walls. All of this, commonplace enough in the great city, had not been seen in the west since Roman times, as the skills of building in stone had been lost in western Christendom.

"After the western lords saw all this, not only did that spell the beginning of a new era in building for the west, but so much did they lust after what they had seen in the great city that some of them were all for forgetting their vows to redeem the holy places in Jerusalem, and instead to turn their military might into conquering this Christian city and empire. It might have happened then, in the very first crusade when they were there in 1097 - it was even discussed in their high council - but as it turned out, they kept their vows and moved on across Anatolia, to eventually take Jerusalem, two years later.

"But as you well know, the Fourth Crusade - a hundred years later in 1204 did finish up there at the great city. It got no further, all thoughts of salvation forgotten in favour of the lust for the wealth and luxury of Constantinople. I know that the military orders, both yours and the Hospitalers were not involved in that disgraceful business. But the western crusaders, our people, drove out the emperor and his Greek Orthodox Christianity and bargained between them who would rule it as a western kingdom, as they did for the next sixty years, under the Roman pope.

"So from the time of the early 1100s then, western lords hired architects and builders from the eastern empire who became a highly-paid privileged class - but one that did not fit into the existing social structures of peasant, priest or nobleman - nor yet of the emerging class of city merchants. Being free, they could please themselves where and for whom they worked and they were quite apart, as were your Templars, of the 'chain-of-duty' feudal system.

"Whole families, including mine, left the eastern empire to take up new residence in the west and whilst the church commissioned them to build mighty cathedrals, the lords employed them to include the latest military technologies in the new stone castles and fortresses. Much of the knowledge for this came from the wars in Outremer.

"So, here we have a few highly skilled experts greatly courted to go to this king or that duke or to some bishop, but independent, outside the chains of feudal duty. They could always please themselves, as can I, whether to accept a commission, or not!"

They both felt some rain drops; the sky looked as though it could go either way. They reached for their cloaks and carried on the conversation.

"Like many great mysteries," Master Peter went on - "religions are the best and most timeless examples - those who have made it to the top realize that their secrets must be safeguarded. So builders, like many trades with their own skills, concentrated in the cities and formed guilds and set standards for new men to meet. Towns started to be rebuilt in brick and wood and local men could be trained in this, and local masters within the towns would emerge and become the leaders of the guild. But unlike the bakers and leather workers and smiths and other tradesmen, the building trade required a special kind of knowledge, beyond cutting, transporting and carving stone, and building scaffolding to erect walls.

"Also, as I said earlier, they had to know that these immense buildings would not fall down, or their roofs collapse. These were the higher engineering skills, somewhere between an art and a science, but based on mathematics. So literacy and draughtsmanship is obligatory and it led to the degree of master mason, men like me and for which you are now being presented as being on the way towards that qualification. Now, enough of your lessons and back to the present!

"I currently have several projects at various stages of building around Christendom. One of them happens to be at the great Munster Church at Freiburg, which you will soon see. There is a local master of works there, who deals with all daily and periodic events with the clients who are the canons of the cathedral, and I have a trained man, a former pupil indeed, with him there who provides the technical knowledge that the locals do not have, and it is he who keeps me informed. This journey for me now is explained by my need to superintend those works. I have other calls in other places.

"That is my work, Brother Paul. It makes me one of the few privileged ones in this feudal world of the west, who can travel widely and come and go as I choose. It also means that great lords and the princes of the church are concerned with my welfare and that I should come to no harm. They all have their projects and without their architect, of whom there are very few, their castles and abbeys don't get built, or do - badly, and then fall down!

"All across the Christian world in every sizeable town and city, as you will find, there are lodges of local masons and I, by certain hand clasps, some words, some signifying, can identify myself and discover the degree of attainment of my interlocutor. As a travelling master I also receive great honour, and whatever assistance I might need.

“Two other matters, Brother Paul. I spoke of Constantinople as where this craft survived but you should know that it was already old before the first stones of Constantine’s new city were laid, a thousand years ago, long before that was built, before all the great buildings of Rome, there were those of Greece which they copied, there were the ziggurats of Babylon and Assyria, the Temple of Solomon itself, after which both your Order and my Companions styled themselves upon. All of these depended on skill and knowledge, hence the calling of the architect.

“Now because I don’t want you to believe that this has all been idle conversation to while away the time, I can tell you that I have already had long conversations with Brother Prior before we left Scotland, about just this. That we both agree that for our new brotherhood which must be so very discreet, there is much that can be learned to the benefit of our cause from the lodge’s structure that I have described, of the organised master masons.”

***

Infrequently on this journey was the monotony of slow progress relieved by anyone overtaking them on the tow path, since the pace was set all along its length by the slow-moving wooden river barges. There were long mule trains regularly travelling on both banks of the river and it seemed ironic that these heavily laden beasts, moving slowly though they were, would still overtake the two barges, this happening sometimes several times a day.

Local peasants and farmers from time to time passed by, leaving a hurried “Praise God” on the air behind them. Rarely indeed did a mounted man other than their own, come by and when so, usually at a trot, but it had been a day or two since last this occurred.

The next day it was Paul’s turn to talk at length. This time he chose to speak, as side by side they were leading the draught horses along the towpath, with the bargees back on board the slow moving barge, having a break.

Paul had promised to tell his story, which he knew by now would look pale by comparison with that of his older companion. But to almost anyone else of his age group and indeed older, it was already quite remarkable, which the master appreciated as Paul's story unfolded.

Despite his youth, he had already travelled extensively. Sent with a group from the Paris Temple in early 1307, through France to the Mediterranean city of Marseilles and joining a Templar galley there, he travelled down the inland sea to Cyprus, where a few days from his 17th birthday, he was formally accepted into the Order of the Temple. As a result he missed the tragic drama that had overtaken his new family, back in the west. During the time of the furore of the news from Paris - of the arrest of their Grand Master and any Templars the king's men could lay their hands on, Paul had been quite unaware of these events, serving as he was across the strait of the eastern Mediterranean from Cyprus, in the garrison of a fortress high in the mountains of Cilicia, the gateway between Syria and Anatolia. There he had been bloodied in war, fighting against the Turkish allies of the Mamelukes who were seeking to control the land route to and from Syria to Anatolia and the eastern empire.

To consolidate their expulsion of Christian forces from the Holy Land, after their capture of the crusader's last stronghold, the port city of Acre, the Mamelukes had tried to subdue the Christian Armenian castles and mountain passes through to Turkish Anatolia, including the few remaining outposts of the military orders, but failed to achieve that, having had only partial success.

It was there that Paul had seen action and whilst on a war footing he and his comrades heard, to their confusion and dismay, of the inexplicable events in France. They were told of the arrest there of the grandmaster, together with the hierarchy of the Order, when his local commander broke the news of it to the assembled Templars; this at a time just before they went into battle. But the commander was unable to give them any explanations.

When Paul's tour of duty was over, he was relieved of garrison duties and returned from Cilicia to Cyprus. There his orders were that he was to move on with a detail from their island fortress, to western Europe. He had been picked to travel, with others, as an aide and escort to the Marshal of the Order. The journey was to go as far as the outermost western fringe of

Christendom at Scotland, which hitherto Paul had only vaguely heard of, there to the Templar's great castle at Aird on the wild Argyllshire coast.

Paul told Master Peter, who listened attentively, of how their party of some dozen men, knights, sergeants and squires, travelled with the Marshal in a war galley of the Order, first from Cyprus to one of the surviving Templar commanderies in Greece, from where they had crossed the Adriatic to Venice. Arriving there by night, their galley had gone straight to the quay of the Teutonic Knights, where they were expected.

The Teutonic Marshal who was an old comrade of the Templar Marshal from the fighting in Acre, had been greatly distressed at what had had happened to the Templars since the French King's treacherous swoop on them in 1307.

The Templars in Scotland had arranged for their safe passage across the North Sea. It was the Teutonic Marshal who dressed them in the overmantles of Teutonic Knights and sent them off, with six of his own men, ostensibly as a sizeable group of Teutons, travelling through the Germanic states to Denmark. Paul described the cities and the sights they had seen traveling through the empire, heading towards the North Sea, which they were to cross to Scotland. But, although the Marshal and his escort completed that journey, Paul had received separate orders to leave them before reaching the North Sea coast. He was to then make his way, in plain garb with only a squire, south to Paris and had coded directions there to find and report to the local clandestine lodge for a special mission.

This was no less than to rescue the Brother Prior, at that time a papal prisoner in a Parisian monastery, and then to spirit him away to Scotland. Paul recounted the main points of how that was achieved and how they then fled Paris, riding north to get to a Flemish North Sea port to cross over to Scotland.

In that northern kingdom, the Templars had not been persecuted at all and the Templar commandery of Aberdeen to which Paul and the rescued prior took ship from Flanders, was still fully functioning, under the command of the new HQ at Castle Aird.

***

Paul knew that without doubt, he was better travelled, even though aged only twenty-five, than most of the people he would ever meet. But his story, though impressive, was eclipsed by the stories the master mason had to tell of his own travels as a young man, as far away as Persia and even northern India to see and learn about their strange societies and extraordinary buildings, which as the days went by, increasingly whetted the appetite of the young knight.

Progress along the Rhine was inevitably slow and punctuated by stops at several cities along the route. The Brethren did not join the bargemen in visiting the rowdier parts of the towns but made a point of mooring outside the cities and staying on board with the cargo. Their mounted companions made camp near the riverbank each night, close by the barges.

Even less would 'the freelances' as they now called themselves, chance going into towns, lest they were confronted and challenged by the watch, individually, or as a group. Being mounted, they instead sent out small groups of foragers to farms along the wayside and scrupulously paid good coin for chickens, vegetables, small beer and other provisions.

The bargees however did go into the towns, with which after all they were familiar, to acquire fresh bread and replenish supplies. But working for their particular master, a merchant member of the order, they had obviously been picked - and were recompensed accordingly - partly because of their sobriety and good sense.

At certain places, passing between the lands of neighbouring magnates, the barges were required to pay a toll and submit to a cursory customs inspection, which usually was just a visual glance, without the toll keepers even coming on board. The bargees were used to the route and were themselves known, so there was never any crisis. The customs tolls were quietly paid and they moved on. The Brethren did not know whether the bargemen were aware of what lay secretly below the ostensible cargoes - nobody ever talked of it.

When the mounted party in turn came up to the tollbooths, they were treated with the respect such well-armed warriors would expect, but they did not seek to bully, as they might. Instead a junior knight would be given the task of cordially telling of their destination as the Black Forest river port of Breisach and paying the small dues required. Neither the leader nor his senior colleagues could be expected to lower themselves to such a purpose. It passed as an explanation, as many travellers including armed horsemen, would follow the river routes on long journeys.

The barge passengers and the horsemen after working a long day until the light had gone, would stroll to meet up and share a meal in the pleasantly warm evenings, discussing what they hoped to do in the following days. Sometimes they could even bring an offering of fish with them to grill over the fire, but although they trailed baited hooks and lines all day behind the barges, seldom did the fish rise to it.

But it was on another long slow afternoon, as they took their ease on the barge deck, when the master mason again talked at length to the young knight. This time he addressed the future.

"Brother Paul, I want to tell you of a decision of the Council which I am charged to pass to you and separately to young Brother Knut. It depends, do I need to tell you, on you both surviving the battles that are to come, when we reach journeys end, which is in a town called Schwyz in Helvetia - and indeed on our mission there being successful. As you have been briefed by the Marshal at the outset of this expedition, there will be heavy fighting, and like Bannockburn, against long odds.

"You see the Council has been thinking of what might be the future and has concluded that our fraternity is admirably equipped to become merchant-venturers. As you know the merchanting arm of the Order has survived in good order, as has the financial investment in the Hanseatic League, so it is a logical way forward extending the known boundaries of commerce, for which in this dangerous world the military skills of the brethren will play their part; not least through their courage and discipline. There is a whole world out there and we in the west know very little about it - except that it is there. That must change. We want the brethren to be at the forefront of new discoveries and in creating trade links, where they don't yet exist.

"It is partly because of your extensive travelling and your military record, plus young Knut's merchanting experience in Bergen, and that both of you have your letters, that you two were selected for this further important mission."

Paul was no longer feeling drowsy in the warm sun, as he had until he heard this, and sat up to be sure to miss nothing.

"You see, our new Order will need to be very different to the Temple in many ways. We have to be secretive as the Templars never needed to be. We cannot rely on any princes - that is the clearest lesson of these past years. We can rely only on ourselves. Maybe the Schwyz forest cantons are indeed the place for the new order, but we must always be looking behind us. If it was known that the Templars had survived and were thriving in their heresy, it would only be a matter of time before some greedy bishops or rulers got together to declare a crusade against us - remember the Cathars in Languedoc a hundred years ago. That crusade went on for all of fifty years, and in the end the Cathars were destroyed, and the survivors murdered by the same Dominicans that tortured your fellow Templars - and my brother - to their deaths.

"So our presence in Schwyz must not attract unusual attention. You and the other mailed fighters being seen on the battlefield will be explained as your being mercenaries from Flanders and the west.

"The Council and our Prior have thought far ahead. The search for other safe places must continue, even if all goes well in Schwyz against the Habsburg Duke. Then, you will learn of another, a further destination planned for you and Brother Knut, but I will tell you more of that once we have arrived in Schwyz, and when we have done there what we have come to do." Paul was intrigued but he could see he would get no more from the master mason until he was ready, which clearly was not yet.

***

THE FREE CITIES

The baggage cart that accompanied the Marshal's mounted group carried a crate of pigeons from which, once a week, was released a bird, reporting their progress. That had, as it turned out, been as uneventful as they had hoped it would be, when after some five weeks journeying on the river, the travellers could see far off across the flatlands, the walled riverport city of Breisach. Its cathedral tower was visible from a great distance in this river plain, standing on its hill behind the city walls, dominating the wide river and all around. To their joy it meant that at last, the long dull, so slow, journey upriver was about to end.

It was now clear to the travellers why it was the master mason who was in charge of the journeying part of the expedition. On the last night before they arrived in Breisach, they gathered around the camp cooking fires, with sentries posted and the bargees left apart as usual to feed the draft horses and, by their own cooking fire, make their own meals beside the two barges.

Servants and squires had another fire to eat by. The knights and some senior sergeants however were grouped in a loose circle, eating the last of the chickens bought along the route and drinking a watered wine, when the master mason, sitting next to the new Marshal, raised his voice slightly and spoke, obviously with authority.

"Tonight, Brother Marshal and I will go into the city with two escorts, to meet the merchant who looks after our interests here.

"Brethren, tomorrow, this is the plan. The two barges will put in at the stonemasons quay where my own people will be expecting us, by about mid-morning - this is some distance on this side of the town quays outside the walls. The boxed statues from my barge will be unloaded by the people there, under supervision, and transferred onto ox-carts.

"Then, these laden carts will move out from the quay to go to the city of

Freiburg, about 15 miles inland, to the cathedral there, where my construction works are going on. Brother Paul and I will go with them. My business there will occupy Paul and me for a few days.

"Another convoy of carts belonging to our merchant friend will arrive at the stonemason's dock during the day. They will be loaded up, this time by all the rest of you, with the pikes, the armour and other weapons, and they will travel south-east, into the edge of the great forest, to the village of Stauffen, near to where there is a silver mine. Our merchant friend will have arranged the carters - local men, and all of you; the remainder of the Marshal's party will ride with them as escorts.

"The lord of these lands, the Baron von Stauffen is with us - he is indeed a former brother Templar who was allowed to leave the order many years ago when his father and elder brother died with no other heir. His castle is our objective for tomorrow night. A transaction is already made. The Marshal will arrange for an additional cargo, ingots of silver from his mine to be collected there at his castle, to be distributed amongst the carts and with these great bales of wool on top of all.

"The barges, after unloading, will wait at the stonemason's quay until we know that all these arrangements are completed. Then our good bargee companions will be released from our service, although I believe Simon, our agent in Breisach, will find them a cargo to take downstream."

"I'll wager there'll be some pigeons, if nothing else" spoke up a voice to general laughter.

"When Paul and I arrive to meet you at Stauffen in a few days' time, coming there from Freiburg, all should be ready for us to depart. We should know the details of how we are to proceed from there to Helvetia. We are to rendezvous at some point we know not now, with our Schwyzer friends who will meet us with the necessary transport.

"The difficult part of this will be passing the city of the Prince Bishop of Basel. This city has a great community of merchants and holds an important fair each year. The Bishop makes much of his income by customs duties on all cargoes crossing his bridges, entering his city, or on his reach of the river. We cannot proceed by river from this point, as it has a series of falls - this is as far as large up-river craft can go. We could of course pay the tolls on the cargo of wool loaded onto smaller craft, but obviously we do not want any inspections.

"This great river narrows down as it goes through their city and whilst most barges have reached journey's end at Basel, we of course have further to go. We are relying on the Schwyzers to tell us how we can cross the Rhine River without alerting the Prince Bishop's people, or indeed the Austrian Duke we have come all this way to fight.

"I have more to say, but any questions so far?"

One of the knights from the mounted party spoke up. "How will we, as freelances, pass through the city? Mounted, armed men in our numbers would be bound to raise concerns."

Another of the mounted party asked his question: "And with all that silver, we presumably will be guarding it, but why would carts laden, just with wool, have armed guards on them? Surely that would raise suspicions?"

"These are good questions but before I answer, has anyone else got concerns?"

"Yes", spoke up Knut. "Since we are carrying wool how do we explain why we are NOT going to the fair at Basel, which would be the natural destination for such a cargo, coming up from the North Sea?"

"That I can answer now," said the master mason. The first two questions I will answer when I have taken counsel from our merchant brother here in Breisach.

"This Norwegian wool is already sold to a trader in Venice. As you know, it is heavy, naturally oiled wool, particularly suitable for seafarers and the wool is genuinely sold at a price that includes delivery in Venice, as I have said. The papers for the transaction made in Bruges three months ago, show why the cargo is not for sale in Basel.

"You probably will not know that this 'Schwyz' is in a country of many lakes and great mountains. The town we go to is on a great lake, called Lucerne. To the south the pass that goes through the mountains, is the main route to Milan, and all of northern Italy, including Venice. When the fighting is done and we can breathe a little, then some will take the wool on packhorses through the pass and then east to Venice. Those who are chosen for that task will be told, but not before the coming battle.

"When we return from our visit this night to Master Simon, the fraternity's agent here, I hope to have the answers to the outstanding questions."

The following morning as the barges reached journey's end, there was a palpable level of excitement after the five-week voyage up river, travelled at such an excruciatingly slow pace for these men of action. The riverbanks here at Breisach were well made and the stonemasons dock was in a cove with, true-to-guild, a stone jetty, where guild labourers were waiting to take off the heavy crates for the cathedral. What lay beneath the layers of straw in the barge was unknown to them, except they would know only that it was not materials for Freiburg.

Two ox-wagons, each with six large crates laid on a straw bed, one with an additional half sized crate, started out on their slow journey which would take most of the day, whilst the master mason and Paul picked out riding horses from the string of re-mounts with the freelancers party. When they had fastened their saddlebags and other travelling possessions, they bade farewell to the Marshal and their friends and re-affirmed the meeting arrangements in Stauffen. As they rode away from the small dock, they were not sorry to see the last of the two barges, but had grasped the hands in farewell of their sturdy bargee companions, themselves looking forward to a much swifter journey downstream, returning to their homes in Flanders - but they would first have to wait to see if the merchants here had a cargo to take downriver.

Breisach was a small ancient city built on a hill, once a Roman river port and town, fully surrounded by a defensive wall coming down to the riverbank where lay the town quay. A bulky citadel imitated real life as it argued domination of the skyline with the twin towers of the cathedral, competing for the most commanding height, whilst the stonemason's dock was below the city, a mile away downstream, outside the walls. The loaded ox wagons now skirted to the east of the city to take the Freiburg road, which was well maintained. Since the time of the Romans, Breisach had been the river port for this capital city of the Black Forest, with the river its highway to the great cities of western Europe. Within minutes Paul and the Master Mason riding swiftly, could see ahead their laden carts on the totally flat land, moving steadily forward, caught them up and fell in behind them. Over to their left a substantial hill rose abruptly out of the landscape, the lower slopes of which the road margined. They could see that much of the hill was planted with row after row of leafy grapevines in concentric circles, which looked well in the morning sunlight.

Walking their horses side by side, Peter Proudhomme now told Paul about the meeting he and the Marshal had had the previous evening with the Templar's commercial agent in Breisach, Master Simon the Jew.

Simon had sent a mounted messenger along the riverbank, to intercept them before the two leaders reached the city. The man told them that his master wanted to meet them in a warehouse by the riverbank, rather than in the city itself. When they got there, Simon explained that he had not wanted them to enter the city because this way, it was not necessary for the town captain to know that they were there. "Discretion made most sense," he pointed out. "Once it was known that a group of fifty mercenaries were in the area, that might draw attention to the barge-loads of 'hardware'," as he called it, "of a kind that would have to be important to the military commander of this city."

The travellers were pleased to accept Simon's advice and indeed his command of the details of the next stages of their journey. He had important news for them from the pigeon post. First that their group of so-called freelances, would find that there was already another similar sized war band, this one of German Templars, waiting at Baron Stauffen's castle for their arrival. They would travel on to Schwyz together, all under the command of the Marshal, Sir Peter Breydel.

"That builds up the strength of the party to more than a hundred - more than a half at least, are fighting men" was Paul's response to the news.

The second piece of important news was that the Schwyzers had sent their man to lead the convoy carts with their loads of silver, and steel pikes, and what had now become their large military escort, towards their destination.

At the Breisach meeting, Simon had told his visitors that he had already met with Franz, the Schwyzer delegate, who had at the Templars request brought with him a number of carrier pigeons that would home in on Schwyz, now to be based at Breisach. Together they had discussed a route for the mounted expedition to move on from Stauffen and bypass the Bishop of Basel's territory to cross the Rhine, and then to avoid the Austrian Duke's roadblocks on the other side.

"This Simon sounds like quite a character," Paul said admiringly.

"I came to the conclusion," Peter Proudhomme replied, "that if our commercial brethren are as able as he is, then our new fraternity is going to do extremely well."

"Before we arrive in this city," the older man said as their horses ambled along behind the laden carts, at the slow pace of the harnessed oxen, "you should know a little more about our project there. It is the building of a massive cathedral; they call it the Munster hereabouts. There is there a local master builder who is master of works - a worthy and skilled man who understands and is responsible for all trades and the progress of the work. But he is not an architect, which is where we come in. I, because I am such a creature, and you, because you have outwardly at any rate, pretensions of becoming one.

"As I tried to explain on the barge, the skills that an architect needs are first to be able to even conceive of a great vaulted building, or a stone bridge or impregnable fortress, and then to know how to construct it. That calls for considerable knowledge, particularly skills in mathematics, because the load bearing has to be calculated. Now consider. No one unlettered and unable to study the writings on this - and they are in Latin translations, some from the Arabic who have well developed this skill, others from the ancient Greeks - will likely be able to master the science of mathematics. It means that even good or great craftsmen, stone workers that can make beautiful things - all the components of a cathedral say, cannot necessarily put them together in such way that building will not fall down.

"But you see that what we master masons do, is a combination of both the science, and the arts. We bring those two desirable conditions together. That, young Paul, is why architects - master masons if you will, have a prestige and a price, which brings out the respect even of arrogant princes, and prideful cardinals. Simply, most of these churchmen seek to build great edifices to their own power and glory. They certainly want their cathedral to be bigger and more magnificent than that of the neighbouring bishop - although they all say it is to God's glory. And yet they themselves don't know how to do it!

"Moreover, so few men do know, that they have become precious and if your neighbouring archbishop employs him, then he is not available to you. It is not just a matter of payment, although that obviously is large. The master mason is a walking treasure house of rare knowledge, which in fact means that he must be cherished. He is outside of their classes of warriors and priests and peasants, leave alone merchants, the system that rules everybody else's lives.

"Now this project of the Munster at Freiburg was conceived and started many years ago by a brother architect, who died a few years back. Then the Archbishop of Constance whose cathedral this is, sent his minions all over Europe to find me and bring me to him, to persuade me to finish his great building. I agreed, on suitable terms, but only on condition that I would at the same time continue on other projects elsewhere. Now that you know the background, presumably you can make intelligent responses, so long," he added drily, "as nobody asks you to work out any stresses, or provide load-bearing calculus."

Intrigued and gratified by the trouble that the Master had taken with him to explain these mysteries; Paul remained silent, except to acknowledge all that information with grateful thanks. Meanwhile his mind dwelt on the great cathedrals he had seen - St. Denis and Notre Dame in Paris, the cathedral at Troyes where the Templar Order was officially founded, at Auxerre, near to his family home at Chatillon on the Seine; St. Mark's Basilica in Venice, the cathedral in Cyprus even. He wondered how this Munster would compare with those marvels. He was intrigued and fell to thinking. Since he was no longer to be a warrior monk, as he had thought to be his future, he wondered whether he might have a calling to follow this man as his genuine student, once their immediate plans in Schwyz had come to fruition. At least, he thought, he could seek to learn this science of mathematics.

The road was metalled with broken stone originally laid in Roman times, which caused a great noise to be made as the iron-shod wheels bit down on the hard surface. Theirs were not the only carts on the road and the nearer they got to the city, the more they travelled along together with mounted men, mainly farmers it seemed, although on two occasions they had made way for well-mounted gentry and attendants, heading in the same direction.

They had seen the many spires and towers of the city for more than an hour before they approached its great walls, and the massive barbican set up at the entrance gates.

But from far off, even before they could make out the walls of the city, they had seen the enormous twin towers, as though dominating the world that could only be those of the Munster.

***

FREIBURG

Outside the walls, there was a brackish moat, not in pristine condition, as was inevitable for a city that had forgotten the last time it was besieged. Beyond this moat, in the long grass, sheep and cattle were contentedly grazing. Around the animals there was the inevitable clutter of poor men's shacks and their mean patches of land with a few scraggy poultry, which surrounded all such great cities that for long, had no more room within their walls. By now it was early afternoon and to Paul, after the long, boring river journey, the sight of the great city and his expectation of so many people, all getting on with their business, acted like a tonic. His joyful mood came down to earth when at the city gate their two carts were halted by the guards. Paul nudged his horse to follow the master mason to the front of the carts where two burly fellows in the uniform of the city watch had crossed their pikes to bar entry.

"These crates are for the Munster" Proudhomme crisply told them. "Where are the papers then?" questioned the senior guard.

"We have just come off the river, where we have been for five weeks past", he replied. "I can't let you in without papers," came the surly reply the man confident in his knowing the rules. "Maybe you should go back down the river and get them." He grinned at his mate, showing a mouthful of bad teeth.

"Look, I'll open a box, so you can see that they are indeed for the Munster", came the reply and the master mason dismounted, went over to the first cart and taking a short iron bar prised open the small box. "Look here!"

The guard leaned over sceptically and then jumped back in horror, crossing himself. His colleague peered over, and was similarly repulsed. In the box out of its straw bed grinned up at him a horribly malevolent grey stone gargoyle, the size of a deformed man, destined for the façade of the cathedral tower.

"Tis the devil himself?", the senior one said horrified, crossing himself again then holding his hand over his mouth, but moving out of their way and waving them on, out of his sight.

The carters knew the way; but all the streets that led from the gates, like this one, made their way to the cathedral close, the very centre of the city itself. Even having seen the twin towers looming closer from such a distance, now right in front of them, the sheer size and bulk of the enormous edifice quite took Paul's breath away. It was truly a magnificent spectacle, but also a very hive of activity with hundreds of workmen like insects all over its giant surfaces, and as he could now see, also within it.

The walls were built and the roof was on, but one of the twin towers was festooned with sturdy wooden scaffolding, its stages linked by wooden ladders, rising up its entire height. The west end of the building, also scaffolded, would become the main entrance. It remained yawning, open and unfinished. As Paul peered inside he could see it was the main access for the large number of tradesmen busily coming and going. In the dark interior he could also see great swarms of workers and internal pillars like a forest of even-sized and spaced stone trees, with around them ladders and more of the storied timber scaffolding that he had seen, climbing the outside of the tower.

In the city square, in the immediate precinct of the great building, was a low timber wall surrounding a half of it, separating the supposedly sacred ground - judging by the tombs there - from the rest of the workaday town centre and market place. There, fine half- timbered buildings and notably, a splendidly ornate guildhall with gilded figurines on its façade, surrounded the Munster, making a complete square out of the city's most important buildings, secular and sacred.

Apart from the hundreds of workmen who could be seen engaged on the building works, the square was full of activity from citizens of all conditions, some just promenading: stall holders, goodwives, horsemen, ox-wagons, priests, merchants, soldiers, children, herdsmen driving beasts. Everywhere Paul looked there was activity and after five weeks of staring at the slow moving Rhine, it looked quite wonderful.

As their laden wagons moved around the building to a delivery point, a clerk came out to inspect the cargo that had just arrived. When he saw that it was Peter Proudhomme bringing these crates, he bowed low and doffed his cap, as did the workmen in the immediate vicinity. "Welcome sir" he said with genuine enthusiasm. "I will send for Master Herman immediately- he is over at the Lodge."

"No need," replied Proudhomme, "we will go to him", and nudging his horse into activity, he rode to a corner of the square with Paul following behind and into a short lane. They dismounted, tossed the reins of their horses to a lad outside, and entered the stonemason's lodge where a figure with a close fitting white cap like those of the two arrivals was poring over a drawing stretched across a great table, with stones weighting each corner to keep it flat.

"Master Herman," Proudhomme called out to the man's back.

A look of surprise becoming evident pleasure, on his face, the Master of Works turned to face them.

"Greetings Master Peter, a thousand fold - you are such a rare treat for my eyes. It must be a year since you were last here - did you bring the apostles?" The words came tumbling out. He advanced his hand out, but Proudhomme clasped him in a warm embrace.

"Good to see you brother," he said. "Hopefully, God has favoured our work"

He looked at Paul still by the door. "Come over and meet my veritable right hand here in Freiburg."

"Master Herman, I present to you my pupil, Brother Paul." The master of works smiled a gap toothed smile and shook hands. "You're a lucky man to pupil with him. I look forward to knowing you better", he said, with a friendly, but evaluating look. "Now Paul", spoke Proudhomme, "do you go over to the works and see our carts safely unloaded. Keep the crates closed. Each has an apostle's name on the box. Have them laid flat, one at the foot of each of the twelve pillars. Then take a look around the interior, and later you can tell me what you observed." He turned to Herman and smiled, "Yes, I have brought the apostles, all the way from Deventer, and they are good. His Grace will, I think, be pleased!"

Paul was leaving as he heard Herman say that the Archbishop was indeed over from Constance, and was in residence in his Freiburg palace. "He will be happy enough to get his apostles here - he has been asking what has become of them. He will be more than pleased to see you back, as well" he added.

The lodge was a two-storied building at the back of the city square and only minutes away from where the two carts stood waiting. Paul walked back and asked the clerk who had first greeted him, to show him the pillars that were to receive the Apostles' statues. Labourers helped the cart drivers to gently lower each box individually onto the ground, as Paul supervised. That done, with the clerk's assistant standing guard over them, the clerk took Paul into the interior of the Munster. Inside it seemed less dimly lit than looking in from the exterior, the light coming in from sizeable window apertures, cut high up on the great walls. The twelve pillars stood in the main body of the church, some of them complete, awaiting only the graven apostle to be placed in the niche already built to receive them. Others still were swathed in timber scaffolding. "If you would walk out with me sir", the clerk said, "I will get the plan, which shows which pillar is named for which apostle."

They walked back into the sunlight, where Paul waited for the clerk to enter his cabin, whilst he drank in all the bustle and activity around. He was not the only observer of the scene. Many a curious face was turned to any small event that had to do with their great building. His being a new face, with the close-fitting white cap of the architect's calling, gained a passing interest from some of those watching. But it was then he noticed that one of the bystanders had a tonsured scalp and was wearing the black robe and white scapula of a Dominican. It seemed to Paul that he was taking more than just a passing interest in this young architect, but then told himself he was over-reacting. Nevertheless, he felt his heart involuntarily pounding.

Master Proudhomme had warned him that there was a Dominican house here in Freiburg, but he knew he had done nothing to provoke interest from them, nor would he do anything to attract their attention.

The building clerk emerged holding a plan and together they re-entered the Munster and made their way around the pillars. The clerk carried a piece of chalk and wrote the saint's name on the paving slab in front of each of the relevant pillars. As they came out again, the clerk hailed a pair of workmen and set them to work taking the boxes, one at a time into the interior. "They can't read," the clerk explained. "Would you sir, check that they leave the right crate at the correct pillar, whilst I watch to see that they handle the crates properly at this end?"

Paul nodded his assent and moving back into the interior risked a glance back towards where the Dominican had previously been standing. Now he saw to his concern that not only was he still there, but that he had a second, an older black-robed friar with him, to whom he was talking animatedly, whilst frequently turning his gaze onto Paul.

Re-entering the dim interior, Paul was relieved by the temporary anonymity it gave him, but the sickening lurch he felt in his gut, reflected his true feelings.

***

Soon after the master mason's party had left for Freiburg, the great carts from Stauffen had arrived at the stonemason's quay. The Marshal had already told Jan Aspach, his master sergeant, and two knights to observe certain precautions and supervise the transhipment from barge to cart. There were four large four-wheeled wagons and under the watchful eye of the two supervisors, the knights and sergeants from the mounted party removed the top layers of straw from the greased steel pike heads and discovering that three per man was a worthy load, they began the long job of transferring 2000 of them, layering straw around them. Gradually, the great carts began to fill up. As each cart completed its load, another team unloading the second barge, brought up items of armour including helmets and breastplates and it could be seen that the four wagons would not be enough.

"Stop there" the Marshal ordered. "Move the wool bales on top to cover that hardware and bring up the cook's wagon. Sergeant," he called Anspach over, "take care of this lot."

The mounted party had brought their own horse-drawn wagons with them, one containing supplies and the cooks equipment, and in this one they proceeded to pile on the items of body armour until now, carried below the cargo of wool. That took a sizeable quantity and then up came the second wagon that contained the baggage and tents for the party. More of the steel accoutrements were loaded into there, but a waterproof canvas covered them. No subterfuge of wool bales was considered necessary for what was after all, transport for a military party. But although the bulky items had all now found a place, there still lay on the ground in piles some two hundred chain mail corselets, of no small weight.

"Right," barked the senior sergeant. "Each mounted man will take four each of these iron shirts, roll them as a pack behind your saddle, drape them over your horses arse, or wear the goddam things. Just get on with it and let's get out of here."

The wagons driven by Stauffen's men were already moving and escorting them, the score of armed men and an equal number of squires and servants were falling in to place, as soon as they had individually figured how best to carry the chainmail shirts.

Within twenty minutes of the carts moving out, the stonemason's quay was quiet and deserted, except for the bargees waiting to be told what cargo, if any, they would be taking back down river.

***

Once the Apostles were allocated and delivered to the correct pillar, the clerk took off about his duties and Paul wandered around the mighty church, marveling at its dimensions and the quality of the workmanship. He nervously noted a black robed priest gliding past him, then saw that this was just a rather benign-appearing old gentleman, a regular canon of the Church. Paul was in no hurry to emerge into the daylight, which was itself beginning to fade. He had assumed that Master Proudhomme would come across to the Munster, once he had got himself up to date with the events of the year that he had been away.

Paul realised why he suddenly felt vulnerable in the face of what might be an unexpected threat. He wore no sword, just a dagger at his girdle, and for the past months he had been within call of armed colleagues in any emergency. Now they were all heading away for this village of Stauffen. His mentor, Master Peter, was elsewhere and probably fully taken up with a new workload. Paul was not ashamed of reacting with a stab of fear at the thought of falling into the hands of the Templar's most dedicated enemies. He knew that if it came to it, they would spare no barbarism in interrogating him, particularly as to what was the mission that brought him to Freiburg.

Many of the workmen had now left, their days work completed. The elderly canon had returned and had noticed him apparently waiting. "Are you here for evensong, dear boy", the old priest asked? "No, no", he answered himself, "I see you wear the architects cap and so must be involved with our great work here, is that so?"

"Indeed Father," replied Paul. "I have just today brought these statues of the twelve apostles, you see they are in their crates there. We came up the river from Flanders."

"Wonderful, I can't wait to see how your sculptor has portrayed St Thomas - 'doubting Thomas'. I imagine a great puzzlement in his features, but all of that would anyway be the artist's imagination. Nobody knows 1300 years later, what they actually looked like, including our Lord, but painters and sculptors have to make an attempt, and hope not to give offence, wouldn't you say?"

Paul was thinking of some intelligent response when the cheery canon saved him the trouble. "I must go, dear boy. Evensong is in that small chapel over there if you feel the need of some spiritual sustenance. Remember, I want to be present when you hoist St Thomas onto his pillar", with which he was off.

Paul walked out of the Munster and across to the clerk's cabin. Discreetly looking around he saw nothing more of the two Dominicans. The Clerk had gone for the night but another man, a watchman had taken his place, who greeted Paul and said, "You Sir, must be the new assistant to Master Proudhomme? I think he is still over at the lodge."

As he looked outside, Paul could see that many of those who had business in the great square had gone. Still there were strollers and horsemen but only a fraction of those earlier.

He walked around the perimeter paling fence, observing that there were many streets and alleys terminating in this great square and he decided to go down the narrow lane to the stonemasons lodge and call in and find Peter Proudhomme.

***

THE INQUISITION

As he reached the lane and turned the corner into it, he was shocked to see the same two black robed monks, together with two uniformed members of the city guard. One of those stepped in Paul's path and said, "Excuse me Sir, but might I trouble you to take off your headgear?"

"Strange", thought Paul but muttered something and removed the cloche shaped cloth helmet as ordered. "Well?" he heard one of the Dominicans, question the other
The younger one that Paul had seen first, was walking around Paul peering closely.

"Enough of this", Paul addressed the guard, a big burly man. "What is going on here, why am I being accosted in this way?"

"Ah well Sir, these reverend gentlemen say that you are a fugitive from justice, they have an open warrant for the arrest of such fugitives and I am obliged to accompany them about the exercise of that warrant."

Paul felt the stab of cold fear he had been trying to keep at bay and started to protest when the younger Dominican, ignoring him completely, said to his companion and the guard. "Yes, this is the man I believed it to be. Take him!"

Paul lunged for his dagger but the second watchman grabbed his wrist. "Help, help me." Paul roared, hoping that they could hear him in the lodge at the next corner. There seemed to be nobody in the immediate vicinity, as the watchmen began to drag him away from that corner of the great square. He struggled, but they knew their business, turned him around and frog-marched him, his heels skidding off the cobblestones as he tried to halt them.

As they left the lit-up city square, he thought he saw in the distance the shocked face of the elderly canon with whom he had talked earlier.

Realising that nobody would even know where he was, Paul shouted, the fear in his voice now obvious for anyone to hear. "Please, somebody," he struggled again, "please tell the Architect what has happened here!" Then the city lights disappeared behind them, as they went further down a cobbled lane.

"Enough of that, Sir Templar," said the younger friar with gloating satisfaction in his voice.

"You've made a big mistake" Paul breathlessly insisted, the two guards having turned him around to face forward again, but keeping up a brisk pace. Within only six or seven minutes they had arrived at a substantial monastic building facing a cobbled small square and the guards hauled him up the front steps. "Will you want us to take him down for you, father?" the older one asked.

"Yes, if you would be so kind, and here for you and your partner", he passed a coin, "…for your trouble." The guards pulled back Paul's arms ignoring his protests, so that they stretched out behind his back like a stiff pair of wings. They clamped iron handcuffs onto his wrists and forced him down a narrow flight of stairs. There they opened a solid small door and pushed him hard into the small cell. His momentum had him heading for the facing stone wall, but he turned his head to take the impact on a shoulder.

***

The long line of wagons and horsemen made their way across the wide plain separating Breisach and the river, from the forest and the village of Stauffen at its edge. It was exceptionally slow going with ox-drawn carts but the horsemen sat easily, using that skill known to cavalrymen throughout the ages, of sleeping in the saddle. All except the scouts that is, because the master sergeant had posted four of them, two well ahead and one as an outrider on each flank. The Marshal himself rode in the lead, alongside his second in command, Sir Geraint of Monmouth.

Greatly relieved after five weeks to be leaving the great river behind them, the two leaders were both conscious that they soon would have to actually cross it, once beyond the territory of the Police Bishop of Basel. They knew their party would be upwards of a hundred horsemen plus the wagons they had now, in addition to more containing the silver bullion they were about to collect at Stauffen. It would be quite an exercise they agreed, and would rely a lot on local knowledge.

As they talked, they saw what from a distance had been a long green line on the horizon expand, gradually taking shape as the edge of the magnificent forest, entirely dominating the skyline, with low green clad hills at the edge, rising sharply beyond. They also saw the most obvious feature in the landscape, just two to three miles distant along this road, a perfect conical hill topped with a stone castle, which they recognised as a seriously strong defensive position commanding one of the roads into and through the forest. One of the scouts came back at the gallop and pulling up with a cloud of dust at the head of the column, reported that a mounted party had left the castle and was making its way towards them. Behind the two leaders rode the senior sergeant Jan Aspach. Geraint, himself straightening up in the saddle, turned and spoke to him, and Jan bellowed back down the line, "Wake up now, dress your ranks, look to your side arms! Shape up now! Don't disgrace me! These are Templars coming to meet us."

"On this occasion Wilfred," Aspach addressed a boyish squire close by him, "you may display Beauséant and stand to, beside the Marshal." The youth shook out the furled banner rolled up on a lance entrusted to him. The flag was of two equal halves, one black one white, and he trotted proudly past the top sergeant, to follow just behind Sir Peter Breughel's right arm.

Their other leading scout cantered in and told the Marshal that there were some twenty horsemen coming including, he added sniffily, "some civilians."

Indeed there were amongst them two young women mounted side-saddle, and a brightly dressed boy about sixteen years old, mounted on a fine horse out in front. A large authoritative bearded figure in half-armour rode leading the column, and the Templars guessed him to be the Baron von Stauffen. Behind them were some twelve pairs of mailed horsemen side by side, by their bearing and dressage, trained cavalry. But today they did not so much look formidable to their viewers, as by their beaming faces delighted to make the rendezvous with other Templars.

His party halted and the baron walked his horse on, right up to the Marshal, where they clasped gauntleted forearms. The commander of the German Templars also rode up, saluted the Marshal, and gripped his hand.

"It does my eyes much good to see that banner once more," he said.

"I broke my own rules in doing so," came the reply. "We managed to resist the urge at Bannockburn and I fear we will not display Beauséant in Schwyz. We don't want to attract a crusade against us, like the Cathars had for fifty years, so we will reserve it for very private occasions, like this one."

***

Paul half lay, half sat, as far as his arms painfully shackled behind him, would allow, on the floor of his small stone chamber. It was dry and it was clean, for which small mercies he was grateful. It also looked as though it had not been occupied for some time.

It was, however, oppressively dark with no window to the outside but a narrow slit, through which air passed, and as Paul took stock of his surroundings, he guessed that would open onto an internal courtyard.

Apart from the pain of his shackled arms, he felt quite paralysed with fear, knowing as did all the surviving Templars, the horrors that these Dominicans of the Inquisition could visit on their victims. But the fear was mixed with some irrational hope, because after all, were there not many armed Templars within a few miles from here, including his own comrades, who would do anything necessary to rescue him? Additionally he had come to greatly respect the master mason Peter Proudhomme, and had to have faith that he would know what to do. But a doubting voice insistently screamed at him, "Nobody knows where you are - how can they rescue you if the city has swallowed you up?"

He reckoned that it was about nine hours of the evening when he heard the cell door opening to see there the younger of the two Dominicans, the first to identify him, though how that had happened, Paul could not guess. He sensed but could not see that there was another figure hovering outside the small cell as the young friar entered. Paul observed that this Dominican and he were about the same age. His features were very sharply defined. Whilst not thin, his flesh was stretched tightly over his facial bones, his nose well sculpted, his pale skin contrasted with his head of jet black tonsured hair. It gave him a positive look and fully suited his black and white vestments. But it was his eyes that struck a chill into Paul's very soul. They were dark and piercing, but they had a light, almost shining from them - the 'light of zeal', he recognised from some of the religious he had come to know.

"Now before you start all your rubbish about a big mistake," the friar stood over him said forcefully, his Spanish accent quite pronounced, "you are identified as a Templar and it was I that did so." Paul looked at him piercingly but could get no clue as to how that might have been.

The friar had a wooden crucifix suspended by a cord around his neck and stood with his hands piously clasped together, intertwined, as if in prayer.

"I am Brother Joacquim. As a novice many years ago, I was attached to the household of our Grand Inquisitor in Paris, the head of our Order in France, Guillaume of Paris. He was, as you may know, also the Confessor to King Phillip and lodged at the royal Palace on the City Island. Does that bring back any memories?"

Paul shook his head. He knew of the evil inquisitor Guillaume as every surviving Templar did, but as to this Joacquim, what memories he meant brought nothing back to him, and he waited for the Dominican to continue.

"One day, it would have been in 1306 or early '07, you came to the palace in uniform, you must have been a squire at that time. I saw you there, requesting audience with Her Majesty. I remember asking myself what would a Templar squire be doing visiting the Queen in her chambers? My master should know of this. Well I found out from within her household that you were a nephew of hers, from her county of Champagne. I was interested enough to follow that up, when your nest of heretics at the Paris Temple was overthrown. When later I had an opportunity, out of curiosity to examine the list of prisoners, I saw that your name, de Chatillon, is it not, possibly valuable to us as being some species of princeling, was not amongst them?"

"So that was many years ago," said Paul, realising he could not succeed in denying who he was and thinking how much he needed some time to work out some story to cling to. "Do you hope I will tell you about that, so long ago?"

"No, Sir Templar. I hope for nothing. What I KNOW is that you WILL tell me everything from that time, right up until now. And for what reason you're here in Freiburg, disguised as an architect. Now you can agree to tell me everything and I will write down your answers. OR, you will tell the entire story - all the truth, when you are examined - it matters little to us. You will then tell all that you know - and beg for the opportunity to be heard."

"But I AM an architect," Paul ventured. "I left the Order long ago."

"We shall see, but I greatly doubt it. We know that your extinguished Order continues to flout the papal bull that followed the Council of Vienne, which abolished the Templars and instructed all members of the former Order still at liberty, to surrender to the justice of their bishop, wherever they found themselves.

"I think Sir Templar that you are such an outlaw, and we can soon verify if you appeared at any bishop's court and what was his verdict - if it was your plan to tell such an unlikely tale. If as I suspect, you are still with the remains of your kind, that new outlaw band that started up in the cursed Kingdom of Scotland, now under interdict, you will tell us.

"I think you were one of those that fought against the English king at Bannockburn, see we know all about you, from others we have caught - and then you will in your examination tell us more. You will tell us everything. Why you are here in Freiburg? Who and where are your associates?"

Paul sat immobile, realising that his only chance was to play for time. That somehow his friends could discover where he was, and in some way act!

Brother Joacquim stepped back to the doorway and beckoned a bulky assistant, a layman servant of the monastery. "Take him through" he ordered but before he stepped out of the way, he fastened his unblinking gaze on Paul and said, "We have sent to our mother house in Strasburg for our expert examiners. We have not often needed them here in Freiburg. The calling of a rack-master is a highly skilled trade. You might know them as something else…"

“Torturers”, Paul broke in bitterly. “Torturers, masquerading as Christians, whilst you, you pious freak, give them their instructions, but keep your own hands lily-white.”

Joacquim laughed. “So you show spirit, Sir Templar. Your kind always start that way but you will finish like all the others, groveling for mercy. Remember, the way that we took you in this city. Nobody knows you are here - and even if they did, who in their right mind would challenge the Holy Inquisition?

“Now”, he spoke more sharply, “the examiners will be here within two to three days and what we do in these circumstances, before we lock you away to wait, is to show you the instruments of examination so that you can reflect alone on what you have seen, before the questions start. Tonight you can still walk. Perhaps, after the questioning begins” his voice slowed in emphasis, “you will never walk again!”

***

Slowly crossing from the meadows close to the village, the combined columns rode together side by side behind Baron von Stauffen and the Marshal. Within the hour they were clattering across the large cobbled yard of the castle. There they noted the presence of the Baron’s own liveried followers. He appeared to employ a lot of soldiers. The newcomers discovered later that this was because the Baron owned a silver mine nearby, and that the huge Black Forest on whose fringe they were had its full quotient of outlaws. In one corner of the courtyard were three solid-looking, sizeable carts with large wheels, empty except for a thin straw base on their planks. Leaning against one of them looking over the arrivals was a large bluff man with a look of rugged independence about him and an air of authority. His carters similarly looked on with particular professional interest at the well-loaded carts that had been brought up from the river. Baron Stauffen nudged his horse, taking the Marshal over to them, and introduced their leader.

“This is Master Franz from Schwyz, come to take you to his country - and journey’s end,” he said. “I present Sir Peter Breydel, Marshal of the Templars - although they call it something else now.”

"Sir Marshal, I am honoured to meet with you. We have heard about your victory over the English king, indeed also that earlier triumph over the French king at the field of Courtrai. All Europe heard of that, and we look forward to your repeating these marvels with our Austrian tyrant, who is after all, a mere duke."

He spoke facetiously, but the Marshal liked his humour.

Sir Peter leaned down and clasped the hand of the Schwyzer. "We have come a long way Sir, and we are not disposed towards any idea that these Austrians could be moving us on even further. So yes Sir, we welcome your comradeship in arms."

Geraint and his comrades from the column dismounted. He was not alone in admiring the two young women also dismounting, who clearly were of the Baron's family and were conscious of the interest being shown in them. "You know," he said to Knut, similarly engaged beside him, "one of the things I like about no longer being a celibate monk is that…" he nodded towards the females. "But living at Aird, was a barracks, not exactly the place to start a romance - an impossibility in fact, and after these weeks on the river, continually on the move, I am definitely feeling a bit frisky."

"Do I not know what you mean?" his Danish friend replied, "but those are the Baron's daughters, not his housemaids, I'll hazard a guess. So unless you want to lose your vital equipment, I counsel you to play the courtier, not the clumsy lover."

"Problems, always there are problems," Geraint sighed. I doubt that we will see any housemaids in the quarters we will be assigned. But maybe when we get to this Schwyz, maybe the grateful women there, knowing we are fighting for their liberty and saving them from being raped by the enemy army, might want to have mercy upon us. Anyway, lucky old Paul is in the city right now. He won't have to worry about upsetting any baron by goosing his daughters. He'll be having a great time tonight, I'll be bound."

"Likely so," Knut agreed with him mournfully, as one who would not.

"Sir Geraint", the Marshal called his name to come over to the Baron's group and meet the Lord of this castle and the two leaders of the German Templars, who had joined them, "this is Sir Geraint of Monmouth, a well experienced soldier and my number two." He introduced him. The Baron nodded cordially and the Schwyzer Franz shook his hand, as did the two German Templars each introducing themselves, their leader Sir Heinrich and his deputy Sir Martin.

"Gentlemen", said the Baron, "I would ask you to attend me in my council room in one hour's time, after you have been shown to your quarters. With Master Franz here we must plan how you are to cross the Rhine and join his people with this precious cargo you have brought, plus the silver bullion purchased from me. With these slow wagons, you certainly will not wish to have to fight your way past the Duke's border patrols.

"At least", he concluded, before entering his castle, "I do believe that we have the advantage of surprise, that nobody knows you have arrived safely here - and if they did, what your mission might be!"

***

Brother Joacquim had led the way with a lanthorn down into a narrow lower corridor, that looked crudely carved from the bedrock. Paul followed. He was bent over, almost doubled up as the Dominican servant held his pinioned arms stretched straight out behind him. Here close to the city drains the stone walls wept with damp, and the smell was fetid. A small solid door opened to the friar's key and followed by the prisoner and his escort they all entered. The size of the chamber was surprisingly large after the narrow approach.

"When your examination begins," Joacquim told him, "I shall sit over there," he nodded to a small table, "with a parchment and pen to write down your answers. The examiners when they get here will do the rest. You see they know just how much pain to inflict for you to tell the truth, in answer to my questions. The rackmaster and his assistant are very skilled, and that Sir Templar, is why we will wait for them. Besides, it may be that our brethren at Strasbourg also will have further questions for you to answer. After all, they are in a big metropolitan city and better know what is happening in the world. This one…" he spoke disparagingly of Freiburg, "doesn't even have a bishop."

"Bring him," the friar ordered, as he walked towards a rough black wooden block of a table with rope loops for a prisoner's ankles and wrists, the rope wound around a windlass at both ends. He slapped its surface familiarly.

"This is the rack you may know of", he said. "It pulls your limbs slowly from their sockets, so even if you are off the table the agony will not cease. Your limbs will no longer work; the sinews will have stretched beyond breaking point. You could be a foot longer - and I say 'longer' not 'taller', a fine point you may think, except that you will never again be able to stand up." Brother Joacquim's unpleasant expression showed how much he was enjoying his power. "No more swordplay for you, Sir Templar, nor will you be able ever to walk again, nor mount a horse.

"Now," he thrust his face into that of the prisoner, his garlic breath offensive, "will you tell me now why you are here in Freiburg? Where are your friends? Tell me now, you fool! You may think you can withstand the torment - you cannot, but if you insist on testing yourself, you cannot then save yourself the mutilation, and having to live on afterwards in permanent agony as a cripple."

Paul was sweating heavily despite the chill, but made no answer. He had no answer!

"So if you think that you can accept the agony and mutilation to save your friends," the friar said it mockingly, "then you will be brought to know pain that you cannot imagine. Your feet here still fettered, will be anointed with oil, 'basted' we might say, as this brazier will be brought up under them full of red-hot coals. Your feet will then be roasted like a pig's trotters, but the difference is that you will still be alive while being roasted and you will pray for death. I can promise you that!"

"One of your comrades in the Temple," he continued in an almost confidential tone, "the day all you Templars in France were arrested, needed this persuasion to confess to his abominable heresies. Somehow he survived. But all the flesh had left the bones of his feet and they fell out. He wore them in a bag around his neck afterwards, as he dragged himself around his cell."

Paul straining against his straight arm manacles could no longer contain himself. "You Dominican filth," he cried out, "you call yourselves 'God's hounds', but you surely serve the devil."

"Take him back!" the Friar ordered.

***

The great hall of Stauffen Castle was impressive with huge black hammer beams holding up the lofty timber roof. Much of the lower walls, instead of being faced with the familiar stone blocks of castle walls, were panelled in carved black oak. Fine woods were in no way scarce or too expensive here, that was obvious. At both ends of the hall there was a great fireplace, but with a moderate temperature outside, no fire was lit. Swords and shields, some of obvious antiquity, decorated the lower walls. From the upper walls heraldic banners of the Stauffen family crest hung lazily in the light draft from the narrow windows below them. The Baron led the other leaders to the back of the dais and through a curtain to a smaller chamber behind dominated by a large black oak table, where already his clerk was waiting for them with large parchment maps in front of him. The Baron waved them all to seats and himself sat in a great carved oak chair with his baronial arms carved on the chair back.

"The map shows the forest land between here and the Rhine and its bridges. Then the second map shows what we know about the route to Schwyz thereafter, and we look to Master Franz here to put us right on that one," the Baron declared.

"Master Franz and I have already talked of this and have proposals to put to you. "We think that you should not linger here but get on your way tomorrow, or the next day," he continued. "Is there any reason why not?"

The Templars looked to their marshal and he in turn looked at Geraint. "Is it not correct" he asked, "that Master Proudhomme and Brother Paul were to come here within a day or two and then our complement would be complete and we could leave?"

"That is my understanding", Geraint confirmed. "But Master Proudhomme," he continued, "was not sure what would be waiting for him in the way of problems at the Munster there. He said that it was a year since he was there and he might not be able to re-join us immediately, but he would try to see that Brother Paul could do so. Master Peter could make his own way to Schwyz, he said, once he is free of whatever problems awaited him in Freiburg."

"Well I would like Brother Paul to be with us before we leave. I believe that Freiburg is little more than an hours brisk riding from here." He turned to the Germans and explained that Paul de Chatillon was one of his valued battalion commanders. "But we cannot hold up a hundred men and our vital cargo for one man, so I propose that we agree to leave here tomorrow and if he has not arrived, leave orders for young Paul to follow after us." There was general assent to that course of action and they turned their attention to the maps.

***

Paul, his arms still pinioned behind him, had just spent the worst night of his life; he had no doubts of that. Nothing had been given him to eat, but the servant who had so easily manhandled him had brought him a jug of water, from which he filled a mug which he placed close to Paul's mouth and helped him to drink .

"You would be better off to tell him what he wants to know," he said, not unkindly. "I can tell you that you will talk - everybody has to when the pain is just too much, and I have had to drag them back here afterwards with ruined limbs, more dead than alive."

Paul grabbed at what appeared to be a chance. "I can pay you 100 marks if you can take a message for me," he said keeping his voice low. The man looked at him scornfully. "Do you not think I know what would be my fate, if I were to do so? This is the Inquisition! There is nowhere you can go, nowhere to hide if they are seeking to find you, and I have seen what happens when they do." He said no more, and stalked out slamming the door behind him.

Sleep, unsurprisingly would not come, but sheer exhaustion had him nodding fitfully, constantly awakening with a start, his faculties straining to identify any noise, real or imagined. He could eventually see from the pale light of the wall slit that daylight had come, and he sat trying to ease the pain in his pinioned arms. He had now gone over his story many times in his mind. He had, he would tell them, been in Cyprus, then served in a

Templar fortress in Cilicia, when the Paris Temple was captured in 1307 which was true. That nobody out there knew what was happening and when his tour of duty in Cilicia was over and he returned to Cyprus, the brethren were told that the Order had been disgraced somehow, by something their Paris house had done - nobody knew, and that the Pope had ordered the arrest of all the Templars in Christendom, which also was true. So far so good, Paul thought.

But the King of Cyprus had no interest in arresting them, he would truthfully say, so the brethren were given a choice by their commanders that they could leave to join the Hospitallers on their island of Rhodes, or be released from their oaths and make their way back to their own countries. He had decided to try to go back to his family home in Burgundy if he could get there, and so joined others on a Templar galley to Venice, where they had split up. He would continue with a story of crossing Austria and the German states, which he had actually done, but as a part of the escort of the Marshal, which he would not tell them. Finally he arrived in Holland. On the journey, as he would say it, he had worked on building sites to have the means to exist and there he had been taken up, being an educated man able to read and write, and offered a place as a pupil to an architect, which is what brought him to the Munster in Freiburg.

He had to rely on the fact that much of it was true - and checkable and he had no doubt that the Master Mason would back his story. But he knew for certain that for Brother Joacquim, whose hatred for him was manifest, having him in his power was less about the truth, and more about destroying him, one way or another. The surviving Templars had discussed between them the papal edict that after their Order was suppressed, all individuals should surrender to their local bishop for his justice. They had scoffed at the idea, but that was back in Scotland in the safety of Castle Aird, surrounded by some of the best warriors in Christendom. None of them of course had surrendered, which made them outlaws.

Paul had never felt so much alone!

It was morning when he heard the noise of men outside his cell door and then the monastery servant of yesterday was unlocking it and he was being dragged out, his stomach, his whole body taut with fear. Two men in the uniform of the city guard were there and pushed him ahead of them up the steps. Paul registered that they were going up, not down to the torture chamber, wondering what this could mean. In the entrance hall of the Friary, there was Brother Joacquim. He was passionately remonstrating with a uniformed city officer standing there, that this was a prisoner of the Holy Inquisition and they could not take him away on anybody's orders. "Sorry Brother," the City officer told him, although he sounded quite indifferent to the Friar's obvious dismay. "Here is the warrant from the Archbishop, who intends to examine the prisoner himself and frankly sir, an Archbishop outranks a friar preacher in our way of looking at things!"

The burly city guards looked askance at the filthy sight and smell of the prisoner as they told him that he was to go before the Archbishop. They told the serving man to remove the iron manacles on Paul's wrists and for the first time in what had seemed like an eternity, he felt the joy of the free movement of these limbs, but gasped at the pain of his blood, now circulating freely. The guards followed their officer down the steps to the street and onwards, each with a restraining hand on Paul's upper arms. They marched briskly down the lanes and alleyways of the city until they came to the Munster and its grand square, but marched on, past the curious and the idle, who watched, wondering what this soiled specimen of humanity had done, and speculating whether for him, it would be the stocks or the gallows. As they passed at a brisk pace, Paul searched the now crowded square no longer regarding the grandeur of the great building, but hoping that by some miracle he might see and perhaps even be seen, by what was his only hope, the comforting presence of Master Proudhomme, but it was not to be.

As they turned into a smaller square with the palace in front of them, the officer stopped and for the first time addressed Paul, wrinkling his nose. "His Grace the Archbishop will question you about what I know not; however, you are altogether too filthy to attend on him as you are." Paul had inevitably soiled himself and his clothes in all the hours of his confinement with his arms pinioned behind him. But he had thought that since there was nothing he could do about it, he had bigger worries. Now the prospect of appearing before a prince of the church with his life at stake, looking and smelling like a drunken vagrant, would not improve his chances.

The Officer continued, "But seemingly you have a friend hereabouts from the Munster, who has arranged with us..." the officer thought of the clinking coins in his purse, "to let you wash up in the guardroom, and has sent some clean clothes."

Paul's relief had little to do with the clothes, welcome though that was. He knew that an Archbishop could order him to the fire if he gave the wrong answers. But it was the realisation that Master Peter somehow had to be behind this change in his fortunes, and that anything must be better than being a helpless victim in the Dominicans torture chamber, the prospect that had so terrified him last night.

***

Morning at Stauffen, some fourteen miles east of the great city of Freiburg, had seen more than the customary bustle, as the newcomers with their mounts and wagons prepared for the day's march. The carts had been reloading since first light, with the Baron's servants assisting the travellers. Master Franz's big wheeled carts from Schwyz had loaded the silver ingots and over the top had piled high the wool bales that had journeyed up the Rhine. The cargo brought up from the river was redistributed between the Schwyzer vehicles and the carts from the stonemason's dock. The armour and armaments were packed over the top of the pike heads hidden below a layer of straw on the floor of other carts. They were after all military goods, consistent with a party of mounted mercenaries heading for a war zone, but they wanted no rumour to get about of a great number of pikes, an infantry weapon, to precede the battle. The Baron had provided teams of draught horses to replace the oxen that had got them there from the river, the yoked oxen were just too slow for the business in hand and they would be returned to the docks at Breisach.

The horsemen had checked their harness and their mounts and the top sergeants were organising them into columns, protective of the wagons. They did not believe that the forest outlaws, who undoubtedly would follow their progress at a distance, like wolves, waiting for a broken down wagon or a lame horse leaving its rider vulnerable, would dare to do more, but they were carrying a great cargo of silver. Desperate men might risk everything for the wealth that promised.

The Baron had much experience of moving his silver from the mine to his castle and his long distance trade in the precious metal was normally under strong guard, down away from the forest to the river at the port of Breisach, to travel downstream to the west. It was the same short route that the Templars had travelled yesterday, through open ground, which did nothing to assist ambushes.

But there were some thirty miles through narrow roads in dense forest to travel to the Rhine Bridge that the commanders had chosen for their crossing. More, the gradients were steep and progress therefore would be slow. Knowing the forest and its hills, he had proposed to them that they would go by a direct route, climbing a track up a steep hill about two miles in length, that with the laden wagons would be extremely hard and slow to climb, but that once achieved, it would be the highest point of the journey. Having painfully got to the summit, it would afterwards be downhill on existing tracks and helped along by the gradient of the slopes, all the way to the distant river.

His planning master-stroke was that the wagons would leave the castle, hauled by their teams of big draught horses, but two miles away at the foot of the long steep track leading up the mountain, all the horses would be unhitched, walked burden-free up the long hillside, and replaced on the wagons by oxen. His young son, Ludo, was leading a party of the Stauffen soldiers, even then going to all the local tenant farmers and commandeering their teams of ploughing oxen and themselves, to serve a day for the Baron. They would return only when the wagons had reached the top of the hill and the horse teams re-hitched. "That way," the baron reasoned, "the horses will still be fresh when the top of the hill is reached and fit for the rest of the journey. After all, the horses could not pull the wagons any quicker up such a hill - it would still be a slow job with either oxen or horses. The Baron, clearly a masterly planner had also put a light cart into the train carrying spare wheels, axles, harness, towing ropes, accompanied by a pair of his own skilled workers to deal with any breakdowns.

The rendezvous with his son was to be anytime soon, as the teams of oxen made their way there from surrounding farms. By eight am the first scouts, the Baron's own men, led the long column out of the castle flying his pennants on their lances and the Stauffen armorial device on their surcoats, the only heraldry to be seen, in contrast to the plain grey steel chain-link armour of the column of Templars and their squires. The long convoy made up now of many wagons, were in the centre of the column, along the road away from the village, with Templar outriders and a rear-guard, amongst which rode the Baron himself and once again his two daughters, to witness such a rare event in their rather commonplace lives.

***

Paul's guards led him into a cobbled yard within the palace complex, which they entered by a side postern. The officer told him to strip off by a barrel of rainwater and the guards dipped buckets in and sluiced him down, whilst he gasped with the shock of the cold water. It reminded him of when he had been a squire at the Paris Temple all those years ago, where the drill sergeants set out to toughen up the young gentlemen entrusted to their robust care. The officer looked at him and his now discarded soiled clothes lying on the cobbles besides him. With one booted toe he turned them over, his nose wrinkling. "Leave them," he ordered, "follow me!" and led the way up some stone steps into a large stone chamber through which other guards and servants were passing about their business. Paul, quite naked, self-consciously clasping his hands in front of his loins to the amusement of the others there, saw that the officer, before departing on his own business, had led him to a neat pile of clothing on top of which were an architect's white smock and cloth helmet and wonder of wonders, a cloth with which he could dry himself.

Not unkindly, the officer who had left meanwhile to talk to a secretary, re-entered the room, finding Paul now dressed and told him to prepare to go before the Archbishop. "He's only here for a few days, so he won't want to waste his time" - the implication being to keep to the point. "He's got someone in with him at this moment. You will probably be next!"

Paul was wishing he could have seen Master Peter to ask him about the many things he did not know and how to reply to questions about them. Fear was creeping back, but it was many degrees less terrifying than the torture chamber that he had expected this morning. At least they were giving him a trial. They would hear his story, before they condemned him.

A black-robed secretary, a small plump man with thinning grey hair, came in, looked at Paul and nodded to the guard officer sprawled in a seat, who got to his feet, signalled to his two guards who again took hold of one arm each They marched the unresisting Paul away down a stone flagged corridor, up a flight of broad stairs and along a black oak floored passage, which led to a pair of wide oak doors.

A household servant in the Archbishop's livery stood doorkeeper, and addressed the officer as soon as he was within earshot "Take him straight in," he ordered. "His Excellency wants this dealt with quickly."

"That did not sound good," thought Paul

The ageing secretary who had summoned them from the guardroom went in first, and Paul coming through the door with his guards saw him bow, and move inside.

It was a high ceilinged stone and oaken chamber with large Flemish tapestries on the walls. The floor was of polished black oak planks and was bare except for a small table for the clerk, and a beautifully carved black oak prie-dieu on which was resting a large Bible closed with a metal clasp. The far end of the hall rose to a dais, on which stood an oak dining table, sitting at which were two men. In the centre was a man who could only be the Archbishop. He was not wearing clerical clothes, but buckskin and a lawn shirt. Were it not for the heavy pectoral cross on a light gold chain and the apostolic ring on a finger, by appearances his calling might have been that of any young vigorous, aristocratic magnate. He was occupied in eating his breakfast. He took a cursory look at the prisoner then carried on talking to his table companion who in front of him, had on the table a model of something sculpted, that he had been explaining to the Archbishop before they were interrupted

Paul still trying to adjust to his situation was at first surprised, and then enormously relieved to see that this other man at the high table was his friend and mentor, Master Peter Proudhomme.

"So Master Proudhomme…" the prelate was speaking. "Yes, I can say that I do like what you have shown me but I will want to carefully choose the Latin inscriptions. After I'm dead and gone and a new man is appointed to the archdiocese, he won't want to be using up a year's revenue to honour his predecessor, nor will he necessarily give much thought to how I am to be described for posterity. So now, you and I have saved him the trouble. I will let you have the text of the inscriptions to go where you showed me and I will give you a commission to your Flemish sculptor who did my apostles. Excellent!"

He looked at Paul. "Now this young man, you tell me, is your pupil?"

"You", he addressed Paul direct. "What is your full name," he nodded at his secretary who had taken up his quill.

"I was born Paul de Chatillon of Burgundy…"

"Wait a minute", the prelate interrupted. "Is that the Chatillon on the Loire, the Marne maybe… or the Seine, or even…" he added as an afterthought, "the Indre?"

"The Seine, your Highness. My father was the Baron."

"So your mother must have been, wait a minute", he thought and resumed, "the Lady Isabel and sister to Blanche of Champagne, Phillip of France's Queen?"

"That is so, your Grace," he replied tonelessly.

Master Proudhomme looked equally surprised.

"My dear boy," the Archbishop said enthusiastically, "come up here, you must have some breakfast." He turned his gaze momentarily to the escort and told them they could go.

The elderly clerk stood respectfully and pointedly coughed, nodding down towards his manuscript.

"Yes, yes, quite right, Otto. We'll get this formal bit done first."

"Now you were a squire in the Order of the Temple and were sent by them to Cyprus where you saw action fighting the Turks in Cilicia, in which you won your spurs, is that not so?" He was reading off a note in front of him. "Master Proudhomme has acquainted me of these matters and how you young Templars were cast adrift over there in Cyprus, and had to make your own way back to the mainland.

"I see that he found you labouring in one of his cathedral projects in Flanders when he came to inspect, he thought you might have the brains to be an architect and so took you on, as his pupil. Is that not so?" He nodded to Otto busily writing this down, without waiting for an answer.

"That all sounds perfectly plausible to me. And now to the edict of Vienne; I was there, you know. It was the coldest winter I can remember, one of the older bishops died there - it went on and on! I want you to know young man, that I voted, as did we all against the condemning of your Order - a terrible business that purge, less so here in the Empire, but absolutely the case in France. It was so obviously a put-up job by French Phillip and that dreadful now departed, Clement, who was bought and paid for. They kept us in session all through the end of the year, but we would not change our minds. Clement ruled that the Order should be terminated - we couldn't stop him. He could do that, but he had to add to the record, at our insistence mind you, that the Order was without sin. Did you know that you should have reported to your local bishop for his dispensation on your future?"

"No!" As was clearly his way, he hardly drew breath before answering his own question, "How could you have known that, moving around building sites, and with no Templar houses remaining in existence."

"Alright", he sat up ready to deliver a formal judgment and looked pointedly at Otto whose quill was poised.

"You have now been examined by an archbishop - did you know that you are in the Archdiocese of Constance? There is no bishop here in Freiburg.

"Like your Order, No! Don't write that bit down Otto," he grumbled, "I find you without sin. I am content that you are working with Master Proudhomme and will award you… ahem…six paternosters, for taking up the time of the court. Now come up and join us for some breakfast."

***

THE BLACK FOREST

The sixteen year-old Ludo of Stauffen had excelled himself. He had started his day at four am to ride around the scattered farmsteads and summon the farm tenants to his father's instructions.

By the time the first of the carts had reached the turn-off to the hill route south, two miles from the castle, he was there waiting for them with several harnessed teams of oxen and the Baron's peasants that managed them. His ten-strong mounted detachment of the Stauffen men at arms, were waiting to lead the unhitched draught horses up the long hill, once the teams were exchanged.

The Marshal appointed Sir Heinrich, the German commander, to be responsible for security for this first day and he sent on an advance guard of some twenty knights and flank guards of a further ten, on each side of the column. Young Ludo went with the advance guard and he proudly wore his family livery, which together with that of the Baron's armed retainers was the only heraldry on display.

The Marshal himself was bringing up the rear-guard with his escort of Templars, all of whom had travelled with him up the Rhine. Baron Stauffen had ridden as far as the turn-off at the start of the long steep hill, and had seen the draught teams exchanged and the great horses led uphill by his mounted men at arms. Despite that they were walking ahead of the bullocks it soon became obvious that they would too quickly outpace the great bovines, so the horse teams, their bridles held by a Stauffen man at arms, were interspersed between the carts, ready to help haul in any emergency.

As the last of the carts swayed away, the sun was climbing high overhead. The Baron said his farewells to the rear-guard, turned his horse and called for his daughters to return with him. "You know," he said as their horses walked back, "we don't often get this much excitement…"

"Father," the eldest, the Lady Melissa interrupted him, "we don't get ANY excitement. All those young men and surely some of them must have been eligible - no?" She didn't wait for an answer. "But they were only with us for one night. Couldn't you have had them stay on for a while?"

"Sorry my darlings" the Baron replied. "There was danger in them staying on - not for us, but what they are doing depends on always keeping surprise on their side. Staying on - that number of troops, many of them obviously knights, mysteriously with no banners, no heraldry on display. That information in the wrong place could mean big trouble for them. It's boring for you, but try to understand!"

They arrived back at Stauffen castle well before noon and the Baron decided to take lunch and relax for a while. He would send some men to follow the convoy but they would soon catch up. He only wanted to discover if they had all got safely to the top of the long hill and then he would know that the most difficult part this side of the Rhine crossing, that his responsibility, was over.

***

Breakfast over, a bemused but deeply relieved Paul was taken by Master Peter to the lodgings he had not yet seen, but where his pack had been left for him. It was on an upper floor of the lodge house where he had last seen the master conferring with his assistant. Master Peter was in a rare good humour as he walked alongside, his hand resting on Paul's shoulder. "That worked out well I must say." he confided quietly as they walked along the alley. "That means that you are now on the record as having been before a bishop, an archbishop even, and dealt with according to law. You are not excommunicated nor can you be arrested on this charge, but it would be prudent - I shall arrange it - that Master Otto back there makes a copy of the judgement, that you can always carry on your person."

"I am so grateful to you" Paul said. "I realised, chained up down there that you were my one hope, but I was worried that you couldn't have known where I was, what had happened. None of the workmen could have seen what happened. They arrested me at a place where there were no witnesses."

“Not quite so”, replied Master Peter. “You had earlier had a conversation with a delightful old gentleman, a canon of the Munster. He had told you, he said, that he wanted to be there when St. Thomas’ effigy was hoisted on to his pillar. It was he that heard your call for help and recognised your voice. When I went looking for you in the Munster he came to me. I asked him if he had seen you and then he told me that he had seen you in some scuffle in the distance, and that the City Guard was involved and what looked like Dominicans.

“After that I went to the City Guard, with whom I have a good relationship, as you may have discovered, and the captain called in the men who arrested you, and then I knew where you were and what the charge would be.

“The really good luck was that His Grace was here in Freiburg. He comes a lot because the Munster is his project, which is why he won’t have a bishop appointed here, but his seat is two days ride away at Constance. As you can see he is not your holiest of priests, indeed by the way he recognised your ancestral house, it was clear that he is more a very well informed politician.

“He told me just now that he studied for his doctorate at the Sorbonne,” Paul added, “and that he is familiar with Burgundy and France in general.

“You won’t forget him in a hurry”, said Peter. “I am sure that he was not what you were expecting?”

“I think he is a great man” Paul replied fervently, “he was so down to earth and he certainly saved my arse. I will always be grateful for that. I was very interested in what he told us about the Church Council at Vienne and how he and his colleagues did what they could to prevent such injustice.”

They had reached the stairs to the lodgings and Master Peter indicated that Paul should go up.

“Look, young Paul. I have another few hours’ work to do, but after that I think we should ride to join our friends at Stauffen. Meantime you get some sleep. I will arrange for the horses and wake you when it is time to go.”

Paul, when he saw the bed, suddenly realised how very tired he was - in his terror he had hardly slept at all last night, his emotions had been racked, even if his body had escaped that fate.

One thing he now even more clearly understood was the depth of hatred some of his fellow knights back in Scotland had for the Inquisitors of the Order of St Dominic. Several had themselves suffered, a few had barely escaped, as had Paul just now. It was unthinkable given the opportunity, that these high-calibre fighting men would meekly accept such treatment from the hands of these over-powerful friars, who terrified all of those about them with their legalised torture chambers.

The old women condemned by them and burned as witches, he reflected, had no defence and no means of striking back. The Templars would he knew, make it their mission. He had no qualms at all about the policy of vengeance that the fraternity had vowed against the black friars, wherever they might find them.

***

Miles away, high up in the mighty forest the laborious long haul of the wagon train was slowly, slowly bringing them up the mountain track, which having achieved the summit would tomorrow first take them across a ridge into the next valley and then downhill, on a better road and in a roundabout fashion, all the way to the river Rhine. Where the track was wide enough, flank guards were riding back and forth, keeping those wagons allotted to their care as far as possible, in sight. But the track, seldom broad, had on the one side a steep bank with a lethal sheer drop down the hillside, to the stream in the narrow valley bottom, far below. The other bank of the road was virgin forest which allowed small margin between the dense growth of thousands of years past, and the ruts of previous wagon wheels on the worn track, with solid packed grass-topped earth almost axle high between them.

At the head of the column guiding them, though in truth the track went nowhere else, rode the young Ludo von Stauffen, resplendent in the colours and heraldic devices of his family. He rode alongside Sir Heinrich who led the advance guard and some four others of his German Templars. Behind them came Baron Stauffen's mounted men, interspersed with the many wagons, each leading a team of the great draught horses who would take over the haulage, once the summit was achieved.

Ludo was feeling pleased with himself. He had thought and discussed with his father the previous evening that the danger of this particular stretch of the way, was clearly of a breakdown or an accident involving a wagon. A delay with the wagon train as a result, or even that it was so slow moving, might seem like an opportunity for the outlaws who from all this activity, undoubtedly would have had the sniff of silver bullion being moved out of Stauffen Castle. An astute bandit leader could see that attacking from the forest onto one stationary wagon could be done, because the defenders on horseback up and down the length of the convoy would be hard to deploy given the lack of space in some places, with the width of the wagons taking almost the whole track. Ludo's suggestion was that his father's huntsmen with their hounds should, with a men-at-arms back-up, patrol uphill through the woods, relying on the hounds to flush out any ambush party in hiding, close to the track. The danger they all recognised was of archers' unseen, firing out of the woodland cover at the wagoners and their escorts. The baron had talked to the Templar leaders who had approved the plan and now Ludo could hear the sound of the hounds baying from within the forest, as they made their way, further ahead up the hill.

Ludo knew that they were now at about half way. The track was certainly no easier higher up. It would take five or six hours start to finish, even if there were no incidents, to climb this three-mile hill. The baron had charged Ludo, when they reached the track at the summit, to guide the convoy down a mile or so along the ridge road, to make camp for the night. As each wagon crested the hill, first the oxen would be unharnessed and replaced by the teams of horses.

Sir Heinrich commanding the advance guard was constantly aware of the sounds, smells and sights of the forest and the convoy he was protecting. His restless senses were attuned to any discordance in the birdsong, the movement of the trees in the light wind, the sounds of the wagons making heavy going of the long climb. But he still was able to chat to the enthusiastic young man beside him. Ludo realised that the life of these Templars was a lot more exciting than his.

"Do you think that the Marshal might accept me into your company," he enquired?

"Well you are not a dubbed knight yet, young Ludo and not experienced enough to be a man at arms, but maybe you could be a squire if any of the knights would take you on," was the reply. "If you do things right, then you should win your spurs, and your father knows that for this to happen you will need to have fought in battle. I can't take you on, I already have a squire, but some of the brethren that came from Scotland didn't have squires with them and we're all going into battle. Talk to your father is my advice, see what he suggests."

They had barely finished their conversation when they heard a series of staccato notes on a hunting horn from down the hill well behind them. It was the agreed signal for a wagon in trouble and stopped. Those notes on the horn would bring the Baron's men who had the spare wheels and other wagon parts making their way towards the sound, but it would almost certainly mean that from the point of the breakdown, the convoy behind would now remain stationary until it was fixed. That in turn would put the escorts on alert. Sir Heinrich told one of his knights to go back downhill to bring him a report on what was the problem. That horseman wheeled his mount and walked him downhill, squeezing past the other wagons still heaving their way forward.

***

Paul threw off his new clothes and sank into the blanket laid on a straw filled mattress. He was quite exhausted by the rush of events and dealing with the fear that had welled up inside him, but there was something else. He recognised an ache in his joints and a heavy feeling on the back of his neck. He was afraid from these symptoms that he was going to have a recurrence of a fever he had first contracted, during his garrison time in Cilicia. Within minutes he was asleep and hardly stirred when the time had come and Master Peter shook him gently, and then more vigorously.

"Sorry" mumbled Paul trying to think. "I've got a fever coming on - it's happened before. I 'll be alright in a minute or two."

The master mason felt his forehead and sure enough a fever had started. "When it happened before - how long did it last?" he asked.

"Not long, three or four days and then the fever breaks and I am on the mend."

The master mason considered that and then said, “Alright, this is what I think we should do. If you are feeling up to it, we ride to Stauffen Castle now; it will only take two hours. If you are going to be ill, better to be there where you are quite safe, and can be taken care of. What do you say?”

“Absolutely, I am on for that.” was the reply. He got up, his limbs ached and he certainly felt fevered. He splashed his face in a bowl of water left there by the bed, and started to pull on his clothes, then followed the older man down the stairs. Their two horses from Breisach, were tethered there and they hefted their packs into the saddle bags.

Led by Peter Proudhomme, the two white cloth helmeted architects, walked their horses to the South Gate, which was about to close at sundown and without any undue haste took the road to the village and castle of Stauffen, some fifteen miles to the south.

***

The disabled wagon was about two thirds of the way back of the convoy so whilst there were several wagons that could still move forward, a sizeable number were halted. The Baron’s repairmen were soon on the scene with their light cart and found that it was one of the armour-carrying wagons that had a damaged axle. It was not a small job to repair, and they so advised the knight sent back from the lead party. He then conferred with Sir Geraint who had been sent forward by the Marshal bringing up the rear. They decided to take the repairmen’s advice to transfer some of the load and attach some of the spare draft horses to the oxen team, to haul the broken wagon off the road and onto the side of the track where it widened, a little further ahead. There, the space would allow the repair work to take place whilst the convoy could keep moving up the hill. Geraint had organised two of the flank riders to travel back down the column to tell each of the wagoners that they would have to pick up a share of the load as they passed the damaged vehicle.

Having set the process in place he was about to ride back to report, when the Marshal and his personal escort came up the track, to find out for himself what was the delay.

The main wagon train now resumed moving again and the knight from the vanguard returned up the hill to inform Sir Heinrich of the situation and the plan.

The Marshal's main concern now was the security of the broken cart with its precious load. "We have a wounded beast here," he commented, "and we have to keep the wolf pack at bay," nodding towards the dense forest.

He ordered a horn signal to bring the Baron's foresters out of the woods back to the track and the slowly moving column. When they appeared he told them he was sending ten dismounted knights with their squires into the woods to form a screen there against any attack on the road. He said he wanted to be sure there could be no arrow attack from cover. "They won't succeed in getting anything from us but I don't want to have the casualties. We have too much to do to have that burden," he muttered to the knights around him.

The foresters with their hounds were told to patrol deeper into the woods, until any of a number of prearranged trumpet signals were heard.

He could hear the hounds baying in the distance as they picked up the scent of the forest raiders but was confident that his precautions, organised with such military precision, were more than any opportunist bandits could deal with. No matter that they were probably numerous, they wisely did not attempt a raid. Any watchers in the greenwood, who could get close enough, would have seen the escorted wagons slowly but steadily, continue to move up the track. Even before the last of them, the kitchen wagon had rattled into sight, the damaged, patched-up wagon with a greatly lightened load had rejoined the line, followed by the mounted rear-guard.

It was about six in the evening when the last of the great carts lumbered behind its ungainly giant oxen over the final ridge, and onto a flat marshalling area. This commanded a view over much of the magnificent landscape of this part of the southern Black Forest. High above them all, a pair of golden eagles soared majestically, riding the warm air currents of early evening. To each of the mounted men as to the carters, after the exertions of the day, it was as though they were being rewarded by being allowed to stand on the roof of their world. In every direction the views were magnificent. Largely wooded, there were green rectangles in the valleys below where the trees had been cleared for husbandry. The lesser ridges and valleys rolled away towards the distant hills they knew to be marking the course of the Rhine, east of Basel. Smoke arose from scattered chimneys and it was just possible to identify a cluster of buildings far off, as a village that they would eventually be passing through. The haze of early evening promised the imminent close of day, a day of unprecedented heavy haulage and hard effort to have travelled so few miles, but so satisfactory to have already conquered the main heights that stood in their path to the river crossing. In fact the best prospect of all was the realisation that from now on, this side of the Rhine, their journey was to be all downhill.

Ludo von Stauffen told his fellows in the advance guard that this long steep hill they had spent the whole day climbing, was in fact a mountain called Belchen and that they had travelled more than 3000 feet up that steep rough track. Now at the top, they had intersected a forest road leading west, he said, which eventually would reach the bank of the Rhine still downstream of the city of Basel, which from that direction would provide the river's crossing place. But their route lay elsewhere, first turning to the east, and in the far distance on the southeastern horizon they could see their way towards the final low hills that hid their view of their destination, that reach of the River Rhine, above Basel.

The Baron had not deceived them about what to expect. From now on it was indeed downhill. The forest carpeted the hillsides and the valleys, but they could see, even though it was getting to be dusk along the winding roads below, open fields, and even villages. On the southern horizon they could pick out the route towards their next destination, Rheinfelden the bridge over the River Rhine in the Habsburg domain, outside the territory of the Prince Bishop of Basel.

The damp surface of the hilltop meadow where the marshalling was taking place, was quickly being churned up by the wheels of the heavily laden wagons; the whole area was abuzz with activity as the remaining teams and their cargo arrived. The teamsters were harnessing up their draught horses, which had been slowly walked unburdened up-hill, as the Baron's peasant farmers unhitched their great oxen that had so well served their purpose. Immediately the farmers started the journey downhill leading their unburdened teams of oxen that even now would never move fast, although the humans were anxious to get back to their farms.

The Marshal and Franz, the Schwyzer wagonmaster, conferred with the Baron's senior man at arms who then led the convoy away to the east, slightly downhill about three miles to a place he had designated as an overnight camp. Already the supply and kitchen carts had been sent on ahead to start making the camp. The Baron's senior man now sent half his mounted soldiers to escort the ox teams going back to Stauffen to travel together with the foresters and their hounds, who had so successfully deterred a raid on the convoy. There still remained a danger of frustrated outlaws trying to raid the ox teams on the downward journey, if only to steal a beast for their dinner.

The rest of the Stauffen guards, it had been agreed, would accompany the Templar convoy leading the way as far as the Rhine and there take their leave, to escort Ludo von Stauffen back to his father's castle.

Later that evening when the cook fires were dying down and the carters, the knights and men at arms were taking their well-earned ease, the Marshal called a meeting of his senior people. The leaders of the Templars from Scotland and those from Germany, who had joined them at Stauffen, were accompanied by Franz the Schwyzer and his son, the Baron's son Ludo, and the captain of the Von Stauffen men at arms. The sky above was sprinkled with stars and a moon had risen, casting its cold light over the men gathered in front of the Marshal's tent. The campfire at which they warmed themselves burned bright, as the Marshal took a stick and with a dagger whittled it to a point, then handed it to Franz.

"Show us if you will, the route we have to follow tomorrow. Say your say, Master Franz, and we can question you afterwards."

The burly wagon master scraped into the packed earth, a broad swathe for the river as well as the line that the road there would take, and described it at each stage. "We are here before the valley of this small river," he told them, "we will continue on the road ahead of us and will pass close by the village of Munstertal, which we do not enter, as our downhill road turns south, just before the village. Now that we have our horses back, we can be past there within an hour of leaving here. So if we leave before first light, we will have already passed the village before they are fully aroused, which must be prudent." He looked at the Marshal, who nodded his approval.

"We continue to follow the valley road, which is of a reasonable width and strength along the river valley. There is likely to be some other traffic on the road, mostly farm or logging carts and probably that is all we will see. Fortunately because of the logging carts, which need to carry the great bulk and weight of some of the giant trees from around here, the surface is in good repair and capable of carrying our own heavy loads.

"By middle afternoon or thereabouts," the big Schweizer continued marking the soil, "we should have reached the village of Steinen - there…" he said pointing to his crude map. "I know a place about a mile beyond the village, here, where I suggest we stop, tend to the horses and prepare for our last stage within the forest, which I propose would be here", he scratched an X in the dirt. "If this is agreed, my suggestion could be that we make all our preparations to cross the river, as Baron von Stauffen recommended at Rheinfelden. The bridge is guarded by a small detachment of the town guard who collect tolls and it will close for the night at about seven hours after noon. Coming from the Steinen direction, we will not come into sight of the bridge until we are almost there, so unless we are betrayed they will not know we are coming."

"I do not presume to say to you military gentlemen…" Franz looked at the Marshal and his circle of knights, "how best to deal with the guard at the crossing of the bridge. What I can say is if we leave it until shortly before they are due to close the bridge, we will have surprise on our side. The river is narrow at this point. We could have our heavy wagons, the light ones and their escorts across the bridge, all taking about thirty minutes, no more. Then I will be with those at the front and we will not linger at all in the town but move on, taking the road leading south away from Rheinfelden towards there," he indicated a point he said was called Nusshof, "about one hour further on. There Sir, with the river crossing accomplished, I propose you call us together again to look at the remainder of the route."

"That is a good plan, Master Franz." the Marshal acknowledged. He looked particularly at the Baron's Captain of his men at arms to see if, as the only other one with local knowledge, he agreed. In fact the soldier deferred to his young master Ludo, who spoke for them both:

"As you know Sir Marshal, my father's orders were for our party from Stauffen Castle to turn back before the bridge, I would suggest we leave you at this last village of Steinen", he scuffed his toe on the earth where Franz's scratching represented that village.

"As you understand, my father needs 'to have not known' about how you might cross the bridge and that our von Stauffen livery is not seen to have been connected with any forcible crossing. He is after all, a local landowner and does not want to start a war with his neighbours, although I must confess Sir that I sorely wish that I was continuing with you."

"You have the right spirit young Ludo," said the Marshal, "but your father has been of the greatest help to us already and we must not prejudice his neighbourly relations. We will follow the route Master Franz has laid out and I thank him for that. We will plan to make the last push towards the bridge so that our wagons start to arrive at the crossing at about six and a half hours after noon - so some thirty minutes before the bridge is due to close for the night. We will discuss the final details at Steinen but my plan at this time is to send ahead about thirty knights and sergeants fully armoured, as if for a fight. It will be our German brethren I think, because of the language in these parts. Their first priority will be to overawe the guard, but my order will actually be to secure the bridge until the last wagon has crossed. Sir Heinrich and Sir Martin, attend upon me now and we will discuss that further.

"One other thing. If anyone, horsemen or others try to pass the convoy to get ahead of us, if they are not content to travel behind, we must temporarily detain them if necessary. No one who has seen us must be allowed to precede us at any point of the journey, to possibly alert any of the villages ahead, and particularly so, the closer we get to the river.

"Therefore both our rear-guard under Sir Geraint and our advance guard as today, commanded by Sir Heinrich; and with you Sir Martin to take the flank guard, all must be fully instructed about that. I assume that you, as you have told us Master Franz, will be with your leading wagon?

"Sleep well, Gentlemen. Tomorrow the successful crossing of the Rhine is our key task of this whole journey."

***

Some fifteen miles away, a short flight for any of the free-floating raptors wheeling high over the forest, at dusk the castle gates had closed for the night. Master Peter Proudhomme and a feverish Paul de Chatillon swathed in a blanket, but both wearing their identifiable mastermason's white cloth helmets, having reached Stauffen village, rode up the spiral road that wound around the hill on which the castle sat. On either side of them on the conical hillside stretched seemingly endless lines of grapevines on cords suspended between their wooden frames. Above them on the castle rampart blazed a torch, which illuminated and reflected off the steel helmets of the guards, who followed their progress up the winding hill, then when they were within earshot, challenged the riders.

"We have business with Baron von Stauffen," called up the master builder and he gave their names.

Within minutes the visitors heard the metallic sound of the great bar on the main gate sliding back, which then promptly opened. As they rode into the peaceful courtyard, a pair of ostlers came up and took their horses and their packs.

"Well Master Peter, better late than never, as they say," boomed the voice of the Baron striding across the cobbled courtyard towards them. "But your friends, they all left early this morning heading for the river - and are well on the way, I am informed."

"Greetings my lord," said Proudhomme, "I will of course tell you everything, as to why we are late, but first of all this young knight, my temporary pupil, has had a bad time - he fell into the hands of the Dominicans in Freiburg."

"Oh my God," broke in the clearly agitated Baron his bonhomie dispersed, looking at the sickly Paul leaning over the neck of his horse, hardly able to sit in his saddle, "was he put to the question? Do the Dominicans know what is afoot? Are we betrayed?"

By his rapid questions his concerns were obvious, but Proudhomme reassured him. "They know nothing," he said firmly, "I will tell you what happened my lord, but Sir Paul here is sick. He has a recurring fever from his time in Outremer and needs to be taken care of."

A female voice, Lady Melissa from behind the Baron, spoke up, "Father, we must get him into bed and leave Master Proudhomme to explain later. She called the ostlers to assist Paul in dismounting. "You are right my dear," her father replied, "let me place him in your care and that of your sister."

For Paul, the next two days passed in a blur of momentary consciousness and long fitful bouts of sleep. What he was vaguely conscious of was the presence of a beautiful young woman by his bedside mopping his forehead and his sweating body with cool damp cloths. He did not know that they were the two von Stauffen sisters taking care of him, but when the fever finally broke, he opened his eyes to see that it was the Lady Melissa who smiled at him. He later realised that in his fevered state he had scarcely made any distinction between her and her younger sister the Lady Helene, since between them they maintained a twenty-four hour watch over him.

After seven years as a Templar, Paul's experience of women was limited. As a pubescent youth his father, the Baron de Chatillon had seen to it, as a part of his preparation for the world that he was instructed in the ways of sex by a comely laundress in their household, and he subsequently had had some sexual engagements with farm girls and domestics. But when he had decided to become a Templar and take his vows, he knew that just as any monk, he would now be required to abandon any thoughts of a family, of sex, or of even casual friendships with any woman. The Order had been very strict about this. Unlike the non-military monks with which they shared much of their Rule, the Templars were not enclosed but out in the world, and so much more subject to temptation. No doubt older knights who were so inclined might in later life find ways around this prohibition, but for the young novices not yet accepted into the Order, they just had to put sex out of their minds. After that, the discipline and sheer volume of their routine and duties, let alone exhaustion from starting each day with the four a.m. mass, followed by a full programme of military exercises and several more masses to follow, each day, ensured that they virtually had no contact with women - which didn't mean they didn't notice them.

The glamour of belonging to this prestigious body of knights had seemed to this idealistic young man, as with many others, to embody the very peak of a chivalrous life - it had been the general view. But as he served his time as a squire, and later became a mature knight of the order, he found it much more difficult to resist his natural sexual urges.

He had taken counselling from a priest of the Order who told him little for his comfort, except that he could always confess his sins, if indeed he had sinned, and any priest was bound to keep it secret. This seemed to make nonsense of his vows, so he continued to wrestle with the problem.

Later in his life he had been stationed at a fortress in Cilicia's Ammanaus Mountains where Templars detached from their own garrisons in Cilicia, had held the castle of an Armenian ally of the Order. The Armenian castellan had a daughter, a beautiful young woman, the Lady Roxanne, and together, they had started discreetly to become close. But whatever might have been, he was suddenly sent for and ordered to return immediately to Cyprus, not even knowing if it was a temporary posting, or as it turned out to be, a permanent move. The relationship with Roxanne was left stranded at that point, as events took over his life. As he had thought about it since, that was now about six years ago - she would, he thought, as a nobleman's shapely daughter with delicate features, almost certainly be married by now.

The young Templar knights who had escaped and met up at Scotland's Castle Aird, after they had heard that their Order was finished and that their vows no longer applied, mostly agreed that whatever else, it would be great relief to live a normal non-monastic life, like any others of their age and class. That and the fact that they no longer needed to attend the mass held at four in the morning and another one at seven plus three more throughout the day - each day; it seemed a notable improvement in their circumstances.

So when Paul had come around, his fever passing, he had at first thought that maybe he had already found his way to Paradise. That of all things this kindly and beautiful young woman, exuding warmth and energy, had unexpectedly entered his life and more, that she had so soon become important to him, little realising that she already felt something of the same about him. Like her younger sister, she was fair of complexion but Melissa had long yellow tresses, which she meticulously brushed, to a shining torrent of gold. Her features were distinctive with her wide blue eyes, with a small slightly tilted nose, that he found quite charming.

Peter Proudhomme, after their arrival, had recounted to the Baron what had happened in Freiburg, and the singular good luck of the Archbishop being in residence there, and in an amiable mood. "It didn't hurt," he mentioned, "that on questioning Paul he discovered that he was related by marriage to the Royal house of France. Since archbishops are primarily politicians rather than priests, he wasn't going to let a bunch of mean-minded Dominicans make off with someone who could perhaps one day be useful to him."

At that, Von Stauffen said, "actually this archbishop is better than most of them." "I know he voted against the suppression of the Templars, and I think that he was genuinely outraged that Phillip of France should have acquired so much power as to get away with this evil deed."

The master mason had decided the day after he had delivered Paul to the castle, that prudence dictated that he himself would make the easy ride back to Freiburg and be available there in the daytime, as long as the archbishop was in the city, but had returned again to sleep at Stauffen late that evening.

It was the morning of the third day after Paul had arrived at the castle, that the Baron passed on the good news from his girls to Proudhomme, that the young knight was better and whilst still a-bed, his fever seemed to have calmed down. Peter went up to his tower chamber to see him, and was impressed with the beautiful Melissa who so tenderly watched over him. Paul was leaning back against great pillows lying on linen sheets and the master mason teased him, "You have probably never before slept in such comfort, my young friend and certainly your nurse is no pinch-faced sister from the convent."

Paul replied sheepishly, "No question of it." whilst Melissa's fair cheeks blushed red.

Peter took in the tenderness with which she surrounded him and despite his pleasure at Paul's obvious improvement, nevertheless registered that this new relationship could possibly become an entanglement for certain plans that he knew of, which the Council had for Paul's future.

"The Baron suggests you might join us at table for supper," the older man told him, "that is if you feel up to it - and if your nurse, is content with that." She looked like she didn't want to share him, but nodded as Paul spoke for himself, that he would be there.

***

THE BRIDGE

When the von Stauffen escort had taken their leave of the convoy at Steinen, the officers and sergeants re-ordered the column as the Marshal had specified for the bridge crossing.

Throughout that days march, as they had passed hamlets and farmhouses where the dogs had alerted all within to their presence, they had attracted the stares of the curious, but no one was about to challenge, nor yet call a greeting to this grim faced body of men at arms and the long and large wagon train.
Most would have assumed that this was a body of mercenaries escorting some nobleman's treasure, since they displayed no banners. The more observant might have seen some von Stauffen surcoats there, which to the well informed would indicate that the cargo of the carts was from the baron's famous silver mines. That would all make sense of it.

Far from any seeking to overtake them on the road, not one of these farmers or peasants in their right senses would risk perhaps provoking the soldiers, by seeking to pass them. The glowering rear-guard reinforced that decision for any waverers.

Nevertheless, the Marshal, now at Steinen village, sent out a patrol ahead of the column with strict instructions to get close to, but stay out of sight of the bridge. They were ordered to intercept and detain anybody who might slip ahead of the column heading for the bridge and hold them if suspicious, or if not, turn them around with advice to try again at any other time, except that evening.

The mounted patrol had now stationed themselves barely a mile from the forest side of the bridge and had allowed to pass them only traffic moving away from the river. Within twenty minutes of the patrol stopping to take up their station, with two horsemen on each side of the road that led downhill to the river town of Rheinfelden and its stone bridge, they heard behind them - and soon saw - the advance guard with Sir Heinrich leader of the Germans and their comrades trotting up, two by two, and once they had passed, fell in behind them. A few hundred paces behind the mounted column made up of the German Templars, was the Marshal with his personal bodyguard, one of his squires behind him carrying a lance with a banner of a black boar on a white field.

The first of the wagons was not yet in sight but the mounted column, apparently unhurried, trotted down the cobbled road leading down to the hinged wooden pole, which was up, and the bridge open with no other travellers to be seen.

The fast-flowing river was not wide here, the bridge's first stone span rested on a small islet continuing through a second span from there on to the nearby southern bank, where it entered the town. The town wall was sheer to the river surface but also served as the back of a row of houses whose rear wall, pierced by windows, this had become. A church steeple rose high above the wall and what to the oncoming riders, midway along the length of the wall, appeared to be the upper level of a modest-sized keep, with a two headed eagle banner flying above its crenellations.

At the bridge, a pair of liveried soldiers of the town guard had, until they heard the sound of a large body of horses, been lounging against the town wall, where there was a small hut, within which was a tally clerk who received the toll duties. Across through the gate, on the other side of the bridgeroad at the town end, another soldier was engaged in talking to a young woman. The leading heavily armed horsemen did not slacken their pace, as they came to the pole barrier before the gate which the soldiers hurriedly were about to lower, but already Sir Heinrich and his leading men had trotted past that minor obstruction.

Sir Heinrich reined in, pulled his mount aside, pushed up his helmet visor and addressed the two by now frightened guards, their hands still on the striped pole whilst his column never broke their stride, moving on across to the far end and into the town beyond.

"What the devil do you think you're doing?" he arrogantly demanded of the foot soldier, "How dare you try to impede the passage of goods for his Grace, the Duke?"

"We were only doing our duty, Sir. We had no knowledge of your coming," the senior soldier hesitantly said.

"Nonsense," was the curt reply. "But who would tell an idiot like you. Where is the town captain?" he now demanded.

"I'll send for him, Sir, immediately," was the nervous reply, but both had seen the single guard at the town end of the bridgeroad leave the girl and run off into the town before the horsemen had got to him, no doubt to inform his superiors.

As ordered, within minutes, the thirty mounted men of the advance guard now held both ends of the bridge and the square beyond, from which as the Schwyzer Franz, had told them, their route departed off to the right, away from the castle keep and the town centre. It was also the main road out of town along the river's southern bank to Basel, but would divide within a mile or so with a road turning south towards Lucerne, and their planned overnight stop at Nusshof.

Now the small honour guard of horsemen surrounding the Marshal appeared, and trotted towards the bridge. They came abreast of Sir Heinrich and the town guards where they halted. The Marshal, whose helmet was embellished for the occasion with a magnificent green and yellow ostrich feather, had its visor up, unlike those of his grim escort.

Sir Heinrich threw an elaborate salute and called, "All is correct, my Lord. Permission to bring up the wagons?"

Inside the tollbooth the clerk witnessing all this, would later report that clearly this was a great lord, but he looked at and failed to recognise his face, which was not a local one. The only evidence of who he was, perhaps, was the banner on the lance, carried by his squire, of a black boar on a white field.

The Marshal quickly took in the whole scene, noted his men controlled both ends of the bridge, nodded his assent and followed by his escort, walked his horse forward across the bridge. Sir Heinrich meanwhile had signalled his messenger to ride back the short distance to the wagons and bring them on.

THE SQUIRE

At Castle Stauffen the Baron was in a good mood as they sat at the broad black oak table in his hall. A pair of outsize shaggy hounds sprawled around his legs and a large log fire blazed in the hearth.

He had placed Paul on his right with his daughter Melissa beyond him. Next to her was her brother Ludo. On his left sat Master Proudhomme and the younger second daughter, the Lady Helene. The baron brandished a chilled silver jug of wine, beads of condensation running down its bulbous shape as he leaned over to fill his guests' silver goblets. "This is our best," he commented. "It is a three year old white and a blend of my own grapes with that of a neighbour whose vineyards are on the route between Breisach and Freiburg - you would have seen the vines," he addressed the Master Mason as he poured, "on your way from the river when you first arrived?" The Master nodded assent as the baron turned to serve Paul.

"Now Sir Paul, I understand that you are from Burgundy, where they also know a thing or two about making wine, but just as they call your wines after your region, so here do we call this wine 'Rhenish'. So let us salute your recovery in good Rhenish my dear boy, and then you must tell us how you first came by this fever in Outremer, and indeed of your time there."

They raised their goblets, drank and Paul set down his wine, preparing to respond. Then the heavy curtain of the abbas at the great door opened, the two hounds sat up and tensed and then relaxed as the Baron's steward hurried in, holding a small silver tray containing a minute ring and a tiny scrap of flattened goatskin bearing some marks.

"The first pigeon has returned", the baron commented non-committedly as he took the message, screwed up his eyes and scrutinised it. "Passed river, no losses," he read out slowly. "Good work my dear friends." he beamed. "At least I have the satisfaction of knowing that my part in this adventure has gone well."

"What now?" he enquired of his two guests, looking first at Peter Proudhomme.

"Well my lord, I have had no chance to discuss this with Sir Paul, but I have thought about what might be our best course of action. He is to be one of the battalion commanders of the Schwyzer pikemen in our scheme of things, and will need to be with his new troops for as long as possible before the big battle. But the Marshal will know that there must have been a mishap for Sir Paul not to have returned to the castle before the column moved out, nor yet to have caught them up. He will be glad to get him back whenever he arrives, and now we know that the bridge is behind them, Master Franz we can be sure, will take the convoy by the fastest route to Schwyz. So they will certainly not be waiting for us, neither him nor me.

"Then there is another matter concerning my Lord Archbishop, who returns to his Archdiocese of Constance in two days' time. It would be imprudent for me not to be there in Freiburg and at his disposal over these next days. I want to give him no cause for dissatisfaction and there is still much for me to do at the Munster.

"Sir Paul's health can only benefit by another two days here," he added. Paul at this point was conscious of a feminine knee pressed gently but firmly against his. He felt his blood course and the first stirrings of a quite different sort of fever from that of his sickness.

"My early presence at Schwyz is not critical", the master builder continued, "but I do represent the Fraternity's High Council and must get there within a reasonable time. So my conclusion is that we wait two more days. I will ride back to Freiburg tomorrow via Breisach, where I want to visit Master Simon, and send a pigeon mail with this good news," he nodded an acknowledgement to von Stauffen. "Then I will go on from there to Freiburg, and over the next two days see how the land lies with the Archbishop and my Munster project.

"I will return in two evenings time and either I will go on the next day with Sir Paul, or he should by then be fit to travel and can go ahead without me. I would follow in my own ways, and at my own time."

"Father," this was from Ludo, in a somewhat strained unnatural voice. He had risen and was standing up at his end of the table. All eyes turned towards him.

"I have a request to make of you, and of Sir Paul. Would you my Lord, allow me to accompany Sir Paul, and Sir Paul, would you take me to serve you as your squire?" He was clearly embarrassed at the directness of his questions, but remained standing, tense as if to hear a verdict.

His father looked studiously at the table in front of him. "Ludo dear boy," he said, "you are certainly of an age to serve as a squire. Moreover, there is a war coming up and without some experience of war it will not be easy for you to win your spurs. I have been thinking, whilst Master Peter explained his position, that it would be prudent now for Sir Paul to travel on through the city of Basel; certainly not across the Rheinfelden bridge. If I know anything, that will by now - too late by far, be bristling with the Duke's men asking many searching questions of any unusual travelers through his domains. The Bishop of Basel however, has no connection with the recent events and for a solitary knight with his squire and servants to make their way over his bridge, through his busy city and along his highways would cause no concern at all. Now I am aware Ludo, that you have travelled with me through Basel and beyond and you could guide Sir Paul that way.

"But what I must say my boy, is that it would be wrong and quite unfair to ask Sir Paul sitting here as our guest, to decide this, based on your rather abrupt request. It is my thought that he might take you to travel on this next stage of his journey in the role of a squire, but without a permanent commitment to take you on beyond that. If so, I will write a letter for you Ludo to take to the Marshal, and ask him if he can place you with one of his knights, not currently served by a squire."

All eyes turned to Paul who felt the knee that had been pressing on his own, had even more delightfully been replaced by a hand. Seeking to concentrate, he cleared his throat and somewhat huskily answered the question.

"I have no squire, my lord. I would be pleased to take on your boy Ludo in that capacity, since he seems so keen to serve. I looked out and saw him at exercise with your master-at-arms this morning, who seems to have done a good job with him. Ludo must know that we are about to enter into a state of war, once we have crossed into the Schwyzer country and there will be much to do."

The hand on his knee had by now stroked its way up to his inner thigh. It had become obvious to him that his body held no mysteries from her. He had realised when he regained consciousness, that he was clean in a way that he had seldom before been clean, and his bed unsoiled, despite that he had suffered his fever there for nearly three days and nights. His feelings for her were mixed between excitement and gratitude, so he was pleased to take on her brother, who was anyway clearly qualified for the role, as she had equally clearly signalled, that she wanted him to do.

"Excellent! That's settled then." and the Baron pounded on the table, jolting the silver goblets and startling his hounds, for his servants to bring the meal to table.

***

RHEINFELDEN TOWN

The Marshal and his escort walked their horses unhurriedly past the end of the bridge and entered the town into the small square beyond, where some twenty fully armoured horsemen now sat their horses in a wide semi-circle, immobile as if on parade. Behind them were a number of two-storey townspeople's houses, of white-painted plaster and wattle, steeply roofed in tightly bound sheaves of straw, with brick chimneys poking through. There was also a smithy there which had closed for the night and an inn with rough wooden tables outside, but no citizens were to be seen, except from behind half-closed shutters.

The Marshal, the leading figure, stopped in the centre and turned his horse, as did his escort, to face towards the town centre which had gone very quiet, although faces peered at them from behind shutters. It was clear that in the near distance, carts were being pulled away and animals driven off from this suddenly taut scene.

The building which was the old Keep, further down the cobbled main street, suddenly debouched some uniformed men, no more than six of them, still pulling on clothing and their helmets and hefting their spears. Then down the steps came striding their under-officer, with the sentry who had run to find him. He was a grizzled veteran and took in the scene at one glance.

He straightened up and adjusted his dress as he walked briskly towards the mounted party, the knights amongst them still had their visors lowered. His small squad following him looking less and less menacing as he approached the horsemen, heading towards the obviously most senior, the be-plumed Marshal.

But before he could reach the mounted semi-circle, a knight detached himself and walked his horse forward to intercept him. It was Sir Martin, the second in command of the German Templars - his leader remained with the troops at the entrance to the bridge. A silence fell, which was disturbed by the distant and growing sound of many iron-shod cartwheels approaching, over the cobbled access road leading down to the bridge.

Sir Martin interposed himself in front of the city officer, lifted his visor and demanded to know his name and station.

"I am Gurt, Sir, deputy to the town captain."

"So, you are not the town captain?" responded the mounted knight

"No Sir, I am the under-officer, he is gone to Zug to report to the Duke's factor."

Hearing this, the Marshal as if in contempt, wheeled his horse and unhurriedly walked him away, his escort behind him, towards the road the convoy would eventually be taking. He was clearly signaling he was not going to talk with this lowly individual, a man beneath his consideration.

"Well Under-officer Gurt," the knight sarcastically articulating the man's rank, spoke with all the arrogance the role demanded. "At any moment - indeed here they come, our wagons will be passing through this funny little town of yours."

"Yes Sir," replied Gurt. "But Sir, may I ask who you are? Our master Duke Leopold will want to know this."

"Your sentry at the bridge told us that he had no knowledge of our coming. Are you telling me that you, Under-officer Gurt, deputy to the town captain, also did not know that we are taking military supplies to His Grace the Duke?"

As he spoke four more mounted men at arms, bearing lances, preceded the first of the great wagons that rumbled across the bridge, with the Schwyzer wagonmaster steering the team of draught horses. Master Franz had pulled the hood of his cloak up covering his head, as did his other teamsters, in case they might be recognized as having travelled that route before. A steady stream of wagons followed, interspersed with strings of spare riding horses with their grooms. Mounted men at arms were on the flanks, whilst squires and servants, smiths, cooks and other tradesmen walked alongside, although some smaller lads were riding on the backs of the carthorses.

They moved across the bridge into the small square where the mounted knights still sat their horses as if on parade. Then without any interruption, the convoy passed through a wide gap in the armoured semi-circle, all maintaining the same steady pace following the lead wagon of Master Franz, taking the road heading west out of the town.

The under-officer stood in dismay, knowing he was helpless, and unable even to follow up his questioning, now simply because of the noise the passing carts created, their iron shod wheels grating on the cobblestones. His men similarly stood back, mere spectators, hoping only that their under-officer would not order them to do something stupid. He could hardly fail to notice that some of the wagons were piled high with the bales of wool that had travelled up the Rhine, which made him wonder about the normal tolls being lost to the Duke. He could not have known that beneath them was a fortune in silver ingots.

Other wagons, heavily laden with unseen pike heads, but with loose armour and bundles of weapons piled above them, to be seen beneath the sailcloth covering, did fill the description of military supplies.

Gurt miserably stood there, watching perhaps a hundred human beings travel through his town, fully half of them of a warlike character. He was thinking primarily of how, and in what terms, he could report his lack of action. When a large wagon was passing and the mounted knight who had addressed him was momentarily distracted, looking it over as well as its cargo, he turned to one of his brighter men and urgently told him to fall-out, run to the stables, there to take a good horse and ride like hell to Zug. He was to look out for the returning town captain on the way and report on these events. But he knew that these grim fighting men would be long gone before any more serious challenge than his half dozen town guards could be offered to them, nor yet if their story was true, should any opposition be offered that might hinder the Duke's war effort.

What he thought that he understood from this short experience was that they appeared to be a war band of freelances, although they were much more orderly and better disciplined than any that he had seen before. It was widely known that the Duke had summoned his vassals to war, to meet at the castle of the lakeside town of Zug, in some few weeks' time. It made sense that mercenaries would also be recruited and probably even bring cartloads of military hardware from some part of Germany, whence they had obviously come. All of that, he thought measured up to what he was witnessing here today, but the great bales of wool bothered him - until as he suddenly realised, it was likely that such people as these had perhaps just helped themselves and commandeered it on the way, from some hapless merchant they had encountered.

That they were some kind of Germans he knew from the direction from which they had come, and the language in which he had been addressed. That they were mercenaries, he assumed, because, apart from their leader's standard on the lance held by his squire, their surcoats showed no coats of arms, although some at least by the quality of their armour, and tellingly their spurs, were plainly dubbed knights.

Within twenty minutes the last cart, that of cooks and clanking kitchen gear, was rolling from the forest bank rattling over the cobbles onto the bridge. When a further ten minutes had elapsed, it could be seen swaying along at the tail end of the long column now leaving town, headed west along the Basel road.

Gurt was surprised, indeed relieved that these troops had not demanded any food or accommodation, which he had at first feared, but reasoned that they were already in or about to join the service of the Duke, and would be unlikely to despoil one of his towns.

The senior knight, who had so superciliously spoken to him, had now wheeled his horse away, the conversation clearly over and he had then ridden out of town, towards the tail end of the column. The horsemen surrounding the square, smartly paired off and followed him, two by two, joining the wagon train as the new rear-guard, the last horse out voiding its bowels onto the cobbles, as though a final comment on this brief transit through the small town.

Gurt continued to stand there and stare after them as the sound faded in the dusk. Why, he wondered, did they take the Basel road and not ride through the town to the east in the opposite direction, on the main road towards the Duke's domains?

THE LASCIVIOUS PLEASING OF A LUTE

For the next two days Paul, although primarily engaged with the tender attentions of the Lady Melissa, prepared for his onwards journey. He had met with the Baron and Ludo to discuss the route to take between Basel and the rebel town of Schwyz. The Baron had told him that the nearest large city, Lucerne, was outside the Duke's domains which covered most of the territory to its north and east. He showed a drawing he had made of the route he believed that Master Franz had chosen for the convoy, which travelled the major well-travelled road from Basel towards Lucerne, but the convoy would skirt the city to the north and when unobserved, double back to the lakeside.

He knew that Franz would send a well-mounted messenger ahead of the slow convoy, the plan being to make a rendezvous on the lakeshore, where barges from the opposite Schwyz shore would transport the convoy across the lake. That would save a further two-day journey of continuing past Lucerne, and going all the way around the lake to the south. It was not sensible for the convoy to continue around the Lake's north side as this was getting uncomfortably close to the Habsburg lands and the very town of Zug, where the Duke held a castle and where his levy was indeed appointed to gather. But heading in that direction, north of Lucerne, would usefully give any witnesses the impression that they must be the Duke's men headed for that destination.

They agreed at the castle that the longer route, right around the south shore was the prudent course for Paul's small party, made up of himself, Ludo, and a mounted servant.

The morning of that second day, the Baron had taken Paul into his stables and had had the grooms take a charger out into the stable yard. "The Marshal told me," he said, "that you travelled up the Rhine on a barge, whilst your colleagues rode their own horses along the riverbank. I would like you to accept this fellow," he slapped the beast's flank, "I could not remount your whole force, which happily was not necessary, but I would like my son's master to be well mounted. Try him!"

A groom quickly slipped his harness on, with which the stallion did little to cooperate. Paul admired the warhorse's points, and then tentatively put his foot in a stirrup trying to judge the beast's temper, as the groom held the bridle. He took the reins and mounted, feeling the muscle power beneath him, whilst the big fellow assessed his rider. They walked a turn around the cobbled yard and then with the Baron looking on approvingly, trotted out into the castle courtyard. They clattered across the open drawbridge, continuing at a walk down the winding road past the rows of vines, to the point where the castle road met the main track on level ground beyond. Then he wheeled and set him to climb the hill they had just descended. "I shall call you Hannibal," he shouted to the horse, who flexed his limbs as the muscle power surged through him.

Hannibal having loosened up on his downhill walk, now opened up and stretched as he accelerated, gaining speed even as the hill became steeper. On the entrance tower over the gate, two sentries looked down admiringly at the show of power on display. For Paul seated firmly, he could not help as he rode, but compare this exhilaration with the utter depths of misery he had experienced so recently, in the cells of the Freiburg Dominicans.

The despair of that episode was such a contrast to the joy and liberation of this moment. Paul was happy and could hardly credit how his luck had changed. The daughter of this amiable nobleman had shown him passion and last night had taken him to new heights of pleasure. His kindly host had entrusted him not only with his only son to be his squire, but had now presented him with this magnificent animal. No doubt it was his gracious way of saying, thank you for taking on Ludo. He already felt, after these few days, that Castle Stauffen was like a home to him, something that as a Templar he had learned to live without. He knew that he must now talk to Melissa about 'them' and their future, and in these strange circumstances, what was to be done.

That evening Master Peter returned. He told them he had concluded that he should not yet leave Freiburg. The Archbishop had again delayed his departure and although he had informed his Grace that he would next be visiting Basel, about some work in the cathedral there, nevertheless, he did not want to leave Freiburg until after the Archbishop had set out for Constance. Also, he said, he was waiting for an answer to his last message from the Prior in Scotland by pigeon-post, which would come via Simon the merchant at Breisach.

So Paul, it was agreed, would travel on the next day as a single knight with his small ménage through Basel. His story if pressed - but why would it be – simply was that he was en route past Lucerne and onwards south, via the Gotthard Pass to Tuscany.

Baron von Stauffen was not unaware that his daughter had developed an attachment to this young Knight. Even if he had been so blind to have not noticed, his other daughter, Helene, the younger of the two girls had also fancied herself with Paul, whose condition, so star-struck was he by the older sister, had quite passed him by.

Plans had been discussed for the journey. At dinner that evening, conversation was warm and cheerful. Paul again felt Melissa's knee beneath the table pressing against his, as though to remind him of what they had agreed. The Baron, to mark the fact that tomorrow was a parting, had engaged some musicians from Breisach, one of whom was a singer who accompanied himself on a lute. The atmosphere was transformed - softened by the entertainment. The plaintive strains he conjured from the instrument charmed the Baron's guests, as his tenor voice spoke of a world of gallant knights and fair damsels, a world of aspiration rather than reality, thought Paul, remembering the bloody field of Bannockburn, and as he readied himself for what was to come in Schwyz.

When the entertainment was over and the musicians had departed, clearing his throat, Paul stood up just as young Ludo had done two nights before, and addressed the Baron, no less nervous than his young squire had been.

"My Lord" he started nervously. "Tomorrow I leave your so very generous hospitality, taking with me not just happy memories of your many kindnesses, but also your boy Ludo for my squire, and a fine warhorse, which I have named for that Carthaginian general Hannibal, who stood against Rome."

The Baron nodded approvingly. "But my Lord," Paul continued, "although I take with me these evidences of your kindness, I leave something behind me." He looked down fondly at the lady at his side, as she met his glance. "My Lord I confess, that have quite lost my heart to the Lady Melissa."

The muscles in the Baron's face worked and his eyes shot up to the ceiling. Paul was not sure if he would now explode at this presumption. Master Proudhomme looked very grave and the young Lady Helene coloured beetroot red. After what seemed to Paul like an eternity, von Stauffen took his gaze from the great cross beams above and looked past Paul at his daughter.

"Melissa, my dear and what say you to this statement. Did you then bewitch your patient?"

She appeared quite composed where the others in one way or another, were not.

"Dearest Father", she replied. "I too am in similar case. I too feel for him, so if and when he speaks of 'us', he speaks for me as well." She flashed her father a brilliant smile.

"Master Proudhomme, what say you? I know that you are one of the senior members of the new Order. How do you regard this declaration?"

"My Lord," the master mason said, "since this is not a celibate Order, the Prior expressly told the brethren that those Templar oaths were null and void, and that indeed for our new Order to have a future, it was expected that the brethren - if they should so wish - would take wives and have families. Having said that, the new Order is on the eve of a great test - we can expect a bloody battle in Helvetia and Sir Paul must necessarily be in the thick of it, and this within a matter of weeks.

"There is another matter. If we carry the day at Schwyz and if Sir Paul survives the battle, I know that the council has him in mind for another mission in distant lands, which might keep him away from here for two years or more. Then if he survives that, I would assume he would be free to return and live perhaps a more normal life, where marriage might then be appropriate."

Paul who knew nothing other than insubstantial hints of this further mission, swallowed hard at the news, but like the others turned his eyes towards the Baron, who spoke out.

"Well there are a lot of 'ifs' there, in what Master Proudhomme has told us. We have little time to ponder this matter, so I will say this. You have your duty to do, as Master Proudhomme has advised us. It is obvious to me that you are on a leadership path within the new fraternity and that must be good.

"I am agreeable that you and my daughter can be considered as betrothed, and let us now see whether you can survive these many hazards and return to us. In these terms, I give you both my blessing."

Neither Paul nor Melissa was interested in the subsequent conversation. They had sprung their big news and now conscious of their limited time together, they looked for an opportunity to leave the table. There was no way that could be done discreetly and when they got up to go, Paul offering his hand to assist her rising, there was a ribald hoot from Ludo and much laughter. Cheeks burning, but wreathed in smiles, both said goodnight to the company and stole away.

The next morning Paul dressed in chain mail and half-armour, had a brief meeting in the courtyard with Master Proudhomme, who himself was departing in the other direction for Ansbach and then Freiburg. He did not, as he might have done, tease the young knight about the past night, but spoke immediately of serious matters.

"Don't ask me now about this foreign mission, I spoke of," the older man warned. That may or may not come off, and you will be well briefed if it does. But right now concentrate only on getting yourself safely to Schwyz and then give all your attention to the duties the Marshal will assign to you. It will be a hard fight. They will be expecting to face only foresters and farmers, and with luck they will know nothing about the Templars they also have to face. But they will be many in number and well-armed. Do not forget that fighting simply is their whole life! Never underestimate your enemy, Paul, as they will undoubtedly underestimate us.

"Now as to your betrothal, the von Stauffens are a fine family and Lady

Melissa is indeed a fair lady. I wish you happiness but again, you cannot turn your attention to your own affairs until you have fulfilled your duties."

"I understand," Paul replied somewhat subdued, as the master builder continued.

"Tell the Marshal please, that I am delayed by waiting on the Archbishop, and also I am waiting for word from the Prior in Scotland. I will follow on, I fully expect to be there certainly some time before the battle is engaged."

Ludo was coming across the courtyard leading Paul's riding hack whilst his charger was being led by the groom who followed him. The servant, Ludo's choice from amongst the castle retainers, was Pipin, a sturdy fellow who looked to be useful in a fight. He led a packhorse with a tent and supplies.

Peter Proudhomme embraced Paul in farewell, mounted and departed on his short journey to Breisach, en route to Freiburg. Paul, who had already said a lengthy and tender farewell to his beloved, nevertheless dodged back into the tower and found her on the steps coming down to see him go. They hugged and kissed yet again on the steps and reluctantly emerged together into the bright light of the courtyard.

All was ready. The Baron was standing by the horses talking to his son. The steward and other household members were gathering to wish good luck to their young master, who was about to become a man.

It was the moment of parting. Paul saluted the Baron and led the way out of the castle turning in his saddle for as long as he could fix his gaze on Melissa. By now many servants had joined in waving goodbye to young Ludo, and their mistress's future husband; wondering, as was the Baron, if either or both of these young men would survive the coming adventures.

***

LAKE LUCERNE

On the evening of the second day after leaving the bridge at Rheinfelden behind them, the convoy was approaching the great lakeside city of Lucerne and nearing its objective. On their first morning on the southern side of the Rhine, the Marshal and Master Franz had conferred. "What I want to do is send my son ahead," the burly wagonmaster explained, "I would ask you to give him a good horse because he has a long way to go in a short time. If this works out as I plan, he will arrange for barges from Schwyz to rendezvous and then take our whole party across the lake from a point on the shore near Lucerne." As was now becoming familiar to both of them, he scratched out a rough plan in the hard soil between them to illustrate his point.

Having dealt with that, they agreed to change the order of march. The treasure wagons laden with silver were disguising their contents with great bales of wool. There were documents showing the wool was intended for Venice and paid for, including delivery to that port city. Master Franz and his drivers, with just these wagons, took the lead in the convoy with a light escort of just four mounted men-at-arms. The Marshal followed on with the military convoy no more than a quarter-mile behind. In addition he had a pair of riders some several miles behind to watch their rear and two others riding side by side, well ahead of the whole party as forward scouts. Following the utility of the trumpet signals when they passed through the Black Forest, he had introduced this as a routine when on the line of march.

The road that they had joined, was the main highway to the south from Basel. It would pass Lucerne and its great lake, and then continue to cross the high Alps through the St. Gotthard Pass into Italy. It had been crossed over for millennia in both directions by countless armies in the past; also by innumerable merchant convoys, superficially not unlike theirs.

The highway was not crossing the property of any single magnate, but in certain places there was a strong castle nearby and inevitably a tollbooth to collect dues on merchandise. This ostensibly was for keeping the roads repaired and safe from outlaws, or rapacious local knights. They had passed two such tollbooths as Master Franz had said they would, and he had paid over the required small toll on the wool bales, without demur.

When the Marshal's column approached the first toll booth, immediately following Franz's wagons, his leading knight had been briefed to rein in and exchange the time of day, plus a little more, whilst the Marshal and his large war band, their accompanying wagons and servants continued serenely on, past the small squad of soldiers on duty there. The one piece of information the knight passed across was that they were freelances under a leader from northern Germany, heading to Zug to join Duke Leopold's army there.

The presence of the city of Lucerne had become obvious as local traffic on the highway became significant. The Marshal's force had closed up with Master Franz's leading party, and now they were once again just one convoy.

It was already late afternoon and they could see the church spires and rooftops of Lucerne in the distance to their south, as they left the main road to skirt its northern flank. About an hour later the town was well behind them, and they were close to the shores of the lake. Franz guided them further to a small promontory with a stretch of shallow shore, on which some fishing boats were drawn up with a solid looking wooden jetty, nearby to two cottages. There the convoy halted. Across the great lake they could see the lights of early evening and Franz made his way to one of the cottages, had a quick conversation at the door, and then went in search of the Marshal.

"We are nearly at journey's end" he said. "Those lights over to the right across the water, are of Schwyz town and district. Our barges will not cross over before dark. All of this was planned before I left, but until they get here, I am not sure how many barges they have, so whether any of them have to make more than one crossing. They tell me at the cottage here - these are our people - that they ferried my son over last night, so all will be prepared."

The Marshal said, "Since we could be here for many hours then I will arrange a defence perimeter and we will post guards, since you tell me that the Duke's domains start close to here".

"Certainly my Lord" replied Franz. "They are still several miles away. Unless we are betrayed, which I think highly unlikely, almost certainly they do not suspect we are here. If this all goes well, by crossing over during the dark hours, we will safeguard the cottagers here from possible questioning by the Duke's men, and keep this route open for future journeys."

***

ZUG CASTLE

That evening, Baron Otto von Cham, castellan of the Duke's castle at the lakeside town of Zug, entertained at supper amongst others, three young knights who had arrived together from Carinthia, seeking employment with the Duke. His orders had been clear. When such volunteers appeared, they were to be questioned as to their military experience, also their families and past or present loyalties. Unless in the castellan's judgement there was a strong reason why not, then they would be taken on the strength and interviewed by Duke Leopold, after he arrived at Zug to take command.

Frequently like these three, they were landless knights, all of them younger brothers and the like, trained to war, but who due to primogeniture would not inherit their father's estates, so had the need to make their own way in the world. A campaign like this one, against foresters and peasants and such inconsequential people, would they were sure mean that the victors stood well to earn themselves estates out of the conquered lands, in fee to the Duke, or one of his great barons, in return for ruling the defeated rebels with an iron hand and using their lands in his economic interests.

In addition to these young men, the castellan had dining at his table the town captain from Rheinfelden with whom he had earlier conferred, away from the others. He had just returned from his town to report further to the Baron, on the incident involving this large military convoy crossing the Rhine, two nights before.

That had taken place on the night that the town captain had been at Zug Castle when his deputy's messenger arrived, alerting him to the passage of this large, warlike party, hastily summoning him back, or to send orders.

The messenger, a young trooper from the town guard could only tell the castellan and his town captain, that a well-armed party of knights and men-at- arms had crossed the bridge with at least ten or more wagons, four of which were heavily laden with bales of wool.

They were still crossing when he had been sent off to Zug to report this and although he had not been near to the short conversation that took place between one of their knights with Gurt, he thought he had heard him say that they were on the way to join up with the Duke's forces and were carrying military supplies for him in the wagons. He was cross-questioned on giving his report and when asked, said that he thought they must be a war band of freelances, certainly professional soldiers, who included by the evidence of their spurs, several knights. He also told them that only the leader displayed heraldic devices, in that his squire carried his banner of a black boar on a white field.

"Means nothing to me," the castellan had observed. "His Grace does not always confide in me about outsiders he might have arranged to serve him, but it sounds like they could be well on the way here by now." "Do you" he had ordered the captain, "go back to Rheinfelden at first light with your trooper, and if you meet them on the way as is probable, send him back to me to report on what you can find out?"

Baron Otto doubled the castle guard that night as a precaution and settled down to wait. Now the town captain had been back and returned to report, having questioned Gurt and others. Not only, he had said, had he not encountered the military convoy on the road, but "the strange thing," he observed, "is that they moved straight on through the town seemingly knowing their way, but then took the road directly away from here, leading to Basel."

"Or possibly to the south, Lucerne - that road forks" the castellan interjected. "But what did Under-officer Gurt report about the knight who addressed him? What did he say about serving the Duke?"

"Well, my lord," came the reply, "it was as my trooper reported to us. This knight who was not the commander - he was too grand, Gurt said, to even talk with him, but obviously the knight who did was a senior man deputed by him. He gave Gurt a hard time, for not knowing and expecting this convoy to cross the river. He took the line that there was clearly inefficiency at work amongst His Grace's retainers. But they didn't hang around to press the point. It turned out that there were fourteen wagons in all and apart from the bales of wool we heard about earlier, Gurt said he could see that most of the wagons did indeed contain steel armour, bundles of lances, helmets, corselets, and the like. Once they had crossed over and as I said, had taken the Basel road, all the company of mounted men quietly filed out of town behind them. They did no damage and stole nothing."

"Well," said the castellan after chewing on the information for a minute or two, "it certainly sounds that they are on the way here, even if in their arrogance they took the wrong turning out of the town, rather than ask directions. Unless it is something to do with the Bishop of Basel, some mischief that we don't yet know about, they will probably arrive here a few days later than they expected. Tell me, what do we know of their numbers and condition? If there is a great lord amongst them, he of the black boar, then I will have to arrange suitable accommodations and also to be prepared for quarters and rations for the whole band."

"This is the tally as best as I can put it together", the captain told him. "Gurt and his men believed that there was this commander who had a great green and yellow plume on his casque, with about fifty or sixty well-mounted men-at-arms, apparently fully equipped for war, including several knights; then about seventy or more assorted squires, grooms, servants and such, carters and their mates and the fourteen wagons. That, they all agreed, was the number of wagons that crossed the bridge."

The castellan deliberated a moment and then decided. "I am going to wait for two days and if they haven't arrived by then I will send a report to Duke Leopold, who I believe may now be on a progress towards Winterthur, gathering up the Habsburg vassals. He is due here in about two to three weeks. But tell me this, was there anything strange or notable that Gurt and his men observed, that might be relevant to my report?"

"Well my lord, only this. We had at first concluded that they were mercenaries, as indeed they perhaps are, but Gurt has seen a few of those in his time. He did say that this lot were very disciplined, not rowdy nor yet bullying, picking fights and that. They made no demands for wine or beer or food, and yet they came from out of the Black Forest and there are no towns nearby where they could have been fed, so they must be self-sufficient in their travelling. Indeed one of their wagons was seen to be a kitchen wagon, which speaks of good organisation, not the usual hallmark of mercenaries. It makes me think Sir, that the key to this is the leader. These could be his household knights, not mercenaries at all. He could perhaps be an ally of His Grace who might want to know sooner rather than later, that he was approaching here."

"You make a good point there," replied the castellan. "You are right. I won't wait two days, indeed I will send you with a small escort to personally search for and report to the Duke wherever you can find him, as of first light tomorrow."

SOUTHBOUND

Paul and his two companions left Castle Stauffen early on a route leading away from the Black Forest to meet the Rhine, a few miles above the river port of Breisach. They planned to join and then follow the main highway on the eastern bank of the great river as it flowed towards the city of Basel and its river port. It was indeed an important road with traffic from Strasburg and beyond, as well as farm wagons loaded with fresh vegetables, mounted groups of merchants with packhorse and mule trains, heading for the famous Basel markets. There were priests trudging along cloaked against the fresh breezes, a farmer with his dogs driving a small herd of cattle, which kept wandering off to the side of the road. A single knight with his squire and servant together with their horses, excited no particular interest and so it remained, until they came to the Bishop's Bridge leading over to the great walled city which spread along the opposite riverbank.

There, a sergeant was in charge of the watch of sentries examining goods and people seeking to enter the city, charging the appropriate tolls on goods for the bishop's exchequer, and a small fee to travelers using the bridge to cross the Rhine. Seldom would the watchmen challenge an armoured knight, but they might respectfully enquire his business in entering the city and note anything unusual for their report.

Paul had determined to make no ripples on the placid surface that offered itself and to avoid drawing attention to himself. When told the bridge fee for his party, he nodded to Ludo to settle it, as beneath his dignity. When politely asked his business in Basel, he affected boredom with the procedure but said languidly that he was passing through on the way to Italy, after spending a night in the city. The watchman stood back respectfully as the three mounted men passed him to cross over the new stone bridge that Ludo had told him had only recently and at great cost, replaced a timber bridge that had served from the time of the Romans.

It was clearly a prosperous city, occupying as it did a conjunction of routes coming up through Helvetia from Italy with its great international ports of Genoa and Venice, joining the Rhine at Basel. This was the main river highway for goods to travel downstream to all the countries between there and the North Sea coast. From Basel they could also travel north to the German states on the Baltic Sea, and goods from all of these in their turn came to the markets of Basel.

The horses of Paul's party clattered across the cobbles of the square that lay beyond the bridge and they were immediately passing through a hive of activity, with market stalls thronged with goodwives shopping for food, and tradesmen offering their wares, as well as foreign merchants with more costly stuff. They could see the cathedral over to their left and a row of guild houses lining the route towards it. Ludo had earlier suggested an inn that his father had taken him to, and Paul told him to take the lead and guide them there.

Pipin dealt with the horses, whilst Paul and Ludo approached the landlord. He had one room he said and gave them a price, and said that the groom could sleep in the stable with the five horses. It all seemed quite satisfactory to Paul and above all, normal! It was late afternoon and Paul said he would take a turn around the city centre and that Ludo should join him. By now some of the stalls were closing down for the day, but they wandered along, indulging their curiosity at some of the goods on display. Paul was intrigued listening to one vendor, a Venetian apparently, asking what seemed to be an enormous price, for the small boxes of black seeds he had on display. That transaction done, Ludo asked the merchant what was it that could command such a high price? "It is called the pepper of the India's, young master" was his reply. "It comes from far beyond the lands of the Saracens and we in Venice buy a cargo annually from Egypt, for these peppercorns do not grow anywhere in Christendom."

"But what are they for?" Ludo persisted, genuinely puzzled.

"You look like you might one day be able to afford to buy our pepper, young sir" the merchant told him, "so I will give you a sample - one single peppercorn". He took one out of the box and handed it to the squire. "Put it into your mouth and then bite down on it."

Ludo did as he was bidden and for a moment did not react. Then his eyes watered and with an exclamation he quickly removed it from his mouth and looked searchingly at the chewed fragment he held between finger and thumb.

"But who is going to choose to eat these seeds that burn in your mouth!" he asked.

"The answer to that", the merchant told him, "is anybody who disliked the sour taste of tainted meat." - "better by far the sharp tang of the black peppercorn," he said, "grated over any questionable cooked meat, before serving it at table. Some just like the sharp taste for itself, or even to impress their friends."

Ludo, having thought about it, then had the good grace to say, "thank you".

"All a part of a young gentleman's education" the merchant responded, with a smile at the knight standing listening to the exchange, who nodded and returned the smile.

They moved on amongst the stalls one of which displayed some beautiful shining fabric, which was particularly attracting women customers. "That looks like very fine work," said Ludo to his master and added shrewdly, "I suspect my sister would welcome such material for herself."

"Yes," Paul said, "that's a good point if we come back this way. It's called silk. I have seen it when I served in Cilicia. They say it is spun by worms, but I could never believe that."

They had wandered to the edge of the market stalls when Paul saw them. Two black robed, tonsured Dominican friars were passing, just ahead of them. Their bony faces intent on some conversation between them, they passed incurious about the young knight.

Despite himself, Paul felt the cold finger of fear on his spine, quickly followed by a sense of loathing. His hand dropped to his sword hilt, which reassuringly was there, unlike the recent time in Freiburg. These friars had taken no interest in the young knight and his squire and certainly he knew he had never seen either of them before. They walked on involved in their conversation, their sandals slapping against the cobblestones. He wondered if he would always react like this when spotting the arch-enemies of his order. He made a mental note that he would one day exact a price from them for the bad time they had given him, from which he had so recently emerged, and for their cruelty to his brother knights at the time of the purge, many of whom had died mutilated - a loathsome death, or survived but forever crippled, as a result.

He took renewed comfort in the small leather pouch under his shirt, suspended with a light cord around his neck. In there was a carefully folded short document, of which the seal of the Archbishop of Constance was the most prominent detail. That was his guarantee that they could never pursue him on the charges they had laid against him in Freiburg. The matter was closed… but he pondered, was it? Here he was a knight on his way to a battlefield, the outcome of which would make for a massive stirring amongst the ruling powers, both secular and ecclesiastical of this part of Christendom.

He had been examined and judged by the Archbishop on the basis that he was now a student architect, a pupil of Master Proudhomme, yet he was about to serve as a senior officer in a rebellion against a great feudal lord belonging to the House of Habsburg, a very powerful one at that. Further reflecting, he wondered what if any, was the relationship between the Archbishop of Constance and the Duke of Austria and resolved to find out when next he saw Master Proudhomme, who seemed to know all such things.

First the battle, he thought, and then worry about any such consequences afterwards. He considered for a moment what the hateful Brother Joaquim of Freiburg might do with such information about his former prisoner's intentions, and did not care for the answer he gave himself!

***

SCHWYZ

It was some two hours after midnight when the first flat-bottomed barge of a convoy of six, was manoeuvred by its oared pinnace up to the side of a solid wooden dock and made secure. The Marshal was handed ashore, followed by his escort. Master Franz had gone ahead in a light cutter to prepare the way, and stood now, together with his son on the dockside, beaming his welcome. There seemed to be many men waiting there in the dark, lit by the light of braziers, and they lost no time in placing a ramp into the barge and dozens of them added their muscle power to that of the big draft horses still standing harnessed to the wagons, yet even then having to remove some of the cargo to be replaced, once on the dock.

A small delegation stood by Franz and these, the Templars realised, must be the leaders of this town. They looked decidedly too solid and prosperous to be rebels. A heavily bearded, big bear of a man, a silver chain of office around his neck with a great mane of hair, stepped forward and introduced himself as Walter Fuerst, burgomeister of the town and district of Schwyz. He wore a long broadsword at his belt and a long woollen tunic down to his gartered leggings, together with a vast fur lined cloak and cap.

The Marshal, no small man himself, found himself unusually looking up into a pair of twinkling friendly eyes, as the large hand was extended in greeting.

"Congratulations, Sir Peter," the big man boomed. "A perfectly executed plan it seems, although I don't want to speak too soon. Two of the barges I understand, must return, to pick up your remaining wagons and the rear-guard." Even as he spoke the second barge was unloading and the first was being hauled away from the dockside by its sixteen oared cutter and turned back towards the far shore.

Master Franz stepped up to introduce the other leaders. Werner Stauffecher was next, a distinguished man of middle years, his greying beard trimmed, by his dress a prosperous merchant. Finally a younger man unbearded, but with a luxuriant and cultivated moustache. He had the bearing of a soldier and under his long cloak his tunic was short, as if not to impede his movements, a serious looking sword hung at his belt. Franz introduced him as Arnold Neirmayer.

The Marshal called over the two leaders of the German contingent of Templars and his own deputy Sir Geraint, to join them and be introduced, now that their barges had docked. It was clear to the new arrivals, from the organised way that the Schwyzers handled the barges and their precious cargos, that there was a high level of competence here. Everything seemed to be well organised.

"Gentlemen," the big man said, "do please call me Walter. I have people here who will straightaway take your warriors and servants to be fed and then to prepared quarters, if you will so authorise, whilst perhaps you gentlemen will join us for some food and have some mulled wine, or try out our beer, which we sometimes prefer to wine in these parts, and we can talk awhile perhaps, before you have a proper sleep."

Within an hour, whilst outside the first hint of dawn was already lightening the eastern sky, the leaders were seated in wood and leather chairs, around a great log fire in the solid timbered mansion that seemed to be Walter's residence, goblets of mulled wine or beer tankards in their hand, helping themselves to minted ribs of lamb from platters offered around by sturdy women servants.

"Franz has told me," said Walter, "that he had little chance to explain the background to our story as the journey required all of your concentration. So I will explain the outline and over the weeks ahead there will be opportunities for telling more detail. But first, you are military men and I will ask Arnold here to quickly appraise the situation."

All eyes turned to the younger man, who self-consciously tweaked his luxuriant moustache and then cleared his throat before speaking. He stood. "I should explain," he said in a pleasant tenor voice, "that because I have had some small experience of war, my friends here asked me to do what I could to organise such warlike resources as we might have."

"Might we know," interjected the Marshal courteously, "of this previous experience of which you speak?"

"Certainly Sir Peter," the young man replied. "I am from these parts, but had been wandering in Greece for some years learning about fighting, with some ex-Templars as it happens, whom I think you will know of - the Company of Catalans. Then I spent three years in Constantinople in the service of the Greek Emperor, but when he was overthrown - I decided it was time to leave to return to the land of my fathers."

"Thank you, Sir. I would talk with you another time about Greece, indeed of Byzantium, but do please give us the appraisal of which Master Walter spoke."

"It is simply this", the young man said. "The Duke is putting together a large force and has appointed his castle of Zug, no great distance away from here as the mustering point by the end of October, so nearly two months away. He has quite a number of ambitious landless knights rallying to him, who can see that they can make their fortunes if they can conquer us. Our information is that some are coming very long distances, but the Duke's own vassals and their troops will account for the backbone of his force.

"They are formidable, hardened professionals who think like all the knightly class that we are merely farm boys and peasants, and all they have to do is sweep us out of the way. My assessment gentlemen, is that just like King Philip at Courtrai and King Edward at Bannockburn, they are greatly overconfident, simply because they believe that armoured cavalry is the only weapon of war that matters. That one serious charge by them will scatter us to the winds. There is a word..." he paused, "*arrogance*, which I believe describes it fully.

"They know we cannot put any such force as theirs into the field and it is this I believe, that can be their undoing. If you gentlemen are able to train our boys as pikemen, with those splendid pikes, even now being unloaded, such that they will hold against a full cavalry charge - and I am told that this is exactly what has happened before under your leadership, then there is the key to our victory. If the momentum and weight of their charge does not break our line, then we have them.

"They will invade us only when they are ready - so we can pick our ground where to make our stand and if that holds, we hopefully will trap them in a killing ground. Gentlemen we have a distance weapon, a powerful version of the crossbow, in which our people excel, largely because many of our men are foresters and are continually exercising those skills. They will pierce armour at sixty paces, in the face of which the armour of the average mounted knight is nearly obsolete, no longer sufficient protection. These same foresters are full-time axe-men, it is what they do year in year out, even if it is performed on trees. When it comes to close quarters fighting, the two-handed axe is indeed a terrible weapon."

There was a thoughtful silence for a few moments during which pause he had resumed his seat, then the giant Walter stood, unwittingly dwarfing the group of seated men.

"Thank you Arnold," he said. "Of course, Sir Peter, now you are here, we regard you as our general; but Arnold here will be your military liaison with our people." The Marshal nodded his acknowledgement, and Walter continued.

"The political situation is this. We have three of what in Helvetia we call cantons. Together they are called the Forest Cantons, roughly the same as your English or French counties - but with one big difference. None of them has, nor has ever had, a count or an earl, or any overlord."

The great fire crackled and in the seductive warmth of journeys end, the new arrivals felt the intimations of drowsiness creeping up on them. Walter noticed and quietly chuckled, "I am sure that you would prefer to hear all this another time gentlemen, but we really can none of us sleep, until those two remaining barges, and all our men are back. So I will continue for a little while."

He spoke again, "The three Forest Cantons, this one Schwyz, with our neighbours Uri and Unterwalden- sometimes called Niderwalden, have since the Romans left, been subject to no laws except the Forest Laws made long ago by our own people, in our traditional way. We elect our leaders, Werner here…" he nodded at his colleague, "and Arnold as well as myself, are elected by a vote of all the citizens. In my case, for five years at a time. Of course we have different classes of citizen. Some own land which in these parts mostly means forests, some are farmers small and great - cattle and horse breeding is the way they are going; merchants like Werner here, who also is our treasurer - he handles our community finances. Some are tradesmen - bakers, butchers and so, most are plain foresters and hunters. Land is owned, much of it in common, but also by individuals, including some outside landowners - magnates in other parts, but their land ownership here no matter how large, gives them only a fair rent, one vote here, and no feudal rights. We accept no overlord and this of course is why the Habsburgs are invading us.

"We are all of us rich or poor, equal citizens, who acknowledge neither hereditary nor any other outside master, except the authority of the Emperor which we can accept. In normal times what is happening now with the Habsburgs, in the past could not have been, because we have held to our ancient rights as free foresters. The old Emperor Frederic put our whole population under his protection more than sixty years ago and we had always paid our taxes to the old Emperor who protected us in his time.

There came a pounding on the great door. A steward quickly went and as quickly returned. "Two barges have been sighted, Sir" he gave his master the message, "and they will be docking within minutes."

The drowsiness quickly disappeared as the company bustled out of the hall into the darkness of the keen night air, and made their way towards the line of glowing braziers.

***

BETTER LATE...

It was three days later before a saddle-weary Paul with his squire and servant found themselves at last having rounded the southeastern corner of Lake Lucerne, which he saw from the signposts was called Uri, only a short distance from the town of Schwyz. He recalled that Uri was the name of one of the cantons he had come to fight for, but he had no contacts and decided to continue with the low profile that had served since they had ridden out of Basel. He had slept the one night there, in his case fitfully, disturbed as he had been by viewing the Dominicans, but as far as he could see, young Ludo on a palliasse in the corner of the chamber slept soundly enough.

They had spent the second night by the side of the road in the tent that Pipin had raised, and again on the third night, they had avoided towns and camped by the roadside. It was now late summer and fortunately the weather was kind.

Before leaving Castle Stauffenburg, the Baron had told him and Ludo that they would best approach Schwyz from the southern side of the lake. He explained that it would have been quicker to cross the lake near Lucerne and that is what Franz was going to organise for the main party. But there was no one that they could trust to ferry them, without telling why they wanted to go to Schwyz, and Paul knew that would be far too dangerous.

He rode along the lakeshore road, his worries and concerns put aside by the sheer dramatic beauty of the scenery all about him. Off to the right, the forest seemingly endless, stretched higher and ever higher, to terminate on snow-covered mountain peaks and further mountains stretching far away behind them. To their left, there was a nearly sheer drop down to the shore of the great lake, that stretched out to more densely forested mountains on the far side, the azure colours of its surface reflecting the brilliant sun that somehow seemed to hold the promise of a cleaner, better world.

Ludo behind him, normally talkative when given the opportunity, was himself unusually silent, absorbing the grandeur of this country, the only sound the occasional metallic jingle of a piece of harness and the soft footfall of their horses on the grass verge, which Paul preferred to the rocky, deeply rutted cart track. They passed occasional cottages set on the hillside above the track but saw little trace of humanity except far out on the lake, where there were pairs of boats laying and hauling nets, or single small fishing boats trailing lines.

Moving along the lakeside, which they had been doing now for two days, they passed what clearly seemed to be an inn, but it was shuttered and silent apart from its guardian dogs, inside, yapping and baying as they approached. The doors were firmly locked; even the stables were empty. Paul had seen a signpost written in German, of which he knew enough, and it seemed that Schwyz was within an hour's steady ride. Pipin took the opportunity of the stop to open a bundle of food - bread and carved chunks off a ham, acquired the previous day, and passed these around together with a flagon of the local beer.

The three of them sat on the grass overlooking the glorious panorama of lake and mountains before them, as their horses cropped at the abundance of green grass by the side of the deserted inn.

"I don't know quite what to make of this", Paul told the others. Judging by the dogs whose noisy complaints had slowed but not ceased, it was clear the place had not long been vacated. On reflection, they agreed that they had not seen any southbound travellers passing them, nor any farm carts or foresters wagons on the road, ever since it had turned north towards their destination.

"What we will do," he finally said, "is ride on a further half-hour and if we have seen no-one to question, then we will move up the hillside into the woods where we can look down on the town, and see what we can see. What we will not do is ride in to discover who knows what - and perhaps not be able to ride out again!"

His head was full of foreboding that perhaps the Marshal had been ambushed, or some treachery had occurred when they had arrived in the town.

They resumed the journey and soon a bend in the road gave him his first glimpse of distant buildings that must be Schwyz. After seeing their proximity he led his small troop off the road and up a cutting into the forest climbing steadily up the hillside, until through a gap in the trees they saw the roofs of Schwyz now closer, yet far below them. He dismounted to look around and then saw in a clearing off the track, a few yards away, an unexpected sight.

Gently grazing were two tethered horses, destriers, the warhorses of the gentry with saddles and other trappings of a military nature. He signalled silence to Ludo behind him, followed by an urgent hand signal to Pipin. He walked his horse back and gave its reins to the lad, signalling Ludo to do likewise and then for Pipin to go back a few paces to conceal them. He whispered to Ludo that he was to draw his sword and follow him quietly, just a few paces behind. Then he carefully moved forward, avoiding stepping on dry twigs or otherwise creating noise, confident his squire was close behind him.

A footpath led the way to a bluff, a point right above the town looking straight down onto the several large and imposing buildings that made up the town centre. It was close enough that he could hear from below a man making a speech, and saw that hundreds of citizens of apparently all conditions, were gathered there listening. Then, he tensed as he saw his quarry - the owners of the destriers, lying flat in the long grass at the very edge of the bluff, staring forward, hands cupped to their ears, the better to hear the words and quite oblivious to Paul's approach. There were two of them, one a heavily moustached older man, the other younger, both in full mail corselets and breeches. Their shields and helmets lay beside them, but their swords were still sheathed at their belts.

Paul waited until Ludo silently emerged from the track behind him and then he pointed and gestured with his sword, before slowly moving forwards. He was already close when the nearer of the knights - the older man sensed him and looked up, his eyes widening. Without hesitating, in one fluid movement, he picked up his shield by the rim and swept it around at Paul's feet, catching him on the knee, bringing him down. But as he fell, Paul poised for the movement, swiped a mighty blow sideways, his whole weight leaning into it behind his drawn sword and felt the keen blade bite through the chainmail into the knight's torso.

His younger companion had reacted more slowly, rolling away whilst trying to draw his sheathed sword. But unsuccessfully, the sword only half drawn, he looked up to see the point of Ludo's naked blade hovering over his face, ready, waiting indeed to stab down.

Paul's stricken adversary groaned in agony, his body arching against the pain of the wound from which blood poured down through a long gash in his right breast and midriff and flowed down through his steel corselet. As if in a reflex of revenge he tried to grasp his sword but could not, and still lying down, choked blood onto the grass.

Paul turned to look at Ludo's prisoner whose eyes were fixed on those of the squire as if to divine whether he was about to stab down.

"Do you submit?" Paul demanded of him.

"Gladly, if you will get this young chap to put his blade away from my face," came the answer. Their eyes still locked, he moved gently to unbuckle his sword belt and slowly sat up, the squire's sword still inches from his nose.

"So you are a spy then", said Paul watching him from one corner of his eye whilst he took a hurried glance down to the town square where the crowd were now applauding.

"I suppose you could call it that," the young knight replied, "but we would call it reconnaissance, no dishonourable thing." He looked over at his dying friend. "Is there anything to be done for him?" he quietly asked.

Paul, the blood heat in him now diminishing, looked again at his recumbent opponent. "Nothing I think, unless you want to shrive him. He might still hear you and respond."

"I am no great hand at that, but I'll see." The young knight knelt by his companion and spoke, "Gilles, can you hear me?" But by the bubble of blood coming from his mouth it was clear he could not, nor ever would hear anything again.

"So who are you - your name, and whom do you serve" demanded Paul. Ludo stood right behind the prisoner, his sword still pointing at him and highly alert, as if willing him to make one wrong move.

The young man looked suddenly weary.

"I am John of Potsdam - knight." he said. "My family are there. I have older brothers and my father remains in rude good health, so it was made clear to me that I should need to follow my sword if I were to make my way in the world... and now" said with a despairing sigh of self-disgust, "I am captured it seems... by a squire!"

Paul didn't comment on that but pressed his question, "So whom do you serve?" he repeated.

The young knight paused and then deciding that he could not afford to give wrong answers, replied. "Strictly speaking I serve no-one, in that I have given no oaths. I am as I have said, a landless knight. I heard that there were opportunities serving under Duke Leopold. I presented myself at the castle of Zug and I was to wait there until the Duke arrives. He then would interview me along with six or seven others already there. I was told and - they said it was a formality, he would offer me a place as his man."

"Yes, I see," said Paul, "and what was this mission that you and Sir Gilles was it, that so occupied you until you were disturbed, a few minutes ago?"

John of Potsdam was speculating whether they would kill him, the young squire behind him looked as though he was ready, indeed quite eager to punch the blade into his back. He could see no alternative than to be open and tell the truth.

"The Castellan at Zug - that's Baron Otto von Cham, told us that since he was feeding the two of us, we could make ourselves useful and it could do our cause no harm, if he was able to give the Duke a good report of us. We were to reconnoitre the approaches to the town here, and to report on any activity of a military character. As you may have noticed, the town meeting below has emptied the countryside, so we were trying to hear what was being announced down there."

"Alright," Paul replied, after a moment's reflection. "Do you Ludo, tie his wrists securely. We'll take him with us."

****

The great meeting in the town square had finished, the crowd was thinning and the townspeople were talking animatedly amongst themselves, whilst the soldierly figures of the newcomers, the former Templars, were interspersed with them, themselves in groups of twos and threes. Then into the square rode a solitary knight walking his charger, followed by a train of horses. He was in chain mail with his helmet off, secured at his saddlebow, revealing a smiling face under the tousled hair. Behind him rode his squire leading a rope, attached to which was another mailed knight walking, disarmed, his wrists bound in front of him. Behind them came a mounted servant holding the leading ropes to four more horses strung out in line, the first of which a still saddled destrier, carried the dead body of another mailed knight, slung over the saddle, with his arms and legs hanging down, tied together under the horses belly.

The silence that this dramatic tableau caused was suddenly broken. Some of Paul's comrades standing amongst the townspeople recognised him and their shouts at what obviously was some triumph, mixed with their greeting, was taken up by the townspeople in a roaring cheer.

Burgomeister Walter and his civic colleagues had just retired into his hall together with the Templar leaders. At the town meeting they had received the townspeople's approval by acclaim, to fight the invaders from Castle Zug, greatly encouraged by the arrival of these professional soldiers with their cargo of weapons. He was organising drinks for his guests when the sound of cheering reached them. To a man they spilled out of his door to see what possibly could have happened and saw Paul leading his small train towards them, some of the dismounted Templar troops walking alongside, talking to Paul and to Ludo, about this adventure, the results of which they could see.

Walter looked confused until the Marshal suddenly exclaimed, "I do believe… yes, it is. It's young Paul. We thought we'd lost him," he explained to the Schwyzers. "We parted with him back on the journey."

Paul was ushered into the mansion whilst sergeants took charge of the prisoner and the corpse. Ludo and Pipin, beaming with their new celebrity, were telling what happened to a widening circle of listeners, as more people joined the crowd around them.

Inside the hall a goblet was thrust into Paul's hand whist the leaders expectantly waited for his story.

He left out the story of the Freiburg Dominicans for his full report to the Marshal later, and just explained that he and the master mason had been delayed there, and then that he had gone sick with his recurring fever, but was safely lodged in Castle Stauffenburg until he recovered. He was able to tell them that the Baron had received the pigeon post after they had successfully crossed the Rhine and had forwarded that news to Scotland. He modestly explained his capture of the young knight outside, and the death of his companion. It was clear that they had been able to hear the speeches below and that if he had not chanced upon them, that information would have gone back to Zug.

The Marshal listened approvingly. "As it happens, Paul, there was no mention of our being Templars. We were explained to the townspeople as 'reinforcements' and as 'professional soldiers'. Nothing so crude as 'mercenaries' although that was what they would have understood, but somehow they also understood that they didn't necessarily need to lock up their daughters."

The Treasurer, Werner Stauffecher spoke up. "Already I have had some of the better-off citizens quietly asking me however will the town pay for the soldiers? I told them the story we had agreed upon. That these men and their commander were survivors of a distant war and that in return for their helping us to survive, that those who so choose will be allowed to settle here and live amongst us."

Walter informed the military men that next he would be bringing to meet them the leaders of their allied cantons, Uri and Unterwalden. The Marshal told the group that together with Master Arnold he would wish to organise the Schwyzer pikemen, and start their training straightaway with the Templars as officers and sergeants. He would need to know the numbers of crossbowmen and axe-men available and decide how best to organise them, and any other mounted fighters with their own horses amongst the local men, which unless they were a significant number, he would probably use as his staff gallopers on the battlefield.

He then called Paul aside and told him to follow him to his quarters and there give his full report.

MYSTERY OF THE BLACK BOAR

Now September, Baron von Cham had all but forgotten the mystery of the disappearing 'Band of the Black Boar' as he had termed that group of mercenaries.

He had of course swiftly reinforced the garrison at Rheinfelden, but the Duke when finally reached, knew nothing of any magnate with the device of a black boar. His chamberlain had looked at his charts of heraldry and found several families around Europe using that device, including in Hungary, Southern Sweden and Flanders, but none of the names meant anything to the Duke, nor was he particularly concerned.

It had possibly something to do with the Bishop of Basel he suggested, but he was not on speaking terms with the Prince Bishop to make such an enquiry. But with so many as sixty men- at- arms with all their baggage carts, it more probably meant that they were headed down the Gotthard pass to Italy. It was well known that the Italian city-states were always hiring mercenaries for their endless wars. Baron Otto could believe that too, but the dressing down described by Gurt, whom he knew to be a steady man, and the mention of 'war supplies for the Duke' that the knight had spoken of at the bridge, got in the way of that explanation. However no further traces of them had been reported so it had to remain in the background as an unsolved mystery.

The castellan's duties in receiving the Duke's levies, plus those soldiers of fortune that still showed up, had kept him more than busy. The latest complication was that the Prince Bishop of Einsiedeln Abbey had just sent an unusual emissary to Zug. The bishop had personally excommunicated his Schwyzer neighbours following the latest quarrel about grazing rights, which Otto knew to be an intractable problem. This messenger was a Dominican friar who despite his simple black robes and sandals, carried with him a sinister aura. That was inevitable, reflected the castellan, since this young Brother Joaquim embodied all the fearful power of the Inquisition. The Prince Bishop, who had endured many years of irritation from these upstart free foresters, had persuaded the Duke to allow him to arrange a team of these black friar Dominicans to accompany the troops, or at least to follow them in their conquest. He had reasoned that like the Cathars, once the foresters had been militarily defeated, then it would take the relentless ways of the Inquisition to root out those who had led these simple country folk into insurrection and excommunication, and to punish them accordingly.

They already had the names of the leaders but there would be many more to be extirpated, before this lawless people would settle down to the feudal condition. Baron Otto did not reflect on this, merely accepted it, his concerns were more the prosaic ones of who would feed and house the unexpected black friars. That problem was solved by this same brother Joacquim, who said that the members of the party of Dominicans were being collected up by their Provincial in Strasburg, whilst he had been sent on from the Dominican house in Freiburg to pave the way. He said that he would be glad temporarily of shelter and food for himself, but his colleagues would be housed by the Abbey of Einsiedeln. He agreed that he would join them there once the date of the Austrian army moving into Schwyz had been determined, and then bring them back to Zug for the muster.

Baron Otto had been exercised by the disappearance of two of the landless knights two weeks before, whom he had sent to reconnoitre the area of the Schwyz town. They probably had been killed by the foresters, indeed that was by far the most likely explanation. But it was always possible he knew, that being landless, and not yet having given their oaths to the Duke, that they might just have ridden on to seek their fortune elsewhere. But those two? He doubted it. The older one needed a safe position at his time of life and where would he do better with any other master? The younger one from Potsdam was like so many that came with little campaigning experience, but seeking to make their fortunes in just such a war as this, by being on the winning side.

The castellan had sent out a larger armed patrol after a few days to look for them, but they had been spotted on the forest tracks by the invisible enemy, greeted with arrows and crossbow bolts, so had thought it prudent to withdraw from such a place.

Now his steward interrupted his thoughts to say that two more landless knights had shown up, which now made thirty that the Castle Zug was having to accommodate. They expected the date for the muster to be late in October and the Duke would want to move out his army, as soon as he was satisfied that those that he was expecting had arrived.

***

THE FREE CANTONS

A month had passed since the Templars had arrived in the Forest Cantons and they had made their presence felt. The general assumption now was that the attack would come by early November, with the harvests in and before the onset of deep winter. Twelve hundred Schwyzer men had been picked for the two battalions of pikemen. They were daily doing regular training with the new weapons so painstakingly brought into their country, and with the Templars acting as drill masters.

The Marshal and his senior officers, that now included Paul, had met with the leaders of the two other Forest Cantons, Uri and Unterwalden, which together with Schwyz, were under threat of immediate invasion by the Habsburgs. That family had long sought to enlarge their existing territories within Helvetia, but only now was this cadet branch of the powerful Habsburg family emboldened to actually invade, to reduce the citizens of these free cantons to the feudal status of serfs, which they had never been.

The three cantons had twenty-four years earlier signed a treaty of alliance, which only now was being tested by the reality of invasion. Their leaders accepted the premier position of Schwyz, which was confirmed by their initiative in bringing in the Templars and their gift of weapons, and for raising the loans in silver now safely stored in the vaults of the Tower, which was Schwyz's centremost point.

The Marshal was conscious of the limited time available to train his troops and needed to know what each of the Cantons would bring to the fight. The results were impressive - he wondered how good the Austrian's intelligence was that they were so blithely expecting to knock these woodsmen down to their knees. But he reflected that they probably didn't regard intelligence - knowledge of the enemy's dispositions as even appropriate. Enough armoured knights, the mantra went, and the peasants - any infantry indeed - will break and run.

The military planning meeting was being held in the centre of Schwyz in what he now knew was called the Bethlehem House, indeed it was where he was lodged as a guest. It was a splendid tall mansion that spoke of prosperity, with solid stone walls inset with aged oak beams, as well as shining oak floors and wall panelling.

He presided at the great polished oak table with, on his right, Schwyz's military delegate Arnold Neirmayer. . The two other Schwyzer leaders were also there - but as observers. The cantons of Uri and Unterwalden had each sent two military delegates who could speak for their fighting men. The two leading German Templars, Sir Heinrich and Sir Martin sat opposite Geraint and Paul, as together these four would be the commanders in the field.

It had been established that the invasion would come on two fronts. There were knights sympathetic to the Forester's cause, or at least hostile to the Habsburgs, whose empire building amongst the Helvetians for more than a generation had been marked by ruthlessness. Some would even fight with the Foresters, but most were content just to send information. It was in this way that the Allies had heard of a second Austrian muster to come into the cantons from the east, through a mountain pass that once traversed would enable them to link up with the army from Zug. It was agreed that Geraint would take command there with ten of the Templars that came with him from Scotland and some 500 men from the canton of Unterwalden where the pass was located. The key to the defence was strictly defensive. There would be built a substantial barrier like a high dam, across a narrow neck of the pass and archers to control the heights above it. Work had already commenced in the necessary logging and stacking of the timber baulks ready to swiftly erect it, planned to be shortly before the date of the muster from when the invasion could be expected. The barrier would be quite impossible for mounted men and would serve as a platform for the crossbowmen of the Canton, with pikemen and axemen to repel assaults. Then there would be a reserve battalion of 500 men under Sir Martin, kept back from both battles, with mounted gallopers in case the commanders on either front were in danger of being over-run.

The first and main attack would almost certainly be from along the most direct land route from Zug to Schwyz, which followed the Zugersee lake shore, at a place where the Habsburg heavy cavalry could deploy in the open. Their only alternative would be a longer circuitous journey on narrow uphill tracks through dense forest, hopeless for heavy cavalry which would allow for numerous ambushes by the foresters. They agreed that Duke Leopold would hardly opt for that, but anyway when they left the castle and city of Zug, if they or some of them were after all to take that route, the Alliance of the Free Cantons would quickly know. They planned to use some of the small boats on the Lake Zugersee as piquets, always fishing offshore, which could cut across the lake to the allied shore with intelligence, once the knights from Zug were on the move.

The Marshal and his senior officers had previously been taken to see the inevitable route the enemy would take, which followed the shore all the way from around the Zugersee, across which their guides had pointed out the distant city of their enemies, Zug, about eight miles directly across the lake and perhaps fifteen miles around it, to the point where their resistance would begin.

"Given our resources," the Marshal said to the table at large, "if I had to design a defensive battlefield for us to meet them on, I wouldn't have made it any different to what I have seen. To put it another way, I would be deeply afraid of failure if I had the responsibility of the other commander."

"Paul, what did you think of the terrain?" he enquired

"Well Sir Peter," Paul confidently said, "we don't know whether it will be, or have recently been, raining. When they are advancing they will be strung out for well more than a mile and that won't make a big difference. But when we confront them if they are checked and they can't advance because of our pikewall, then those heavy horses will churn the ground up in no time, into a quagmire. It is even more so on the edge of the lake. I have noticed that once off the metalled cart track, which is really all that this lakeside road really is, the ground falls quickly into marshland on the lakes edge. If we can drive the leaders back into their own still advancing tail, we could push riders off the firm ground. The key to all of that of course is the pikewall and where to locate it, but that is perfectly answered by the terrain we have."

He looked around at the other Templars. "We agreed," he said as they nodded, "that the ideal place is just beyond where the lake road eventually turns away from the water, where it is densely wooded on both sides. They will be expecting an ambush there, but I propose we let them come on. Draw them in. It is the road to Schwyz. Less than half a mile along that from the lake, you will recall Sir, there is a large clearing, an open space where they will be able to deploy in line in front of a giant stone bluff blocking the road, indeed the whole small valley at that point. It's a rock formation like a fortress, where at some time in history, someone has cut a passage through and made a road, so a wide cart could pass straight through the gap and continue up on the road to Schwyz beyond.

"That sir, the stone bluff is where our pikemen should make their stand. I would propose that we deploy perhaps in three ranks each of a hundred men in front of the gap, with another similar number in ranks to replace those fallen or exhausted, stationed just behind the three front ranks. Then again in reserve on the other side of the gap, out of sight behind the stone bluff, our second, fresh battalion, made up in the same way. When the charge is finally blunted, that will be the time for us to advance, just as we did at Bannockburn.

"If the battalion to first engage after a long stand, is in trouble, then the hidden battalion can act as a reserve. But if the front battalion holds, then ideally the reserve will pass through those in our deployed ranks that would by then have taken the brunt of the attack, and will be fresh for our counter-attack and taking the fight to the Austrians. But that is not all…" he said.

"In support, we should station as many archers and crossbowmen as we can, in the woods and on the top of the stone bluff - it's like the gate towers of a castle. Give them a massive extra supply of bolts and they will keep up a deadly lethal rain against the cavalry massed down there below them, who will surely be trying to outflank our position. Between the crossbows and the natural terrain they will not be able to flank us, or we would be in trouble in the centre."

The Marshal reflected. He knew the features of the terrain and had come to similar conclusions himself. "Yes, we are lucky with the lie of the land. That will be where we take our stand. You didn't say it, but if things went badly wrong for us, that narrow gap made for the road is highly defensible, even if all our people were withdrawn behind it. The enemy could only come at us two mounted men at a time, or five or six men on foot. They will of course once they are checked there at the bluff, try to outflank us, mounted or on foot, they don't have many options. Anyway they should throw whatever infantry that they have got past the lakeshore by that time, at the flanks of the bluff. So we must have sufficient crossbows and axemen high up in the woods on both sides of that fortress of a rock. Now Sir Paul, I wish you to command the first battalion of pikemen whose training I have already assigned to you. You Sir Heinrich, will please continue with the command of the second battalion that will be in reserve during their first assault and will then lead the counterattack when I signal it."

"Sir Peter," interjected the local leader who the Templars now referred to as 'Arnold the soldier', "I am sure that you had not overlooked the fact that, as Sir Paul has said, the enemy will be strung out in a narrow column for perhaps two miles or more, along the lakeside track. That track of course has the lake along one side but for more than a mile has a steep hill with dense woodlands coming down on the other side, looking down on the lake. The Austrians will be expecting to be attacked from there. I am sure that you are not going to disappoint them?"

"You are absolutely right Master Arnold", replied the Marshal, "Please give us your advice as to how to do this most effectively."

"Frankly Sir, if you and your 'reinforcements' had not joined us, that is where we would have made our main stand. It's too steep for horses, and fighting in the forest is not the best place for armoured knights. What we have already prepared is a large number of tree trunks all trimmed, so they will roll down what look like firebreaks we have already cut, back in the summer. They are pegged in position. Remove the great pegs and they will roll, accelerate and crush whatever is in their path. That path is the lakeside track - everything between the woods and the water, down into to the lake itself!

"Of course," he continued, "because they will be expecting attacks from the forest, they will have foot soldiers and crossbowmen of their own that they will send up the hill. They will probably have their big war hounds and will send those ahead of them, once they get amongst the trees. We are working on an idea about that, but it will be a hard fight once they get amongst us."

"Yes, two things I wish to say about that," replied the Marshal. "First of all I would be glad, Master Arnold, if you would take command of that sector. We should concentrate axemen for your defence but I believe that nearly every one of your forest axemen is also a crossbowman, so you have both offence and defence.

"You have heard the plan for the pikemen. I don't know yet how many of the troops that travelled with us, will be needed as leaders of the pikemen there, but the battle pivots on our getting that right. I will send you as many as I can spare to assist you in close quarter fighting against the Duke's infantry, if indeed - as we must expect - they come up the hill to find you.

"I suggest that you take under your command the entire remaining force from Schwyz, that is the men that you know have not already been allocated to be pikemen. I will ask Uri to provide their axemen and crossbowmen to the stone bluff, where we will make our stand with the wall of pikes." He looked over to the representatives from the Uri canton, who nodded their answer.

"There is one other critical point about your command Master Arnold, and that is the timing. I want you not to attack, not to release any of the great logs nor to start any offensive downhill, until you get a horn signal from me. I plan to find a place high up in the woods where I can see most of what is going on and I will have riders, trumpeters and staff officers, as well obviously as an escort. The enemy array will almost certainly be a long column of their most formidable cavalry with most of the important leaders; followed by the infantry strung out in column, including archers. Then the final third will be their remaining cavalry, led by the less important magnates but because they are seeking reputations, just as, if not more formidable than the vanguard.

"No matter how vulnerable or how tempting the enemy may appear, I want to get the vanguard, the greater part of their leading horsemen safely past the point where the lakeside road turns away from the water and heads up to where our pikewall is waiting for them. Our tactics are best when the enemy is massed, his ranks close together when the shock of our pikes stops the charge, and starts to kill the horses and bring down their riders. Those knights behind the front ranks who can't see what is happening will press forward. Confusion reigns! So long as the pikewall holds, in such circumstances gentlemen, we have them.

"My worst fear, other of course than the pikewall failing, is that if you, Master Arnold were to be too successful, too soon, with your logs and missiles and discourage them from getting as far as our strong point. Then they might ride back where they came from and come up with an even bigger army, or a more subtle plan of attack for another day.

"What I am saying is that we must seek to finish it in such a way that this generation of invaders, or as many of them as survive, are not likely to repeat the experience in their lifetimes."

All of those present, nodded in assent.

***

THE PRISONER

Paul managed to get an interview with the Marshal later that evening to ask about the policy on prisoners. "I assume that those who ask for quarter and throw down their arms will get it," he enquired, "but what then?"

"I will have to consult with the locals about that" said the Marshal. "Remembering that we are in Schwyz to earn our right to make a home here," he continued, "I think we should be as merciful as circumstances allow. The ordinary rank and file who are captured should I think be handed over to the foresters. Many will be local men perhaps pressed into the Duke's service, but let them be the judge of the locals. After this is over, it will be our task to build up a permanent force for an independent little republic, which will need some fulltime soldiers.

"Obviously knights will be ransomed and the benefit of that, their arms and so on should go to their captor. But we are expecting Master Peter Proudhomme. He and I as Council members have the authority together to decide such issues. What happens in some realms is that the king receives 30 per cent of the ransom, the rest going to the captor. That could be a group of these woodsmen, or it could be individuals like you. In our case the realm would become the free cantons that will surely form a state if we can beat the Austrians. Then there is the matter of our own Council as the authority that we are subject to. Is that what you are asking?"

"Well in a way it is" replied Paul. "I am thinking of the young chap, Sir John of Potsdam. I took him prisoner - he yielded to me - and my servant has hold of his arms and armour, plus his horse. But what is to happen to him now?"

"Well, on the basis of what I have just said, as he is your prisoner, it is for you to decide but of course if he is to be set at liberty or even paroled, it will have to be after they attack - if he reported back at all to the Austrians about all these men at arms amongst the woodsmen, that would tip off our enemies. Another thing, he was you said, a landless knight like a lot of the Duke's recruits for this war. Apart from the value of his horse and arms I wouldn't expect to see much more from him. If you are being just a bit too fastidious, just ask me and I will have my Sergeant Jan Ansbach, 'take care' of him."

"No, no…" protested Paul. "That's not what I have in mind. He is my prisoner and will remain so until his ransom is paid - which is likely to be never. So he remains my prisoner for the same length of time. Truth is that I rather liked him and definitely feel sorry, that really for one bad fall of the dice, he should lose everything."

"This side of the invasion he is clearly a security risk; after that he is not. Then do what you will.

"If our local friends will excuse us now, I have some Brotherhood business to transact." He paused as the locals left, leaving Paul and the two German commanders.

"Now I have something I can tell you, at this moment in confidence, although I will discreetly tell the other Templar commanders. The Schwyzers have a spy amongst the servants in Zug castle - the servants are local men after all," he added, as though any explanation was necessary.

"It is of course very valuable to us. The connection is through young 'Arnold the soldier' who now reports to me. It seems that the invading army will be accompanied by some unusual allies. They are a group of eight Dominican friars who are expecting after the Austrian victory to put our Schwyzer friends to the question, all of whom of course, as you know, are excommunicates regarded as enemies of the Church - and thus suspected heretics.

"I know of at least six of the fifty or so Templars with us, that were in their prisons and suffered rather worse than you did. I am going to appoint a small squad who on my orders, once the battle has turned our way, will head for those bloody hounds of God, to the exclusion of other enemies and capture or kill these black Dommies when it is possible. You will notify all of the Templars in your command, that in the battle, Dommies spotted are prime targets. It is important than none of them survive to tell the story. They amongst all of our foes might make the connection about us being here, in the Foresters ranks. The Council from the beginning has said that we must remain submerged - our survival strategy is to just become forgotten. The warning for us has always been the Cathars. The crusade against them lasted fifty years and even now, a century later, the Black Dommies are continually combing the Languedoc sniffing out their descendants.

"You are too important in this battle as a battalion commander, to be on this snatch squad, but I want you to know that after the battle, and I will keep the locals out of this, those of our brethren that suffered at their hands - and I include you Paul- will sit in judgement on any survivors we can take. We might be able in Schwyz to pay off some old scores of our own, as well as deal with these Austrians.

THE EVE OF BATTLE

Ludo, on Paul's authority, had been taking meals to their prisoner - the young knight from Potsdam, who was locked up in a windowless basement in the town hall. His guards were the constables who kept the civil peace and before the hostilities they normally would have nothing more serious to deal with than drunkenness. But they had been told that this was one prisoner who absolutely must not escape. Ludo saw him regularly and despite the fact that he was once near to killing him, now found a kind of friendship forming. John had asked Ludo what he thought the chances were of his getting a release.

"I would say it's certain, but not before the battle" the squire told him. "After that, one of two things could happen. If your side wins, they will release you. If we win I think my master will try to find an honourable way to at least get you out of here. Perhaps, Sir John, it is you who should be thinking what you can offer for your liberty, since you have already told him you will not be ransomed by your family."

The prisoner replied, "I have indeed been thinking about that. Look, since I am not sworn to the Duke or any of his people, I am free to give my oath to your side or to Sir Paul personally, if he would accept that. That way I could join you in the fight - it is after all what I am good for. Every day for years, in all weathers, slogging away for hours in the castle yard against my father's master-at-arms, and my brothers. You may know something of that life?"

"Well, apart from the brothers - I have none, yes I certainly do know about that."

"So it has to be wrong for me to be down here in a windowless cell, whilst the butchers and bakers and scullions of this town are battling it out in the forest with the Duke's trained soldiers. My place is in a fighting line."

"I will tell him what you say Sir John. Don't despair. Sir Paul is a good man and a worthy knight."

"I don't doubt it my young friend, but ask him how might he like a personal bodyguard, to literally guard his back? Ask him that!"

Walking back across the town square where he had first followed Sir Paul into this town, Ludo was intercepted by a stooped and elderly clerk from the Burgomeister's office. "Do you know young Sir", he enquired, "where is Sir Paul? Can you take a message to him?"

"He is exercising his battalion", the squire replied, "but I know where he is. What is the message?"

"It is from your Marshal, to say that he has had a signal that Master Peter Proudhomme will get here by this evening. There will be a meeting. Please tell him that."

"At once" replied Ludo, as he set off to saddle his horse.

Paul had now been training these men every day for four weeks. He had been obliged to wait for several of them until the harvest was in but he knew that the enemy would be having the same problem with their footmen. His first two hundred swelled to become four and then six hundred - its full complement. Each Monday for the benefit of the new intake, he repeated his little lecture on the pike as a superior weapon when properly deployed. He was assisted in this training by the Marshal's top sergeant, Jan Ansbach, who had fought with the chief not only the previous year in the battalion of King Robert at Bannockburn, but even back years earlier at the battle of Courtrai, when Sir Peter's part in defeating the army of French Phillip was rewarded with a knighthood in the field. Jan, as well as knocking some basic discipline into these willing volunteers, was primarily selecting men to be section leaders, corporals and sergeants, whilst the Templars for the most part, were the officers and senior sergeants.

Paul told his assembled volunteers about the Greek and Macedonian hoplites and of the Spartans at Thermopolae, the way that spears became defensive weapons against cavalry, and how the shafts got longer. Then in addition to the spear point for stabbing, a blade was added for cutting, and a hook for pulling armoured men off their horses. Each of these techniques was demonstrated by the top sergeant, using some of the unhappy mounted squires as 'demo' opponents. "And thus," Paul always concluded, "the pike was born."

The men themselves had to believe against all their instincts, that if they could stand firm, the armoured mounted knights would be halted, their warhorses unable to go forward against the forest of steel spikes. Then and only then, the horsemen would be really vulnerable to counter-attack from the knife-men ducking below their horses, and crossbowmen from above, whilst the press of fresh riders of their own side behind them, would prevent their retreat.

"That is the point," Paul had told them, "when this piece of land in front of you becomes a killing ground." Using some mounted squires to demonstrate against men with wooden shafts without their steel heads, he had the horsemen charge at the unmoving thicket of poles to show that the horses could not break through, and would indeed refuse. Then Sergeant Jan did his demonstration of the hook to snag in armour and tug men out of their saddles, a bruising process which the mounted squires did not care for at all.

Paul knew that the men were about as ready as they were going to be and had taken them discreetly away from the town, to the actual rock bluff that they would be defending near to the lake, with his battalion in the front. There he and Sir Heinrich rehearsed their troops in the tactics they had planned for the day itself. They had jointly met with the leaders of the Uri fighting men who would provide their crossbowmen and forest fighters to cover the wooded flanks of their position. Volunteers from amongst their smaller, nimbler men had agreed to be skirmishers, to move in and out of the pikemen's ranks as knifemen, to despatch dismounted fallen knights, and dodge back to safety.

It was at the close of the afternoon before Paul could give his attention to Ludo, who had brought up his horse and waited for him to finish that day's exercises.

"Sir Paul, I am to tell you that Master Proudhomme will be arriving tonight in Schwyz." Paul warmed to the news. He had the highest regard for the master builder who was in fact so much more than that, not to mention the gratitude he owed him for saving him from the Dominicans in Freiburg.

"I also have a message from your prisoner, Sir John" upon which Ludo passed on the gist of it. "He wants to be your man, to give you his oath and show he can be useful, but he wants in to this fight, to do what he is trained to do."

"You like him don't you, Ludo?"

"In truth Sir Paul, I do."

"So do I," the knight said. "The danger he represents no longer exists once their army is on the move. They will find out very soon that they are up against other professionals and not just foresters, but they won't change their plans because of that. Since Master Proudhomme will be here tonight I will ask for his advice, but my instinct is to take our prisoner's oath of fealty, tell him his duties, but release him only on the morning of the invasion after we have heard that the enemy have left Zug castle. That would comply with the Marshal's orders, when if we were wrong about him, there is nothing useful he could tell them anyway."

***

On the evening of the arrival in Schwyz of Master Proudhomme, he had been introduced to the leaders of the free cantons. All the military leaders were present for this was to be the final council of war. The intelligence from Zug was quite clear. The Habsburg levy almost in its entirety had reported there. The Duke himself, with his household knights and war captains, were also now resident at the castle. Everything pointed to the invasion coming in one more days' time on November 15th and the same intelligence was coming from the second invasion front in the canton of Unterwalden, in this case from a sympathetic knight who was himself a part of the Habsburg levy.

The Marshal asked for Geraint's report on his planned defence tactics and details of the liaison with central headquarters high up in the forest, overlooking the bluff and the lake. Sir Geraint and his principal lieutenants from the Unterwalden contingent having reported, concluding that as they had a journey to get back to their positions, they needed the maximum time to finish their preparations. Satisfied, the Marshal wished them luck and gave permission for them to leave. As they left the room, came the farewells poignant before a battle, as they clasped hands with those friends who remained to fight the main army on the shores of Lake Zugensee. When Geraint reached Paul, like the old comrades they had become, they embraced and wished each other good luck.

Those Templars under Geraint's command, were waiting mounted outside with his saddled horse, and the sound of iron-shod horses on the cobblestones made their departure resound, echoing through the town square and off the buildings.

"So gentlemen," spoke the Marshal, "I will take a report from each battalion commander in our order of battle starting with Master Arnold, whose force will probably be the first to encounter the enemy." All the captains listened to each of the section reports, so by the end they all knew the overall plan and where their units fitted into it.

The leader of the Uri crossbowmen repeated his responsibilities out loud, as did his colleague in charge of the axemen, protecting the pike battalion's flanks. Their orders there would come from Sir Paul, when his battalion was at the front of the line and from Sir Heinrich once his battalion had moved through the front lines, to start the counter attack. Trumpet signals were agreed and a muted version demonstrated.

When all seemed to be over, the Marshal asked a further question. "We appear to be well prepared," he told them, "and that is a core element in good leadership, but a good general must also ask about what might happen that is unexpected. In other words, if we were attacking and not defending, what would you have in your minds to catch us off balance?" He looked around for an answer.

"Well, Sir Peter," spoke up the German commander, "they could assume we know that they are to attack us in the morning tomorrow and instead make it a night attack tonight. That is what I might do."

"And very enterprising too," the Commander replied. "But we do have the spy boats on the lake who could get across to us much faster than the enemy could march around the lake."

"Paul?" He saw him rising to speak.

"I have worried about them sending a powerful group in boats tonight. They will know which are our spy boats and will have their own out there and could eliminate them. Now if they sent a strong group, tonight, let us say to come up to the shore where the road moves away from the lake and scout what their main army will have to overcome. If they took us by surprise not in a defensive array, they could seek to hold the bluff until the main army reaches them, and reinforce themselves with the small boats. That could turn our defensive plan onto its head."

"So," came the reply, "what then is your solution?"

"I will treble the guard tonight, have my entire battalion camping by the bluff and position a spy boat close to our shore, in case they can spot any movement on the lake and give us maximum warning. In that case, I would organise squads to meet the enemy in the shallows with pikes, stop them landing, and kill them there."

Sir Peter looked around and noted approval on all faces. "Very well," he said, as he stood up. "We now have our plan."

***

EXODUS NOVEMBER 15TH 1315

It was like a Biblical event, the castellan mused. After his massive organisational effort, which had started months before, the great host in all its power and splendour was finally on its way. He stood now on the castle's highest tower watching them below, wending through the crowded cobbled streets of the ancient lakeside town of Zug, towards the outskirts and the road that followed the lakeshore, leading to the rebel canton of Schwyz. Out on the shimmering surface of the lake he could see fishing boats and he knew that some amongst those would be spying for the enemy. There would be little for their comfort, he reflected.

The November sun was now emerging, more bright than hot, after overnight rain. As ever, the splendour of the vista, a dense blue sky with green forested, snow-capped mountains, and the deep azure of the lake, was healing to the soul. The Baron von Cham had every reason to be content. He had fulfilled his duty in preparing for today's invasion. Now it was up to the younger men, the Duke's war captains, to bring this business to its conclusion.

Von Cham had conducted his liege lord Duke Leopold Habsburg, to the mounting block in the castle courtyard and once in the saddle, had kissed his gauntleted hand. Surrounded by his mounted escort, the superbly armoured magnate then walked his great warhorse, hooves drumming across the drawbridge and trotted away towards the city gate, his squire just behind, proudly holding his banner. Behind him followed a long line of mounted, armoured men, stretching out along the narrow cobbled lane, the clatter of their horses' iron-shod hooves reverberating off the buildings in the narrow lanes, and drenching the small town with the martial noise.

The Duke had risen early and enjoyed a vast breakfast surrounded by his nobility, jesting about being too busy hunting down the survivors amongst the peasantry, to expect to eat again before evening. "First the small war and then the great hunt, eh your Highness?" enquired one of his leading tenants, catching the general mood. Indeed the Duke had thought in similar terms, once he knew for certain that he would have under his orders between two and three thousand mounted knights and men- at- arms. He smiled his agreement then turned, specifying to von Cham, what in particular he would wish served up that evening for his victory feast.

Now the castellan could see the armoured knights below. He knew that there would be so many of them at the muster, their squires in close attendance emerging from the city gates and forming up outside, with the marshals placing them in the order of march. On each side of the road he could see where the infantry had bivouacked for the past few nights whilst the last elements of the army came together. It was Baron Otto, to whom had fallen the massive job of feeding them and organising the camps and horse lines in lanes, and areas for each contingent. All were supplied with latrines, with tents and when those had run out, with lean-to shelters for the late arrivals. His clerks had noted the attendance of each of the Duke's vassals, great and small, and what they had brought to the muster, compared with their obligations. In addition there were the volunteers and soldiers of fortune, most of whom he had concluded were of prideful and prickly disposition, but each had to be allocated to a subsidiary military leader

It had all taken a lot of progressively harder work, it had been many months - years even, in the making. Now he was gratified to see the results of his labours as the great host streamed away along the lakeside road in an orderly river of brightly caparisoned horses, their steel-clad riders in multi-coloured surcoats, each apart from the Duke's mesnie with their Habsburg double-headed eagles insignia, displaying their unique heraldic devices, with a veritable forest of lance points held high, the shafts carrying their bannerets.

Even from this distance, von Cham could pick out the heraldry of the great houses amongst the chieftains, each followed by his household knights and tenants.

Interspersed after the first thousand or so of the heavy cavalry, the veritable point and weight of the mighty sword that the Duke wielded against the Foresters, came the first contingents of footmen. There were crossbowmen and men at arms who were ready to counter attack against any ambush from the forest, where they expected on past history for the enemy to be concealed. At least fifteen large hounds were being led along with them, the hounds being trained to fight against men.

He saw that waiting at the rear of the column, behind them all on the road, came the tonsured Dominicans in their distinctive black robes and sandals. Brother Joacquim had brought them to Zug from Einsiedeln Abbey the previous evening. They had requested his Highness to allow them to hold a service for the army before it moved off, but he dismissed that idea in short order. "This is not a bloody holy war," he had said. "Their fight with Einsiedeln Abbey was about land and pasturing rights - and that is what my fight with them is about!"

There were eight of the black friars now walking in pairs, the front pair carrying a processional cross and a swinging chained censer. No doubt, he speculated, they would all be chanting some dirge. Even looking at them from this distance caused him involuntarily to shudder. All Christian men had cause to fear them, he thought - these Hounds of God, perpetually sniffing out 'error' to be punished in the cruelest ways. Not a philosophical man, nevertheless in his secret heart, the Castellan wondered how the cruel Dominicans had thrived in their religion, based as it was upon a self-sacrificing gentle saviour, who spoke the riddle of 'loving your enemies'. He quickly banished such thoughts as just the sort of reflection that if ever given voice, could condemn him. Nevertheless he was glad to have them away from his castle and thought it would be unlikely they would be back. Now their work would be amongst the broken remains of the foresters and the ceaseless striving for men's souls by use of red-hot irons, thumbscrews and the rack.

The remaining heavy cavalry had now formed up and taken their place in the long procession, around another thousand, he remembered from the planned order of march. These, for all their bright heraldry and formidable appearance were for the most part the Duke's less prestigious smaller vassals and those of his allies, the great men insisting, as usual, on the most exposed leading positions at the front of the battle - at least during the march to get there. Having arrived, as he recalled, youthful valour would be allowed to take precedence over seniority.

As the last of the great host swung out along the roads, more than five thousand men in all, the Baron could no longer see the vanguard. At that rate of progress he calculated it would be about three hours before they would be at the edge of Schwyzer territory. He knew from the scouts who had gone out the previous day that there was nothing in the way of fortifications or obstructions along the lakeside road, but it changed when the scouts had tentatively followed the road, as it led away from the lake into the forest towards Schwyz. Then as he would have expected, crossbow bolts and arrows had immediately started to fly, causing the scouts to withdraw.

They did report however that there were a number of firebreaks - lanes downhill through that part of the forest that bordered the lake, which hadn't been there before.

The Baron knowing the terrain, had given his opinion at the previous night's council of war, that the enemy would attack down the steep hillside from the forest, as the Habsburg army was strung out in column along the lake road. Probably, he suggested, these firebreaks were to allow them to make massed attacks. One of the Duke's captains agreed and was for concentrating the infantry and crossbowmen to enter the forest, as soon as they knew from what part of the frontage the attack came from, but they would wait to respond until the enemy betrayed their positions. Meanwhile he would mass them at the forest edge in front of these firebreaks, ready to absorb any attack and then hit them hard. The bulk of the army, the heavy cavalry, of course would continue to proceed along the lake road and would deploy into line on His Highness's orders, as soon as his people could see the nature of the Forester's defences, further along the road to Schwyz.

Baron Otto felt the tug of the instincts of his youth and that he should be out there riding to do battle against his liege's enemies. But he knew that today his duty was otherwise, and that now he had to prepare for a returning flow of injured - and dead - if they were too important to leave on the battlefield, and then over a day or two, a lot of hungry and probably drunken soldiery making their ways back to Zug.

First however in his concerns must be the victory feast for the Duke, his principal guests and warriors planned for this night, and he left his observation point to go down and attend to the detail.

DAY OF DESTINY: THE BATTLE OF MORGARTEN

The boatmen had the first count but information was streaming by runners into the Marshal's headquarters and it seemed that Duke Leopold did indeed have more than 2,000 - nearer 2,500 armoured knights and men at arms, each mounted on a great warhorse with more than half of this force leading the army's advance. It was a massive weight of arms and armour that could be expected to smash through all conceivable infantry formations. Indeed, except against a similar or greater sized cavalry opponent, military convention would say they must prevail. To be sure, the Duke knew that there would be no cavalry force in the field apart from his own. He expected his 3000 or so infantry would have a tough fight and take casualties in the forests, whilst the sheer weight of his main armoured attack on the road would clear aside any resistance or obstacles, and allow the cavalry to ride all the way to take possession of Schwyz town.

There they expected to be joined by the smaller second force invading the cantons from a different direction, that through Unterwalden. The attacks had been co-ordinated to commence soon after dawn this morning and after some early rain, the skies cleared and the road to Schwyz, alongside the lake at any rate, seemed firm enough for this martial traffic.

The Duke himself with his cavalry captains rode in the vanguard, walking their horses with a screen of mounted scouts well ahead. The long armoured snake had slimmed down over the march from the start, now with cavalry riding two by two, rather than the five and six abreast, as had been easy leaving the castle and the town. But once away from the busy farmsteads and cottages, that road, strengthened to take laden carts, was not much more than a single cart's width and already the rain-softened turf on each side had turned into mud. Now the procession stretched out over some two miles and moved at a speed no greater than that of the infantry in the elongated centre of the column.

When the Duke looked back at a curve in the road, he felt the pride of leading such a glorious host of horsemen, the sun now reflecting off steel armour and thousands of steel points on spears and lances high above their heads. The surcoats of so many colours emblazoned with their wearer's heraldic devices were repeated on their shields mostly slung on the saddlebows, and on the pennants and banners flying from lances that each squire carried behind his master. He was not so pleased to see on the road at the back of the column, the black crows of Dominicans, no doubt chanting their doleful stuff and depressing their hearers, who he was sure would much prefer a rousing marching song.

He looked over at the heavily timbered mountain slope on his left and agreed with the opinion of his foot captain that they must certainly expect an attack from there. In anticipation of that he saw that several hundred infantrymen and scores of crossbowmen had now left the main column and were doubling over towards the forest fringe. They would be ready to react to any attack from that quarter, once they could determine from where it came within that mile long stretch of seemingly impenetrable woodland.

He saw the wide swathe-like lanes cut down the mountainside, which if it hadn't have been a war situation he would have taken to be the good husbandry of firebreaks. But his scouts had said they were new, and so their purpose must surely be to concentrate their attackers to speed down en masse, rather than emerge from the forest fringe in ones and twos. Still, he pondered, they could equally serve to send his infantry up the mountainside, without fighting from tree to tree as they had expected. He could see that his captains were concentrating the troops in ranks at the mouth of each firebreak, ready to contain the furious downhill charge of foresters that they expected, and it looked to be well done.

But looking at the peacefulness of the forest, the sun now shining brightly overhead, the only sounds the steady rat-a-tat tat of the drummer boys, of jangling harness and the excited war hounds - but they would bark anyway - it was easy to imagine that their enemies were not even there; that they were massing somewhere else in fact. That brought him back to speculating what kind of a barrier the foresters would have built across the road, once it left the lakeside. The enemy had been expecting spies and he had received no information from that source, but that those sent had been pierced by the crossbow bolts that remained in their recovered dead bodies.

He knew that he must expect a barrier across the road, probably a massive timber affair but once in the forest, he should be able to flank it, perhaps on both sides, before he charged. He would of course give pride of position to the younger men when it came to the actual assault. It would never do for him to be caught up in the melee before whatever the barrier was, unable to direct his forces. He wondered then whether these quarrelsome foresters had been able to agree on a single leader. He doubted it.

The scouts had earlier passed along the road where it turned up into the forest at the end of the lake. They came galloping back. One of them, a bright young knight from his own mesnie saluted, and breathlessly reported. "They are defending a position, Your Highness, about a quarter to half of a mile from this bend in the road where it is well wooded and there are steep slopes rising on both sides of the road. There seems to be an outcrop of rock on both sides of the road and I would guess that they have built a barrier in between."

"Why do you 'guess'?" the Duke asked disapprovingly. "Why don't you know?"

"Yes sir," the knight replied nervously, "but we could go no further. They set up a barrage of bolts as soon as they saw us; they obviously have the approaches covered by crossbowmen. But your Highness, the reason I couldn't see what the barrier was made of, was because they had hundreds of men, many with helmets and some armour and spears, standing in front, in array - on *our* side of the barrier" his voice reflected his amazement.

"Hallelujah" the Duke said incredulously! "Perhaps the bloody fools don't know about a heavy cavalry charge - a thousand warhorses with armoured riders, each one weighing a ton, galloping down on them… and they are all footmen formed up on our side of the barrier, you say?"

His captains had heard the whole exchange and he reined in his charger and turned to them. "So gentlemen, what say you?"

One turned to the scout who had reported. "Does the space on the road between the trees on both sides, widen? Can we deploy into line for the charge?"

"No question Sir," the knight replied, "I would say that the enemy was in formation in a line maybe a hundred or more men wide, and to some depth unknown. It's a valley but not a wide one. In the available space we could probably have our ranks each of 50 to 60 chargers for an initial attack, but as I said Sir, they have crossbowmen, I would estimate on both flanks of the road"

"So shields up," the Duke retorted, "and we will form up as soon as the space is available to us. On my trumpet signal, we will attack."

All along the line, visors were being pulled down, knights were receiving their lances from the squires behind them, girths were being checked and shields unslung from the saddlebows, and when the first trumpet signal sounded, a mass of warhorses swung off the road and deployed onto the soft verges beyond them.

The Duke allowed his captains to lead the column away from the lakeside, following the road up into the forest. He and his bodyguards and squires fell back several ranks and off to one side, with his trumpeter and the scouts as messengers. The column widening as far as the space now allowed, followed the captains into the gap, which enabled them to see their enemy for the first time. No more than eighty yards ahead, drawn up in proper ranks was the force that opposed them. This was no rabble, they could see that. All wore the red scarves that matched the crimson banners of Schwyz that fluttered overhead their position, competing in the air only with the banners of the giant black and white bull's heads of Uri. They looked disciplined and formidable. Many were equipped in steel body armour and helmets which gleamed in the early light; their lines bristled with regularly spaced sixteen foot long shafted pikes angled outwards to the height of a horse's breast, the shafts rooted in the ground beside them; their great number of shining steel points and blades looking lethal to the attackers. It was a giant steel hedgehog that the Duke's horsemen had to overcome.

"Christ Jesu!" exclaimed one rugged looking captain. "Pikes! This is the 'Golden Spurs' again." He referred to the Flanders battle not many years before where pikes first withstood heavy cavalry. "I would hope not," said another veteran. "I want to survive this lot. There's no glory in going down to a bunch of farmers."

"True," said his colleague," but do they look to you like farmers?"

"Whatever! As usual we will do our duty," came the reply as he spurred his horse forward, his colleague alongside him. The Duke had now taken in what his force was up against. Clearly the bloody Schwyzers had brought in mercenaries, but he still had more than two and half thousand horsemen and this was just a few hundred pikemen. He motioned to his trumpeter who blew the charge.

The notes had hardly faded away before they heard another trumpet signal, high up above them in the forest. Even before the charge commenced and drowned out the sound, there was a distant rumble from far back behind them, out of their sight along the lakeside road. Down each of the 'firebreaks' on the mountainside came scores of giant trimmed tree trunks, tumbling, bouncing high and rolling, an elemental force gathering momentum as they crashed into, through and over the horror-struck and suddenly helpless companies of the Duke's infantry, now crushed, waiting there in formation for the assault of the wild foresters for which they had prepared.

Hundreds, perhaps thousands of tons of timber rolled on after destroying the ranks of formed-up infantry, sweeping the column of riders clear off the road and into the lake. Behind the logs then indeed came a torrent of the screaming wild foresters, wielding two-handed axes and other close quarter weapons, smashing through the shattered remains of the infantry formations and on, to engage the main column that had been marching along the lakeside, where all suddenly was death and confusion.

The second great formation of the Duke's mounted men, formidable enough, was not far behind. They quickly moved to engage the teeming foresters ahead of them. Orders were shouted, visors came down and a line of battle started to form up on the soft ground off the road. Before they were ready to charge, another trumpet call came out of the high forest and to the amazement of the mounted soldiers this apparent peasant rabble smartly disengaged, and streamed back towards the firebreaks and up the steep slopes, melting away into the trees. The rear-guard cavalry commander ordered the charge, leaving individual riders to try to ride down some of the fugitives before they could escape, some sizeable groups of whom formed up, the blood of battle roused, were hefting their axes and standing their ground.

***

Paul had suffered a sleepless night. He had managed to convince himself that there would be a night attack, once he had suggested that possibility at the war council, but it had not happened. Jan Ansbach, had been seconded to Paul for the battle, to stiffen the men that they had jointly trained. He had tried to persuade Paul to get some sleep but he had probably had no more than two hours over the whole night. Few of the Schwyzer pikemen had slept much either, knowing that some, perhaps many of them, would not survive the coming battle.

They knew the whereabouts of the invading force because of the early intelligence from the boatmen. There could be no surprise attacks after that and Paul and his fellow officers made sure their men had been well fed, and as prepared as they could ever be, before they were ordered into line. Even then as runners came regularly out of the forest to report on the position and deployment of the cavalry column, Jan Ansbach still had them practicing the drills their lives depended on, that day.

The sun had come out, although there were rain clouds scudding along. It was a crisp day to which the sun did make a noticeable difference when it had emerged. Although the army had no musicians accompanying the force, detachments did have their drummers whose marching beat could be heard in the distance, before the sound of jingling harness and metal accoutrements of these thousands of heavy cavalry horses and their armoured riders.

Paul understood the dread, many perhaps most of his men, would be experiencing at this moment, simply because he felt it himself. He had fought at the bloody field of Bannockburn on less favourable ground than this, and the measured struggle of pikes against armoured horsemen was a confrontation in which he could feel some confidence. But he still remembered with some horror, the intensive hand to hand fighting that day that followed the counterattack, and finished for him fighting waist high in the chill water of the Bannock stream. In that kind of brutal close fighting, against desperate men, he knew that luck was a large factor in determining who got in the way of a swung blade or random arrow, or was struck down from behind by an unseen assailant.

Also, he knew his military theory well enough, to understand that the main enemy of pikemen were archers. From what he knew of the enemy dispositions they did not have longbowmen but rather crossbows, lethal at close quarters. But of course, so did the men of Uri there in large numbers, whom they hoped could neutralise them. Paul, like his Templar colleagues had the view that the military arrogance of the magnates and their armoured knights, would crowd out all other forms of arms in 'the positions of honour' - at least in the early charges. After that his hope was that the constant arrival of new horsemen, manoeuvering into the limited area before the lines of pikemen, together with the dead and wounded, would eventually cause sufficient chaos to allow a counterattack to be ordered. But timing would be everything. They knew that high above them on the forested mountain slope, the Marshal would be watching up in his field HQ - the foresters had built him a viewing platform up there - and deciding, as though in a chess competition, when to make the moves for his trumpets to announce.

All the ranks were ready and saw the Habsburg mounted scouts as they cautiously emerged from the river road. Paul heard the top sergeant's hoarse reassuring voice, "Steady lads, this isn't it. They're just taking a look at us."

Paul saw the Uri leader signal his men, although it was at the edge of their range, and heard the thwang of crossbows as a flight of bolts sped towards the mounted men who wisely turned about and disappeared.

Now they knew it could only be minutes before the attack and indeed, to the accompanying beat of drums, long columns came into sight of magnificently caparisoned warhorses with their armoured riders sitting them like giants, great lance shafts in their mailed fists. Paul was relieved to see no archers or crossbowmen preceding the cavalry. He noticed with his professional eye, that the riders all had their shields on one arm with the reins bunched in the same grip. Obviously the brief experience of their scouts had had its effect. He also knew that those shields would be of little use against pikes and be more of an encumbrance than a protection, once the charge commenced.

As they deployed into a rough line Paul could not but admire their sheer magnificence, the gorgeous spectacle that they made, even though he knew that it could be lethal for him personally. He could see why they could never countenance the idea in all that glory that they could ever be defeated, other than perhaps by a larger number of their own kind. He also was confident that whatever they saw, as they were looking at him and his men, it was not at all what they had been expecting.

"Steady lads" he heard the sergeant behind him say again. "They'll be here soon enough."

There was a sudden silence. Both sides now faced the other across the forest clearing, through which the road to Schwyz made its way.

Paul suddenly remembered the pause before the storm at Bannockburn, a year before. Now as then, for a few heartbeats nothing moved except for the crowd of crows, just as in the battle in Scotland a mystery, flying in from all directions, occupying and weighting down the available branches in this greenwood arena. The only sound now was their harsh cawing, the sound of the harbinger of death.

The boys with water skins had done their rounds and retired out of sight. The nervous jesting and ribbing that had been going on earlier had stopped now. Each man was holding his own silence. Paul knew that more than one with bladder strained, unable to break ranks, would be pissing himself, but the sergeant had told them earlier that they shouldn't worry about that. It was totally unimportant compared with each man holding his place in the line and he knew that for their mounted adversaries opposite, it would be just the same.

Paul himself carried a pike, as did Ludo his squire who had materialised from the men behind him. He also noticed that an armed and armoured John of Potsdam was standing behind Ludo. The squire had taken him out of the jail and given him back his weapons and his ringmail corselet on which a scarlet scarf was clearly in evidence. This was by agreement with Master Proudhomme the condition fulfilled, that the Austrian army was already on the march.

The previous night, after the council of war, Paul with Ludo, had visited the young knight in his cell and had taken his oath of loyalty. It was the first time anyone had sworn loyalty to him personally, his folded hands clasped in those of his feudal leader, and Paul strangely felt not a little embarrassed by it.

"I will release you from all that when the time is right," Paul told him reassuringly.

"Well, that is very civil of you," spoke up the young knight, "but I have the feeling that I might do quite well as your man. It might not be so easy to get rid of me." Now John of Potsdam his sword sheathed, carried a plain shield on his arm with a short handled axe in one hand and a long slender dagger in his belt. "Since I am not a pikeman," he said, "I thought I would be most useful nipping out and seeing off dismounted knights before they can get up, and start being a nuisance again." That, Paul reflected, would be one of the most dangerous tasks on the battlefield.

The Habsburg captains had now got their front rank of some sixty mounted men lined up, with a second similar line coming together behind it, and a third behind that. Several of the riders had to be restrained from attacking single-handedly, so conditioned were they to the idea that no foot soldier could stand up to an armoured charge - that they would surely break and run. The Duke himself, off to one side, had needed to move his command group back because of speculative crossbow shots in his direction. He could see all was ready and ordered his trumpeter to sound the charge, then like all the others listened surprised, to hear what sounded to be an answering trumpet from high up in the forest. The Duke sent an aide to bring him a captain of foot soldiers.

The pikemen were in their three ranks closed up together, each rank a line of a hundred. Behind the walls of spikes Paul and his officers and sergeants moved up and down, dressing the ranks and encouraging the men. He had about eighty of the Uri crossbowmen also in line behind the front rank of pikes, for close quarters support. The orders were drilled into them to aim to shoot the horses that were larger targets, less well armoured, and created chaos when they were brought down.

Another two hundred or more pikemen at the back were reserves, to drag away their dead and wounded to the rear, and replace them in the ranks.

Behind the road-wide gap that pierced the great rock, Paul was comforted to know that his efficient German comrade, Sir Heinrich, had a similar force to his own, who would at some point relieve Paul's battalion. He knew that whatever the outcome for the Foresters and for himself personally, that nothing had been neglected by himself or his comrades in preparing for what was now upon them. He stopped reflecting and fully concentrated on the moment, hefted his pike ready to step into any breach. As he saw the cavalry line opposite begin to surge towards them, he called out, "Steady lads", a cry taken up along the long line of sturdy foresters and their Templar allies.

For only a few moments more this quiet little valley, hidden by the forest, would continue with the silence that it had known for millennia..

The long rows of foresters, both pikemen and crossbow men that blocked the passage of these hundreds of heavy cavalrymen, pounding towards them, now began to shout their defiance against the deep rumbling of the oncoming hundreds of armoured warhorses, their riders dressed from head to toe in steel. From this moment on, silence was banished from the land for all the time it would take for sanity to return.

***

THE SHOCK OF BATTLE

The thunder of the hooves was immense; the steel helmets bowed down just above the horses' heads as the steel crossbow bolts began to fly. The silent pikemen stood shifting and nervously re-shifting their suddenly sweaty grasp on the pike shafts, as they waited for the crash, now only seconds away

The mass of horsemen had now reached the embedded many-pointed steel caltrops that could cripple a horse. One horse was down and then another, and more, still more as the flights of steel bolts struck home, causing widespread havoc with those that followed them. The line was now ragged, hardly a line any more, but were clusters of a massive tonnage of horse and riders with lances couched, still apparently overwhelming - except that in their turn, the pikes didn't waver. At the moment of impact, most horses refused to skewer themselves, whilst their riders wrestled the reins for control. Riders went crashing into the wall of pikes, their own lances short of a target, but the points of the pikes finding the horses as they had been trained to do. One great horse rose up hooves flailing, pinned there by several upthrust pikes, before crashing down, his rider already gone, the beast causing destruction to both pikemen and other horses as he fell. The sergeants hurried reserves over, tugging at the fallen pikemen and dragging them away, whilst others were thrust into gaps in the line.

Behind the first wave of cavalry, the second and third lines were immediately engaged by the disappearance of so many of those leading the attack. In that confined space and charging with such momentum a downed horse and rider entangled their near neighbours, who then had to struggle not to be brought down themselves. To the Duke watching at a distance, the momentum had given way to a confused milling of frustrated horsemen, unable to make their horses crash through the pikewall. The riders could not strike a target with their lances and sometimes in frustration finally hurled these over the top of the pikes like spears, and fell back on waving their swords and maces.

Some unhorsed knights managed to get up and came on foot against the implacable array of pike heads, trying to chop their way though. The crossbowmen standing with the pikes had a point blank target, as the armoured men struggled to find a way through the forest of steel points. Others stumbled back dazed and concussed, towards their starting point, a target now for the many crossbowmen high on the flanks rising to the forest on either side of the array of pikemen. The remainder still struggled to get from underneath their fallen steeds, or lay still.

"Now!" Paul waved out the skirmishers including John of Potsdam, who passed through the ranks of pikes and fell to attacking the armoured men on the ground. It was a bloody business of slashing throats, sliding the point of a dagger into a slit in the armour or chopping down with an axe, which was the preferred local way of making sure that enemy would never rise again.

The young boys now were passing along the pikemens' ranks with the water skins and above all the gravelly voice of the top sergeant could be heard up and down the line saying, "Well done lads, they'll be back, but now you know you've got the beating of them."

Paul looking out for the next attack saw more and more fresh horsemen continuously entering the battlefield and the ranks for a charge forming up, without any apparent change of tactics. He sent the horn signal for his skirmishers to immediately withdraw behind his lines.

The Habsburg trumpet blew for their attack and another two or three hundred men on their giant horses in close ranks, started to work up their momentum, to become what should have been an unstoppable force. Lances couched, helmeted heads low down over their horses' necks, onwards they came, filling all the space available that the pikemen could see.

This time the crossbowmen of Uri above him and on his flanks started to fire high into the charging mass at the edge of their range and immediately got results in spectacular spills and crashes. Paul saw that there were groups of horsemen behind the central charging body that were slanting off towards both his flanks, obviously to see if they could outflank the defenders. But the ground beyond the line of this pikewall on both sides started to sharply rise up to the forest that dominated the clearing, which had so quickly become a battlefield. Paul was not the only one to see the danger. Again from high above them in the forest, came a clear trumpet signal to the men of Uri protecting the pikemens' flanks. With hardly a break, the shower of steel bolts that had been wreaking such damage on the main attack, was switched onto the knights that were coming to test the flanks; the nearer they came, the more of their number went down. But they were determined and the crossbowmen slowly pulled back into the fringes of the forest. The horsemen then had to halt their charge and swords drawn, slow down as they entered the forest to get around the trees. Then, with a burst of cheering, came a downhill counter attack from the burly foresters that had been waiting there, now running, wielding their favoured two handed axes, chopping at the legs of the chargers and their riders alike, driving the survivors out of the forest and away across the open space back to their starting point, accompanied by a blizzard of lethal steel bolts and the screams of the mortally injured, both horses and men.

By now the great clash had recurred in the main assault with the same result as before. Most horses at the last moment had refused in front of the levelled pikes and swerved away, crashing into other horses, going down in a tangle of limbs and steel and harness. A few had run right onto the pikes, which stood firm, skewering the animals and dumping their riders into the chaos before them.

While the next rank piled on to the churning mass of broken animals and men, with the tangle of lances and shields piling up, it had made a new and formidable wall of obstruction, ahead of the front rank of pikemen. Frustrated survivors wheeled their mounts, looking for a way to engage, but instead faced the implacable faces of the unbroken ranks of pikemen, steadfast and unyielding, hurling challenges and abuse at them.

As the survivors retreated, more and more fresh horsemen were entering the small clearing and joining the fray without orders, merely on the instinct to engage. The crossbow bolts hummed ceaselessly through the air, many finding their targets of man or beast. Pressure on the defenders ranks once again eased.

The skirmishers went out again and did their butchers work. Paul saw his new vassal dragging back into his lines the recumbent body of a knight in magnificent armour. He saw Paul watching and called out, "Got a Count here, at least." Clearly the young knight had had the time recently, to reflect on the value of ransoms.

The space near to Duke Leopold and his command group was fast filling up with the constant stream of new arrivals from the lakeshore road. A rider reported directly to him who was a captain of foot soldiers, who had been sent for earlier. He reported on the forester's tree trunk ambush from the so-called firebreaks and the large estimated losses. The particular units that had been swept away into the lake were mostly crossbowmen coming up to support the main assault, news of which further depressed the Duke who, too late, realised that the assault should never have started without his own archers in place. He needed crossbowmen to thin out the ranks of the pikemen who, standing in line without shields, were particularly vulnerable to arrows - their worst fear. The captain said he would get as many together as he could organise up to the front and was about to leave on this mission, when the Duke stopped him.

"I want you to get a force into the woods and take the hounds, but not to chase those men who ambushed you. There is a higher priority… Up there!" he pointed, "somewhere, is the leader of these mercenaries. He knows his business, unluckily for us. It is his trumpet signals that those men, obey," he indicated nodding towards the lines of the defenders. "I want him found and killed, or better captured, so we can find out how these forest peasants got a trained force like this together. If we can isolate their head, then we can take care of what is left of the body. If you can bring me his head, or alive, you will have a barony."

The cavalry captains were trying to restore their authority over the assault which had become ever more difficult as more and more fresh horsemen kept arriving, seeking to join in the fray. One of the captains, he who had spoken of the 'Battle of the Golden Spurs', before fighting commenced, spoke to the group who gathered around him: "We are only going to break through those three ranks up front if we can make the horses keep going and not refuse. Here is what I want you to do and I will do this with you. We have to blindfold the horses so they can't see the steel, with scarves, sacks, anything you can find, and I want a line of fifty like that, we will ride stirrup to stirrup, the riders with their shields up, swords or maces in hand.

"Never mind lances at that stage. We have to burst through and then the ranks behind must exploit the gaps we make. The fight will then be at close quarters but in amongst their ranks. Now go and find some sort of horse blindfolds and get back into line."

Paul could see the large number of knights conferring as their excited mounts wheeled about that group, but he couldn't see what they were going to do next. Jan Ansbach, his sergeant came hurrying over and said, "I think they are blindfolding their horses, Sir - and you know what that means."

Paul did, and it was a worrying development. They would sacrifice their mounts by using them as a battering ram to find the weakest points in the hundred men long line. From the defenders point of view they wouldn't know where in that long line they would need to reinforce, until the enemy were already through, and the line could then roll up as new mounted men kept arriving to exploit the gap.

"Sergeant Ansbach - Jan," he said. "My compliments to Brother Heinrich. Explain our position. I am going to take our three ranks a little way forward, up closer to the line of wreckage of the horses and men we have already brought down, which I hope will snag them. I reckon they haven't counted on that with blindfolded horses. Suggest to Brother Heinrich that he may care to draw up his battalion in full array behind us, in case we go down. That way they would have done for us, but would be no nearer breaking through."

"Very good Sir, and good luck" and the sergeant was pushing his way back through the remainder of the reserves.

Paul found the leader of his crossbowmen, Hans, who like his men wore a magnificent full faced black and white Bull of Uri on his surcoat, and explained to him what was happening. The Uri men had taken no losses so far and trusted Paul's judgement. He explained that bringing down horses whilst they were blindfolded, could massively increase the enemy's problems The knights with their visors down had a restricted field of vision and expected their steeds to navigate all normal obstacles. Riding stirrup to stirrup would mean that just land a lethal bolt on one horse, and inevitably it will bring down others. He asked for more Uri bowmen to go immediately behind the first rank of his pikemen, to keep up a storm of missiles at the closest range and also asked that they used loaders and spare crossbows, to keep up the supply to their best shots.

He collected his other Templar officers who each commanded a section of the line and quickly explained what was happening. He could see across the field that the enemy were having quite some difficulty getting their now unsighted horses into some kind of formation. He had time he reckoned, and told his officers to immediately march their men a few steps backwards to a new line and set up just sufficient distance from the wrack of the earlier attacks, that the heavy horses would trip over the wreckage of horses, knights, their armour, broken lances and other weapons. Or in slowing, would lose the momentum on which they counted to burst through the pikewall.

Out of the corner of his eye he saw Heinrich's second battalion filing through the gap they were all defending and forming up in long ranks in the space to his rear. Jan came doubling back and saw that that Paul's officers were moving the ranks smartly forward and reported, "Second Battalion is moving into position Sir. I suggest we take our own reserves and the skirmishers, as a mobile force to go to any place they might break through."

"Yes, Jan - and would you please take personal command of that group."

They both looked across the battlefield, which was still milling with riders now hoping that their blindfold tactics would work and that this charge would make gaps sufficient to let them individually break through.

"Here they come," the Sergeant quietly said. "Good luck, sir" and turned away to organise the mobile reserve.

***

FIELD HEADQUARTERS

High up above the fray, in his field command headquarters, the Marshal was pleased with the progress of the battle so far. What had worked so well for him was the restricted space in front of his pikemen, and the inability of the enemy to flank the position. The tree trunk ruse had worked a treat, and happily, although the Marshal did not know this, had taken out a large body of crossbowmen, which the Duke would by now have discovered, that he could hardly do without.

He was concerned about the ability of the pikemen to continue to hold, against the continual assaults of the armoured cavalry and he could see that hours after the battle had commenced, fresh horsemen were arriving still and further crowding the restricted space before the defensive positions.

He was contemplating resting his first battalion by replacing them with Heinrich's and then he saw that indeed Heinrich's battalion was taking up positions previously held by Paul, whose ranks were moving back a few feet. From this distance he realised that they were reacting to some threat he could not see from the next mounted attack, which even then was forming up, somewhat clumsily, he thought. Then he understood.

The horsemen were running out of options, he realised. Incredibly, they hadn't brought up or used archers or crossbowmen, and now they were going to try to burst through with the sheer weight of their blindfolded horses. Paul and Heinrich were putting their whole strength where it could react if the riders successfully got past the first battalion's pikewall. It was the right move he thought, and was glad he had such field commanders who could so sensibly use their initiative.

He was up on his platform, built of sturdy timbers at his request at a point in the higher forest, where without being seen, he could view much of the battlefield. He had some six personal guards with him, all Templars, plus despatch riders and runners, and his key man - the trumpeter.

When he had heard the hounds for the first time nearby, he quickly realised that they might have been sent to look for him. The appropriate move, he thought, and one that, in the Duke's position, he would have also taken.

The deep ominous baying of the great hounds was then answered from a different direction but echoed almost on the level of comedy, by an outbreak of many more dogs' high-pitched barking, yapping even, more shrill and certainly not the ominous sound of the dogs of war. It came from further away, as though from a village, but he knew of no such village in that part of the forest.

The Templar officer commanding his escort looked up at him and saw that the Marshal had taken it all on board. Their planning had considered the security of the location that the Marshal had selected. They could not afford to draw too many men away from the battle, so had agreed on horn signals to summon reinforcements from the foresters within hearing. Now they knew or were sufficiently sure that the enemy was moving seriously against him, it was time to summon help. The Marshal ordered it done and then as the signals rang out over the forest saw that there was a disturbance at the point where the uphill track entered his headquarters area. It was a messenger who had arrived- a youth who had been delegated as a runner from a signal station the Marshal had set up on a mountain nearer to Schwyz, to keep in touch with developments in Unterfelden. The signal was one of several flag signals, which had previously been agreed. What had come through was a positive result, success! No detail of course, but they would now not need the reserve force of 500 men under the German Templar, Sir Martin, that the Marshal had held back and stationed where they could be sent to Unterfelden, if needed.

"Excellent," he said to his escort commander who had brought the lad over to him. "That means that the attack has failed or that they can contain it. We'll know in due course, but it's good news. Do you…" he said to the officer, "write this order. I will sign it and the messenger can get back a signal to Sir Martin with the reserve, who must be two hours from here. I want them here as soon as possible, but when they are just an hour away, he is to send a fast rider on to me here, so that we can decide exactly where they are to join into the battle."

Down below, the Marshal could see that the charge had commenced with about seventy or more knights in the front rank, riding as he had guessed, blindfolded horses. They were certainly riding as close, stirrup-to-stirrup, as if they were tied together. Another rank following had also launched in close order and a further one readying behind them. There were about two hundred and fifty men and horses in this charge, and a similar number milling about in the restricted space behind them in no formation, but waiting to exploit any gaps the charge could make. In the leading ranks the attackers had now abandoned lances, and held close-quarter weapons, swords, maces and axes. The Marshal realised that the battle probably now pivoted on this charge. He knew although he could not see them, that hundreds of crossbow bolts would be in the air and yes, now he could see horses and riders going down in swathes.

Still the monolithic mass of armoured horses and men swept on, now three ranks and behind them forming up, the remainder of the mounted men at arms. His lines of defenders looked puny from this distance but he knew that whether they could contain this massive onslaught had much to do with the Austrians gamble of blindfolding the horses, so they would not refuse in the face of the levelled pikes. Even that, he knew, was not the whole story. It was inevitable, he thought, with their sheer weight, that some at least of the mounted knights would break through. A few, the defenders could deal with, but if a long section of their pikewall collapsed, the individual mounted knights following, would roll up the line and make a great slaughter.

The future of the whole enterprise lay down there below him. Down there, ever more crows as spectators, occupied already laden branches. Above him and far above the tall trees that surrounded him, a pair of red kites sailed lazily, riding the air currents, impervious to the doings of mere men.

***

THE PIKEWALL

The thunder of the hooves of hundreds of warhorses was indeed a fearsome noise. They were no more than two minutes away and apart from the sergeants scolding and encouraging their men, there was little sound from the defenders. Then within one minute the sound of a hundred crossbows at more or less point blank range, was followed by the awful screams of dozens of the great beasts and their stricken riders and the crashing of their going down in a tangled chaos of steel and flesh. It was the pattern of the earlier charges with the deadly crossbows concentrating on the horses.

But now the damage was worse. The unsighted horses on either side of them had no means of avoiding collisions as the stricken beasts swerved in their pain and the second rank of attackers in their enthusiasm had come up too close to avoid the chaos. Most of the bolts hit a target and the second volley from preloaded weapons followed up the slaughter. Perhaps eighty or a hundred bolts had already struck home, the evidence of which was the shattered debris of men and horses that were down, many of whom would never rise.

The bowmen now rapidly withdrew behind the pikes to reload and prepare to fire again. Paul and all his officers and sergeants took up the chorus of 'stand fast now' and the like, as the well-thinned first rank of cavalry towered above them and the battalion's 300 pikes firmly extended in their direction. A coherent line of attack barely existed but still scores of horsemen were attacking them with the blindfolded steeds in the lead. The dangers were immense. In groups of four and five, the attackers could still achieve the objective of blasting through the pikewall and opening up gaps, for the hundreds of following riders to exploit.

Then the attackers, now only a few feet dividing them from the massed pikes on which they planned to sacrifice their mounts and break the line, were caught up in their headlong dash by a chaotic barrier of hundreds of sprawling dead and dying warhorses and men, broken lances and lost armour strewn before them from every earlier attack. It rose in places several feet high and had no order in terms of width. These knights were all expert horsemen, but their giant horses laden with their own armour and that of their heavy riders, were not for the hunting field, nor able to jump a fence. Moreover, blindfolded as they were, only the rider could steer their course and jumping with unsighted horses was not possible. The momentum of the charge necessary to be able to break through the pikes, meant that rein back as they might, they now could not avoid crashing into and tripping over the long line of the debris and bodies of these scores of casualties from earlier charges.

The cavalry in these few minutes had mostly destroyed itself, before it could quite reach the pikewall. Some managed to steer around the wreckage and the blindfolds worked as their great horses broke through, although pierced over and again by levelled pikes. In three places, they burst right through the lines of pikes, crushing pikemen under their horses and scattering their neighbours, as they pushed on through the second and third ranks. But of the whole cavalry host, no more than ten or so horsemen had broken through.

Where Paul had chosen to stand was one such place. The giant horse in front of him pierced by the pikes reared up, its hooves flailing lethally, striking a glancing blow which scraped off Paul's helmet, stunning him. Its rider, a dazed Paul now saw, wearing a horned helmet, was striking out with a great sword. He was caught off balance, his battle instinct for survival frustrated as he had no chance of blocking the blow in time. The weapon slashed down with a mighty blow, which didn't after all strike him, as had seemed unavoidable. But it made a fearful noise as it struck and glanced off an unexpected shield held above him. His saviour was his new vassal of one day, whom he had forgotten having told earlier to watch his back, rather than going out picking the pockets of the dead. John of Potsdam quickly reacted to the blow to his shield, wasting no time in stabbing his sword right up into the mounted man's throat, who disappeared on the other side of his horse that then collapsed on top of him.

Heinrich in the front of his three ranks, could see that Paul's pikewall was swiftly being restored, and partly broke his formation to send men to overwhelm those few mounted knights who had got through, and who were still fighting the lightly armed skirmishers.

Paul's officers knew what they must do, despite the desperate hand-to-hand fighting just a few yards to their rear. They had to look to the front and take second row men to close up the front ranks and to restore the pikewall. They left the reserve and skirmishers under Sergeant Jan and now some of Sir Heinrich's men, to use their pikes to hook the armoured riders who had got through and drag them off their now terrified horses, then fall on them with whatever weapons came to hand.

Outside the now re-forming pikewall, hundreds of the Habsburg cavalry were crowding in, whose task it had been to exploit the gaps. They were fruitlessly riding up and down the outside of the now greatly enlarged barrier of dead and dying horses, colliding with each other, as they sought to cross it and close with the pikemen. Then the openings in the pikewall had been sealed. The opportunity had passed. There were no more gaps. Hans' crossbowmen calmly stepped up behind Paul's first line, coolly selected their new targets and at point blank range, systematically shot the mounted men down.

Paul winded by his short encounter, was leaning on a pike in the second row when Hans approached him. "We are close to running out of bolts for the crossbows, Sir. We don't have enough for another attack like that one" he reported.

"I am giving my best shots the remaining bolts and after that, the rest of our Uri lads will have to become axe-men."

Paul called for Ludo, who had been running messages for him throughout the day.

"Get yourself up to the Marshal," he said wearily, his head throbbing. "You know how to get to his command post... yes?"

Give him my compliments and tell him that we've held, but that the Uri boys are down to a few dozen crossbow bolts, not enough Herr Hans tells me, for another attack like the last one.

He looked around and saw the exhausted faces of his men now bloodied from the breakthrough they had repulsed. "Tell him also that we are in good heart and think we have the beating of them." As he spoke he watched the milling mass of horsemen frustrated by the once more impervious wall of lethal steel points, reduced to shouting insults, as the remorseless steel crossbow bolts tore into their armour and removed more and more of them from their saddles, forcing the survivors to turn around, back towards their starting point.

"I think he will have seen what happened here" Paul added wearily. "The main point is, can he get us a new supply of crossbow bolts? On your way, young Ludo. Oh, and don't try to be a hero."

The skirmishers were brutally seeing off the last of the dying knights who had managed to burst through, and the reserve pikemen were hauling away the wounded and the dead, as well as the enormous carcases of the horses that had fallen onto their ranks. With all the enemy riders still out there, just praying for a chance to kill some of this infuriating infantry who blocked them, it was just too soon for the skirmishers to slip out and kill those downed knights between the lines who were not yet dead.

Then from the heights of the forest thrillingly came the clear, clean, unmistakable notes of a trumpet signal. They thrilled because they recognised it as that which announced that the pikemen were now to take the offensive. It said that the battle had turned! Now defence at last, could give way to attack!

Behind Paul's men, with a great noise of clattering arms and armour, of hundreds of warriors suddenly on the move, Heinrich's battalion smartly formed up behind him, pikes raised and ready, passed through the weary ranks of Paul's men, who called out those sarcastic greetings to their fresh replacements, as could be expected in such a situation. Heinrich's men were well drilled and unbloodied, their red scarves looking pristine; they looked not only smart but formidable, led by their sergeants and Templar officers, some of whom who called out complimentary remarks to Paul as they passed him. They made their way forward through the front line, pikes now at the slope and swiftly formed up in new lines, grounding their pikes, a hundred men long and four lines deep, which took just about all the available width in this forest clearing. The frustrated Austrian cavalry moving up and down on the other side of the barrier of their destroyed companions, looked in vain to see where they might find a point of attack, but found instead that they had to back their horses away from the bristling spikes of the giant hedgehog formation, that stepping over the ruined line of the last attack, now had started to move, slowly yet remorselessly towards them.

Back on the killing field, young Schwyzer lads ran up and down the lines with water skins, whilst wounded were being helped off the field. With Heinrich's battalion having relieved him, a weary, slightly stunned Paul, sitting legs sprawled on the rump of the dead horse that nearly killed him, looked up and saw a bloody Jan Ansbach coming towards him.

"Not mine", he said seeing Paul's worried look at the blood all over him. "The lads did well, Sir" he said typically. "They'll not be back I'm thinking." jerking his head towards the enemy. They looked over to where the second battalion still slowly and implacably moved forward, keeping near perfect formation with a forest of pike shafts preceding them. Their sergeants shouted at them to keep the line straight, which they did, except where they needed to step over dead horses or riders, the product of the Uri men's earlier culling. All could see the large body of heavily armoured horsemen waiting their chance, but quite unable to deal with this remorseless infantry advance. There was still a press of those just recently arrived in the narrow valley from the lakeside road, obviously quite unaware of events and trying to get to the front, blocked eventually by the majority of horsemen moving slowly backwards, hurling abuse but giving ground, at the slow, remorseless pace of the pikemen's advance.

"I daresay Sir," the top sergeant offered to the weary Paul, "that the Marshal would like us to get up and give our friends out there some support, just in case."

"Absolutely right, Jan. Get the men fell in if you will, I reckon we have about a hundred men down with one thing and another, so shortened lines I would suggest, and we divide our force to face out to both his flanks, when the ground widens on either side of Sir Heinrich's lads.

***

THE MESSENGER

Ludo knew that the Marshal's observation point must have given him a better view of the battle, than anyone else could have had. He had already taken a message up there earlier in the day. There was a track up between the dense undergrowth, too steep to ride up, so along the way, riders dismounted and led their horses. In front of him Ludo saw another messenger doing just that with a red scarf tied to his arm, but too far away to hail.

Then there was a sudden flurry of activity up ahead as two armoured men on foot appeared from the undergrowth with drawn swords, and attacked the messenger. Ludo broke into a run as he unsheathed his weapon and saw the messenger struck, although he had brought down one of his assailants. The horse had taken fright and bolted uphill towards the field HQ, which Ludo realised, would alert the camp.

The other attacker had lifted his weapon to deliver the swift fatal blow when he saw and heard Ludo's intervention. He looked to be a senior armoured knight, whilst the wounded messenger was a forester, no older than himself. Ludo was young but well-built and well-armoured. His sword raised, he didn't hesitate to attack the knight who was wearing chainmail on his head and no helmet. Neither of the two men on the ground were dead but the other man-at-arms was near the end, whilst the young messenger although bleeding profusely, was still holding his sword with which he suddenly slashed out at the knights' ankle. The eyes in the knight's florid face were facing Ludo, like a cobra, and he didn't see the blow coming from beneath him. The blow lacked power but cut into his chainmail painfully and diverted him from Ludo's sword for long enough for the young squire to fiercely thrust the point of his blade into his opponents' throat. Blood spurted and choking, the knight sank down to his knees, dropping his sword and then pitching over to lie near to his man at arms.

Ludo sank down beside the messenger and saw that his wound was bad. He cushioned the youth's head on his lap as he struggled to speak, "… message…" he choked and forced himself to continue, "for the Marshal… the reserve is coming fast and should be here in… forty minutes, they are on..." his voice became a whisper, "the main road from Schwyz." He was going. Ludo clutched his hand and repeatedly told him, "You did well, you did very well." Then he was gone. When Ludo looked up it was into the eyes of several of the Marshal's guards arriving with drawn weapons. "He's alright," one of them said of him. "He was here earlier. He's Sir Paul's squire - you hurt, son?"

They helped him up. "Seemingly you had quite a scrap here," one remarked, casually looking for valuables, turning over the body of the dead knight.

Paul told them what had happened and that he needed to get the message to the Marshal. At that, two of them hurried him along up the hill, and eventually into the clearing on top.

The Marshal was on top of his platform and told his officer to send Ludo up to him. The Marshal of course remembered him well from his father's castle, and the long convoy through the Black Forest.

Before he could open his mouth, the Marshal pointed down at the battlefield below.

"Your master has done brilliantly today, young Ludo and now I do believe that Sir Heinrich is going to push them into the lake." Looking down it was as though at a world in miniature, too far for more than the generalised background noise of battle. Too far for the shrieks of wounded horses and men alike to reach them, a sound which Ludo would never forget after this day.

It was a strange picture down below them in front of the now cobalt blue lake, with the late afternoon sun still reflecting off its surface. There were the ordered ranks, with hundreds of the Schwyzer men, purposefully if slowly sweeping away the great confused steel clad masses facing them, in no apparent order, and now leaderless - he had seen the Duke earlier being hurried away from the battlefield, by his close aides. Even now the invading army was larger in numbers than that of the defending foresters, but had no coherence except a frustrated need to attack, without the means of doing so.

"What is your message then?" the Marshal asked.

Ludo told him of the lack of crossbow bolts and the commander reflected on that. "What else?" he demanded. Then the squire told him of the fight of a few minutes back and the message of the whereabouts of the reserve.

"Good man" the Commander told him. "Can you ride, are you fit to ride? We saw the young man's horse. That's why we sent to investigate." As he spoke they saw the bodyguards carrying the young messenger's body into the clearing where they laid it down gently.

Ludo was given a message and told to repeat it, then taken and assisted to collect and mount his horse. With a slap on the animal's rump, he was off down the hill.

A guard spoke to the Marshal's Officer who then walked over to report. "It seems sir, that one of these two enemies, a man-at-arms was not quite dead, we are questioning him now." Later he reported back to the commander. "He told our men that the knight that got killed by young Ludo was no less than a captain of Duke Leopold's infantry, looking to capture or kill you sir, for some great reward. It seems that when he got amongst their men with the war dogs that they went streaming off before they could stop them. He and the captain got separated from them.

"Why I asked him, did the captain want to stop them, and he said he had come across that dog's trick before, with the hounds."

"And what trick is that?" The Marshal absently enquired, concentrating on the scene below him.

"Well Sir, if I tell you that you could probably scour Schwyz and Uri and Unterwalden and nowhere find a bitch on heat, you would then know what that second bunch of dogs yapping, we heard earlier, was all about."

The tension that the Marshal had been under all day suddenly eased. He laughed and he laughed uproariously, and it was infectious, all the men around him joined in.

***

Ludo had his horse walk down the track, which left the woods on the further side of the great rock outcrop that they had been defending all day. As he rode away from the fight he could now travel fast. The road in front of him was empty.

It was no more than twenty minutes before he could see up ahead a cloud of dust, within which he could distinguish lances and red banners. As he approached, two mounted scouts, both Templars he was relieved to see, were riding to challenge him when he was recognised. Another armoured figure galloped ahead of the throng.

"It's von Stauffenberg's boy, Sir Paul's squire" a scout called back to the leader as he came closer.

It was Sir Martin, the leader of the reserve which included some fifteen mounted Templars with squires, and another large mounted group of crossbowmen from Schwyz. It looked as though they had raided the local delivery carts to get their nags. But at least it gave them mobility and put them ahead of the axemen, who trudged along, far behind. Sir Martin saw Ludo looking at his column wide-eyed and demanded to know where was the messenger he had sent.

Ludo quickly explained what had happened and how he had been sent by the Marshal to intercept the reserve column with new orders.

"Which are…" the knight demanded brusquely?

"Sir, The Marshal said that your crossbows with all spare ammunition- he stressed that- should join those from Uri and place themselves under the command of Herr Franz attached to the First Battalion - straight ahead down this road. Any other footmen are to go there also, to the command of Sir Paul. He ordered me to request you and all mounted Templar personnel to follow me, and I am to conduct you to his headquarters."

"Very well" said the knight. "You can tell me how the battle is going as we ride." He returned to the main body of his troops and gave his orders following which a body of mounted Templar knights displaying the red scarf of Schwyz, fell into a column with squires riding behind each of the knights. Sir Martin took the lead alongside Ludo, a banner of a plain red cloth square was carried behind him on his squire's lance.

Signaling alternate stretches of trotting and gallops, he questioned Ludo about the day's events. The squire did his best to answer in a military fashion. The crossbowmen and their grinding supply cart were making slower but steady progress behind them, as the armoured knights drew further ahead with every minute that passed.

Soon they saw the great rock, on the other side of which, all resistance had been based and they could hear the distant sound of battle, where thousands were still engaged. With Ludo leading, they turned onto the track into the forest that led up to the field headquarters. He passed the spot where only an hour or so ago, he had himself been engaged in that desperate short fight, in which the young messenger had been killed.

Sir Martin's Templars were now dismounted, leading their steeds, strung out in single file behind them, and then they were challenged by the guards at the entrance to the clearing. Sir Martin going first, Ludo found himself scrambling up the wooden platform steps behind the Templar knight, as the Marshal turned around and smiled his welcome. They could see the valley below them up to the shores of the lake and the main confrontation and still a great host of mounted men swirling about in a tight area, with a solid phalanx of infantry squared off, slowly pushing them back.

"I am pleased indeed to see you," he greeted Sir Martin and added, "well done young Ludo."

"Look down there" he said to the Templar officer as he pointed out the salient factors of the battlefield beneath them. Many of the newcomer knights were peering through the trees seeing what they could.

"Do you see the Second battalion, Sir Heinrich's boys, and beyond, behind them that's Sir Paul's slightly battered first battalion? They broke the cavalry after countless charges, now they are supporting the counter attack, the object of which is no less than to drive the enemy into the lake. They don't need support other than crossbows and I expect your bowmen will soon be down there with them - did you have supplies of bolts, because..."

"Yes Sir indeed, they are on their way." The answer interrupted him.

"Now I have special task for you, Sir Martin. This is Templar business and I don't want to involve our good Schwyzer friends. First I want you to lead your horses down through the forest, I have a guide for you, a forester who knows the woods perfectly. You will emerge on the lakeside road, see there…" he pointed. "You will come out of the trees behind their main force. I will see you as you emerge and I will give a trumpet signal when I want you to attack. You are to spread out your full force, squires and all in line, to look more of a company than you are. Then sir, a full scale cavalry charge along the road from behind them and to the left of the road, if you please, lances, swords whatever, a lot of noise, shouting - but not 'Beauséant, Beauséant,' you understand", he added softly and smiled. He continued: "They don't know what's going on down there, their leaders have left the battlefield.

"I want you to panic them into retreating away from you, which crowds them up to their own people that are up against our pike boys. The trick is to leave the right side of the road, that area between the road and the lake entirely clear, and they will be bound to try to get away on that, en masse I expect… What they are unlikely to know is that just a few yards away from the road it is just too marshy there to support a horse and rider. They will be trapped in a bog and the lake will do our work for us."

"I understand, Sir."

"Hold. You may soon see others hanging back on the road there, see them? Those black crows down there, my friend, are Dominicans!

"You have in your command a brother knight, Sir Roger of Gloucester. He, I know was their prisoner and was severely tortured by the Dommies.

As soon as you have made your main charge on the Austrians - and keep on harassing their rear, detach Roger with six men to capture that Dommie Devil Spawn.

"We will have some justice here, as well as helping our Schwyzer friends to become independent. The same man who will guide you down there is now with me, my man - and is reliable. He will maintain silence on the topic He is to go with your Sir Roger. He knows where I want the Dommie prisoners to be taken. They must of course be kept apart from all other prisoners, and indeed from the locals here. This is as I have already said, Templar business, not to be discussed with those who are not brethren. Better that they don't know."

"I will delay you just one minute more. Lend me your sword," he ordered.

The recently arrived Templars seeing this, crowded below the platform.

"Come here Ludo. Did you know the man that you killed on the track was a senior captain of the Duke's infantry, coming of course to try to kill me? By rights, he should have eaten you for breakfast.

"No? I can see you didn't know. You have done well today, young man. Now kneel!"

Ludo, hardly understanding, went down on one knee on the coarsely cut timber platform, as the sword touched one shoulder and then the other.

"You are to become the first today to be knighted in the field. Rise up Sir Ludoviç von Stauffen. I will be pleased to tell your father of your conduct today, and he will be proud of you, as are we all."

The watching Templars shouted approval and applauded enthusiastically, yet strangely quietly, with their steel chain-mail gauntlets. Sir Martin grinned, took back and sheathed his sword, removed one gauntlet and shook Ludo's hand, then clattered down the wooden steps calling his men behind him, to where his squire held his charger. Following the guide from the Marshal's staff, the column led their horses in single file and quickly disappeared from sight, down a track into the forest.

***

AN ACCOUNTING

Later that night, two boats left the lakeshore about a mile from where the hard fought battle had taken place. In the first sat in the stern, a one-armed man, dressed similarly to the six cloaked oarsmen, who rowed steadily, towing the second boat and its inactive occupants behind them. There was no moon that night, but the numerous spot fires near to the killing ground showed where the Schwyzers were still sorting out the enemy dead from their wounded, and no doubt separating the corpses from their valuables.

There was a light wind, enough to disturb the surface of the lake and from the boats it was just possible to see the glow above the lakeside town of Zug, some seven miles away over the placid water. There for hours now, dejected remnants of the defeated Habsburg army had been straggling in. Of the Duke himself, it was said that he did not draw rein after leaving the field of battle, until he reached his castle of Winterthur, some twenty miles away to the north.

The oarsmen were all Templars, one of them Paul, who had each in some way been in the power of the Inquisition, tortured by the Dominicans, during the years that followed King Phillip's coup of 1307. The passengers in the second boat were eight black-robed Dominicans, shackled to each other, the chains passing under the stout timber cross beams that strengthened the hull and provided seating.

Earlier they had been identified by name and produced before a rudimentary tribunal in the forest hut, where they had been confined. Accusations were made by different Templars which collectively told a horrific story. The friars' initial defiance included issuing threats, then finally to pleading for forgiveness, but when the Templars there were asked at the end, if any wanted mercy for any individual Dominican, the silence spoke volumes.

When the boats were about two miles offshore, well away from the normal fishing grounds, the Templar leader, Sir Roger of Gloucester with just one eye and one arm - all that the torturers had left him with - ordered his colleagues to ship oars. The lead rope was tightened and the second boat pulled close. Then Paul and another Templar put aside their cloaks and with short axes in hand, crossed over into the second boat. Paul was highly conscious of the glare of frustrated hate mingled with terror that the Spanish friar Joacquim directed at him.

As the Dominicans shrank away from them, the two knights attacked not the friars but the planks at the bottom of the boat, both fore and aft, until water started to flow powerfully through. Then the two Templars clambered back onto their leading boat. The eight Dominicans struggling against their shackles, at last fully understanding what was to be their fate, set up a mighty din in which towards the end, some prayers could be discerned amongst the babble and the screams.

As the lead boat returned alone to the shore, they passed in the soft deep marshland of the lakeshore the evidence of the corpses of many men and horses, the flower of Austrian chivalry that had drowned, trapped in the deep mud along the lake shore. They had been amongst the last to leave the fight, but seeking to evade the pikemen in the fast closing trap in which they found themselves, fatally took the unobstructed route along the lake edge.

Meanwhile on the shore, the spot fires grew brighter and shapes of the living were framed against the light, but all around them, the wreckage of men and horses obscenely littered the weapon-strewn ground. It was a harvest of death.

***

WEDDING PLANS

The worst of the harsh winter had finally let up, for a while at least, on the village and castle of Stauffenberg. The great forest that surrounded them, perhaps the largest in Europe, was blanketed in a thin layer of frozen snow that hugged the ground. It was too soon for the forest to have reached even the early stage of recovering its leafy canopy to reclothe the legions of gaunt skeletal trees, stretching far out of sight. Paul and his party had been there since before Christmas. This had been his well-earned leave, commencing some days after the triumph of the battle of Morgarten, in November. But the big event of this Christmas of 1315 was his wedding to the Lady Melissa, daughter of the Baron von Stauffen in the family's great castle on the western fringe of the Black Forest, facing the river Rhine.

It was February 1316 and, despite everything, his career was blossoming. Now aged twenty-six, in the last two years he had taken part as a battalion commander in two great battles, and had been picked to lead a new mission traveling away from Christendom to the edge of the known world, and beyond. This journey was to commence in Venice in just four weeks' time. His party now about to depart, were mounting up, whilst servants and squires sorted out the pack animals

But what a Christmas it had been! He had enjoyed his best time ever. He had married the Lady Melissa with the full approval of her father the Baron, who had himself as a young man, served as a Templar. Paul had been surrounded by friends, and to everyone's surprise even his top commander, the Prior of the Order, had been there.

The great castle high on its conical hill was a joyous place. Four weeks before Yuletide, Paul, together with Ludo, the baron's heir, newly knighted on the field at Morgarten, had returned home to a hero's welcome from a proud and mightily relieved father, and his daughters together. He had also brought home from the wars, Ludo's servant Pippin whose own family, indeed whose whole life until now had been at the castle. In addition there was another member of Paul's train, a completely new character to the good people of the family and household. This was Sir John of Potsdam, a young knight pledged to Paul who had captured and later paroled him, in time for the Morgarten fight, a decision that had already saved Paul's life at the hottest point of the battle. This was when John alongside him, by interposing his shield, took the blow from a mighty sword thrust from a mounted knight, directed at a dismounted Paul who had been caught, off balance, in the fray. Had it not been for the young German knight, that fierce downstroke would have ended Paul's promising career, and indeed his story. Their arrival for the homecoming had been announced by Pipin riding ahead, reaching the castle about two hours before the trio of warriors, including Ludo the newly minted knight and heir to the domain, and Paul the betrothed of the Lady Melissa. That was time enough to ensure that the courtyard was full of happy smiling greetings for the young warriors; the Baron and Melissa waiting for them on the steps of the Keep. The other daughter, the Lady Helene was watching from her room at the top of the tower as the mounted party arrived.

Although she was somewhat envious of her older sister, because she too had nursed Paul when he was laid low, the last time he was there, she thought she should not now crowd her sister at this joyful reunion. But there was her brother Ludo below, also in the party and returned a hero. The knights had their helmets off and on their saddlebows, and it was then she observed the third knight in the party, a stranger, a rather well set-up young man. This was enough to set her off to bustling down the spiral stair. Could he, she told herself, he really might be, the answer to the proverbial maiden's prayer, living in this isolated castle?

So she tore down the steps and arrived onto the cobbles somewhat flushed. She tightly hugged her brother, pecked Paul chastely on the cheek and then was introduced to their companion, Sir John of Potsdam. He bowed somewhat formally, as they sized each other up. He was really rather gorgeous, as she told her sister later, who was rejoicing at her own new happiness. For his part the young John squeezed Ludo's arm and said, "You didn't tell me that you had another beautiful sister". The Baron, who in his time had seen everything, understood everything. His two daughters had constantly complained to him, that year around, they never met any eligible young men in that isolated place, which he knew to be true. Yet suddenly, his courtyard was alive with them.

Paul, before leaving Schwyz, had been able to requisition one of the carrier pigeons that 'homed in' on Castle Stauffenberg. Thus he had been able to signal ahead to the Stauffen family the success of the military mission at the seminal battle of Morgarten; that Ludo had won his spurs, and that including Pippin, all were safe. He had estimated a date of their return to be home before the Christmas feast, and sent a special message for Melissa that he loved her and was coming to marry her.

So there had been adequate time for Melissa, her sister and the Baron, to plan the wedding feast and it had originally been decided, that there would be time for this to take place before the celebrations for Christmas.

Yet this all had to change when the Baron told them one morning that he had received a coded pigeon message. It had relayed the news from Flanders that a military escort party was bringing the Bishop of Bangor up from the Flemish coast, following the Rhine. Nothing more. But it was the route that would bring the party to Castle Stauffenberg, only a few days after Paul's party had arrived from Schwyz. The fact that it was a carrier bird from the Stauffen flock, said that it was Templar business. It was clearly a warning to expect distinguished arrivals, although the mystery of who this bishop might be eluded them all.

Then a second pigeon arrived a day later, making no reference to the first message, or to travelling arrangements. It simply said that the Baron might be pleased to learn that the Prior of Aird had been elevated to the Bishopric of Bangor. Unsigned, no more, no less.

The Baron and Melissa decided that since this Bishop's party could be expected to arrive before Christmas, the Yuletide feast and that for his daughter's wedding would be merged. Neither Paul nor Melissa had any concerns about that, since the young betrothed couple were happily in private fully taken up with each other, anticipating the formal wedding, catching up for their lost time since Paul had ridden away to war in Schwyz.

FRIENDS REUNITED

Every evening since the return, the enlarged family met in the great hall to share the evening meal. It was on one such occasion that the Baron's steward interrupted them at table to deliver a verbal message to the Baron that a horseman had just brought. It seemed that the Bishop of Bangor and his escort anticipated arriving on the afternoon of the following day. Having heard this, the Baron indicated for Paul to follow him to the kitchens. There they found the messenger, who Paul immediately recognised, a Danish Templar, a sergeant who had served under his command in Scotland. He stood up awkwardly, since he was holding a bowl of steaming hot stew, as he had been warming himself sitting on a stool by the great fireplace.

"Brother Paul" he said, putting the food aside, as he stood smiling.

"Welcome Sergeant... Brother Kurt, isn't it?" said Paul as he embraced him. "Indeed it is" the man acknowledged. "This, Brother Kurt, is the Baron von Stauffenberg,"Paul told him. "My lord," the messenger said, bowing, in acknowledgement.

"Wine," the Baron called, looking around for his steward, hovering nearby, "for the messenger, and cups also for Sir Paul and myself." The cooks brought over a bench on which the two men then sat, waving Kurt back to his seat by the fire, as the jug of wine arrived and the steward started to pour. "Eat up sergeant," the Baron told him, and he added, "and then we want to hear of your long journey."

Kurt told them in between mouthfuls, referring only to 'the Bishop,' that his escort was of thirty fighting men - knights and sergeants, with their servants, squires, grooms, a farrier, cooks, altogether a mounted party of some fifty, and some eighty horses, together with carts carrying tents, kitchen supplies, and other goods from Castle Aird. The Baron looked around to see that his steward had taken all of this in.

"The Bishop told me to apologise on his behalf for landing all of this number on you over the Yuletide season" said Brother Kurt.

The Baron nodded. "Go on," he replied.

"I left the Bishop's party to the west, about fifteen miles short of Breisach, about to make camp, my Lord, and in their last stage they intend to bypass Breisach as I did, and perhaps any wagging tongues there, which should bring them here by tomorrow afternoon. I had the directions how to get here, but that was simple enough, just following the river and then before Breisach, taking the road into the forest, signed towards Stauffen. I brought a spare horse, so I made it in about four hours. Fortunately, there was little snow on the roads, which was my good luck."

He told them that they had not dallied in the cities, along the Rhine, sending in the cooks to buy fresh bread, chickens, river fish and such, whilst the main party stayed on the river road, or if that were not possible, they went around the outskirts of the towns, aiming always to average about thirty miles a day. There were certain safe places where they could stay overnight, but for security reasons they hadn't notified any of the brethren in the upper Rhineland.

In Scotland, they had, before they took ship, sent a small advance party to the tried and trusted brethren in Flanders. They it was who would see them off their ship from Scotland, provisioned and well mounted, and get them on their way. So they had tents for when no better arrangements were possible and additional horse blankets for sleeping under. Sleeping in this way, he said, because of the cold, was the worst part of the journey.

Ludo had quietly come in and stood against the wall, followed by his sisters and a rather bemused John of Potsdam, from which vantage point they had picked up the essentials of the news brought by the Templar sergeant. Melissa detached herself from the others and went to confer with the slightly shaken steward. They discussed the food and drink situation, also sleeping arrangements for 'the bishop' and his knights. The steward then left to go and find the stable master, and the captain of the Baron's troopers, to prepare them for the new arrivals, beasts and men.

The following day all was activity, in the castle, in its adjoining barracks and particularly in the kitchens, in anticipation of feeding the arriving host. The Baron had scouts positioned on the road to Breisach and just as he had welcomed the Marshal and his troopers from Scotland, back in the summer, so he rode out once again, accompanied as before by his son, Ludo, and this time with Paul, to welcome them, together with an escorting troop from the castle's garrison. They met the travellers amidst the open meadows flanking the same country road from the river port of Breisach, which led to the village and castle of Stauffen and into the Black Forest.

Paul knew that 'the bishop' could only be the Prior, the leader of his order and observed, as he rode alongside, that the man he so admired, in a black fur hat and swathed in folds of black wool with a large silver crucifix on his chest, sitting on a rich red leather saddle on a milk-white mare, fully looked the part.

"So Paul, we meet again in happy circumstances" he said, stretching out his gloved hand to clasp the arm of Paul, who rode alongside him.

"The business in Schwyz was well handled and you and your brethren can be proud of yourselves. It has all worked out very well, I must say. I and my colleagues on the Council, are now moving up to Schwyz. The others are making their own ways there. No matter how good our security, we couldn't risk some awful chance by all travelling together, of putting the larger part of our council into the enemy's hands.

"You will have realised from this that we have now vacated Castle Aird, which has served its purpose. But it could no more have been a secret from the Dominicans. England right now is in chaos, with the second Edward facing a serious revolt. The church is without a pope. France has a new king. Scotland, for the first time in generations, is quiet and not facing an invasion from England, but our good friend King Robert, is in indifferent health. Now that the church has dissolved the Templar Order and disposed of our property, frankly, with the exception of course of the Dominicans, nobody cares about us at all. With this move to central Europe and covering our tracks in Scotland, we are to all of them now, just where we want to be… Gone! No longer of concern to anyone; just history."

Back at the castle, the Brethren's leader and senior knights followed the

Baron to be introduced to his daughters, with Paul proudly standing beside Melissa who took his arm. "So I heard you are to be married," the Prior said, "and I am glad to be here in time. What of a priest?" he enquired.

Melissa looked at Paul pointedly.

"Well as you may know," Paul spoke for them both, "hereabouts in the German confederation, at any rate, the only requirement for a legal marriage is to have a witness, To have a priest is optional and we thought with the Fraternity's security in mind, that we would not bring a priest into the castle at this time, a potential informant against us all, since we are no favourites of the church."

"Splendid!" replied the Prior. "I am not, as of course you well know, the Bishop of Bangor or of any other place - we only picked that identity because that bishopric in the north of Ireland is close to the western ocean - about as remote as you can get in western Christendom. However, although no bishop, I remain an ordained Templar priest, and having served for years in the Papal Curia had the opportunity to study at close quarters the ways of many of those princes of the church. If you young people and the good Baron here are willing, I will be delighted to officiate."

"Wonderful!" Melissa replied for all of them, as to his surprise and pleasure, she leaned forward and pecked the Prior's cheek.

***

THE WEDDING FEAST

Over the next few days the leaders talked, and agreed at the outset, that just as on the march to get there, the Prior during his stay would always be referred to and addressed as a bishop, so the Baron's people, the servants from the village and his tenants could not inadvertently know more than was prudent, for the demands of security.

During this time the Baron's people prepared the castle for the celebrations. The great hall was to be the centre of activities and the steward together with Melissa, busily planned and supervised every detail.

The steward had sent to the village for additional help for the great feast when the brother soldiers of the Templar escort party, would join them at table in the great hall.

For days, men had gone out into the woodlands that surrounded them, bringing back cartloads of mossy green boughs, sacks full of stems of shiny green holly leaves studded with crimson berries; long strings of white mistletoe gathered in coils from the upper branches of the trees. The great hall itself had its rush-covered plank floors cleared, swept, washed and re-covered with fresh sweet smelling rushes. The steward had disappeared with a large cart for the food market in Breisach, accompanied by the two cooks that had arrived with the Bishop's party. They had previously been the cooks at the Scottish Castle of Aird, and were now a part of the move to Schwyz. When they returned from the market they could be seen unloading swans, eels, pike and other fish, together with sacks of flour and other grains, The castle farm was providing quantities of chickens, geese, ducks, and eggs by the hundred.

The Baron's huntsmen could be seen bringing in the eviscerated carcasses of boar, along with joints of venison from deer shot by the archers, and unmade in the forest. There were hares and dozens of rabbits. The kitchens were a very hive of preparation with several of the castle's men at arms, sitting on stools in a semi-circle in the yard outside the kitchen door, plucking the fowls and skinning the rabbits.

Quantities of green boughs were strewn decoratively about the hall and along the foot of the dais where stood the top table. The trestle tables were covered for the occasion in white linen cloths on which clumps of holly and strings of mistletoe were interwoven in the centre, down the length of the table. From the great oak hammer beams above, dangled more bunches of holly and mistletoe in profusion. Big fat candles in pewter holders were brought out and positioned to illuminate each table, being side sprigs off the top table that stretched from the dais, down the length of the great hall. Apart from the most senior knights of the Templar escort to be on the dais, there were also there the Baron's chief tenants, his daughter Helene and next to her, Melissa had arranged to place John of Potsdam. The wedding ceremony would be short and precede the feast.

When the big day came and all was in place, with sixty or so guests at table and standing around in the hall behind them, the young couple stood together on the dais in front of the top table, behind which stood the 'Bishop' with the Baron at his side.

All noise from the guests had ceased and there was a sudden turmoil at the kitchen entrance as the staff in their kitchen clothes crowded out to see the young mistress marry her knight.

The Prior spoke into the silence. He asked them their names and station in life.

She was the first to be addressed and answered, "Melissa von Stauffen, maid, of Stauffenberg in the Barony of Stauffen."

Paul then spoke up, "Paul of Chatillon in the County of Burgundy, knight."

The Prior asked each in turn if they wished to marry the other, and having received their assent, spoke a few words, gave them a blessing and pronounced them man and wife. At this, the assembled crowd cheered, banged pots on the tables, stamped and noisily called out raucous and vulgar advice, as the Baron stepped up to be the witness and attach his signature to a document his clerk offered to him.

The steward escorted Paul and Melissa and seated them at the head of the table in the place of honour, normally occupied by the Baron, after which the feasting commenced. The Baron's cupbearer passed along the top table, pouring his lord's best vintage, as the host told the Prior whilst his goblet was being filled, along with his customary discourse comparing Rhine wine with the vintages of Burgundy. The long tables below had some sixty guests, mainly the Baron's largest tenants and the Templars of the escort, for whom numerous jugs of wine were on the table, with barrels for refilling over against the wall.

Below the dais, the long table stretched down the hall, the floor covered in fresh rushes, towards the second fireplace, which like the first, up on the dais, was blazing in its great hearth with pinecones crackling as the pyramid of great logs burned away, broadcasting waves of heat.

The Baron had arranged for musicians from Freiburg to entertain, and they struck up a lively air, whilst relays of serving staff two by two, filed out of the kitchen into the great hall bearing the handles of great trenchers of pike-perch, and eels, which was the first course.

The day progressed into evening as course had followed course. To the accompaniment of a drum roll from the musicians, the roast swan had been carried on its great silver dish, by four men each bearing a handle of the wooden stretcher on which it sat, decorated with its own feathers. Once it had been seen and admired by all it was taken to the top table and placed before the Baron with a carving knife and fork. He looked at it, nodded and told the bearers to put it in front of Paul who rising to the occasion, carved a slice and placed it on the trencher in front of his new wife, and then the same for the Prior on his other side, whilst the guests all cheered. Other servers brought in numberless dishes of cooked vegetables. The steward then sent the bearers back to a carving table where he took over the disjointing of the giant bird, and serving out portions for the servers to put before the rest of the top table and all the other guests. Soon afterwards, a similar process took place, this time with a boar's head glazed in honey being the centre piece, surrounded by joints piled high with roast chestnuts.

By now, the short winter day had already passed evening and turned into night, as measured by the candles being lit. This was the time that the ladies withdrew, as Paul and his bride tried quietly to slip away, but with no success. So openly, Paul beaming, with Melissa rather more reserved, made their exit whilst the whole assembly stood up, banged the table, roared and hooted, happily shouting coarse advice. Helene saw her opportunity and took it. She and Melissa had earlier done the seating plan together, where they had placed John by her side, so she touched his shoulder and got up. He was not slow to follow. Whilst the guests were hurrahing the bride and groom, she and John slipped out of another door and she led him to the top of her tower. There the silence was profound, and just the two of them were all that mattered.

Once the top table guests had retired, the Baron asked his son Ludo to help him up the stone steps to his chamber - the outward veneer of some semblance of order, in the great gave way to the reality of hard drinking. This led to frequent visits to the torch-lit courtyard for the guests to relieve themselves, throw up, or whatever else they had to do. For many of the Prior's escort the great feasting was something they hadn't done since before they had first become Templars. Before they had escaped to Scotland, they had lived in monastic surroundings where five masses a day were the norm and no talking took place at rather frugal meals, whilst a junior knight at the lectern, read from the lives of the saints. Although Castle Aird in Scotland had not in any way been religiously observant, as had been the Templar Order before their betrayal by the then pope, there was still a military discipline. Restrained habits and the practice of moderation had become second nature. But Castle Aird anyway, was primarily a military fortress not noted for lavish entertainment, although they had held a great celebratory feast there, after the critical victory at the Battle of Bannockburn.

This gargantuan kind of Black Forest feast was neither unique nor unknown, because the many knights amongst them had been brought up in baronial surroundings as pages, where feasting for them was very different. Then before being accepted into the Order, they had usually served as squires, where they would have had to wait upon their masters at the feasts they attended. Here, they now were, in this Black Forest castle, the leader of the Order presiding, nearing the end of a long and tedious journey to a new land. There they could and would live normal lives, forming the nucleus of the standing army of the nascent Swiss republic with its original forest cantons who had thrown off the Austrian yoke.

Although all of these roistering excesses were now available to them, the habit of moderation had taken hold and so whilst they feasted and drank the good wine, nevertheless few of them took these pleasures to excess. The Baron's retainers and tenants of course were under no such self-imposed restraint.

There was little restraint either in the great tower at the top of which was Melissa's room, where the young newlyweds threw off their clothing and rejoiced in each other's arms. Soon after he had returned from Schwyz, she had told him that she was pregnant from the pleasures they had shared in the summer before he went off to battle. Her father knew, she told him, but the Baron, ever practical, had responded that they were betrothed, and that was good enough for him. He had observed back then there had been no guarantees that Paul would survive the battle he was headed for, and anyway, he looked forward to having grandchildren about the place.

She had a feeling that her sister and Paul's young German household knight, had clearly fallen for each other, in the time since the men had returned. Possibly she knew, they might even be talking about betrothal for the same reasons as she and Paul had, before the men went off back to their duties in such a short time - and for how long nobody knew.

Indeed the days following the feast were spent in preparation for the Prior's party to head off to cross the Rhine, and travel on to Schwyz. The Baron's pigeon-master had been kept busy with the return of long unseen birds from his flock, carrying messages for the Prior and his aides. After they had rested with the celebrations over, when the weather improved, Paul had planned to travel on with them guiding them to Schwyz, the new Swiss Headquarters of the Order, where were already situated the Marshal, Sir Peter Breydel, and Master Proudhomme, the only members of the Council so far to get there. Others of the Council were at different stages of transferring by different routes, from Scotland.

None of these recent arrivals had been with the Templar convoy the previous year that, before the battle, en route to Schwyz, had memorably crossed the great river Rhine at Rhinefelden bridge, with a plain display of raw power. It was decided that this was the safest route, now as then. It was necessary to bypass the city of Basel. The ruler of that city was its powerful Prince Bishop. If he were told the 'Bishop of Bangor' was passing through, he would certainly seek to meet him. That would obviously be disastrous, and so the decision was made easy.

So Paul's party became a part of the Templar Prior's train, indeed an advance guard since they knew the way - they all set out at the same time to get to Schwyz and journey's end for the Prior's group. But it would be only the first stage for Paul's party where he would get his final instructions from the Council, collect the cargo of oiled wool for Venice and pick up the rest of the personnel for his new expedition.

Leaving Stauffen this time had really been hard. He knew that this was now his home and his thoughts were of Melissa and their baby, due in the late Spring.

Riding alongside him was his liegeman Sir John, who had declared on the last night that Helene and he were betrothed. They had asked the Baron's permission and this was readily given, although they all knew that the expedition in which he was to accompany Paul was inevitably dangerous, from which one or both might never return. The same applied to the Baron's son Ludo, who was also going on this mission. Now he was knighted, he had said, with no disrespect to his father, that he would decide, and since Paul was agreeable, he would accompany him on this adventure. Pippin too had requested to come and Paul and the Baron were happy to accept his travelling along, looking after the young warriors' domestic needs, and perhaps also to share in their adventure.

So with the sisters alternately sobbing and smiling, the young men of the family rode out at the front of the Prior's large party, and Ludo led the way, since he was the only one among them that had travelled the route through the forest from Stauffen to the great river, and to the bridge at Rheinfelden.

Beyond that, none knew for certain what would happen. For Paul and his friends and close colleagues, another chapter of the adventure was about to begin.

***

EPILOGUE

THE VATICAN

It was a baking hot July afternoon in 2014 when Brother Aloysius Daly SJ wearing a casual shirt and cotton trousers, with sun glasses protecting his eyes from the blazing sun, made his way through the crowded St Peter's Square. There, thousands milled around, hoping perhaps that something unexpected might happen, silently praying that perhaps the Pope himself would suddenly make an unscheduled appearance, up on his balcony. The many devout pilgrims, as they would call themselves, tended to cluster in groups, many of the laywomen wearing those shapeless starched head cloths, inspired perhaps by a nun's coif. Quite usually they would be in the charge of their parish priest. Daly was interested, but not surprised, that snatches of their conversations suggested that many were Polish. He chided himself for pretending to have deduced this, when he had walked past several buses parked as close as they were allowed, which clearly were from Poland. That in turn reminded him of a conversation he had had a few days back, when his interlocutor had told him that the shrines at Lourdes, at Santiago de Compostella, and at Fatima, plus some new place in Croatia - he had forgotten the name - let alone Rome itself, were enjoying a considerable uptick in pilgrims. This ancient traffic, thanks to the lifting of 'the Iron Curtain' had re-established the now firmly capitalist Polish and Lithuanian travel businesses.

He turned left off the great Square past the ice cream sellers, away from the crowds and the fierce heat and then right into the quiet and blessedly shaded Via del Santo Spiritu. Before him on his left were the offices of the Curia of the Societe Saint Iesu housed in a large and anonymous looking grey stone block, taking up much of one side of the street. He looked at his watch, still fifteen minutes before his appointment with the Jesuit Father General, which seemed about right.

The crisply efficient woman on the reception desk inside the entrance door recognised him, since he had a small office in this building, although he was seldom there, but importantly his clerk was.

"Are you to see the Father General?" she enquired, looking in the appointments screen. "Yes, I see you are" she answered herself, as she picked up the internal phone, and announced him before he had replied. "You're to go up straight away," she told him.

He had already submitted his interim report, and as he went up the stairs, rehearsed a little of what he might say in front of the great man of his Order.

At the precise time of his appointment he was shown in from the outer office to find the lanky Father General of the Jesuit Order in well-cut slacks, and open necked shirt with his brogue encased feet up, legs crossed at the ankles, on the desk. . Seemingly he was absorbed in what to Al Daly appeared to be his already submitted report. Half-moon spectacles propped up near the end of his nose, he acknowledged Al's presence, simultaneously waving him into a seat. This was only the fourth time that the lowly Brother Daly had met his high-flying boss, but he was beginning to get the picture.

He looked around and noted the large, rather magnificent terrestrial globe off to one side of the desk, what might have been expected in the inner sanctum of a medieval Italian prince. Very appropriate, he was thinking, when the German accented, New England Yankee voice, cut in on his reverie.

"So, Al, You were right about them going to Switzerland or what did they call it then… Schwyz? … sounds quite ugly when you say it like that." He referred back to the paper. "I remember from my history lessons that in the Middle Ages, Swiss pikemen were in demand all over Europe - the kings of France for example. That particular lot in the Confederation's three valleys went for Calvinism a century later - I wonder how much the influence of the Templars in their midst had to do with that", he murmured reflectively?

"Strange isn't it, that all of the Holy Fathers, from sometime after that battle that led to Swiss independence, hired the Swiss Guard - their barracks are right behind us, just back across the road from us here in the Vatican. Since another chunk of this newly independent nation retained the faith, presumably they recruit from there. I don't think Christ's vicar on earth needs to worry about the orthodoxy of his bodyguards, but their fame as pikemen, for which their country was famous in Europe, might well have started up, as a result of the battle of Morgarten.

"So the 'Geraint papers' as you say here," he nodded towards the report, "were your best source - in telling you effectively what to look for when you checked out Schwyz?"

"That is certainly the case," Al replied. "I realised, when I had taken in the implications of the surviving Templars starting up again in Schwyz, that of course they brought their banking business with them. Also, some of those same people I met there and talked with, about the battle of Morgarten - my cover was that I was a history professor - could be the descendants of the probable thousands, of no longer celibate, outlawed Templars, who made their ways from across Europe to those valleys after the battle, and settled there.

"It was also true," Al continued, "that the locals, all of them in Schwyz, had previously been excommunicated by the Prince Bishop of the local abbey at Einsiedeln, over decades of arguing about grazing rights - would you believe - so there were no priests and no serious church history locally from that time, for quite a while. That meant a gap with no parish records of births and deaths etc. that could have given us a handle from the frequency of non-local names.

"But I am pretty sure that the whole purpose for the Templars in fighting for the Schwyzers, was to find themselves a safe home," he continued, "and in the 14th century, what a good choice that turned out to be!

"I also mentioned in my first report that the Scottish castle of Aird was returned to the MacDonalds of the Isles, from whom they had previously leased it, at just about the same time. So they were gone from there long ago."

"Did you get anything - help I mean, from the Dominicans?" the General asked.

"Do you know Father General," Al replied, "I don't think they approve of us Jesuits doing this investigation. They have been almost resentful, certainly non-cooperative. But they did grudgingly say that their records tell that they lost several of their mendicant brethren, eight they said, who were chaplains with the Austrian army in that battle of Morgarten. They must have been killed, because no trace of any of them, they said, was ever found."

"So what's your next move?" asked the General.

"In a sense, that is the foundation story in Europe," Al replied. "We know now what happened after Bannockburn. We know they also made the difference at Morgarten, as a result of which they were able to bring in their wandering bands from across Europe, to Switzerland and settle down …and all of that without publicity or any involvement of the Church, which was temporarily missing in that area.

"It could indicate from a present-day perspective that they knew how to game that. After all, their 'bounce-back' after their Order was stamped upon in 1307, by Philip of France and Pope Clement V and then being officially wound up at the Council of Vienne in 1312, took place in Scotland. It was at the time, the only realm in all Europe, where the Papal writ did not run. The church in Scotland happened to be under interdict at that time, with Robert the Bruce being excommunicated earlier, for the murder of his rival for the throne.

"Then this was followed up by supporting the independence of the excommunicated Swiss foresters who had approached them via their secret, still functioning commercial arm, who had a branch at Breisach on the river Rhine. As I just said, for the 14th century - before the Reformation, it is quite amazing in itself. Just as in Scotland, another area under interdict and at the right time! Schwyz was also tailor-made for them."

"So now the search takes on another dimension," said the General. "After seven hundred years, they must have spread out from there… some of them might have gone in for cuckoo clocks," he added sarcastically, "but the possible banking line has got to be more interesting for us".

"It would be a reasonable guess that at least one- maybe more - of those secretive Swiss Banks was, and maybe still is, controlled by them, if as we presume, they still exist in some form. Get your researcher", he ordered, "to check out *all* the Swiss Banks, private and public for what information is in the public domain about them. What we want to narrow down are some likely candidates, the earliest in terms of when they or their predecessors were founded. Then we can consider how to proceed.

Meanwhile, this overseas trading lead you have, from Sir Geraint's account which I have read or tried to read, with great interest, is where you should next concentrate.

"It certainly seems colourful - Egypt: St Katherine's in the Sinai desert, yet this Welsh Templar never seems to be sure where he is after that, except that it's very hot, and foreign, and that they went by sea. But they were involved, he says, when they got there with both Christians and Jews, so it logically would have been some part of the Middle East, except that it couldn't be! No Europeans could possibly be living or working there, so soon after the Crusades and the fall of Acre, with Islam riding high.

"So Al. This is good work, he nodded down at the report, "and, as usual, Good luck!"

***

About the author and the series…..

Clive Lindley turned to writing after a successful career as a business entrepreneur who founded and operated a number of prosperous companies, including involvement in the oil industry, sport, crowd events, catering, commercial radio and magazine publishing. The best known of these is Roadchef plc, now the UK's largest national chain of motorway service areas.

Success in business enabled him to indulge his passion for serious world travel. This melded with a number of other broad interests that he was able to develop further.

Among these interests is absorption with medieval history, especially the extraordinary accomplishments of the medieval military monks: the Knights Hospitaller, the Teutonic Knights and for him most importantly, the Knights Templar.

His special fascination has long been focused on the Templars. He visited their former fortresses and bases in today's Syria, Israel, Jordan, Cyprus, Majorca, Spain and Portugal. Clive continued this self-imposed mission throughout Europe, particularly in Spain, Portugal and France. There he lived for several years on Paris's Rue du Temple, close to Templar headquarters, where evidence of their history is still omni-present. Despite there being a wealth of knowledge about the Templars, during their near two centuries of existence as an order of the Church, it suddenly all stopped. It came to an abrupt end, seven hundred years ago in 1314 when our first volume, "End of an Epoch" also closes, with many questions unanswered.

After that… officially nothing, but Lindley wouldn't leave it there. As a former multinational chief executive, he felt it just not credible, that outside of France, an elite transnational force with large undiscovered, portable funds, unquestionably a mercantile empire to boot, plus a raging desire for revenge, could have just 'disappeared'. Lindley set out to develop a plausible sequence of events based on available pointers and traditions, where for lack of concrete evidence, some parts of the Templar story could not be dealt with by academic historians. Not the least of these is the widely credited connection with Freemasonry, a subject on which he has lectured. The relationship is now defined, in this "Templar Knights Secret History".

THE SERIES

Volume 1 "End of an Epoch" describes the drama of the 'end-days' for the Templars. The shock for those of the fighting brethren still engaged in Cilicia, now SE Turkey, where action has continued after the Crusaders are thrown out of the Holy Land. There, on the fighting line against the Turks, they first hear the incomprehensible news that their two centuries old military Order, throughout France, has been seized by the French King, with the Pope their ultimate commander, apparently acquiescing and all Templars including themselves, subject to arrest.

It tells of how the French King 'Phillip the Fair,' springs his trap on the Templars, having lured their grandmaster from his HQ in Cyprus, back to Paris, there to be arrested and tortured on charges of ***heresy***, and throughout France their branches and assets seized. How the survivors scattered across Europe, thus avoiding arrest, set out to reorganise when the Pope eventually issues a Bull calling on all Christian kings to arrest those Templars in their realms (which many of the kings, knowing the greed of King Philip, at first resisted). So outside of France, most Templars had adequate time to move themselves – and did! How Scotland was the first and obvious choice as a refuge, because it was now the only European realm where the Pope's writ did not run. This was because their King, Robert the Bruce, was already excommunicated and the nation under interdict, from earlier succession quarrels there.

The story tells how those Templars now re-established in Scotland answer the call for aid from the Scottish king, who is about to be invaded by a large English army. Hence to the story of the Battle of Bannockburn, on the outcome of which, Scottish independence was determined.

How the High Council of the Church meeting at Vienne, defies the Pope by refusing to find the Templars guilty of heresy and the Pope, fearful of his 'master' King Phillip, using an administrative technicality, closes them down anyway. Then, on to the future role the revived Temple (now calling themselves "the Brethren"), will fulfil.

Finally, there is a description of the outcome for each of the key players in this story.

Volume 2: "Birth of a Nation" takes the story to Switzerland where a year after Scotland's independence was assured at Bannockburn, the Templars critical help, requested by the Swiss foresters, ensures that the pivotal Battle of Morgarten was won, securing Switzerland's independence as a new nation. In return for their vital assistance, the Templars now renamed "the Brotherhood", and incidentally Europe's first bankers, are invited to relocate their organisation to the new Swiss Republic.

The significant role the Templars, Europe's military elite, played in both successful independence campaigns, is explored through a cast of characters we know from Volume 1, and their relationship with the 14th century's proto-freemasons, the operative cathedral builders, is described.

This 'secret history' is the thread that animates this series. By intermingling known and previously unpublished facts, with plausible explanations - including circumstantial evidence that the Templars may still in some form continue to exist today - Clive has developed a compelling story that will surely interest all lovers of medieval history.

***

Our web site www.templarsecrethistory.com is available for those who wish to follow the secret history, and order the new book and those to come, or they might have further evidence of events to contribute. It will carry news of future publications and related events.

AFTERWORD

This, as a writing project, has been a long time in the making. Volume One was eventually completed (with the assured independence of Scotland), before the 700th anniversary of Bannockburn, from which I plunged straight into Volume Two, the core of which is Switzerland's independence, achieved through the pivotal battle of Morgarten, just one year later than Scotland - so now, also seven centuries ago.

For much of the writing, I was living in Paris's Rue du Temple, about 200 metres from the previously fortified 130 hectares site of 'The Temple,' which centuries ago was European HQ of the Knights Templar, located within the Paris city walls. I like to think that this proximity gave me inspiration. From there I travelled once by rivercraft from Holland, but mostly by car, up and down the Rhine, enjoying taking in swathes of Germany's vast Black Forest, the upper Rhine and Switzerland's Schwyz town, meadows, lakes and forests.

I have been greatly helped along the way by family and friends, particularly by Maureen Lindley my wife, herself a successful novelist, who created the conditions for me to write this work.

From beginning to end, my long time secretary Trina Middlecote, worked on innumerable drafts of the two volumes of this project. I am enormously grateful to her for her good sense and good temper, doing all of this alongside other responsibilities. The book itself was designed and produced for printing, by my long-time friend and colleague, Angel Kaushish from Webseamsters.com in Pune. I am grateful to many who helped me alomg the way, particularly Mike Clancy and Peter Grose, to Peter Crisell and Roger AV Ward, in all cases for helpfully reading through and offering sound advice and encouragement. Olivier Salvatori in France throughout has been of great, even critical help in research matters and generally. In Monmouth, Daphne Smith was of great assistance in research and liberal encouragement.

Clive Lindley

Made in the USA
Charleston, SC
13 January 2017